GHOST Stories

GHOST Stories

CHILLING SUPERNATURAL TALES

ARCTURUS

ARCTURUS

This edition published in 2019 by Arcturus Publishing Limited
26/27 Bickels Yard, 151–153 Bermondsey Street,
London SE1 3HA

ISBN: 978-1-78950-295-4
AD007128UK

Printed in China

CONTENTS

INTRODUCTION

Ghosts have always fascinated us. Whether they are vengeful spirits returning to haunt those who wronged them in life or mournful figures trapped on earth until they can pass into a peaceful rest, there is something both terrifying and comforting about these ethereal beings. Combining the suspense of the thriller with the mystery of the detective story, ghost stories often provide an unforgettable experience.

At one time or another, many leading writers have tried their hand at perfecting the classic ghost story. Charles Dickens in 'No. 1 Branch Line: The Signal-man' features mysterious warning bells, a series of accidents and a terrifying apparition in one of his most unique works. Ambrose Bierce, a veteran of the American Civil War, was a prolific short story writer and accomplished journalist, who underwent a spooky end himself, disappearing in December 1913 after travelling to Mexico. In 'The Boarded Window', he tells of a widower living in a cabin haunted by the ghost of his wife.

Other authors spent their careers mastering the genre. Montague Rhodes James, a medieval scholar at King's College Cambridge, honed his craft by trying out his terrors on his students. 'O, Whistle and I'll Come to You My Lad' is the atmospheric tale of a sinister ghost haunting a Cambridge academic. Edward Frederic Benson could make even the mundane frightening by adding subtle touches of the supernatural that hinted at a malevolent power lurking just out of sight. In 'The Bus-Conductor' he turns an everyday journey into a deeply unsettling experience.

These are just a few of the terrors that await you. The ghosts come in all shapes and sizes and appear in every corner imaginable, but it is in the haunted characters themselves that are at the centre of every story.

These stories are sure to terrify and entertain in equal measure. There are strange and terrible things lurking in the pages ahead. Begin reading, if you dare …

O, Whistle and I'll Come to You My Lad

MONTAGUE RHODES JAMES

'I suppose you will be getting away pretty soon, now Full term is over, Professor,' said a person not in the story to the Professor of Ontography, soon after they had sat down next to each other at a feast in the hospitable hall of St. James's College.

The Professor was young, neat, and precise in speech.

'Yes,' he said; 'my friends have been making me take up golf this term, and I mean to go to the East Coast – in point of fact to Burnstow – (I dare say you know it) for a week or ten days, to improve my game. I hope to get off tomorrow.'

'Oh, Parkins,' said his neighbour on the other side, 'if you are going to Burnstow, I wish you would look at the site of the Templars' preceptory, and let me know if you think it would be any good to have a dig there in the summer.'

It was, as you might suppose, a person of antiquarian pursuits who said this, but, since he merely appears in this prologue, there is no need to give his entitlements.

'Certainly,' said Parkins, the Professor: 'if you will describe to me whereabouts the site is, I will do my best to give you an idea of the lie of the land when I get back; or I could write to you about it, if you would tell me where you are likely to be.'

'Don't trouble to do that, thanks. It's only that I'm thinking of taking my family in that direction in the Long, and it occurred to me that, as very few of the English preceptories have ever been properly planned, I might have an opportunity of doing something useful on off-days.'

The Professor rather sniffed at the idea that planning out a preceptory could be described as useful. His neighbour continued:

'The site – I doubt if there is anything showing above ground – must be down quite close to the beach now. The sea has encroached tremendously, as you know, all along that bit of coast. I should think, from the map, that it must be about three-quarters of a mile from the Globe Inn, at the north end of the town. Where are you going to stay?'

'Well, *at* the Globe Inn, as a matter of fact,' said Parkins; 'I have engaged a room there. I couldn't get in anywhere else; most of the lodging-houses are shut up in winter, it seems; and, as it is, they tell me that the only room of any size I can have is really a double-bedded one, and that they haven't a corner in which to store the other bed, and so on. But I must have a fairly large room, for I am taking some books down, and mean to do a bit of work; and though I don't quite fancy having an empty bed – not to speak of two – in what I may call for the time being my study, I suppose I can manage to rough it for the short time I shall be there.'

'Do you call having an extra bed in your room roughing it, Parkins?' said a bluff person opposite. 'Look here, I shall come down and occupy it for a bit; it'll be company for you.'

The Professor quivered, but managed to laugh in a courteous manner.

'By all means, Rogers; there's nothing I should like better. But I'm afraid you would find it rather dull; you don't play golf, do you?'

'No, thank Heaven!' said rude Mr. Rogers.

'Well, you see, when I'm not writing I shall most likely be out on the links, and that, as I say, would be rather dull for you, I'm afraid.'

'Oh, I don't know! There's certain to be somebody I know in the place; but, of course, if you don't want me, speak the word, Parkins; I shan't be offended. Truth, as you always tell us, is never offensive.'

Parkins was, indeed, scrupulously polite and strictly truthful. It is to be feared that Mr. Rogers sometimes practised upon his knowledge of these characteristics. In Parkins's breast there was a conflict now raging, which for a moment or two did not allow him to answer. That interval being over, he said:

'Well, if you want the exact truth, Rogers, I was considering whether the room I speak of would really be large enough to accommodate us both comfortably; and also whether (mind, I shouldn't have said this if you hadn't pressed me) you would not constitute something in the nature of a hindrance to my work.'

Rogers laughed loudly.

'Well done, Parkins!' he said. 'It's all right. I promise not to interrupt your work; don't you disturb yourself about that. No, I won't come if you don't want me; but I thought I should do so nicely to keep the ghosts off.' Here he might have been seen to wink and to nudge his next neighbour. Parkins might also have been seen to become pink. 'I beg pardon, Parkins,' Rogers continued; 'I oughtn't to have said that. I forgot you didn't like levity on these topics.'

'Well,' Parkins said, 'as you have mentioned the matter, I freely own that I do *not* like careless talk about what you call ghosts. A man in my position,' he went on, raising his voice a little, 'cannot, I find, be too careful about appearing to sanction the current beliefs on such subjects. As you know, Rogers, or as you ought to know; for I think I have never concealed my views—'

'No, you certainly have not, old man,' put in Rogers *sotto voce*.

'—I hold that any semblance, any appearance of concession to the view that such things might exist is to me a renunciation of all that I hold most sacred. But I'm afraid I have not succeeded in securing your attention.'

'Your *undivided* attention, was what Dr. Blimber actually *said,'* Rogers interrupted, with every appearance of an earnest desire for accuracy. 'But I beg your pardon, Parkins: I'm stopping you.'

'No, not at all,' said Parkins. 'I don't remember Blimber; perhaps he was before my time. But I needn't go on. I'm sure you know what I mean.'

'Yes, yes,' said Rogers, rather hastily – 'just so. We'll go into it fully at Burnstow, or somewhere.'

In repeating the above dialogue I have tried to give the impression which it made on me, that Parkins was something of an old woman – rather henlike, perhaps, in his little ways; totally destitute, alas! of the sense of humour, but at the same time dauntless and sincere in his convictions, and a man deserving of the greatest respect. Whether or not the reader has gathered so much, that was the character which Parkins had.

On the following day Parkins did, as he had hoped, succeed in getting away from his college, and in arriving at Burnstow. He was made welcome at the Globe Inn, was safely installed in the large double-bedded room of which we have heard, and was able before retiring to rest to arrange his materials for work in apple-pie order upon a commodious table which occupied the outer end of the room, and was surrounded on three sides by windows looking out seaward; that is to say the central window looked straight out to sea, and those on the left and right commanding prospects along the shore to the north and south respectively. On the south you saw the village of Burnstow. On the north no houses were to be seen, but only the beach and the low cliff backing it. Immediately in front was a strip – not considerable – of rough grass, dotted with old anchors, capstans, and so forth; then a broad path; then the beach. Whatever may have been the original distance between the Globe Inn and the sea, not more than sixty yards now separated them.

The rest of the population of the inn was, of course, a golfing one, and included few elements that call for a special description. The most conspicuous figure was, perhaps, that of an *ancien militaire*, secretary of a London club, and possessed of a voice of incredible strength, and of views of a pronouncedly Protestant type. These were apt to find utterance after his attendance upon the ministrations of the Vicar, an estimable man with inclinations towards a picturesque ritual, which he gallantly kept down as far as he could out of deference to East Anglian tradition.

Professor Parkins, one of whose principal characteristics was pluck, spent the greater part of the day following his arrival at Burnstow in what he had called improving his game, in company with this Colonel Wilson: and during the afternoon – whether the process of improvement were to blame or not, I am not sure – the Colonel's demeanour assumed a colouring so lurid that even Parkins jibbed at the thought of walking home with him from the links. He determined, after a short and furtive look at that bristling moustache and those incarnadined features, that it would be wiser to allow the influences of tea and tobacco to do what they could with the Colonel before the dinner-hour should render a meeting inevitable.

'I might walk home to-night along the beach,' he reflected – 'yes, and take a look – there will be light enough for that – at the ruins of which Disney was talking. I don't exactly know where they are, by the way; but I expect I can hardly help stumbling on them.'

This he accomplished, I may say, in the most literal sense, for in picking his way from the links to the shingle beach his foot caught, partly in a gorse-root and partly in a biggish stone, and over he went. When he got up and surveyed his surroundings, he found himself in a patch of somewhat broken ground covered with small depressions and mounds. These latter, when he came to examine them, proved to be simply masses of flints embedded in mortar and grown over with turf. He must, he quite rightly concluded, be on the site of the preceptory he had promised to look at. It seemed not unlikely to reward the spade of the explorer; enough of the foundations was probably left at no great depth to throw a good deal of light on the general plan. He remembered vaguely that the Templars, to whom this site had belonged, were in the habit of building round churches, and he thought a particular series of the humps or mounds near him did appear to be arranged in something of a circular form. Few people can resist the temptation to try a little amateur research in a department quite outside their own, if only for the satisfaction of showing how successful they would have been had they only taken it up seriously. Our Professor, however, if he felt something of this mean desire, was also truly anxious to oblige Mr. Disney. So he paced with care the circular area he had noticed, and wrote down its rough dimensions in his pocket-book. Then he proceeded to examine an oblong eminence which lay east of the centre of the circle, and seemed to his thinking likely to be the base of a platform or altar. At one end of it, the northern, a patch of the turf was gone – removed by some boy or other creature *feræ naturæ*. It might, he thought, be as well to probe the soil here for evidences of masonry, and he took out his knife and began scraping away the earth. And now followed another little discovery: a portion of soil fell inward as he scraped, and disclosed a small cavity. He lighted one match after another to help him to see of what nature the hole was, but the wind was too strong for them all. By tapping and scratching the sides with his knife, however, he was able to make out that it must be an artificial hole in masonry. It was rectangular, and the sides, top, and bottom, if not actually plastered, were smooth and regular. Of course it was empty. No! As he withdrew the knife he heard a metallic clink, and when he introduced his hand it met with a cylindrical object lying on the floor of the hole. Naturally enough, he picked it up, and when he brought it into the light, now fast fading, he could see that it, too, was of man's making – a metal tube about four inches long, and evidently of some considerable age.

By the time Parkins had made sure that there was nothing else in this odd receptacle, it was too late and too dark for him to think of undertaking any further search. What he had done had proved so unexpectedly interesting that he determined to sacrifice a little more of the daylight on the morrow to archæology. The object which he now had safe in his pocket was bound to be of some slight value at least, he felt sure.

Bleak and solemn was the view on which he took a last look before starting homeward. A faint yellow light in the west showed the links, on which a few figures moving towards the club-house were still visible, the squat martello tower, the lights of Aldsey village, the pale ribbon of sands intersected at intervals by black wooden groynings, the dim and murmuring sea. The wind was bitter from the north, but was at his back when he set out for the Globe. He quickly rattled and clashed through the shingle and gained the sand, upon which, but for the groynings which had to be got over every few yards, the going was both good and quiet. One last look behind, to measure the distance he had made since leaving the ruined Templars' church, showed him a prospect of company on his walk, in the shape of a rather indistinct personage in the distance, who seemed to be making great efforts to catch up with him, but made little, if any, progress. I mean that there was an appearance of running about his movements, but that the distance between him and Parkins did not seem materially to lessen. So, at least, Parkins thought, and decided that he almost certainly did not know him, and that it would be absurd to wait until he came up. For all that, company, he began to think, would really be very welcome on that lonely shore, if only you could choose your companion. In his unenlightened days he had read of meetings in such places which even now would hardly bear thinking of. He went on thinking of them, however, until he reached home, and particularly of one which catches most people's fancy at some time of their childhood. 'Now I saw in my dream that Christian had gone but a very little way when he saw a foul fiend coming over the field to meet him.' 'What should I do now,' he thought, 'if I looked back and caught sight of a black figure sharply defined against the yellow sky, and saw that it had horns and wings? I wonder whether I should stand or run for it. Luckily, the gentleman behind is not of that kind, and he seems to be about as far off now as when I saw him first. Well, at this rate he won't get his dinner as soon as I shall; and, dear me! it's within a quarter of an hour of the time now. I must run!'

Parkins had, in fact, very little time for dressing. When he met the Colonel at dinner, Peace – or as much of her as that gentleman could manage – reigned once more in the military bosom; nor was she put to flight in the hours of bridge that followed dinner, for Parkins was a more than respectable player. When, therefore, he retired towards twelve o'clock, he felt that he had spent his evening in quite a satisfactory way, and that, even for so long as a fortnight or three weeks, life at the Globe would be supportable under similar conditions – 'especially,' thought he, 'if I go on improving my game.'

As he went along the passages he met the boots of the Globe, who stopped and said:

'Beg your pardon, sir, but as I was a-brushing your coat just now there was somethink fell out of the pocket. I put it on your chest of drawers, sir, in your room, sir – a piece of a pipe or somethink of that, sir. Thank you, sir. You'll find it on your chest of drawers, sir – yes, sir. Good-night, sir.'

The speech served to remind Parkins of his little discovery of that afternoon. It was with some considerable curiosity that he turned it over by the light of his candles. It was of bronze, he now saw, and was shaped very much after the manner of the modern dog-whistle; in fact it was – yes, certainly it was – actually no more nor less than a whistle. He put it to his lips, but it was quite full of a fine, caked-up sand or earth, which would not yield to knocking, but must be loosened with a knife. Tidy as ever in his habits, Parkins cleared out the earth on to a piece of paper, and took the latter to the window to empty it out. The night was clear and bright, as he saw when he had opened the casement, and he stopped for an instant to look at the sea and note a belated wanderer stationed on the shore in front of the inn. Then he shut the window, a little surprised at the late hours people kept at Burnstow, and took his whistle to the light again. Why, surely there were marks on it, and not merely marks, but letters! A very little rubbing rendered the deeply-cut inscription quite legible, but the Professor had to confess, after some earnest thought, that the meaning of it was as obscure to him as the writing on the wall to Belshazzar. There were legends both on the front and on the back of the whistle. The one read thus:

FUR FLA FLE BIS

The other:

✠ QUIS EST ISTE QUI UENIT ✠

'I ought to be able to make it out,' he thought; 'but I suppose I am a little rusty in my Latin. When I come to think of it, I don't believe I even know the word for a whistle. The long one does seem simple enough. It ought to mean, "Who is this who is coming?" Well, the best way to find out is evidently to whistle for him.'

He blew tentatively and stopped suddenly, startled and yet pleased at the note he had elicited. It had a quality of infinite distance in it, and, soft as it was, he somehow felt it must be audible for miles round. It was a sound, too, that seemed to have the power (which many scents possess) of forming pictures in the brain. He saw quite clearly for a moment a vision of a wide, dark expanse at night, with a fresh wind blowing, and in the midst a lonely figure – how employed, he could not tell. Perhaps he would have seen more had not the picture been broken by the sudden surge of a gust of wind against his casement, so sudden that it made him look up, just in time to see the white glint of a sea-bird's wing somewhere outside the dark panes.

The sound of the whistle had so fascinated him that he could not help trying it once more, this time more boldly. The note was little, if at all, louder than before, and repetition broke the illusion – no picture followed, as he had half hoped it might. 'But what is this? Goodness! what force the wind can get up in a few minutes! What a tremendous gust! There! I knew that window-fastening was no use! Ah! I thought so – both candles out. It is enough to tear the room to pieces.'

The first thing was to get the window shut. While you might count twenty Parkins was struggling with the small casement, and felt almost as if he were pushing back a sturdy burglar, so strong was the pressure. It slackened all at once, and the window banged to and latched itself. Now to relight the candles and see what damage, if any, had been done. No, nothing seemed amiss; no glass even was broken in the casement. But the noise had evidently roused at least one member of the household: the Colonel was to be heard stumping in his stockinged feet on the floor above, and growling.

Quickly as it had risen, the wind did not fall at once. On it went, moaning and rushing past the house, at times rising to a cry so desolate that, as Parkins disinterestedly said, it might have made fanciful people feel quite uncomfortable; even the unimaginative, he thought after a quarter of an hour, might be happier without it.

Whether it was the wind, or the excitement of golf, or of the researches in the preceptory that kept Parkins awake, he was not sure. Awake he remained, in any case, long enough to fancy (as I am afraid I often do myself under such conditions) that he was the victim of all manner of fatal disorders: he would lie counting the beats of his heart, convinced that it was going to stop work every moment, and would entertain grave suspicions of his lungs, brain, liver, etc. – suspicions which he was sure would be dispelled by the return of daylight, but which until then refused to be put aside. He found a little vicarious comfort in the idea that someone else was in the same boat. A near neighbour (in the darkness it was not easy to tell his direction) was tossing and rustling in his bed, too.

The next stage was that Parkins shut his eyes and determined to give sleep every chance. Here again over-excitement asserted itself in another form – that of making pictures. *Experto crede,* pictures do come to the closed eyes of one trying to sleep, and often his pictures are so little to his taste that he must open his eyes and disperse the images.

Parkins's experience on this occasion was a very distressing one. He found that the picture which presented itself to him was continuous. When he opened his eyes, of course, it went; but when he shut them once more it framed itself afresh, and acted itself out again, neither quicker nor slower than before. What he saw was this:

A long stretch of shore – shingle edged by sand, and intersected at short intervals with black groynes running down to the water – a scene, in fact, so like that of his afternoon's walk that, in the absence of any landmark, it could not be distinguished therefrom. The light was obscure, conveying an impression of gathering storm, late winter evening, and slight cold rain. On this bleak stage at first no actor was visible. Then, in the distance, a bobbing black object appeared; a moment more, and it was a man running, jumping, clambering over the groynes, and every few seconds looking eagerly back. The nearer he came the more obvious it was that he was not only anxious, but even terribly frightened, though his face was not to be distinguished. He was, moreover, almost at the end of his strength. On he came; each successive obstacle seemed to cause him more difficulty than the last. 'Will he get over this next one?' thought Parkins; 'it seems a little higher than the others.' Yes; half climbing, half throwing himself, he did get over, and fell all in a heap on the other side (the side nearest to the spectator). There, as if really unable to get up again, he remained crouching under the groyne, looking up in an attitude of painful anxiety.

So far no cause whatever for the fear of the runner had been shown; but now there began to be seen, far up the shore, a little flicker of something light-coloured moving to and fro with great swiftness and irregularity. Rapidly growing larger, it, too, declared itself as a figure in pale, fluttering draperies, ill-defined. There was something about its motion which made Parkins very unwilling to see it at close quarters. It would stop, raise arms, bow itself toward the sand, then run stooping across the beach to the water-edge and back again; and then, rising upright, once more continue its course forward at a speed that was startling and terrifying. The moment came when the pursuer was hovering about from left to right only a few yards beyond the groyne where the runner lay in hiding. After two or three ineffectual castings hither and thither it came to a stop, stood upright, with arms raised high, and then darted straight forward towards the groyne.

It was at this point that Parkins always failed in his resolution to keep his eyes shut. With many misgivings as to incipient failure of eyesight, overworked brain, excessive smoking, and so on, he finally resigned himself to light his candle, get out a book, and pass the night waking, rather than be tormented by this persistent panorama, which he saw clearly enough could only be a morbid reflection of his walk and his thoughts on that very day.

The scraping of match on box and the glare of light must have startled some creatures of the night – rats or what not – which he heard scurry across the floor from the side of his bed with much rustling. Dear, dear! the match is out! Fool that it is! But the second one burnt better, and a candle and book were duly procured, over which Parkins pored till sleep of a wholesome kind came upon him, and that in no long space. For about the first time in his orderly and prudent life he forgot to blow out the candle, and when he was called next morning at eight there was still a flicker in the socket and a sad mess of guttered grease on the top of the little table.

After breakfast he was in his room, putting the finishing touches to his golfing costume – fortune had again allotted the Colonel to him for a partner – when one of the maids came in.

'Oh, if you please,' she said, 'would you like any extra blankets on your bed, sir?'

'Ah! thank you,' said Parkins. 'Yes, I think I should like one. It seems likely to turn rather colder.'

In a very short time the maid was back with the blanket.

'Which bed should I put it on, sir?' she asked.

'What? Why, that one – the one I slept in last night,' he said, pointing to it.

'Oh yes! I beg your pardon, sir, but you seemed to have tried both of 'em; leastways, we had to make 'em both up this morning.'

'Really? How very absurd!' said Parkins. 'I certainly never touched the other, except to lay some things on it. Did it actually seem to have been slept in?'

'Oh yes, sir!' said the maid. 'Why, all the things was crumpled and throwed about all ways, if you'll excuse me, sir – quite as if anyone 'adn't passed but a very poor night, sir.'

'Dear me,' said Parkins. 'Well, I may have disordered it more than I thought when I unpacked my things. I'm very sorry to have given you the extra trouble, I'm sure. I expect a friend of mine soon, by the way – a gentleman from Cambridge – to come and occupy it for a night or two. That will be all right, I suppose, won't it?'

'Oh yes, to be sure, sir. Thank you, sir. It's no trouble, I'm sure,' said the maid, and departed to giggle with her colleagues.

Parkins set forth, with a stern determination to improve his game.

I am glad to be able to report that he succeeded so far in this enterprise that the Colonel, who had been rather repining at the prospect of a second day's play in his company, became quite chatty as the morning advanced; and his voice boomed out over the flats, as certain also of our own minor poets have said, 'like some great bourdon in a minster tower'.

'Extraordinary wind, that, we had last night,' he said. 'In my old home we should have said someone had been whistling for it.'

'Should you, indeed!' said Parkins. 'Is there a superstition of that kind still current in your part of the country?'

'I don't know about superstition,' said the Colonel. 'They believe in it all over Denmark and Norway, as well as on the Yorkshire coast; and my experience is, mind you, that there's generally something at the bottom of what these country-folk hold to, and have held to for generations. But it's your drive' (or whatever it might have been: the golfing reader will have to imagine appropriate digressions at the proper intervals).

When conversation was resumed, Parkins said, with a slight hesitancy:

'Apropos of what you were saying just now, Colonel, I think I ought to tell you that my own views on such subjects are very strong. I am, in fact, a convinced disbeliever in what is called the "supernatural."'

'What!' said the Colonel, 'do you mean to tell me you don't believe in second-sight, or ghosts, or anything of that kind?'

'In nothing whatever of that kind,' returned Parkins firmly.

'Well,' said the Colonel, 'but it appears to me at that rate, sir, that you must be little better than a Sadducee.'

Parkins was on the point of answering that, in his opinion, the Sadducees were the most sensible persons he had ever read of in the Old Testament; but, feeling some doubt as to whether much mention of them was to be found in that work, he preferred to laugh the accusation off.

'Perhaps I am,' he said; 'but – Here, give me my cleek, boy! – Excuse me one moment, Colonel.' A short interval. 'Now, as to whistling for the wind, let me give you my theory about it. The laws which govern winds are really not at all perfectly known – to fisher-folk and such, of course, not known at all. A man or woman of eccentric habits, perhaps, or a stranger, is seen repeatedly on the beach at some unusual hour, and is heard whistling. Soon afterwards a violent wind rises; a man who could read the sky perfectly or who possessed a barometer could have foretold that it would. The simple people of a fishing-village have no barometers, and only a few rough rules for prophesying weather. What more natural than that the eccentric personage I postulated should be regarded as having raised the wind, or that he or she should clutch eagerly at the reputation of being able to do so? Now, take last night's wind: as it happens, I myself was whistling. I blew a whistle twice, and the wind seemed to come absolutely in answer to my call. If anyone had seen me—'

The audience had been a little restive under this harangue, and Parkins had, I fear, fallen somewhat into the tone of a lecturer; but at the last sentence the Colonel stopped.

'Whistling, were you?' he said. 'And what sort of whistle did you use? Play this stroke first.' Interval.

'About that whistle you were asking, Colonel. It's rather a curious one. I have it in my – No; I see I've left it in my room. As a matter of fact, I found it yesterday.'

And then Parkins narrated the manner of his discovery of the whistle, upon hearing which the Colonel grunted, and opined that, in Parkins's place, he should himself be careful about using a thing that had belonged to a set of Papists, of whom, speaking generally, it might be affirmed that you never knew what they might not have been up to. From this topic he diverged to the enormities of the Vicar, who had given notice on the previous Sunday that Friday would be the Feast of St. Thomas the Apostle, and that there would be service at eleven o'clock in the church. This and other similar proceedings constituted in the Colonel's view a strong presumption that the Vicar was a concealed Papist, if not a Jesuit; and Parkins, who could not very readily follow the Colonel in this region, did not disagree with him. In fact, they got on so well together in the morning that there was no talk on either side of their separating after lunch.

Both continued to play well during the afternoon, or, at least, well enough to make them forget everything else until the light began to fail them. Not until then did Parkins remember that he had meant to do some more investigating at the preceptory; but it was of no great importance, he reflected. One day was as good as another; he might as well go home with the Colonel.

As they turned the corner of the house, the Colonel was almost knocked down by a boy who rushed into him at the very top of his speed, and then, instead of running away, remained hanging on to him and panting. The first words of the warrior were naturally those of reproof and objurgation, but he very quickly discerned that the boy was almost speechless with fright. Inquiries were useless at first. When the boy got his breath he began to howl, and still clung to the Colonel's legs. He was at last detached, but continued to howl.

'What in the world is the matter with you? What have you been up to? What have you seen?' said the two men.

'Ow, I seen it wive at me out of the winder,' wailed the boy, 'and I don't like it.'

'What window?' said the irritated Colonel. 'Come, pull yourself together, my boy.'

'The front winder it was, at the 'otel,' said the boy.

At this point Parkins was in favour of sending the boy home, but the Colonel refused; he wanted to get to the bottom of it, he said; it was most dangerous to give a boy such a fright as this one had had, and if it turned out that people had been playing jokes, they should suffer for it in some way. And by a series of questions he made out this story: The boy had been playing about on the grass in front of the Globe with some others; then they had gone home to their teas, and he was just going, when he happened to look up at the front winder and see it a-wiving at him. *It* seemed to be a figure of some sort, in white as far as he knew – couldn't see its face; but it wived at him, and it warn't a right thing – not to say not a right person. Was there a light in the room? No, he didn't think to look if there was a light. Which was the window? Was it the top one or the second one? The seckind one it was – the big winder what got two little uns at the sides.

'Very well, my boy,' said the Colonel, after a few more questions. 'You run away home now. I expect it was some person trying to give you a start. Another time, like a brave English boy, you just throw a stone – well, no, not that exactly, but you go and speak to the waiter, or to Mr. Simpson, the landlord, and – yes – and say that I advised you to do so.'

The boy's face expressed some of the doubt he felt as to the likelihood of Mr. Simpson's lending a favourable ear to his complaint, but the Colonel did not appear to perceive this, and went on:

'And here's a sixpence – no, I see it's a shilling – and you be off home, and don't think any more about it.'

The youth hurried off with agitated thanks, and the Colonel and Parkins went round to the front of the Globe and reconnoitred. There was only one window answering to the description they had been hearing.

'Well, that's curious,' said Parkins; 'it's evidently my window the lad was talking about. Will you come up for a moment, Colonel Wilson? We ought to be able to see if anyone has been taking liberties in my room.'

They were soon in the passage and made as if to open the door. Then he stopped and felt in his pockets.

'This is more serious than I thought,' was his next remark. 'I remember now that before I started this morning I locked the door. It is locked now, and, what is more, here is the key.' And he held it up. 'Now,' he went on, 'if the servants are in the habit of going into one's room during the day when one is away, I can only say that – well, that I don't approve of it at all.' Conscious of a somewhat weak climax, he busied himself in opening the door (which was indeed locked) and in lighting candles. 'No,' he said, 'nothing seems disturbed.'

'Except your bed,' put in the Colonel.

'Excuse me, that isn't my bed,' said Parkins. 'I don't use that one. But it does look as if someone had been playing tricks with it.'

It certainly did: the clothes were bundled up and twisted together in a most tortuous confusion. Parkins pondered.

'That must be it,' he said at last: 'I disordered the clothes last night in unpacking, and they haven't made it since. Perhaps they came in to make it, and that boy saw them through the window and then they were called away and locked the door after them. Yes, I think that must be it.'

'Well, ring and ask,' said the Colonel, and this appealed to Parkins as practical.

The maid appeared, and, to make a long story short, deposed that she had made the bed in the morning when the gentleman was in the room, and hadn't been there since. No, she hadn't no other key. Mr. Simpson he kep' the keys; he'd be able to tell the gentleman if anyone had been up.

This was a puzzle. Investigation showed that nothing of value had been taken, and Parkins remembered the disposition of the small objects on tables and so forth well enough to be pretty sure that no pranks had been played with them. Mr. and Mrs. Simpson furthermore agreed that neither of them had given the duplicate key of the room to any person whatever during the day. Nor could Parkins, fair-minded man as he was, detect anything in the demeanour of master, mistress, or maid that indicated guilt. He was much more inclined to think that the boy had been imposing on the Colonel.

The latter was unwontedly silent and pensive at dinner and throughout the evening. When he bade good-night to Parkins, he murmured in a gruff undertone:

'You know where I am if you want me during the night.'

'Why, yes, thank you, Colonel Wilson, I think I do; but there isn't much prospect of my disturbing you, I hope. By the way,' he added, 'did I show you that old whistle I spoke of? I think not. Well, here it is.'

The Colonel turned it over gingerly in the light of the candle.

'Can you make anything of the inscription?' asked Parkins, as he took it back.

'No, not in this light. What do you mean to do with it?'

'Oh, well, when I get back to Cambridge I shall submit it to some of the archaeologists there, and see what they think of it; and very likely, if they consider it worth having, I may present it to one of the museums.'

''M!' said the Colonel 'Well, you may be right. All I know is that, if it were mine, I should chuck it straight into the sea. It's no use talking, I'm well aware, but I expect that with you it's a case of live and learn. I hope so, I'm sure, and I wish you a good night.'

He turned away, leaving Parkins in act to speak at the bottom of the stair, and soon each was in his own bedroom.

By some unfortunate accident, there were neither blinds nor curtains to the windows of the Professor's room. The previous night he had thought little of this, but to-night there seemed every prospect of a bright moon rising to shine directly on his bed, and probably wake him later on. When he noticed this he was a good deal annoyed, but, with an ingenuity which I can only envy, he succeeded in rigging up, with the help of a railway-rug, some safety-pins, and a stick and umbrella, a screen which, if it only held together, would completely keep the moonlight off his bed. And shortly afterwards he was comfortably in that bed. When he had read a somewhat solid work long enough to produce a decided wish for sleep, he cast a drowsy glance round the room, blew out the candle, and fell back upon the pillow.

He must have slept soundly for an hour or more, when a sudden clatter shook him up in a most unwelcome manner. In a moment he realized what had happened: his carefully constructed screen had given way, and a very bright frosty moon was shining directly on his face. This was highly annoying. Could he possibly get up and reconstruct the screen? or could he manage to sleep if he did not?

For some minutes he lay and pondered over the possibilities; then he turned over sharply, and with all his eyes open lay breathlessly listening. There had been a movement, he was sure, in the empty bed on the opposite side of the room. To-morrow he would have it moved, for there must be rats or something playing about in it. It was quiet now. No! the commotion began again. There was a rustling and shaking: surely more than any rat could cause

I can figure to myself something of the Professor's bewilderment and horror, for I have in a dream thirty years back seen the same thing happen; but the reader will hardly, perhaps, imagine how dreadful it was to him to see a figure suddenly sit up in what he had known was an empty bed. He was out of his own bed in one bound, and made a dash towards the window, where lay his only weapon, the stick with which he had propped his screen. This was, as it turned out, the worst thing he could have done, because the personage in the empty bed, with a sudden smooth motion, slipped from the bed and took up a position, with outspread arms, between the two beds, and in front of the door. Parkins watched it in a horrid perplexity. Somehow, the idea of getting past it and escaping through the door was intolerable to him; he could not have borne – he didn't know why – to touch it; and as for its touching him, he would sooner dash himself through the window than have that happen. It stood for the moment in a band of dark shadow, and he had not seen what its face was like. Now it began to move, in a stooping posture, and all at once the spectator realized, with some horror and some relief, that it must be blind, for it seemed to feel about it with its muffled arms in a groping and random fashion. Turning half away from him, it became suddenly conscious of the bed he had just left, and darted towards it, and bent and felt over the pillows in a way which made Parkins shudder as he had never in his life thought it possible. In a very few moments it seemed to know that the bed was empty, and then, moving forward into the area of light and facing the window, it showed for the first time what manner of thing it was.

Parkins, who very much dislikes being questioned about it, did once describe something of it in my hearing, and I gathered that what he chiefly remembers about it is a horrible, an intensely horrible, face *of crumpled linen*. What expression he read upon it he could not or would not tell, but that the fear of it went nigh to maddening him is certain.

But he was not at leisure to watch it for long. With formidable quickness it moved into the middle of the room, and, as it groped and waved, one corner of its draperies swept across Parkins's face. He could not, though he knew how perilous a sound was – he could not keep back a cry of disgust, and this gave the searcher an instant clue. It leapt towards him upon the instant, and the next moment he was halfway through the window backwards, uttering cry upon cry at the utmost pitch of his voice, and the linen face was thrust close into his own. At this, almost the last possible second, deliverance came, as you will have guessed: the Colonel burst the door open, and was just in time to see the dreadful group at the window. When he reached the figures only one was left. Parkins sank forward into the room in a faint, and before him on the floor lay a tumbled heap of bed-clothes.

Colonel Wilson asked no questions, but busied himself keeping everyone else out of the room and in getting Parkins back to his bed; and himself, wrapped in a rug, occupied the other bed, for the rest of the night. Early on the next day Rogers arrived, more welcome than he would have been a day before, and the three of them held a very long consultation in the Professor's room. At the end of it the Colonel left the hotel door carrying a small object between his finger and thumb, which he cast as far into the sea as a very brawny arm could send it. Later on the smoke of a burning ascended from the back premises of the Globe.

Exactly what explanation was patched up for the staff and visitors at the hotel I must confess I do not recollect. The Professor was somehow cleared of the ready suspicion of delirium tremens, and the hotel of the reputation of a troubled house.

There is not much question as to what would have happened to Parkins if the Colonel had not intervened when he did. He would either have fallen out of the window or else lost his wits. But it is not so evident what more the creature that came in answer to the whistle could have done than frighten. There seemed to be absolutely nothing material about it save the bed-clothes of which it had made itself a body. The Colonel, who remembered a not very dissimilar occurrence in India, was of opinion that if Parkins had closed with it it could really have done very little, and that its one power was that of frightening. The whole thing, he said, served to confirm his opinion of the Church of Rome.

There is really nothing more to tell, but, as you may imagine, the Professor's views on certain points are less clear cut than they used to be. His nerves, too, have suffered: he cannot even now see a surplice hanging on a door quite unmoved, and the spectacle of a scarecrow in a field late on a winter afternoon has cost him more than one sleepless night.

HE?

GUY DE MAUPASSANT

My dear friend, you cannot understand it by any possible means, you say, and I perfectly believe you. You think I am going mad? It may be so, but not for the reasons which you suppose.

Yes, I am going to get married, and I will give you what has led me to take that step.

My ideas and my convictions have not changed at all. I look upon all legalized cohabitation as utterly stupid, for I am certain that nine husbands out of ten are cuckolds; and they get no more than their deserts for having been idiotic enough to fetter their lives, and renounce their freedom in love, the only happy and good thing in the world, and for having clipped the wings of fancy, which continually drives us on towards all women, &c., &c., &c. You know what I mean. More than ever I feel that I am incapable of loving one woman alone, because I shall always adore all the others too much. I should like to have a thousand arms, a thousand mouths, and a thousand – *temperaments*, to be able to strain an army of these charming creatures in my embrace at the same moment.

And yet I am going to get married!

I may add that I know very little of the girl who is going to become my wife tomorrow; I have only seen her four or five times. I know that there is nothing unpleasing about her, and that is enough for my purpose. She is small, fair, and stout; so of course the day after tomorrow I shall ardently wish for a tall, dark, thin woman.

She is not rich, and belongs to the middle-classes. She is a girl such as you may find by the gross, well adapted for matrimony, without any apparent faults, and with no particularly striking qualities. People say of her:

'Mlle. Lajolle is a very nice girl,' and tomorrow they will say: 'What a very nice woman Madame Raymon is.' She belongs, in a word, to that immense number of girls whom one is glad to have for one's wife till the moment comes, when one discovers that one happens to prefer all the other women to that particular woman whom one has married.

'Well,' you will say to me, 'what on earth did you get married for?'

I hardly like to tell you the strange and seemingly improbable reason that urged me on to this senseless act; the fact, however, is that I am frightened of being alone!

I don't know how to tell you or to make you understand me, but my state of mind is so wretched that you will pity me and despise me.

I do not want to be alone any longer at night; I want to feel that there is someone close to me, touching me, a being who can speak and say something, no matter what it be.

I wish to be able to awaken somebody by my side, so that I may be able to ask some sudden question, a stupid question even if I feel inclined, so that I may hear a human voice, and feel that there is some waking soul close to me, someone whose reason is at work; so that when I hastily light the candle I may see some human face by my side – because – because – I am ashamed to confess it – because I am afraid of being alone.

Oh! you don't understand me yet.

I am not afraid of any danger; if a man were to come into the room I should kill him without trembling. I am not afraid of ghosts, nor do I believe in the supernatural. I am not afraid of dead people, for I believe in the total annihilation of every being that disappears from the face of this earth.

Well, – yes, well, it must be told; I am afraid of myself, afraid of that horrible sensation of incomprehensible fear.

You may laugh, if you like. It is terrible, and I cannot get over it. I am afraid of the walls, of the furniture, of the familiar objects, which are animated, as far as I am concerned, by a kind of animal life. Above all, I am afraid of my own dreadful thoughts, of my reason, which seems as if it were about to leave me, driven away by a mysterious and invisible agony.

At first I feel a vague uneasiness in my mind which causes a cold shiver to run all over me. I look round, and of course nothing is to be seen, and I wish there were something there, no matter what, as long as it were something tangible: I am frightened, merely because I cannot understand my own terror.

If I speak, I am afraid of my own voice. If I walk, I am afraid of I know not what, behind the door, behind the curtains, in the cupboard, or under my bed, and yet all the time I know there is nothing anywhere, and I turn round suddenly because I am afraid of what is behind me, although there is nothing there, and I know it.

I get agitated; I feel that my fear increases, and so I shut myself up in my own room, get into bed, and hide under the clothes, and there, cowering down rolled into a ball, I close my eyes in despair, and remain thus for an indefinite time, remembering that my candle is alight on the table by my bedside, and that I ought to put it out, and yet – I dare not do it!

It is very terrible, is it not, to be like that?

Formerly I felt nothing of all that; I came home quite comfortably, and went up and down in my rooms without anything disturbing my calmness of mind. Had anyone told me that I should be attacked by a malady – for I can call it nothing else – of most improbable fear, such a stupid and terrible malady as it is, I should have laughed outright. I was certainly never afraid of opening the door in the dark; I went to bed slowly without locking it, and never got up in the middle of the night to make sure that everything was firmly closed.

It began last year in a very strange manner, on a damp autumn evening. When my servant had left the room, after I had dined, I asked myself what I was going to do. I walked up and down my room for some time, feeling tired without any reason for it, unable to work, and even without energy to read. A fine rain was falling, and I felt unhappy, a prey to one of those fits of despondency, without any apparent cause which makes us feel inclined to cry, or to talk, no matter to whom, so as to shake off our depressing thoughts.

I felt that I was alone, and my rooms seemed to me to be more empty than they had ever done before, while I was surrounded by a sensation of infinite and overwhelming solitude. What was I to do? I sat down, but then a kind of nervous impatience agitated my legs, so I got up and began to walk about again. I was rather feverish, for my hands, which I had clasped behind me, as one often does when walking slowly, almost seemed to burn one another. Then suddenly a cold shiver ran down my back, and I thought the damp air might have penetrated into my room, so I lit the fire for the first time that year, and sat down again and looked at the flames. But soon I felt that I could not possibly remain quiet, and so I got up again and determined to go out, to pull myself together, and to find a friend to bear me company.

I could not find anyone, so I went on to the boulevards to try and meet some acquaintance or other there.

It was wretched everywhere, and the wet pavement glistened in the gaslight, while the oppressive warmth of the almost impalpable rain lay heavily over the streets and seemed to obscure the light from the lamps.

I went on slowly, saying to myself, 'I shall not find a soul to talk to.'

I glanced into several cafés, from the Madeleine as far as the Faubourg Poissonière, and saw many unhappy-looking individuals sitting at the tables, who did not seem even to have enough energy left to finish the refreshments they had ordered.

For a long time I wandered aimlessly up and down, and about midnight I started off for home; I was very calm and very tired. My concierge* opened the door at once, which was quite unusual for him, and I thought that another lodger had no doubt just come in.

When I go out I always double-lock the door of my room, and I found it merely closed, which surprised me; but I supposed that some letters had been brought up for me in the course of the evening.

I went in, and found my fire still burning, so that it lighted up the room a little, and, in the act of taking up a candle, I noticed somebody sitting in my armchair by the fire, warming his feet, with his back towards me.

I was not in the slightest degree frightened. I thought very naturally that some friend or other had come to see me. No doubt the porter, whom I had told when I went out, had lent him his own key. In a moment I remembered all the circumstances of my return, how the street door had been opened immediately, and that my own door was only latched, and not locked.

I could see nothing of my friend but his head, and he had evidently gone to sleep while waiting for me, so I went up to him to rouse him. I saw him quite clearly; his right arm was hanging down and his legs were crossed, while his head, which was somewhat inclined to the left of the armchair, seemed to indicate that he was asleep. 'Who can it be?' I asked myself. I could not see clearly, as the room was rather dark, so I put out my hand to touch him on the shoulder, and it came in contact with the back of the chair. There was nobody there; the seat was empty.

I fairly jumped with fright. For a moment I drew back as if some terrible danger had suddenly appeared in my way; then I turned round again, impelled by some imperious desire of looking at the armchair again, and I remained standing upright, panting with fear, so upset that I could not collect my thoughts, and ready to drop.

But I am a cool man, and soon recovered myself. I thought: 'It is a mere hallucination, that is all,' and I immediately began to reflect about this phenomenon. Thoughts fly very quickly at such moments.

---

* Hall-porter.

I had been suffering from a hallucination, that was an incontestable fact. My mind had been perfectly lucid and had acted regularly and logically, so there was nothing the matter with the brain. It was only my eyes that had been deceived; they had had a vision, one of those visions which lead simple folk to believe in miracles. It was a nervous accident to the optical apparatus, nothing more; the eyes were rather congested, perhaps.

I lit my candle, and when I stooped down to the fire in so doing, I noticed that I was trembling, and I raised myself up with a jump, as if somebody had touched me from behind.

I was certainly not by any means quiet.

I walked up and down a little, and hummed a tune or two.

Then I double-locked my door, and felt rather reassured; now, at any rate, nobody could come in.

I sat down again, and thought over my adventure for a long time; then I went to bed, and blew out my light.

For some minutes all went well; I lay quietly on my back, but then an irresistible desire seized me to look round the room, and I turned on to my side.

My fire was nearly out, and the few glowing embers threw a faint light on to the floor by the chair, where I fancied I saw the man sitting again.

I quickly struck a match, but I had been mistaken, for there was nothing there; I got up, however, and hid the chair behind my bed, and tried to get to sleep as the room was now dark, but I had not forgotten myself for more than five minutes when in my dream I saw all the scene which I had witnessed as clearly as if it were reality. I woke up with a start, and having lit the candle, I sat up in bed, without venturing even to try and go to sleep again.

Twice, however, sleep overcame me for a few moments in spite of myself, and twice I saw the same thing again, till I fancied I was going mad; when day broke, however, I thought that I was cured, and slept peacefully till noon.

It was all past and over. I had been feverish, had had the nightmare; I don't know what. I had been ill, in a word, but yet I thought that I was a great fool.

I enjoyed myself thoroughly that evening; I went and dined at a restaurant; afterwards I went to the theatre, and then started home. But as I got near the house I was seized by a strange feeling of uneasiness once more; I was afraid of *seeing* him again. I was not afraid of him, not afraid of his presence, in which I did not believe; but I was afraid of being deceived again; I was afraid of some fresh hallucination, afraid lest fear should take possession of me.

Far more than an hour I wandered up and down the pavement; then I thought that I was really too foolish, and at last I returned home. I panted so that I could scarcely get upstairs, and I remained standing outside my door for more than ten minutes; then suddenly I took courage, and screwed myself together. I inserted my key into the lock, and went in with a candle in my hand. I kicked open my half-open bedroom door, and gave a frightened look towards the fireplace; there was nothing there. A – h!

What a relief and what a delight! What a deliverance! I walked up and down briskly and boldly, but I was not altogether reassured, and kept turning round with a jump; the very shadows in the corner disquieted me.

I slept badly, and was constantly disturbed by imaginary noises, but I did not see *him*; no, that was all over.

Since that time I have been afraid of being alone at night. I feel that the spectre is there, close to me, around me; but it has not appeared to me again. And supposing it did, what would it matter, since I do not believe in it, and know that it is nothing?

It still worries me, however, because I am constantly thinking of it: *his right arm hanging down and his head inclined to the left like a man who was asleep* . . . Enough of that, in Heaven's name! I don't want to think about it!

Why, however, am I so persistently possessed with this idea? His feet were close to the fire!

He haunts me; it is very stupid, but so it is. Who and what is HE? I know that he does not exist except in my cowardly imagination, in my fears, and in my agony! There – enough of that! . . .

Yes, it is all very well for me to reason with myself, *to stiffen myself*, so to say; but I cannot remain at home, because I know he is there. I know I shall not see him again; he will not show himself again; that is all over. But he is there all the same in my thoughts. He remains invisible, but that does not prevent his being there. He is behind the doors, in the closed cupboards, in the wardrobe, under the bed, in every dark corner. If I open the door or the cupboard, if I take the candle to look under the bed and throw a light on to the dark places, he is there no longer, but I feel that he is behind me. I turn round, certain that I shall not see him, that I shall never see him again; but he is, for all that, none the less behind me.

It is very stupid, it is dreadful; but what am I to do? I cannot help it.

But if there were two of us in the place, I feel certain that he would not be there any longer, for he is there just because I am alone; simply and solely because I am alone!

The Room in the Tower

Edward Frederic Benson

It is probable that everybody who is at all a constant dreamer has had at least one experience of an event or a sequence of circumstances which have come to his mind in sleep being subsequently realized in the material world. But, in my opinion, so far from this being a strange thing, it would be far odder if this fulfilment did not occasionally happen, since our dreams are, as a rule, concerned with people whom we know and places with which we are familiar, such as might very naturally occur in the awake and daylit world. True, these dreams are often broken into by some absurd and fantastic incident, which puts them out of court in regard to their subsequent fulfilment, but on the mere calculation of chances, it does not appear in the least unlikely that a dream imagined by anyone who dreams constantly should occasionally come true. Not long ago, for instance, I experienced such a fulfilment of a dream which seems to me in no way remarkable and to have no kind of psychical significance. The manner of it was as follows.

A certain friend of mine, living abroad, is amiable enough to write to me about once in a fortnight. Thus, when fourteen days or thereabouts have elapsed since I last heard from him, my mind, probably, either consciously or subconsciously, is expectant of a letter from him. One night last week I dreamed that as I was going upstairs to dress for dinner I heard, as I often heard, the sound of the postman's knock on my front door, and diverted my direction downstairs instead. There, among other correspondence, was a letter from him. Thereafter the fantastic entered, for on opening it I found inside the ace of diamonds, and scribbled across it in his well-known handwriting, 'I am sending you this for safe custody, as you know it is running an unreasonable risk to keep aces in Italy.' The next evening I was just preparing to go upstairs to dress when I heard the postman's knock, and did precisely as I had done in my dream. There, among other letters, was one from my friend. Only it did not contain the ace of diamonds. Had it done so, I should have attached more weight to the matter, which, as it stands, seems to me a perfectly ordinary coincidence. No doubt I consciously or subconsciously expected a letter from him, and this suggested to me my dream. Similarly, the fact that my friend had not written to me for a fortnight suggested to him that he should do so. But occasionally it is not so easy to find such an explanation, and for the following story I can find no explanation at all. It came out of the dark, and into the dark it has gone again.

All my life I have been a habitual dreamer: the nights are few, that is to say, when I do not find on awaking in the morning that some mental experience has been mine, and sometimes, all night long, apparently, a series of the most dazzling adventures befall me. Almost without exception these adventures are pleasant, though often merely trivial. It is of an exception that I am going to speak.

It was when I was about sixteen that a certain dream first came to me, and this is how it befell. It opened with my being set down at the door of a big red-brick house, where, I understood, I was going to stay. The servant who opened the door told me that tea was being served in the garden, and led me through a low dark-panelled hall, with a large open fireplace, on to a cheerful green lawn set round with flower beds. There were grouped about the tea-table a small party of people, but they were all strangers to me except one, who was a schoolfellow called Jack Stone, clearly the son of the house, and he introduced me to his mother and father and a couple of sisters. I was, I remember, somewhat astonished to find myself here, for the boy in question was scarcely known to me, and I rather disliked what I knew of him; moreover, he had left school nearly a year before. The afternoon was very hot, and an intolerable oppression reigned. On the far side of the lawn ran a red-brick wall, with an iron gate in its centre, outside which stood a walnut tree. We sat in the shadow of the house opposite a row of long windows, inside which I could see a table with cloth laid, glimmering with glass and silver. This garden front of the house was very long, and at one end of it stood a tower of three storeys, which looked to me much older than the rest of the building.

Before long, Mrs. Stone, who, like the rest of the party, had sat in absolute silence, said to me, 'Jack will show you your room: I have given you the room in the tower.'

Quite inexplicably my heart sank at her words. I felt as if I had known that I should have the room in the tower, and that it contained something dreadful and significant. Jack instantly got up, and I understood that I had to follow him. In silence we passed through the hall, and mounted a great oak staircase with many corners, and arrived at a small landing with two doors set in it. He pushed one of these open for me to enter, and without coming in himself, closed it after me. Then I knew that my conjecture had been right: there was something awful in the room, and with the terror of nightmare growing swiftly and enveloping me, I awoke in a spasm of terror.

Now that dream or variations on it occurred to me intermittently for fifteen years. Most often it came in exactly this form, the arrival, the tea laid out on the lawn, the deadly silence succeeded by that one deadly sentence, the mounting with Jack Stone up to the room in the tower where horror dwelt, and it always came to a close in the nightmare of terror at that which was in the room, though I never saw what it was. At other times I experienced variations on this same theme. Occasionally, for instance, we would be sitting at dinner in the dining-room, into the windows of which I had looked on the first night when the dream of this house visited me, but wherever we were, there was the same silence, the same sense of dreadful oppression and foreboding. And the silence I knew would always be broken by Mrs. Stone saying to me, 'Jack will show you your room: I have given you the room in the tower.' Upon which (this was invariable) I had to follow him up the oak staircase with many corners, and enter the place that I dreaded more and more each time that I visited it in sleep. Or, again, I would find myself playing cards still in silence in a drawing-room lit with immense chandeliers, that gave a blinding illumination. What the game was I have no idea; what I remember, with a sense of miserable anticipation, was that soon Mrs. Stone would get up and say to me, 'Jack will show you your room: I have given you the room in the tower.' This drawing-room where we played cards was next to the dining-room, and, as I have said, was always brilliantly illuminated, whereas the rest of the house was full of dusk and shadows. And yet, how often, in spite of those bouquets of lights, have I not pored over the cards that were dealt me, scarcely able for some reason to see them. Their designs, too, were strange: there were no red suits, but all were black, and among them there were certain cards which were black all over. I hated and dreaded those.

As this dream continued to recur, I got to know the greater part of the house. There was a smoking-room beyond the drawing-room, at the end of a passage with a green baize door. It was always very dark there, and as often as I went there I passed somebody whom I could not see in the doorway coming out. Curious developments, too, took place in the characters that peopled the dream as might happen to living persons. Mrs. Stone, for instance, who, when I first saw her, had been black-haired, became grey, and instead of rising briskly, as she had done at first when she said, 'Jack will show you your room: I have given you the room in the tower,' got up very feebly, as if the strength was leaving her limbs. Jack also grew up, and became a rather ill-looking young man, with a brown moustache, while one of the sisters ceased to appear, and I understood she was married.

Then it so happened that I was not visited by this dream for six months or more, and I began to hope, in such inexplicable dread did I hold it, that it had passed away for good. But one night after this interval I again found myself being shown out onto the lawn for tea, and Mrs. Stone was not there, while the others were all dressed in black. At once I guessed the reason, and my heart leaped at the thought that perhaps this time I should not have to sleep in the room in the tower, and though we usually all sat in silence, on this occasion the sense of relief made me talk and laugh as I had never yet done. But even then matters were not altogether comfortable, for no one else spoke, but they all looked secretly at each other. And soon the foolish stream of my talk ran dry, and gradually an apprehension worse than anything I had previously known gained on me as the light slowly faded.

Suddenly a voice which I knew well broke the stillness, the voice of Mrs. Stone, saying, 'Jack will show you your room: I have given you the room in the tower.' It seemed to come from near the gate in the red-brick wall that bounded the lawn, and looking up, I saw that the grass outside was sown thick with gravestones. A curious greyish light shone from them, and I could read the lettering on the grave nearest me, and it was, 'In evil memory of Julia Stone.' And as usual Jack got up, and again I followed him through the hall and up the staircase with many corners. On this occasion it was darker than usual, and when I passed into the room in the tower I could only just see the furniture, the position of which was already familiar to me. Also there was a dreadful odour of decay in the room, and I woke screaming.

The dream, with such variations and developments as I have mentioned, went on at intervals for fifteen years. Sometimes I would dream it two or three nights in succession; once, as I have said, there was an intermission of six months, but taking a reasonable average, I should say that I dreamed it quite as often as once in a month. It had, as is plain, something of nightmare about it, since it always ended in the same appalling terror, which so far from getting less, seemed to me to gather fresh fear every time that I experienced it. There was, too, a strange and dreadful consistency about it. The characters in it, as I have mentioned, got regularly older, death and marriage visited this silent family, and I never in the dream, after Mrs. Stone had died, set eyes on her again. But it was always her voice that told me that the room in the tower was prepared for me, and whether we had tea out on the lawn, or the scene was laid in one of the rooms overlooking it, I could always see her gravestone standing just outside the iron gate. It was the same, too, with the married daughter; usually she was not present, but once or twice she returned again, in company with a man, whom I took to be her husband. He, too, like the rest of them, was always silent. But, owing to the constant repetition of the dream, I had ceased to attach, in my waking hours, any significance to it. I never met Jack Stone again during all those years, nor did I ever see a house that resembled this dark house of my dream. And then something happened.

I had been in London in this year, up till the end of the July, and during the first week in August went down to stay with a friend in a house he had taken for the summer months, in the Ashdown Forest district of Sussex. I left London early, for John Clinton was to meet me at Forest Row Station, and we were going to spend the day golfing, and go to his house in the evening. He had his motor with him, and we set off, about five of the afternoon, after a thoroughly delightful day, for the drive, the distance being some ten miles. As it was still so early we did not have tea at the club house, but waited till we should get home. As we drove, the weather, which up till then had been, though hot, deliciously fresh, seemed to me to alter in quality, and become very stagnant and oppressive, and I felt that indefinable sense of ominous apprehension that I am accustomed to before thunder. John, however, did not share my views, attributing my loss of lightness to the fact that I had lost both my matches. Events proved, however, that I was right, though I do not think that the thunderstorm that broke that night was the sole cause of my depression.

Our way lay through deep high-banked lanes, and before we had gone very far I fell asleep, and was only awakened by the stopping of the motor. And with a sudden thrill, partly of fear but chiefly of curiosity, I found myself standing in the doorway of my house of dream. We went, I half wondering whether or not I was dreaming still, through a low oak-panelled hall, and out onto the lawn, where tea was laid in the shadow of the house. It was set in flower beds, a red-brick wall, with a gate in it, bounded one side, and out beyond that was a space of rough grass with a walnut tree. The facade of the house was very long, and at one end stood a three-storeyed tower, markedly older than the rest.

Here for the moment all resemblance to the repeated dream ceased. There was no silent and somehow terrible family, but a large assembly of exceedingly cheerful persons, all of whom were known to me. And in spite of the horror with which the dream itself had always filled me, I felt nothing of it now that the scene of it was thus reproduced before me. But I felt intensest curiosity as to what was going to happen.

Tea pursued its cheerful course, and before long Mrs. Clinton got up. And at that moment I think I knew what she was going to say. She spoke to me, and what she said was:

'Jack will show you your room: I have given you the room in the tower.'

At that, for half a second, the horror of the dream took hold of me again. But it quickly passed, and again I felt nothing more than the most intense curiosity. It was not very long before it was amply satisfied.

John turned to me.

'Right up at the top of the house,' he said, 'but I think you'll be comfortable. We're absolutely full up. Would you like to go and see it now? By Jove, I believe that you are right, and that we are going to have a thunderstorm. How dark it has become.'

I got up and followed him. We passed through the hall, and up the perfectly familiar staircase. Then he opened the door, and I went in. And at that moment sheer unreasoning terror again possessed me. I did not know what I feared: I simply feared. Then like a sudden recollection, when one remembers a name which has long escaped the memory,

I knew what I feared. I feared Mrs. Stone, whose grave with the sinister inscription, 'In evil memory,' I had so often seen in my dream, just beyond the lawn which lay below my window. And then once more the fear passed so completely that I wondered what there was to fear, and I found myself, sober and quiet and sane, in the room in the tower, the name of which I had so often heard in my dream, and the scene of which was so familiar.

I looked around it with a certain sense of proprietorship, and found that nothing had been changed from the dreaming nights in which I knew it so well. Just to the left of the door was the bed, lengthways along the wall, with the head of it in the angle. In a line with it was the fireplace and a small bookcase; opposite the door the outer wall was pierced by two lattice-paned windows, between which stood the dressing-table, while ranged along the fourth wall was the washing-stand and a big cupboard. My luggage had already been unpacked, for the furniture of dressing and undressing lay orderly on the wash-stand and toilet-table, while my dinner clothes were spread out on the coverlet of the bed. And then, with a sudden start of unexplained dismay, I saw that there were two rather conspicuous objects which I had not seen before in my dreams: one a life-sized oil painting of Mrs. Stone, the other a black-and-white sketch of Jack Stone, representing him as he had appeared to me only a week before in the last of the series of these repeated dreams, a rather secret and evil-looking man of about thirty. His picture hung between the windows, looking straight across the room to the other portrait, which hung at the side of the bed. At that I looked next, and as I looked I felt once more the horror of nightmare seize me.

It represented Mrs. Stone as I had seen her last in my dreams: old and withered and white-haired. But in spite of the evident feebleness of body, a dreadful exuberance and vitality shone through the envelope of flesh, an exuberance wholly malign, a vitality that foamed and frothed with unimaginable evil. Evil beamed from the narrow, leering eyes; it laughed in the demon-like mouth. The whole face was instinct with some secret and appalling mirth; the hands, clasped together on the knee, seemed shaking with suppressed and nameless glee. Then I saw also that it was signed in the left-hand bottom corner, and wondering who the artist could be, I looked more closely, and read the inscription, 'Julia Stone by Julia Stone.'

There came a tap at the door, and John Clinton entered.

'Got everything you want?' he asked.

'Rather more than I want,' said I, pointing to the picture.

He laughed.

'Hard-featured old lady,' he said. 'By herself, too, I remember. Anyhow she can't have flattered herself much.'

'But don't you see?' said I. 'It's scarcely a human face at all. It's the face of some witch, of some devil.'

He looked at it more closely.

'Yes; it isn't very pleasant,' he said. 'Scarcely a bedside manner, eh? Yes; I can imagine getting the nightmare if I went to sleep with that close by my bed. I'll have it taken down if you like.'

'I really wish you would,' I said. He rang the bell, and with the help of a servant we detached the picture and carried it out onto the landing, and put it with its face to the wall.

'By Jove, the old lady is a weight,' said John, mopping his forehead. 'I wonder if she had something on her mind.'

The extraordinary weight of the picture had struck me too. I was about to reply, when I caught sight of my own hand. There was blood on it, in considerable quantities, covering the whole palm.

'I've cut myself somehow,' said I.

John gave a little startled exclamation.

'Why, I have too,' he said.

Simultaneously the footman took out his handkerchief and wiped his hand with it. I saw that there was blood also on his handkerchief.

John and I went back into the tower room and washed the blood off; but neither on his hand nor on mine was there the slightest trace of a scratch or cut. It seemed to me that, having ascertained this, we both, by a sort of tacit consent, did not allude to it again. Something in my case had dimly occurred to me that I did not wish to think about. It was but a conjecture, but I fancied that I knew the same thing had occurred to him.

The heat and oppression of the air, for the storm we had expected was still undischarged, increased very much after dinner, and for some time most of the party, among whom were John Clinton and myself, sat outside on the path bounding the lawn, where we had had tea. The night was absolutely dark, and no twinkle of star or moon ray could penetrate the pall of cloud that overset the sky. By degrees our assembly thinned, the women went up to bed, men dispersed to the smoking or billiard room, and by eleven o'clock my host and I were the only two left. All the evening I thought that he had something on his mind, and as soon as we were alone he spoke.

'The man who helped us with the picture had blood on his hand, too, did you notice?' he said.

'I asked him just now if he had cut himself, and he said he supposed he had, but that he could find no mark of it. Now where did that blood come from?'

By dint of telling myself that I was not going to think about it, I had succeeded in not doing so, and I did not want, especially just at bedtime, to be reminded of it.

'I don't know,' said I, 'and I don't really care so long as the picture of Mrs. Stone is not by my bed.'

He got up.

'But it's odd,' he said. 'Ha! Now you'll see another odd thing.'

A dog of his, an Irish terrier by breed, had come out of the house as we talked. The door behind us into the hall was open, and a bright oblong of light shone across the lawn to the iron gate which led on to the rough grass outside, where the walnut tree stood. I saw that the dog had all his hackles up, bristling with rage and fright; his lips were curled back from his teeth, as if he was ready to spring at something, and he was growling to himself. He took not the slightest notice of his master or me, but stiffly and tensely walked across the grass to the iron gate. There he stood for a moment, looking through the bars and still growling. Then of a sudden his courage seemed to desert him: he gave one long howl, and scuttled back to the house with a curious crouching sort of movement.

'He does that half-a-dozen times a day,' said John. 'He sees something which he both hates and fears.'

I walked to the gate and looked over it. Something was moving on the grass outside, and soon a sound which I could not instantly identify came to my ears. Then I remembered what it was: it was the purring of a cat. I lit a match, and saw the purrer, a big blue Persian, walking round and round in a little circle just outside the gate, stepping high and ecstatically, with tail carried aloft like a banner. Its eyes were bright and shining, and every now and then it put its head down and sniffed at the grass.

I laughed.

'The end of that mystery, I am afraid,' I said. 'Here's a large cat having Walpurgis night all alone.'

'Yes, that's Darius,' said John. 'He spends half the day and all night there. But that's not the end of the dog mystery, for Toby and he are the best of friends, but the beginning of the cat mystery. What's the cat doing there? And why is Darius pleased, while Toby is terror-stricken?'

At that moment I remembered the rather horrible detail of my dreams when I saw through the gate, just where the cat was now, the white tombstone with the sinister inscription. But before I could answer the rain began, as suddenly and heavily as if a tap had been turned on, and simultaneously the big cat squeezed through the bars of the gate, and came leaping across the lawn to the house for shelter. Then it sat in the doorway, looking out eagerly into the dark. It spat and struck at John with its paw, as he pushed it in, in order to close the door.

Somehow, with the portrait of Julia Stone in the passage outside, the room in the tower had absolutely no alarm for me, and as I went to bed, feeling very sleepy and heavy, I had nothing more than interest for the curious incident about our bleeding hands, and the conduct of the cat and dog. The last thing I looked at before I put out my light was the square empty space by my bed where the portrait had been. Here the paper was of its original full tint of dark red: over the rest of the walls it had faded. Then I blew out my candle and instantly fell asleep.

My awaking was equally instantaneous, and I sat bolt upright in bed under the impression that some bright light had been flashed in my face, though it was now absolutely pitch dark. I knew exactly where I was, in the room which I had dreaded in dreams, but no horror that I ever felt when asleep approached the fear that now invaded and froze my brain. Immediately after a peal of thunder crackled just above the house, but the probability that it was only a flash of lightning which awoke me gave no reassurance to my galloping heart. Something I knew was in the room with me, and instinctively I put out my right hand, which was nearest the wall, to keep it away. And my hand touched the edge of a picture-frame hanging close to me.

I sprang out of bed, upsetting the small table that stood by it, and I heard my watch, candle, and matches clatter onto the floor. But for the moment there was no need of light, for a blinding flash leaped out of the clouds, and showed me that by my bed again hung the picture of Mrs. Stone. And instantly the room went into blackness again. But in that flash I saw another thing also, namely a figure that leaned over the end of my bed, watching me. It was dressed in some close-clinging white garment, spotted and stained with mould, and the face was that of the portrait.

Overhead the thunder cracked and roared, and when it ceased and the deathly stillness succeeded, I heard the rustle of movement coming nearer me, and, more horrible yet, perceived an odour of corruption and decay. And then a hand was laid on the side of my neck, and close beside my ear I heard quick-taken, eager breathing. Yet I knew that this thing, though it could be perceived by touch, by smell, by eye and by ear, was still not of this earth, but something that had passed out of the body and had power to make itself manifest. Then a voice, already familiar to me, spoke.

'I knew you would come to the room in the tower,' it said. 'I have been long waiting for you. At last you have come. Tonight I shall feast; before long we will feast together.'

And the quick breathing came closer to me; I could feel it on my neck.

At that the terror, which I think had paralysed me for the moment, gave way to the wild instinct of self-preservation. I hit wildly with both arms, kicking out at the same moment, and heard a little animal-squeal, and something soft dropped with a thud beside me. I took a couple of steps forward, nearly tripping up over whatever it was that lay there, and by the merest good-luck found the handle of the door. In another second I ran out on the landing, and had banged the door behind me. Almost at the same moment I heard a door open somewhere below, and John Clinton, candle in hand, came running upstairs.

'What is it?' he said. 'I sleep just below you, and heard a noise as if – Good heavens, there's blood on your shoulder.'

I stood there, so he told me afterwards, swaying from side to side, white as a sheet, with the mark on my shoulder as if a hand covered with blood had been laid there.

'It's in there,' I said, pointing. 'She, you know. The portrait is in there, too, hanging up on the place we took it from.'

At that he laughed.

'My dear fellow, this is mere nightmare,' he said.

He pushed by me, and opened the door, I standing there simply inert with terror, unable to stop him, unable to move.

'Phew! What an awful smell,' he said.

Then there was silence; he had passed out of my sight behind the open door. Next moment he came out again, as white as myself, and instantly shut it.

'Yes, the portrait's there,' he said, 'and on the floor is a thing – a thing spotted with earth, like what they bury people in. Come away, quick, come away.'

How I got downstairs I hardly know. An awful shuddering and nausea of the spirit rather than of the flesh had seized me, and more than once he had to place my feet upon the steps, while every now and then he cast glances of terror and apprehension up the stairs. But in time we came to his dressing-room on the floor below, and there I told him what I have here described.

The sequel can be made short; indeed, some of my readers have perhaps already guessed what it was, if they remember that inexplicable affair of the churchyard at West Fawley, some eight years ago, where an attempt was made three times to bury the body of a certain woman who had committed suicide. On each occasion the coffin was found in the course of a few days again protruding from the ground. After the third attempt, in order that the thing should not be talked about, the body was buried elsewhere in unconsecrated ground. Where it was buried was just outside the iron gate of the garden belonging to the house where this woman had lived. She had committed suicide in a room at the top of the tower in that house. Her name was Julia Stone.

Subsequently the body was again secretly dug up, and the coffin was found to be full of blood.

No. 1 Branch Line: The Signal-Man

CHARLES DICKENS

'Halloa! Below there!'

When he heard a voice thus calling to him, he was standing at the door of his box, with a flag in his hand, furled round its short pole. One would have thought, considering the nature of the ground, that he could not have doubted from what quarter the voice came; but instead of looking up to where I stood on the top of the steep cutting nearly over his head, he turned himself about, and looked down the Line. There was something remarkable in his manner of doing so, though I could not have said for my life what. But I know it was remarkable enough to attract my notice, even though his figure was foreshortened and shadowed, down to the deep trench, and mine was high above him, so steeped in the glow of an angry sunset, that I had shaded my eyes with my hand before I saw him at all.

'Hallow! Bellow!'

From looking down the Line, he turned himself about again, and, raising his eyes, saw my figure high above him.

'Is there any path by which I can come down and speak to you?'

He looked up at me without replying, and I looked down at him without pressing him too soon with a repetition of my idle question. Just then there came a vague vibration in the earth and air, quickly changing into a violent pulsation, and an oncoming rush that caused me to start back, as though it had force to draw me down. When such vapour as rose to my height from this rapid train had passed me, and was skimming away over the landscape, I looked down again, and saw him refurling the flag he had shown while the train went by.

I repeated my inquiry. After a pause, during which he seemed to regard me with fixed attention, he motioned with his rolled-up flag towards a point on my level, some two or three hundred yards distant. I called down to him, 'All right!' and made for that point. There, by dint of looking closely about me, I found a rough zigzag descending path notched out, which I followed.

The cutting was extremely deep, and unusually precipitate. It was made through a clammy stone, that became oozier and wetter as I went down. For these reasons, I found the way long enough to give me time to recall a singular aid of reluctance or compulsion with which he had pointed out the path.

When I came down low enough upon the zigzag descent to see him again, I saw that he was standing between the rails on the way by which the train had lately passed, in an attitude as if he were waiting for me to appear. He had his left hand at his chin, and that left elbow rested on his right hand, crossed over his breast. His attitude was one of such expectation and watchfulness that I stopped a moment, wondering at it.

I resumed my downward way, and stepping out upon the level of the railroad, and drawing nearer to him, saw that he was a dark sallow man, with a dark beard and rather heavy eyebrows. His post was in as solitary and dismal a place as ever I saw. On either side, a dripping-wet wall of jagged stone, excluding all view but a strip of sky; the perspective one way only a crooked prolongation of this great dungeon; the shorter perspective in the other direction terminating in a gloomy red light, and the gloomier entrance to a black tunnel, in whose massive architecture there was a barbarous, depressing, and forbidding air. So little sunlight ever found its way to this spot, that it had an earthy, deadly smell; and so much cold wind rushed through it, that it struck chill to me, as if I had left the natural world.

Before he stirred, I was near enough to him to have touched him. Not even then removing his eyes from mine, he stepped back one step, and lifted his hand.

This was a lonesome post to occupy (I said), and it had riveted my attention when I looked down from up yonder. A visitor was a rarity, I should suppose; not an unwelcome rarity, I hoped? In me, he merely saw a man, who had been shut up within narrow limits all his life, and who, being at last set free, had a newly-awakened interest in these great works. To such purpose I spoke to him; but I am far from sure of the terms I used; for, besides that I am not happy in opening any conversation, there was something in the man that daunted me.

He directed a most curious look towards the red light near the tunnel's mouth, and looked all about it, as if something were missing from it, and then he looked at me.

That light was part of his charge? Was it not?

He answered in a low voice, – 'Don't you know it is?'

The monstrous thought came into my mind, as I perused the fixed eyes and the saturnine face, that this was a spirit not a man. I have speculated since, whether there may not have been infection in his mind.

In my turn, I stepped back. But in making the action, I detected in his eyes some latent fear of me. This put the monstrous thought to flight. 'You look at me,' I said, forcing a smile, 'as if you had a dread of me.'

'I was doubtful,' he returned, 'whether I had seen you before.'

'Where?'

He pointed to the red light he had looked at.

'There?' I said.

Intently watchful of me, he replied (but without sound), 'Yes.'

'My good fellow, what should I do there? However, be that as it may, I never was there, you may swear.'

'I think I may,' he rejoined. 'Yes; I am sure I may.'

His manner cleared, like my own. He replied to my remarks with readiness, and in well-chosen words. Had he much to do there? Yes;

that was to say, he had enough responsibility to bear; but exactness and watchfulness were what was required of him, and of actual work – manual labour – he had next to none. To change that signal, to trim those lights, and to turn this iron handle now and then, was all he had to do under that head. Regarding those many long and lonely hours of which I seemed to make so much, he could only say that the routine of his life had shaped itself into that form, and he had grown used to it. He had taught himself a language down here, – if only to know it by sight, and to have formed his own crude ideas of its pronunciation, could be called learning it. He had also worked at fractions and decimals, and tried a little algebra; but he was, and had been as a boy, a poor hand at figures. Was it necessary for him when on duty always to remain in that channel of damp air, and could he never rise into the sunshine from between those high stone walls? Why, that depended upon times and circumstances. Under some conditions there would be less upon the Line than under others, and the same held good as to certain hours of the day and night. In bright weather, he did choose occasions for getting a little above these lower shadows; but, being at all times liable to be called by his electric bell, and at such times listening for it with redoubled anxiety, the relief was less than I would suppose.

He took me into his box, where there was a fire, a desk for an official book in which he had to make certain entries, a telegraphic instrument with its dial, face, and needles, and the little bell of which he had spoken. On my trusting that he would excuse the remark that he had been well educated, and (I hoped I might say without offence), perhaps educated above the station, he observed that instances of slight incongruity in such wise would rarely be found wanting among large bodies of men; that he had heard it was so in workhouses, in the police force, even in that last desperate resource, the army; and that he knew it was so, more or less, in any great railway staff. He had been, when young (if I could believe it, sitting in that hut, – he scarcely could), a student of natural philosophy, and had attended lectures; but he had run wild, misused his opportunities, gone down, and never risen again. He had no complaint to offer about that. He had made his bed, and he lay upon it. It was far too late to make another.

All that I have here condensed he said in a quiet manner, with his grave dark regards divided between me and the fire. He threw in the word, 'Sir,' from time to time, and especially when he referred to his youth – as though to request me to understand that he claimed to be nothing but what I found him. He was several times interrupted by the little bell, and had to read off messages, and send replies. Once he had to stand without the door, and display a flag as a train passed, and make some verbal communication to the driver. In the discharge of his duties, I observed him to be remarkably exact and vigilant, breaking off his discourse at a syllable, and remaining silent until what he had to do was done.

In a word, I should have set this man down as one of the safest of men to be employed in that capacity, but for the circumstance that while he was speaking to me he twice broke off with a fallen colour, turned his face towards the little bell when it did NOT ring, opened the door of the hut (which was kept shut to exclude the unhealthy damp), and looked out towards the red light near the mouth of the tunnel. On both of those occasions, he came back to the fire with the inexplicable air upon him which I had remarked, without being able to define, when we were so far asunder.

Said I, when I rose to leave, 'You almost make me think that I have met with a contented man.'

(I am afraid I must acknowledge that I said it to lead him on.)

'I believe I used to be so,' he rejoined, in the low voice in which he had first spoken; 'but I am troubled, Sir, I am troubled.'

He would have recalled the words if he could. He had said them, however, and I took them up quickly.

'With what? What is your trouble?'

'It is very difficult to impart, Sir. It is very, very difficult to speak of. If ever you make me another visit, I will try to tell you.'

'But I expressly intend to make you another visit. Say, when shall it be?'

'I go off early in the morning and I shall be on again at ten tomorrow night, Sir.'

'I will come at eleven.'

He thanked me, and went out at the door with me. 'I'll show my white light, Sir,' he said, in his peculiar low voice, 'till you have found the way up. When you have found it, don't call out! And when you are at the top, don't call out!'

His manner seemed to make the place strike colder to me, but I said no more than, 'Very well.'

'And when you come down tomorrow night, don't call out! Let me ask you a parting question. What made you cry, "Halloa! Below there!" tonight?"

'Heavens knows,' said I. 'I cried something to that effect ...'

'Not to that effect, Sir. Those were the very words. I know them well.'

'I admit those were the very words. I said them no doubt, because I saw you below.'

'For no other reason?'

'What other reason could I possibly have?'

'You had no feeling that they were conveyed to you in any supernatural way?'

'No.'

He wished me good night, and held up his light. I walked by the side of the down Line of rails (with a very disagreeable sensation of a train coming behind me) until I found the path. It was easier to mount than to descend, and I got back to my inn without any adventure.

Punctual to my appointment, I placed my foot on the first notch of the zigzag next night, as the distant clocks were striking eleven. He was waiting for me at the bottom, with his white light on. 'I have not called out,' I said, when we came close together; 'may I speak now?'

'By all means, Sir.'

'Goodnight, then, and here's my hand.'

'Goodnight, Sir, and here's mine.' With that we walked side by side to his box, entered it, closed the door, and sat down by the fire.

'I have made up my mind, Sir,' he began, bending forward as soon as we were seated, and speaking in a tone but a little above a whisper, 'that you shall not have to ask me twice what troubles me. I took you for someone else yesterday evening. That troubles me.'

'That mistake?'

'No. That someone else.'

'Who is it?'

'I don't know.'

'Like me?'

'I don't know. I never saw the face. The left arm is across the face and the right arm is waved – violently waved. This way.'

I followed his action with my eyes, and it was the action of an arm gesticulating with the utmost passion and vehemence, 'For God's sake, clear the way!'

'One moonlight night,' said the man, 'I was sitting here, when I heard a voice cry, "Halloa! Below there!" I started up, looked from that door, and saw this Some one else standing by the red light near the tunnel, waving as I just now showed you. The voice seemed hoarse with shouting, and it cried, "Look out! Look out!" And then again, "Halloa! Below there! Look out!" I caught up my lamp, turned it on red, and ran towards the figure, calling "What's wrong? What has happened? Where?" It stood just outside the blackness of the tunnel. I advanced so close upon it that I wondered at its keeping the sleeve across its eyes. I ran right up at it, and had my hand stretched out to pull the sleeve away, when it was gone.'

'Into the tunnel?' said I.

'No. I ran on into the tunnel, five hundred yards. I stopped, and held my lamp above my head, and saw the figures of the measured distance, and saw the wet stains stealing down the walls and trickling through the arch. I ran out again faster than I had run in (for I had a mortal abhorrence of the place upon me), and I looked all round the red light with my own red light, and I went up the iron ladder to the gallery atop of it, and I came down again, and ran back here. I telegraphed both ways. "An alarm has been given. Is anything wrong?" The answer came back, both ways, "All well."'

Resisting the slow touch of a frozen finger tracing out my spine, I showed him how that this figure must be a deception of his sense of sight; and how that figures, originating in disease of the delicate nerves that minister to the functions of the eye, were known to have become conscious of the nature of their affliction, and had even proved it by experimenting upon themselves. 'As to an imaginary cry,' said I, 'do but listen for a moment to the wind in this unnatural valley while we speak so low, and to the wild harp it makes of the telegraph wires.'

That was all very well, he returned, after we had sat listening for a while, and he ought to know something of the wind and the wires, – he who so often passed long winter nights there, alone and watching. But he would beg to remark that he had not finished.

I asked his pardon, and he slowly added these words, touching my arm,—

'Within six hours after the Appearance, the memorable accident on this Line happened, and within ten hours the dead and wounded were brought along through the tunnel over the spot where the figure had stood.'

A disagreeable shudder crept over me, but I did my best against it. It was not to be denied, I rejoined, that this was a remarkable coincidence, calculated deeply to impress his mind. But it was unquestionable that remarkable coincidence did continually occur, and they must be taken into account in dealing with such a subject. Though to be sure I must admit, I added (for I thought I saw that he was going to bring the objection to bear upon me), men of common sense did not allow much for coincidences in making the ordinary calculations of life.

He again begged to remark that he had not finished.

I again begged his pardon for being betrayed into interruptions.

'This,' he said, again laying his hand upon my arm, and glancing over his shoulder with hollow eyes, 'was just a year ago. Six or seven months passed, and I had recovered from the surprise and shock, when one morning, as the day was breaking, I, standing at the door, looked towards the red light, and saw the spectre again.' He stopped, with a fixed look at me.

'Did it cry out?'

'No. It was silent.'

'Did it wave its arm?'

'No. It leaned against the shaft of light, with both hands before the face. Like this.'

Once more I followed his action with my eyes. It was an action of mourning. I have seen such an attitude in stone figures on tombs.

'Did you go up to it?'

'I came in and sat down, partly to collect my thoughts, partly because it had turned me faint. When I went to the door again, daylight was above me, and the ghost was gone.'

'But nothing followed? Nothing came of this?'

He touched me on the arm with his forefinger twice or thrice, giving a ghastly nod each time:

'That very day, as a train came out of the tunnel, I noticed, at a carriage window on my side, what looked like a confusion of hands and heads, and something waved. I saw it just in time to signal the driver, Stop! He shut off, and put his brake on, but the train drifted past here a hundred and fifty yards or more. I ran after it, and, as I went along, heard terrible screams and cries. A beautiful young lady had died instantaneously in one of the compartments, and was brought in here, and laid down on this floor between us.'

Involuntarily I pushed my chair back, as I looked from the boards at which he pointed to himself.

'True, Sir. True. Precisely as it happened, so I tell it you.'

I could think of nothing to say, to any purpose, and my mouth was very dry. The wind and wires took up the story with a long lamenting wail.

He resumed. 'Now, Sir, mark this, and judge how my mind is troubled. The spectre came back a week ago. Ever since, it has been there, now and again, by fits and starts.'

'At the light?'

'At the Danger-light.'

'What does it seem to do?'

He repeated, if possible with increased passion and vehemence, that former gesticulation of 'For God's sake, clear the way!'

Then he went on. 'I have no peace or rest for it. It calls to me, for many minutes together, in an agonised manner, "Below there! Look out!" It stands waving to me. It rings my little bell …'

I caught at that. 'Did it ring your bell yesterday evening when I was here, and you went to the door?'

'Twice.'

'Why, see,' said I, 'how your imagination misleads you. My eyes were on the bell, and my ears open to the bell, and if I am a living man, it did NOT ring at those times. No, nor at any other time, except when it was rung in the natural course of physical things by the station communicating with you.'

He shook his head. 'I have never made a mistake as to that yet, Sir. I have never confused the spectre's ring with the man's. The ghost's ring is a strange vibration in the bell that it derives from nothing else, and I have not asserted that the bell stirs to the eye. I don't wonder that you failed to hear it. But I heard it.'

'And did the spectre seem to be there, when you looked out?'

'It WAS there.'

'Both times?'

He repeated firmly: 'Both times.'

'Will you come to the door with me, and look for it now?'

He bit his under-lip as though he were somewhat unwilling, but he arose. I opened the door, and stood on the step, while he stood in the doorway. There was the Danger-light. There was the dismal mouth of the tunnel. There were the high, wet stone walls of the cutting. There were the stars above them.

'Do you see it?' I asked him, taking particular note of his face. His eyes were prominent and strained, but not very much more so, perhaps, than my own had been when I had directed them earnestly towards the same spot.

'No,' he answered. 'It is not there.'

'Agreed,' said I.

We went in again, shut the door, and resumed our seats. I was thinking how best to improve this advantage, if it might be called one, when he took up the conversation in such a matter-of-course way, so assuming that there could be no serious question of the fact between us, that I felt myself placed in the weakest of positions.

'By this time you will fully understand, Sir,' he said, 'that what troubles me so dreadfully is the question, What does the spectre mean?'

I was not sure, I told him, that I did fully understand.

'What is its warning against?' he said, ruminating, with his eyes on the fire, and only by times turning them on me. 'What is the danger? Where is the danger? There is danger overhanging somewhere on the Line. Some dreadful calamity will happen. It is not to be doubted this third time, after what has gone before. But surely this is a cruel haunting of me. What can I do?'

He pulled out his handkerchief, and wiped the drops from his heated forehead.

'If I telegraph Danger, on either side of me, or on both, I can give no reason for it,' he went on, wiping the palms of his hands. 'I should get into trouble, and do no good. They would think I was mad. That is the way it would work: – Message: "Danger! Take care!" Answer. "What danger? Where?" Message: "Don't know. But for God's sake, take care!" They would displace me. What else could they do?'

His pain of mind was most pitiable to see. It was the mental torture of a conscientious man, oppressed beyond endurance by an unintelligible responsibility involving life.

'When it first stood under the Danger-light,' he went on, putting his dark hair back from his head, and drawing his hands outward and across his temples in an extremity of feverish distress, 'why not tell me where that accident was to happen, – if it must happen? Why not tell me how it could be averted, – if it could have been averted? When on its second coming it hid its face, why not tell me, instead, "She is going to die. Let them keep her at home"? If it came, on those two occasions, only to show me that its warnings were true, and so to prepare me for a third, why not warn me plainly now? And I, Lord help me! A mere poor signal-man on this solitary station! Why not go to somebody with credit to be believed, and power to act?'

When I saw him in this state, I saw that for the poor man's sake, as well as for public safety, what I had to do for the time was to compose his mind. Therefore, setting aside all question of reality or unreality between us, I represented to him that whoever thoroughly discharged his duty must do well, and that at least it was his comfort that he understood his duty, though he did not understand these confounding Appearances. In this effort I succeeded far better than in the attempt to reason him out of his conviction. He became calm; the occupations incidental to his post as the night advanced began to make larger demands on his attention: and I left him at two in the morning. I had offered to stay through the night, but he would not hear of it.

That I more than once looked back at the red light as I ascended the pathway, that I did not like the red light, and that I should have slept poorly if my bed had been under it, I see no reason to conceal. Nor did I like the two sequences of the accident and the dead girl. I see no reason to conceal that either.

But what ran most in my thoughts was the consideration how ought I to act, having become the recipient of this disclosure? I had proved the man to be intelligent, vigilant, painstaking, and exact; but how long might he remain so, in his state of mind? Though in a subordinate position, still he held a most important trust, and would I (for instance) like to stake my own life on the chances of his continuing to execute it with precision?

Unable to overcome a feeling that there would be something treacherous in my communicating what he had told me to his superiors in the Company, without first being plain with himself and proposing a middle course to him, I ultimately resolved to offer to accompany him (otherwise keeping his secret for the present) to the wisest medical practitioner we could hear of in those parts, and to take his opinion. A change in his time of duty would come round next night, he had apprised me, and he would be off an hour or two after sunrise, and on again soon after sunset. I had appointed to return accordingly.

Next evening was a lovely evening, and I walked out early to enjoy it. The sun was not yet quite down when I traversed the field-path near the top of the deep cutting. I would extend my walk for an hour, I said to myself, half an hour on and half an hour back, and it would then be time to go to my signal-man's box.

Before pursuing my stroll, I stepped to the brink, and mechanically looked down, from the point from which I had first seen him. I cannot describe the thrill that seized me, when, close at the mouth of the tunnel, I saw the appearance of a man, with his left sleeve across his eyes, passionately waving his right arm.

The nameless horror that oppressed me passed in a moment, for in a moment I saw that this appearance of a man was a man indeed, and that there was a little group of other men, standing at a short distance, to whom he seemed to be rehearsing the gesture he made. The Danger-light was not yet lighted. Against its shaft, a little low hut, entirely new to me, had been made of some wooden supports and tarpaulin. It looked no bigger than a bed.

With an irresistible sense that something was wrong, – with a flashing self-reproachful fear that fatal mischief had come of my leaving the man there, and causing no one to be sent to overlook or correct what he did, – I descended the notched path with all the speed I could make.

'What is the matter?' I asked the men.

'Signal-man killed this morning, Sir.'

'Not the man belonging to that box?'

'Yes, Sir.'

'Not the man I know?'

'You will recognise him, Sir, if you knew him,' said the man who spoke for the others, solemnly uncovering his own head, and raising an end of the tarpaulin, 'for his face is quite composed.'

'O, how did this happen, how did this happen?' I asked, turning from one to another as the hut closed in again.

'He was cut down by an engine, Sir. No man in England knew his work better. But somehow he was not clear of the outer rail. It was just at broad day. He had struck the light, and had the lamp in his hand. As the engine came out of the tunnel, his back was towards her, and she cut him down. That man drove her, and was showing how it happened. Show the gentleman, Tom.'

The man, who wore a rough dark dress, stepped back to his former place at the mouth of the tunnel.

'Coming round the curve in the tunnel, Sir,' he said, 'I saw him at the end, like as if I saw him down a perspective-glass. There was no time to check speed, and I knew him to be very careful. As he didn't seem to take heed of the whistle, I shut it off when we were running down upon him, and called to him as loud as I could call.'

'What did you say?'

'I said, "Below there! Look out! Look out! For God's sake, clear the way!"'

I started.

'Ah! it was a dreadful time, Sir. I never left off calling to him. I put this arm before my eyes not to see, and I waved this arm to the last; but it was of no use.'

Without prolonging the narrative to dwell on any one of its curious circumstances more than on any other, I may, in closing it, point out the coincidence that the warning of the Engine-Driver included, not only the words which the unfortunate Signal-man had repeated to me as haunting him, but also the words which I myself – not he – had attached, and that only in my own mind, to the gesticulation he had imitated.

From *All the Year Round, 1866*

An Account of Some Strange Disturbances in Aungier Street

SHERIDAN LE FANU

It is not worth telling, this story of mine – at least, not worth writing. Told, indeed, as I have sometimes been called upon to tell it, to a circle of intelligent and eager faces, lighted up by a good after-dinner fire on a winter's evening, with a cold wind rising and wailing outside, and all snug and cosy within, it has gone off – though I say it, who should not – indifferent well. But it is a venture to do as you would have me. Pen, ink, and paper are cold vehicles for the marvellous, and a 'reader' decidedly a more critical animal than a 'listener'. If, however, you can induce your friends to read it after nightfall, and when the fireside talk has run for a while on thrilling tales of shapeless terror; in short, if you will secure me the *mollia tempora fandi,* I will go to my work, and say my say, with better heart. Well, then, these conditions presupposed, I shall waste no more words, but tell you simply how it all happened.

My cousin (Tom Ludlow) and I studied medicine together. I think he would have succeeded, had he stuck to the profession; but he preferred the Church, poor fellow, and died early, a sacrifice to contagion, contracted in the noble discharge of his duties. For my present purpose, I say enough of his character when I mention that he was of a sedate but frank and cheerful nature; very exact in his observance of truth, and not by any means like myself – of an excitable or nervous temperament.

My Uncle Ludlow – Tom's father – while we were attending lectures, purchased three or four old houses in Aungier Street, one of which was unoccupied. *He* resided in the country, and Tom proposed that we should take up our abode in the untenanted house, so long as it should continue unlet; a move which would accomplish the double end of settling us nearer alike to our lecture-rooms and to our amusements, and of relieving us from the weekly charge of rent for our lodgings.

Our furniture was very scant – our whole equipage remarkably modest and primitive; and, in short, our arrangements pretty nearly as simple as those of a bivouac. Our new plan was, therefore, executed almost as soon as conceived. The front drawing-room was our sitting-room. I had the bedroom over it, and Tom the back bedroom on the same floor, which nothing could have induced me to occupy.

The house, to begin with, was a very old one. It had been, I believe, newly fronted about fifty years before; but with this exception, it had nothing modern about it. The agent who bought it and looked into the titles for my uncle, told me that it was sold, along with much other forfeited property, at Chichester House, I think, in 1702; and had belonged to Sir Thomas Hacket, who was Lord Mayor of Dublin in James II.'s time. How old it was *then*, I can't say; but, at all events, it had seen years and changes enough to have contracted all that mysterious and saddened air, at once exciting and depressing, which belongs to most old mansions.

There had been very little done in the way of modernising details; and, perhaps, it was better so; for there was something queer and by-gone in the very walls and ceilings – in the shape of doors and windows – in the odd diagonal site of the chimney-pieces – in the beams and ponderous cornices – not to mention the singular solidity of all the woodwork, from the banisters to the window-frames, which hopelessly defied disguise, and would have emphatically proclaimed their antiquity through any conceivable amount of modern finery and varnish.

An effort had, indeed, been made, to the extent of papering the drawing-rooms; but somehow, the paper looked raw and out of keeping;

and the old woman, who kept a little dirt-pie of a shop in the lane, and whose daughter – a girl of two and fifty – was our solitary handmaid, coming in at sunrise, and chastely receding again as soon as she had made all ready for tea in our state apartment; – this woman, I say, remembered it, when old Judge Horrocks (who, having earned the reputation of a particularly 'hanging judge,' ended by hanging himself, as the coroner's jury found, under an impulse of 'temporary insanity,' with a child's skipping-rope, over the massive old bannisters) resided there, entertaining good company, with fine venison and rare old port. In those halcyon days, the drawing-rooms were hung with gilded leather, and, I dare say, cut a good figure, for they were really spacious rooms.

The bedrooms were wainscoted, but the front one was not gloomy; and in it the cosiness of antiquity quite overcame its sombre associations. But the back bedroom, with its two queerly-placed melancholy windows, staring vacantly at the foot of the bed, and with the shadowy recess to be found in most old houses in Dublin, like a large ghostly closet, which, from congeniality of temperament, had amalgamated with the bedchamber, and dissolved the partition. At night-time, this 'alcove' – as our 'maid' was wont to call it – had, in my eyes, a specially sinister and suggestive character. Tom's distant and solitary candle glimmered vainly into its darkness. *There* it was always overlooking him – always itself impenetrable. But this was only part of the effect. The whole room was, I can't tell how, repulsive to me. There was, I suppose, in its proportions and features, a latent discord – a certain mysterious and indescribable relation, which jarred indistinctly upon some secret sense of the fitting and the safe, and raised indefinable suspicions and apprehensions of the imagination. On the whole, as I began by saying, nothing could have induced me to pass a night alone in it.

I had never pretended to conceal from poor Tom my superstitious weakness; and he, on the other hand, most unaffectedly ridiculed my tremors. The sceptic was, however, destined to receive a lesson, as you shall hear.

We had not been very long in occupation of our respective dormitories, when I began to complain of uneasy nights and disturbed sleep. I was, I suppose, the more impatient under this annoyance, as I was usually a sound sleeper, and by no means prone to nightmares. It was now, however, my destiny, instead of enjoying my customary repose, every night to 'sup full of horrors'. After a preliminary course of disagreeable and frightful dreams, my troubles took a definite form, and the same vision, without an appreciable variation in a single detail, visited me at least (on an average) every second night in the week.

Now, this dream, nightmare, or infernal illusion – which you please – of which I was the miserable sport, was on this wise:—

I saw, or thought I saw, with the most abominable distinctness, although at the time in profound darkness, every article of furniture and accidental arrangement of the chamber in which I lay. This, as you know, is incidental to ordinary nightmare. Well, while in this clairvoyant condition, which seemed but the lighting up of the theatre in which was to be exhibited the monotonous tableau of horror, which made my nights insupportable, my attention invariably became, I know not why, fixed upon the windows opposite the foot of my bed; and, uniformly with the same effect, a sense of dreadful anticipation always took slow but sure possession of me. I became somehow conscious of a sort of horrid but undefined preparation going forward in some unknown quarter, and by some unknown agency, for my torment; and, after an interval, which always seemed to me of the same length, a picture suddenly flew up to the window, where it remained fixed, as if by an electrical attraction, and my discipline of horror then commenced, to last perhaps for hours. The picture thus mysteriously glued to the window-panes, was the portrait of an old man, in a crimson flowered silk dressing-gown, the folds of which I could now describe, with a countenance embodying a strange mixture of intellect, sensuality, and power, but withal sinister and full of malignant omen. His nose was hooked, like the beak of a vulture; his eyes large, grey, and prominent, and lighted up with a more than mortal cruelty and coldness. These features were surmounted by a crimson velvet cap, the hair that peeped from under which was white with age, while the eyebrows retained their original blackness. Well I remember every line, hue, and shadow of that stony countenance, and well I may! The gaze of this hellish visage was fixed upon me, and mine returned it with the inexplicable fascination of nightmare, for what appeared to me to be hours of agony. At last—

The cock he crew, away then flew

the fiend who had enslaved me through the awful watches of the night; and, harassed and nervous, I rose to the duties of the day.

I had – I can't say exactly why, but it may have been from the exquisite anguish and profound impressions of unearthly horror, with which this strange phantasmagoria was associated – an insurmountable antipathy to describing the exact nature of my nightly troubles to my friend and comrade. Generally, however, I told him that I was haunted by abominable dreams; and, true to the imputed materialism of medicine, we put our heads together to dispel my horrors, not by exorcism, but by a tonic.

I will do this tonic justice, and frankly admit that the accursed portrait began to intermit its visits under its influence. What of that? Was this singular apparition – as full of character as of terror – therefore the creature of my fancy, or the invention of my poor stomach? Was it, in short, *subjective* (to borrow the technical slang of the day) and not the palpable aggression and intrusion of an external agent? That, good friend, as we will both admit, by no means follows. The evil spirit, who enthralled my senses in the shape of that portrait, may have been just as near me, just as energetic, just as malignant, though I saw him not. What means the whole moral code of revealed religion regarding the due keeping of our own bodies, soberness, temperance, etc.? here is an obvious connexion between the material and the invisible; the healthy tone of the system, and its unimpaired energy, may, for aught we can tell, guard us against influences which would otherwise render life itself terrific. The mesmerist and the electro-biologist will fail upon an average with nine patients out of ten – so may the evil spirit. Special conditions of the corporeal system are indispensable to the production of certain spiritual phenomena. The operation succeeds sometimes – sometimes fails – that is all.

I found afterwards that my would-be sceptical companion had his troubles too. But of these I knew nothing yet. One night, for a wonder, I was sleeping soundly, when I was roused by a step on the lobby outside my room, followed by the loud clang of what turned out to be a large brass candlestick, flung with all his force by poor Tom Ludlow over the banisters, and rattling with a rebound down the second flight of stairs; and almost concurrently with this, Tom burst open my door, and bounced into my room backwards, in a state of extraordinary agitation.

I had jumped out of bed and clutched him by the arm before I had any distinct idea of my own whereabouts. There we were – in our shirts – standing before the open door – staring through the great old banister opposite, at the lobby window, through which the sickly light of a clouded moon was gleaming.

'What's the matter, Tom? What's the matter with you? What the devil's the matter with you, Tom?' I demanded, shaking him with nervous impatience.

He took a long breath before he answered me, and then it was not very coherently.

'It's nothing, nothing at all – did I speak? – what did I say? – where's the candle, Richard? It's dark; I – I had a candle!'

'Yes, dark enough,' I said; 'but what's the matter? – what *is* it? – why don't you speak, Tom? – have you lost your wits? – what is the matter?'

'The matter? – oh, it is all over. It must have been a dream – nothing at all but a dream – don't you think so? It could not be anything more than a dream.'

'Of *course*,' said I, feeling uncommonly nervous, 'it *was* a dream.'

'I thought,' he said, 'there was a man in my room, and – and I jumped out of bed; and – and – where's the candle?'

'In your room, most likely,' I said, 'shall I go and bring it?'

'No; stay here – don't go; it's no matter – don't, I tell you; it was all a dream. Bolt the door, Dick; I'll stay here with you – I feel nervous. So, Dick, like a good fellow, light your candle and open the window – I am in a *shocking state*.'

I did as he asked me, and robing himself like Granuaile in one of my blankets, he seated himself close beside my bed.

Every body knows how contagious is fear of all sorts, but more especially that particular kind of fear under which poor Tom was at that moment labouring. I would not have heard, nor I believe would he have recapitulated, just at that moment, for half the world, the details of the hideous vision which had so unmanned him.

'Don't mind telling me anything about your nonsensical dream, Tom,' said I, affecting contempt, really in a panic; 'let us talk about something else; but it is quite plain that this dirty old house disagrees with us both, and hang me if I stay here any longer, to be pestered with indigestion and – and – bad nights, so we may as well look out for lodgings – don't you think so? – at once.'

Tom agreed, and, after an interval, said—

'I have been thinking, Richard, that it is a long time since I saw my father, and I have made up my mind to go down to-morrow and return in a day or two, and you can take rooms for us in the meantime.'

I fancied that this resolution, obviously the result of the vision which had so profoundly scared him, would probably vanish next morning with the damps and shadows of night. But I was mistaken. Off went Tom at peep of day to the country, having agreed that so soon as I had secured suitable lodgings, I was to recall him by letter from his visit to my Uncle Ludlow.

Now, anxious as I was to change my quarters, it so happened, owing to a series of petty procrastinations and accidents, that nearly a week elapsed before my bargain was made and my letter of recall on the wing to Tom; and, in the meantime, a trifling adventure or two had occurred to your humble servant, which, absurd as they now appear, diminished by distance, did certainly at the time serve to whet my appetite for change considerably.

A night or two after the departure of my comrade, I was sitting by my bedroom fire, the door locked, and the ingredients of a tumbler of hot whisky-punch upon the crazy spider-table; for, as the best mode of keeping the

Black spirits and white,
Blue spirits and grey,

with which I was environed, at bay, I had adopted the practice recommended by the wisdom of my ancestors, and 'kept my spirits up by pouring spirits down'. I had thrown aside my volume of Anatomy, and was treating myself by way of a tonic, preparatory to my punch and bed, to half-a-dozen pages of the *Spectator*, when I heard a step on the flight of stairs descending from the attics. It was two o'clock, and the streets were as silent as a churchyard – the sounds were, therefore, perfectly distinct. There was a slow, heavy tread, characterised by the emphasis and deliberation of age, descending by the narrow staircase from above; and, what made the sound more singular, it was plain that the feet which produced it were perfectly bare, measuring the descent with something between a pound and a flop, very ugly to hear.

I knew quite well that my attendant had gone away many hours before, and that nobody but myself had any business in the house. It was quite plain also that the person who was coming down stairs had no intention whatever of concealing his movements; but, on the contrary, appeared disposed to make even more noise, and proceed more deliberately, than was at all necessary. When the step reached the foot of the stairs outside my room, it seemed to stop; and I expected every moment to see my door open spontaneously, and give admission to the original of my detested portrait. I was, however, relieved in a few seconds by hearing the descent renewed, just in the same manner, upon the staircase leading down to the drawing-rooms, and thence, after another pause, down the next flight, and so on to the hall, whence I heard no more.

Now, by the time the sound had ceased, I was wound up, as they say, to a very unpleasant pitch of excitement. I listened, but there was not a stir. I screwed up my courage to a decisive experiment – opened my door, and in a stentorian voice bawled over the banisters, 'Who's there?' There was no answer but the ringing of my own voice through the empty old house – no renewal of the movement; nothing, in short, to give my unpleasant sensations a definite direction. There is, I think, something most disagreeably disenchanting in the sound of one's own voice under such circumstances, exerted in solitude, and in vain. It redoubled my sense of isolation, and my misgivings increased on perceiving that the door, which I certainly thought I had left open, was closed behind me; in a vague alarm, lest my retreat should be cut off, I got again into my room as quickly as I could, where I remained in a state of imaginary blockade, and very uncomfortable indeed, till morning.

Next night brought no return of my barefooted fellow-lodger; but the night following, being in my bed, and in the dark – somewhere, I suppose, about the same hour as before, I distinctly heard the old fellow again descending from the garrets.

This time I had had my punch, and the *morale* of the garrison was consequently excellent. I jumped out of bed, clutched the poker as I passed the expiring fire, and in a moment was upon the lobby. The sound had ceased by this time – the dark and chill were discouraging; and, guess my horror, when I saw, or thought I saw, a black monster, whether in the shape of a man or a bear I could not say, standing, with its back to the wall, on the lobby, facing me, with a pair of great greenish eyes shining dimly out. Now, I must be frank, and confess that the cupboard which displayed our plates and cups stood just there, though at the moment I did not recollect it. At the same time I must honestly say, that making every allowance for an excited imagination, I never could satisfy myself that I was made the dupe of my own fancy in this matter; for this apparition, after one or two shiftings of shape, as if in the act of incipient transformation, began, as it seemed on second thoughts, to advance upon me in its original form. From an instinct of terror rather than of courage, I hurled the poker, with all my force, at its head; and to the music of a horrid crash made my way into my room, and double-locked the door. Then, in a minute more, I heard the horrid bare feet walk down the stairs, till the sound ceased in the hall, as on the former occasion.

If the apparition of the night before was an ocular delusion of my fancy sporting with the dark outlines of our cupboard, and if its horrid eyes were nothing but a pair of inverted teacups, I had, at all events, the satisfaction of having launched the poker with admirable effect, and in true 'fancy' phrase, 'knocked its two daylights into one', as the commingled fragments of my tea-service testified. I did my best to gather comfort and courage from these evidences; but it would not do. And then what could I say of those horrid bare feet, and the regular tramp, tramp, tramp, which measured the distance of the entire staircase through the solitude of my haunted dwelling, and at an hour when no good influence was stirring? Confound it! – the whole affair was abominable. I was out of spirits, and dreaded the approach of night.

It came, ushered ominously in with a thunder-storm and dull torrents of depressing rain. Earlier than usual the streets grew silent; and by twelve o'clock nothing but the comfortless pattering of the rain was to be heard.

I made myself as snug as I could. I lighted *two* candles instead of one. I forswore bed, and held myself in readiness for a sally, candle in hand; for, *coûte qui coûte*, I was resolved to *see* the being, if visible at all, who troubled the nightly stillness of my mansion. I was fidgetty and nervous and tried in vain to interest myself with my books. I walked up and down my room, whistling in turn martial and hilarious music, and listening ever and anon for the dreaded noise. I sate down and stared at the square label on the solemn and reserved-looking black bottle, until 'FLANAGAN & CO'S BEST OLD MALT WHISKY' grew into a sort of subdued accompaniment to all the fantastic and horrible speculations which chased one another through my brain.

Silence, meanwhile, grew more silent, and darkness darker. I listened in vain for the rumble of a vehicle, or the dull clamour of a distant row. There was nothing but the sound of a rising wind, which had succeeded the thunder-storm that had travelled over the Dublin mountains quite out of hearing. In the middle of this great city I began to feel myself alone with nature, and Heaven knows what beside. My courage was ebbing. Punch, however, which makes beasts of so many, made a man of me again – just in time to hear with tolerable nerve and firmness the lumpy, flabby, naked feet deliberately descending the stairs again.

I took a candle, not without a tremor. As I crossed the floor I tried to extemporise a prayer, but stopped short to listen, and never finished it. The steps continued. I confess I hesitated for some seconds at the door before I took heart of grace and opened it. When I peeped out the lobby was perfectly empty – there was no monster standing on the staircase; and as the detested sound ceased, I was reassured enough to venture forward nearly to the banisters. Horror of horrors! within a stair or two beneath the spot where I stood the unearthly tread smote the floor. My eye caught something in motion; it was about the size of Goliath's foot – it was grey, heavy, and flapped with a dead weight from one step to another. As I am alive, it was the most monstrous grey rat I ever beheld or imagined.

Shakespeare says – 'Some men there are cannot abide a gaping pig, and some that are mad if they behold a cat.' I went well-nigh out of my wits when I beheld this *rat'*; for, laugh at me as you may, it fixed upon me, I thought, a perfectly human expression of malice; and, as it shuffled about and looked up into my face almost from between my feet, I saw, I could swear it – I felt it then, and know it now, the infernal gaze and the accursed countenance of my old friend in the portrait, transfused into the visage of the bloated vermin before me.

I bounced into my room again with a feeling of loathing and horror I cannot describe, and locked and bolted my door as if a lion had been at the other side. D—n him or *it*; curse the portrait and its original! I felt in my soul that the rat – yes, the *rat*, the RAT I had just seen, was that evil being in masquerade, and rambling through the house upon some infernal night lark.

Next morning I was early trudging through the miry streets; and, among other transactions, posted a peremptory note recalling Tom. On my return, however, I found a note from my absent 'chum', announcing his intended return next day. I was doubly rejoiced at this, because I had succeeded in getting rooms; and because the change of scene and return of my comrade were rendered specially pleasant by the last night's half ridiculous half horrible adventure.

I slept extemporaneously in my new quarters in Digges' Street that night, and next morning returned for breakfast to the haunted mansion, where I was certain Tom would call immediately on his arrival.

I was quite right – he came; and almost his first question referred to the primary object of our change of residence.

'Thank God,' he said with genuine fervour, on hearing that all was arranged. 'On *your* account I am delighted. As to myself, I assure you that no earthly consideration could have induced me ever again to pass a night in this disastrous old house.'

'Confound the house!' I ejaculated, with a genuine mixture of fear and detestation, 'we have not had a pleasant hour since we came to live here'; and so I went on, and related incidentally my adventure with the plethoric old rat.

'Well, if that were *all*,' said my cousin, affecting to make light of the matter, 'I don't think I should have minded it very much.'

'Ay, but its eye – its countenance, my dear Tom,' urged I; 'if you had seen *that*, you would have felt it might be *anything* but what it seemed.'

'I am inclined to think the best conjurer in such a case would be an able-bodied cat,' he said, with a provoking chuckle.

'But let us hear your own adventure,' I said tartly.

At this challenge he looked uneasily round him. I had poked up a very unpleasant recollection.

'You shall hear it, Dick; I'll tell it to you,' he said. 'Begad, sir, I should feel quite queer, though, telling it *here*, though we are too strong a body for ghosts to meddle with just now.'

Though he spoke this like a joke, I think it was serious calculation. Our Hebe was in a corner of the room, packing our cracked delft tea and dinner-services in a basket. She soon suspended operations, and with mouth and eyes wide open became an absorbed listener. Tom's experiences were told nearly in these words:—

'I saw it three times, Dick – three distinct times; and I am perfectly certain it meant me some infernal harm. I was, I say, in danger – in *extreme* danger; for, if nothing else had happened, my reason would most certainly have failed me, unless I had escaped so soon. Thank God. I *did* escape.

'The first night of this hateful disturbance, I was lying in the attitude of sleep, in that lumbering old bed. I hate to think of it. I was really wide awake, though I had put out my candle, and was lying as quietly as if I had been asleep; and although accidentally restless, my thoughts were running in a cheerful and agreeable channel.

'I think it must have been two o'clock at least when I thought I heard a sound in that – that odious dark recess at the far end of the bedroom. It was as if someone was drawing a piece of cord slowly along the floor, lifting it up, and dropping it softly down again in coils. I sate up once or twice in my bed, but could see nothing, so I concluded it must be mice in the wainscot. I felt no emotion graver than curiosity, and after a few minutes ceased to observe it.

'While lying in this state, strange to say; without at first a suspicion of anything supernatural, on a sudden I saw an old man, rather stout and square, in a sort of roan-red dressing-gown, and with a black cap on his head, moving stiffly and slowly in a diagonal direction, from the recess, across the floor of the bedroom, passing my bed at the foot, and entering the lumber-closet at the left. He had something under his arm; his head hung a little at one side; and, merciful God! when I saw his face.'

Tom stopped for a while, and then said—

'That awful countenance, which living or dying I never can forget, disclosed what he was. Without turning to the right or left, he passed beside me, and entered the closet by the bed's head.

'While this fearful and indescribable type of death and guilt was passing, I felt that I had no more power to speak or stir than if I had been myself a corpse. For hours after it had disappeared, I was too terrified and weak to move. As soon as daylight came, I took courage, and examined the room, and especially the course which the frightful intruder had seemed to take, but there was not a vestige to indicate anybody's having passed there; no sign of any disturbing agency visible among the lumber that strewed the floor of the closet.

'I now began to recover a little. I was fagged and exhausted, and at last, overpowered by a feverish sleep. I came down late; and finding you out of spirits, on account of your dreams about the portrait, whose *original* I am now certain disclosed himself to me, I did not care to talk about the infernal vision. In fact, I was trying to persuade myself that the whole thing was an illusion, and I did not like to revive in their intensity the hated impressions of the past night – or to risk the constancy of my scepticism, by recounting the tale of my sufferings.

'It required some nerve, I can tell you, to go to my haunted chamber next night, and lie down quietly in the same bed,' continued Tom. 'I did so with a degree of trepidation, which, I am not ashamed to say, a very little matter would have sufficed to stimulate to downright panic. This night, however, passed off quietly enough, as also the next; and so too did two or three more. I grew more confident, and began to fancy that I believed in the theories of spectral illusions, with which I had at first vainly tried to impose upon my convictions.

'The apparition had been, indeed, altogether anomalous. It had crossed the room without any recognition of my presence: I had not disturbed *it*, and *it* had no mission to *me*. What, then, was the imaginable use of its crossing the room in a visible shape at all? Of course it might have *been* in the closet instead of *going* there, as easily as it introduced itself into the recess without entering the chamber in a shape discernible by the senses. Besides, how the deuce *had* I seen it? It was a dark night; I had no candle; there was no fire; and yet I saw it as distinctly, in colouring and outline, as ever I beheld human form! A cataleptic dream would explain it all; and I was determined that a dream it should be.

'One of the most remarkable phenomena connected with the practice of mendacity is the vast number of deliberate lies we tell ourselves, whom, of all persons, we can least expect to deceive. In all this, I need hardly tell you, Dick, I was simply lying to myself, and did not believe one word of the wretched humbug. Yet I went on, as men will do, like persevering charlatans and impostors, who tire people into credulity by the mere force of reiteration; so I hoped to win myself over at last to a comfortable scepticism about the ghost.

'He had not appeared a second time – that certainly was a comfort; and what, after all, did I care for him, and his queer old toggery and strange looks? Not a fig! I was nothing the worse for having seen him, and a good story the better. So I tumbled into bed, put out my candle, and, cheered by a loud drunken quarrel in the back lane, went fast asleep.

'From this deep slumber I awoke with a start. I knew I had had a horrible dream; but what it was I could not remember. My heart was thumping furiously; I felt bewildered and feverish; I sate up in the bed and looked about the room. A broad flood of moonlight came in through the curtainless window; everything was as I had last seen it;

and though the domestic squabble in the back lane was, unhappily for me, allayed, I yet could hear a pleasant fellow singing, on his way home, the then popular comic ditty called, 'Murphy Delany.' Taking advantage of this diversion I lay down again, with my face towards the fireplace, and closing my eyes, did my best to think of nothing else but the song, which was every moment growing fainter in the distance:—

"Twas Murphy Delany, so funny and frisky,
Stept into a shebeen shop to get his skin full;
He reeled out again pretty well lined with whiskey,
As fresh as a shamrock, as blind as a bull.'

'The singer, whose condition I dare say resembled that of his hero, was soon too far off to regale my ears any more; and as his music died away, I myself sank into a doze, neither sound nor refreshing. Somehow the song had got into my head, and I went meandering on through the adventures of my respectable fellow-countryman, who, on emerging from the 'shebeen shop', fell into a river, from which he was fished up to be 'sat upon' by a coroner's jury, who having learned from a 'horse-doctor' that he was 'dead as a door-nail, so there was an end', returned their verdict accordingly, just as he returned to his senses, when an angry altercation and a pitched battle between the body and the coroner winds up the lay with due spirit and pleasantry.

'Through this ballad I continued with a weary monotony to plod, down to the very last line, and then *da capo*, and so on, in my uncomfortable half-sleep, for how long, I can't conjecture. I found myself at last, however, muttering, '*dead* as a door-nail, so there was an end'; and something like another voice within me, seemed to say, very faintly, but sharply, 'dead! dead! *dead*! and may the Lord have mercy on your soul!' and instantaneously I was wide awake, and staring right before me from the pillow.

'Now – will you believe it, Dick? – I saw the same accursed figure standing full front, and gazing at me with its stony and fiendish countenance, not two yards from the bedside.'

Tom stopped here, and wiped the perspiration from his face. I felt very queer. The girl was as pale as Tom; and, assembled as we were in the very scene of these adventures, we were all, I dare say, equally grateful for the clear daylight and the resuming bustle out of doors.

'For about three seconds only I saw it plainly; then it grew indistinct; but, for a long time, there was something like a column of dark vapour where it had been standing, between me and the wall; and I felt sure that he was still there. After a good while, this appearance went too. I took my clothes downstairs to the hall, and dressed there, with the door half open; then went out into the street, and walked about the town till morning, when I came back, in a miserable state of nervousness and exhaustion. I was such a fool, Dick, as to be ashamed to tell you how I came to be so upset. I thought you would laugh at me; especially as I had always talked philosophy, and treated *your* ghosts with contempt. I concluded you would give me no quarter; and so kept my tale of horror to myself.

'Now, Dick, you will hardly believe me, when I assure you, that for many nights after this last experience, I did not go to my room at all. I used to sit up for a while in the drawing-room after you had gone up to your bed; and then steal down softly to the hall-door, let myself out, and sit in the 'Robin Hood' tavern until the last guest went off; and then I got through the night like a sentry, pacing the streets till morning.

'For more than a week I never slept in bed. I sometimes had a snooze on a form in the 'Robin Hood', and sometimes a nap in a chair during the day; but regular sleep I had absolutely none.

'I was quite resolved that we should get into another house; but I could not bring myself to tell you the reason, and I somehow put it off from day to day, although my life was, during every hour of this procrastination, rendered as miserable as that of a felon with the constables on his track. I was growing absolutely ill from this wretched mode of life.

'One afternoon I determined to enjoy an hour's sleep upon your bed. I hated mine; so that I had never, except in a stealthy visit every day to unmake it, lest Martha should discover the secret of my nightly absence, entered the ill-omened chamber.

'As ill-luck would have it, you had locked your bedroom, and taken away the key. I went into my own to unsettle the bedclothes, as usual, and give the bed the appearance of having been slept in. Now, a variety of circumstances concurred to bring about the dreadful scene through which I was that night to pass. In the first place, I was literally overpowered with fatigue, and longing for sleep; in the next place, the effect of this extreme exhaustion upon my nerves resembled that of a narcotic, and rendered me less susceptible than, perhaps, I should in any other condition have been, of the exciting fears which had become habitual to me. Then again, a little bit of the window was open, a pleasant freshness pervaded the room, and, to crown all, the cheerful sun of day was making the room quite pleasant. What was to prevent my enjoying an hour's nap *here*? The whole air was resonant with the cheerful hum of life, and the broad matter-of-fact light of day filled every corner of the room.

'I yielded – stifling my qualms – to the almost overpowering temptation; and merely throwing off my coat, and loosening my cravat, I lay down, limiting myself to *half*-an-hour's doze in the unwonted enjoyment of a feather bed, a coverlet, and a bolster.

'It was horribly insidious; and the demon, no doubt, marked my infatuated preparations. Dolt that I was, I fancied, with mind and body worn out for want of sleep, and an arrear of a full week's rest to my credit, that such measure as *half*-an-hour's sleep, in such a situation, was possible. My sleep was death-like, long, and dreamless.

'Without a start or fearful sensation of any kind, I waked gently, but completely. It was, as you have good reason to remember, long past midnight – I believe, about two o'clock. When sleep has been deep and long enough to satisfy nature thoroughly, one often wakens in this way, suddenly, tranquilly, and completely.

'There was a figure seated in that lumbering, old sofa-chair, near the fireplace. Its back was rather towards me, but I could not be mistaken; it turned slowly round, and, merciful heavens! there was the stony face, with its infernal lineaments of malignity and despair, gloating on me. There was now no doubt as to its consciousness of my presence, and the hellish malice with which it was animated, for it arose, and drew close to the bedside. There was a rope about its neck, and the other end, coiled up, it held stiffly in its hand.

'My good angel nerved me for this horrible crisis. I remained for some seconds transfixed by the gaze of this tremendous phantom. He came close to the bed, and appeared on the point of mounting upon it. The next instant I was upon the floor at the far side, and in a moment more was, I don't know how, upon the lobby.

'But the spell was not yet broken; the valley of the shadow of death was not yet traversed. The abhorred phantom was before me there; it was standing near the banisters, stooping a little, and with one end of the rope round its own neck, was poising a noose at the other, as if to throw over mine; and while engaged in this baleful pantomime, it wore a smile so sensual, so unspeakably dreadful, that my senses were nearly overpowered. I saw and remember nothing more, until I found myself in your room.

'I had a wonderful escape, Dick – there is no disputing *that* – an escape for which, while I live, I shall bless the mercy of heaven. No one can conceive or imagine what it is for flesh and blood to stand in the presence of such a thing, but one who has had the terrific experience. Dick, Dick, a shadow has passed over me – a chill has crossed my blood and marrow, and I will never be the same again – never, Dick – never!'

Our handmaid, a mature girl of two-and-fifty, as I have said, stayed her hand, as Tom's story proceeded, and by little and little drew near to us, with open mouth, and her brows contracted over her little, beady black eyes, till stealing a glance over her shoulder now and then, she established herself close behind us. During the relation, she had made various earnest comments, in an undertone; but these and her ejaculations, for the sake of brevity and simplicity, I have omitted in my narration.

'It's often I heard tell of it,' she now said, 'but I never believed it rightly till now – though, indeed, why should not I? Does not my mother, down there in the lane, know quare stories, God bless us, beyant telling about it? But you ought not to have slept in the back bedroom. She was loath to let me be going in and out of that room even in the day time, let alone for any Christian to spend the night in it; for sure she says it was his own bedroom.'

'*Whose* own bedroom?' we asked, in a breath.

'Why, *his* – the ould Judge's – Judge Horrock's, to be sure, God rest his sowl'; and she looked fearfully round.

'Amen!' I muttered. 'But did he die there?'

'Die there! No, not quite *there*,' she said. 'Shure, was not it over the banisters he hung himself, the ould sinner, God be merciful to us all? and was not it in the alcove they found the handles of the skipping-rope cut off, and the knife where he was settling the cord, God bless us, to hang himself with? It was his housekeeper's daughter owned the rope, my mother often told me, and the child never throve after, and used to be starting up out of her sleep, and screeching in the night time, wid dhrames and frights that cum an her; and they said how it was the speerit of the ould Judge that was tormentin' her; and she used to be roaring and yelling out to hould back the big ould fellow with the crooked neck; and then she'd screech 'Oh, the master! the master! he's stampin' at me, and beckoning to me! Mother, darling, don't let me go!' And so the poor crathure died at last, and the docthers said it was wather on the brain, for it was all they could say.'

'How long ago was all this?' I asked.

'Oh, then, how would I know?' she answered. 'But it must be a wondherful long time ago, for the housekeeper was an ould woman, with a pipe in her mouth, and not a tooth left, and better nor eighty years ould when my mother was first married; and they said she was a rale buxom, fine-dressed woman when the ould Judge come to his end; an', indeed, my mother's not far from eighty years ould herself this day; and what made it worse for the unnatural ould villain, God rest his soul, to frighten the little girl out of the world the way he did, was what was mostly thought and believed by every one. My mother says how the poor little crathure was his own child; for he was by all accounts an ould villain every way, an' the hangin'est judge that ever was known in Ireland's ground.'

'From what you said about the danger of sleeping in that bedroom,' said I, 'I suppose there were stories about the ghost having appeared there to others.'

'Well, there was things said – quare things, surely,' she answered, as it seemed, with some reluctance. 'And why would not there? Sure was it not up in that same room he slept for more than twenty years? and was it not in the *alcove* he got the rope ready that done his own business at last, the way he done many a betther man's in his lifetime? – and was not the body lying in the same bed after death, and put in the coffin there, too, and carried out to his grave from it in Pether's churchyard, after the coroner was done? But there was quare stories – my mother has them all – about how one Nicholas Spaight got into trouble on the head of it.'

'And what did they say of this Nicholas Spaight?' I asked.

'Oh, for that matther, it's soon told,' she answered.

And she certainly did relate a very strange story, which so piqued my curiosity, that I took occasion to visit the ancient lady, her mother, from whom I learned many very curious particulars. Indeed, I am tempted to tell the tale, but my fingers are weary, and I must defer it. But if you wish to hear it another time, I shall do my best.

When we had heard the strange tale I have *not* told you, we put one or two further questions to her about the alleged spectral visitations, to which the house had, ever since the death of the wicked old Judge, been subjected.

'No one ever had luck in it,' she told us. 'There was always cross accidents, sudden deaths, and short times in it. The first that tuck, it was a family – I forget their name – but at any rate there was two young ladies and their papa. He was about sixty, and a stout healthy gentleman as you'd wish to see at that age. Well, he slept in that unlucky back bedroom; and, God between us an' harm! sure enough he was found dead one morning, half out of the bed, with his head as black as a sloe, and swelled like a puddin', hanging down near the floor. It was a fit, they said. He was as dead as a mackerel, and so *he* could not say what it was; but the ould people was all sure that it was nothing at all but the ould Judge, God bless us! that frightened him out of his senses and his life together.

'Some time after there was a rich old maiden lady took the house. I don't know which room *she* slept in, but she lived alone; and at any rate, one morning, the servants going down early to their work, found her sitting on the passage-stairs, shivering and talkin' to herself, quite mad; and never a word more could any of *them* or her friends get from her ever afterwards but, 'Don't ask me to go, for I promised to wait for him.' They never made out from her who it was she meant by *him*, but of course those that knew all about the ould house were at no loss for the meaning of all that happened to her.

'Then afterwards, when the house was let out in lodgings, there was Micky Byrne that took the same room, with his wife and three little children; and sure I heard Mrs. Byrne myself telling how the children used to be lifted up in the bed at night, she could not see by what mains; and how they were starting and screeching every hour, just all as one as the housekeeper's little girl that died, till at last one night poor Micky had a dhrop in him, the way he used now and again; and what do you think in the middle of the night he thought he heard a noise on the stairs, and being in liquor, nothing less id do him but out he must go himself to see what was wrong. Well, after that, all she ever heard of him was himself sayin', 'Oh, God!' and a tumble that shook the very house; and there, sure enough, he was lying on the lower stairs, under the lobby, with his neck smashed double undher him, where he was flung over the banisters.'

Then the handmaiden added—

'I'll go down to the lane, and send up Joe Gavvey to pack up the rest of the taythings, and bring all the things across to your new lodgings.'

And so we all sallied out together, each of us breathing more freely, I have no doubt, as we crossed that ill-omened threshold for the last time.

Now, I may add thus much, in compliance with the immemorial usage of the realm of fiction, which sees the hero not only through his adventures, but fairly out of the world. You must have perceived that what the flesh, blood, and bone hero of romance proper is to the regular compounder of fiction, this old house of brick, wood, and mortar is to the humble recorder of this true tale. I, therefore, relate, as in duty bound, the catastrophe which ultimately befell it, which was simply this – that about two years subsequently to my story it was taken by a quack doctor, who called himself Baron Duhlstoerf, and filled the parlour windows with bottles of indescribable horrors preserved in brandy, and the newspapers with the usual grandiloquent and mendacious advertisements. This gentleman among his virtues did not reckon sobriety, and one night, being overcome with much wine, he set fire to his bed curtains, partially burned himself, and totally consumed the house. It was afterwards rebuilt, and for a time an undertaker established himself in the premises.

I have now told you my own and Tom's adventures, together with some valuable collateral particulars; and having acquitted myself of my engagement, I wish you a very good night, and pleasant dreams.

Canon Alberic's Scrap-Book

Montague Rhodes James

St. Bertrand de Comminges is a decayed town on the spurs of the Pyrenees, not very far from Toulouse, and still nearer to Bagnères-de-Luchon. It was the site of a bishopric until the Revolution, and has a cathedral which is visited by a certain number of tourists. In the spring of 1883 an Englishman arrived at this old-world place – I can hardly dignify it with the name of city, for there are not a thousand inhabitants. He was a Cambridge man, who had come specially from Toulouse to see St. Bertrand's Church, and had left two friends, who were less keen archæologists than himself, in their hotel at Toulouse, under promise to join him on the following morning. Half an hour at the church would satisfy *them* and all three could then pursue their journey in the direction of Auch. But our Englishman had come early on the day in question, and proposed to himself to fill a note-book and to use several dozens of plates in the process of describing and photographing every corner of the wonderful church that dominates the little hill of Comminges. In order to carry out this design satisfactorily, it was necessary to monopolize the verger of the church for the day. The verger or sacristan (I prefer the latter appellation, inaccurate as it may be) was accordingly sent for by the somewhat brusque lady who keeps the inn of the Chapeau Rouge; and when he came, the Englishman found him an unexpectedly interesting object of study. It was not in the personal appearance of the little, dry, wizened old man that the interest lay, for he was precisely like dozens of other church-guardians in France, but in a curious furtive, or rather hunted and oppressed, air which he had. He was perpetually half glancing behind him; the muscles of his back and shoulders seemed to be hunched in a continual nervous contraction, as if he were expecting every moment to find himself in the clutch of an enemy. The Englishman hardly knew whether to put him down as a man haunted by a fixed delusion, or as one oppressed by a guilty conscience, or as an unbearably henpecked husband. The probabilities, when reckoned up, certainly pointed to the last idea; but, still, the impression conveyed was that of a more formidable persecutor even than a termagant wife.

However, the Englishman (let us call him Dennistoun) was soon too deep in his note-book and too busy with his camera to give more than an occasional glance to the sacristan. Whenever he did look at him, he found him at no great distance, either huddling himself back against the wall or crouching in one of the gorgeous stalls. Dennistoun became rather fidgety after a time. Mingled suspicions that he was keeping the old man from his *déjeuner,* that he was regarded as likely to make away with St. Bertrand's ivory crozier, or with the dusty stuffed crocodile that hangs over the font, began to torment him.

'Won't you go home?' he said at last; 'I'm quite well able to finish my notes alone; you can lock me in if you like. I shall want at least two hours more here, and it must be cold for you, isn't it?'

'Good heavens!' said the little man, whom the suggestion seemed to throw into a state of unaccountable terror, 'such a thing cannot be thought of for a moment. Leave monsieur alone in the church? No, no; two hours, three hours, all will be the same to me. I have breakfasted, I am not at all cold, with many thanks to monsieur.'

'Very well, my little man,' quoth Dennistoun to himself: 'you have been warned, and you must take the consequences.'

Before the expiration of the two hours, the stalls, the enormous dilapidated organ, the choir-screen of Bishop John de Mauléon, the remnants of glass and tapestry, and the objects in the treasure-chamber, had been well and truly examined; the sacristan still keeping at

Dennistoun's heels, and every now and then whipping round as if he had been stung, when one or other of the strange noises that trouble a large empty building fell on his ear. Curious noises they were sometimes.

'Once,' Dennistoun said to me, 'I could have sworn I heard a thin metallic voice laughing high up in the tower. I darted an inquiring glance at my sacristan. He was white to the lips. "It is he – that is – it is no one; the door is locked," was all he said, and we looked at each other for a full minute.'

Another little incident puzzled Dennistoun a good deal. He was examining a large dark picture that hangs behind the altar, one of a series illustrating the miracles of St. Bertrand. The composition of the picture is well-nigh indecipherable, but there is a Latin legend below, which runs thus:

> 'Qualiter S. Bertrandus liberavit hominem quem diabolus diu volebat strangulare.' (How St. Bertrand delivered a man whom the Devil long sought to strangle.)

Dennistoun was turning to the sacristan with a smile and a jocular remark of some sort on his lips, but he was confounded to see the old man on his knees, gazing at the picture with the eye of a suppliant in agony, his hands tightly clasped, and a rain of tears on his cheeks. Dennistoun naturally pretended to have noticed nothing, but the question would not go away from him, 'Why should a daub of this kind affect anyone so strongly?' He seemed to himself to be getting some sort of clue to the reason of the strange look that had been puzzling him all the day: the man must be a monomaniac; but what was his monomania?

It was nearly five o'clock; the short day was drawing in, and the church began to fill with shadows, while the curious noises – the muffled footfalls and distant talking voices that had been perceptible all day – seemed, no doubt because of the fading light and the consequently quickened sense of hearing, to become more frequent and insistent.

The sacristan began for the first time to show signs of hurry and impatience. He heaved a sigh of relief when camera and note-book were finally packed up and stowed away, and hurriedly beckoned Dennistoun to the western door of the church, under the tower. It was time to ring the Angelus. A few pulls at the reluctant rope, and the great bell Bertrande, high in the tower, began to speak, and swung her voice up among the pines and down to the valleys, loud with mountain-streams, calling the dwellers on those lonely hills to remember and repeat the salutation of the angel to her whom he called Blessed among women. With that a profound quiet seemed to fall for the first time that day upon the little town, and Dennistoun and the sacristan went out of the church.

On the doorstep they fell into conversation.

'Monsieur seemed to interest himself in the old choir-books in the sacristy.'

'Undoubtedly. I was going to ask you if there were a library in the town.'

'No, monsieur; perhaps there used to be one belonging to the Chapter, but it is now such a small place—' Here came a strange pause of irresolution, as it seemed; then, with a sort of plunge, he went on: 'But if monsieur is *amateur des vieux livres*, I have at home something that might interest him. It is not a hundred yards.'

At once all Dennistoun's cherished dreams of finding priceless manuscripts in untrodden corners of France flashed up, to die down again the next moment. It was probably a stupid missal of Plantin's printing, about 1580. Where was the likelihood that a place so near Toulouse would not have been ransacked long ago by collectors? However, it would be foolish not to go; he would reproach himself for ever after if he refused. So they set off. On the way the curious irresolution and sudden determination of the sacristan recurred to Dennistoun, and he wondered in a shame-faced way whether he was being decoyed into some purlieu to be made away with as a supposed rich Englishman. He contrived, therefore, to begin talking with his guide, and to drag in, in a rather clumsy fashion, the fact that he expected two friends to join him early the next morning. To his surprise, the announcement seemed to relieve the sacristan at once of some of the anxiety that oppressed him.

'That is well,' he said quite brightly – 'that is very well. Monsieur will travel in company with his friends; they will be always near him. It is a good thing to travel thus in company – sometimes.'

The last word appeared to be added as an afterthought, and to bring with it a relapse into gloom for the poor little man.

They were soon at the house, which was one rather larger than its neighbours, stone-built, with a shield carved over the door, the shield of Alberic de Mauléon, a collateral descendant, Dennistoun tells me, of Bishop John de Mauléon. This Alberic was a Canon of Comminges from 1680 to 1701. The upper windows of the mansion were boarded up, and the whole place bore, as does the rest of Comminges, the aspect of decaying age.

Arrived on his doorstep, the sacristan paused a moment.

'Perhaps,' he said, 'perhaps, after all, monsieur has not the time?'

'Not at all – lots of time – nothing to do till to-morrow. Let us see what it is you have got.'

The door was opened at this point, and a face looked out, a face far younger than the sacristan's, but bearing something of the same distressing look: only here it seemed to be the mark, not so much of fear for personal safety as of acute anxiety on behalf of another. Plainly, the owner of the face was the sacristan's daughter; and, but for the expression I have described, she was a handsome girl enough. She brightened up considerably on seeing her father accompianied by an able-bodied stranger. A few remarks passed between father and daughter, of which Dennistoun only caught these words, said by the sacristan, 'He was laughing in the church,' words which were answered only by a look of terror from the girl.

But in another minute they were in the sitting-room of the house, a small, high chamber with a stone floor, full of moving shadows cast by a wood-fire that flickered on a great hearth. Something of the character of an oratory was imparted to it by a tall crucifix, which reached almost to the ceiling on one side; the figure was painted of the natural colours, the cross was black. Under this stood a chest of some age and solidity, and when a lamp had been brought, and chairs set, the sacristan went to this chest, and produced therefrom, with growing excitement and nervousness, as Dennistoun thought, a large book, wrapped in a white cloth, on which cloth a cross was rudely embroidered in red thread. Even before the wrapping had been removed, Dennistoun began to be interested by the size and shape of the volume. 'Too large for a missal,' he thought, 'and not the shape of an antiphoner; perhaps it may be something good, after all.' The next moment the book was open, and Dennistoun felt that he had at last lit upon something better than good. Before him lay a large folio, bound, perhaps, late in the seventeenth century, with the arms of Canon Alberic de Mauléon stamped in gold on the sides. There may have been a hundred and fifty leaves of paper in the book, and on almost every one of them was fastened a leaf from an illuminated manuscript. Such a collection Dennistoun had hardly dreamed of in his wildest moments. Here were ten leaves from a copy of Genesis, illustrated with pictures, which could not be later than 700 AD. Further on was a complete set of pictures from a Psalter, of English execution, of the very finest kind that the thirteenth century could produce; and, perhaps best of all, there were twenty leaves of uncial writing in Latin, which, as a few words seen here and there told him at once, must belong to some very early unknown patristic treatise. Could it possibly be a fragment of the copy of Papias 'On the Words of Our Lord,' which was known to have existed as late as the twelfth century at Nimes?* In any case, his mind was made up; that book must return to Cambridge with him, even if he had to draw the whole of his balance from the bank and stay at St. Bertrand

* We now know that these leaves did contain a considerable fragment of that work, if not of that actual copy of it.

till the money came. He glanced up at the sacristan to see if his face yielded any hint that the book was for sale. The sacristan was pale, and his lips were working.

'If monsieur will turn on to the end,' he said.

So monsieur turned on, meeting new treasures at every rise of a leaf; and at the end of the book he came upon two sheets of paper, of much more recent date than anything he had yet seen, which puzzled him considerably. They must be contemporary, he decided, with the unprincipled Canon Alberic, who had doubtless plundered the Chapter library of St. Bertrand to form this priceless scrap-book. On the first of the paper sheets was a plan, carefully drawn and instantly recognisable by a person who knew the ground, of the south aisle and cloisters of St. Bertrand's. There were curious signs looking like planetary symbols, and a few Hebrew words in the corners; and in the north-west angle of the cloister was a cross drawn in gold paint. Below the plan were some lines of writing in Latin, which ran thus:

> 'Responsa 12^{mi} Dec. 1694. Interrogatum est: Inveniamne? Responsum est: Invenies. Fiamne dives? Fies. Vivamne invidendus? Vives. Moriarne in lecto meo? Ita.' (Answers of the 12th of December, 1694. It was asked: Shall I find it? Answer: Thou shalt. Shall I become rich? Thou wilt. Shall I live an object of envy? Thou wilt. Shall I die in my bed? Thou wilt.)

'A good specimen of the treasure-hunter's record – quite reminds one of Mr. Minor-Canon Quatremain in "Old St. Paul's,"' was Dennistoun's comment, and he turned the leaf.

What he then saw impressed him, as he has often told me, more than he could have conceived any drawing or picture capable of impressing him. And, though the drawing he saw is no longer in existence, there is a photograph of it (which I possess) which fully bears out that statement. The picture in question was a sepia drawing at the end of the seventeenth century, representing, one would say at first sight, a Biblical scene; for the architecture (the picture represented an interior) and the figures had that semi-classical flavour about them which the artists of two hundred years ago thought appropriate to illustrations of the Bible. On the right was a King on his throne, the throne elevated on twelve steps, a canopy overhead, soldiers on either side – evidently King Solomon. He was bending forward with outstretched sceptre, in attitude of command; his face expressed horror and disgust, yet there was in it also the mark of imperious command and confident power. The left half of the picture was the strangest, however. The interest plainly centred there. On the pavement before the throne were grouped four soldiers, surrounding a crouching figure which must be described in a moment. A fifth soldier lay dead on the pavement, his neck distorted, and his eyeballs starting from his head. The four surrounding guards were looking at the King. In their faces the sentiment of horror was intensified; they seemed, in fact, only restrained from flight by their implicit trust in their master. All this terror was plainly excited by the being that crouched in their midst. I entirely despair of conveying by any words the impression which this figure makes upon anyone who looks at it. I recollect once showing the photograph of the drawing to a lecturer on morphology – a person of, I was going to say, abnormally sane and unimaginative habits of mind. He absolutely refused to be alone for the rest of that evening, and he told me afterwards that for many nights he had not dared to put out his light before going to sleep. However, the main traits of the figure I can at least indicate. At first you saw only a mass of coarse, matted black hair; presently it was seen that this covered a body of fearful thinness, almost a skeleton, but with the muscles standing out like wires. The hands were of a dusky pallor, covered, like the body, with long, coarse hairs, and hideously taloned. The eyes, touched in with a burning yellow, had intensely black pupils, and were fixed upon the throned King with a look of beast-like hate. Imagine one of the awful bird-catching spiders of South America translated into human form, and endowed with intelligence just less than human, and you will have some faint conception of the terror inspired by the appalling effigy. One remark is universally made by those to whom I have shown the picture: 'It was drawn from the life.'

As soon as the first shock of his irresistible fright had subsided, Dennistoun stole a look at his hosts. The sacristan's hands were pressed upon his eyes; his daughter, looking up at the cross on the wall, was telling her beads feverishly.

At last the question was asked, 'Is this book for sale?'

There was the same hesitation, the same plunge of determination, that he had noticed before, and then came the welcome answer, 'If monsieur pleases.'

'How much do you ask for it?'

'I will take two hundred and fifty francs.'

This was confounding. Even a collector's conscience is sometimes stirred, and Dennistoun's conscience was tenderer than a collector's.

'My good man!' he said again and again, 'your book is worth far more than two hundred and fifty francs, I assure you – far more.'

But the answer did not vary: 'I will take two hundred and fifty francs, not more.'

There was really no possibility of refusing such a chance. The money was paid, the receipt signed, a glass of wine drunk over the transaction, and then the sacristan seemed to become a new man. He stood upright, he ceased to throw those suspicious glances behind him, he actually laughed or tried to laugh. Dennistoun rose to go.

'I shall have the honour of accompanying monsieur to his hotel?' said the sacristan.

'Oh no, thanks! it isn't a hundred yards. I know the way perfectly, and there is a moon.'

The offer was pressed three or four times, and refused as often.

'Then, monsieur will summon me if – if he finds occasion; he will keep the middle of the road, the sides are so rough.'

'Certainly, certainly,' said Dennistoun, who was impatient to examine his prize by himself; and he stepped out into the passage with his book under his arm.

Here he was met by the daughter; she, it appeared, was anxious to do a little business on her own account; perhaps, like Gehazi, to 'take somewhat' from the foreigner whom her father had spared.

'A silver crucifix and chain for the neck; monsieur would perhaps be good enough to accept it?'

Well, really, Dennistoun hadn't much use for these things. What did mademoiselle want for it?

'Nothing – nothing in the world. Monsieur is more than welcome to it.'

The tone in which this and much more was said was unmistakably genuine, so that Dennistoun was reduced to profuse thanks, and submitted to have the chain put round his neck. It really seemed as if he had rendered the father and daughter some service which they hardly knew how to repay. As he set off with his book they stood at the door looking after him, and they were still looking when he waved them a last good-night from the steps of the Chapeau Rouge.

Dinner was over, and Dennistoun was in his bedroom, shut up alone with his acquisition. The landlady had manifested a particular interest in him since he had told her that he had paid a visit to the sacristan and bought an old book from him. He thought, too, that he had heard a hurried dialogue between her and the said sacristan in the passage outside the *salle à manger*; some words to the effect that 'Pierre and Bertrand would be sleeping in the house' had closed the conversation.

At this time a growing feeling of discomfort had been creeping over him – nervous reaction, perhaps, after the delight of his discovery. Whatever it was, it resulted in a conviction that there was someone behind him, and that he was far more comfortable with his back to the wall. All this, of course, weighed light in the balance as against the obvious value of the collection he had acquired. And now, as I said, he was alone in his bedroom, taking stock of Canon Alberic's treasures, in which every moment revealed something more charming.

'Bless Canon Alberic!' said Dennistoun, who had an inveterate habit of talking to himself. 'I wonder where he is now? Dear me! I wish that landlady would learn to laugh in a more cheering manner; it makes one feel as if there was someone dead in the house. Half a pipe more, did you say? I think perhaps you are right. I wonder what that crucifix is that the young woman insisted on giving me? Last century, I suppose. Yes, probably. It is rather a nuisance of a thing to have round one's neck – just too heavy. Most likely her father has been wearing it for years. I think I might give it a clean up before I put it away.'

He had taken the crucifix off, and laid it on the table, when his attention was caught by an object lying on the red cloth just by his left elbow. Two or three ideas of what it might be flitted through his brain with their own incalculable quickness.

'A penwiper? No, no such thing in the house. A rat? No, too black. A large spider? I trust to goodness not – no. Good God! a hand like the hand in that picture!'

In another infinitesimal flash he had taken it in. Pale, dusky skin, covering nothing but bones and tendons of appalling strength; coarse black hairs, longer than ever grew on a human hand; nails rising from the ends of the fingers and curving sharply down and forward, grey, horny and wrinkled.

He flew out of his chair with deadly, inconceivable terror clutching at his heart. The shape, whose left hand rested on the table, was rising to a standing posture behind his seat, its right hand crooked above his scalp. There was black and tattered drapery about it; the coarse hair covered it as in the drawing. The lower jaw was thin – what can I call it? – shallow, like a beast's; teeth showed behind the black lips; there was no nose; the eyes, of a fiery yellow, against which the pupils showed black and intense, and the exulting hate and thirst to destroy life which shone there, were the most horrifying feature in the whole vision. There was intelligence of a kind in them – intelligence beyond that of a beast, below that of a man.

The feelings which this horror stirred in Dennistoun were the intensest physical fear and the most profound mental loathing. What did he do? What could he do? He has never been quite certain what words he said, but he knows that he spoke, that he grasped blindly at the silver crucifix, that he was conscious of a movement towards him on the part of the demon, and that he screamed with the voice of an animal in hideous pain.

Pierre and Bertrand, the two sturdy little serving-men, who rushed in, saw nothing, but felt themselves thrust aside by something that passed out between them, and found Dennistoun in a swoon. They sat up with him that night, and his two friends were at St. Bertrand by nine o'clock next morning. He himself, though still shaken and nervous, was almost himself by that time, and his story found credence with them, though not until they had seen the drawing and talked with the sacristan.

Almost at dawn the little man had come to the inn on some pretence, and had listened with the deepest interest to the story retailed by the landlady. He showed no surprise.

'It is he – it is he! I have seen him myself,' was his only comment; and to all questionings but one reply was vouchsafed: 'Deux fois je l'ai vu; mille fois je l'ai senti.' He would tell them nothing of the provenance of the book, nor any details of his experiences. 'I shall soon sleep, and my rest will be sweet. Why should you trouble me?' he said.*

We shall never know what he or Canon Alberic de Mauléon suffered. At the back of that fateful drawing were some lines of writing which may be supposed to throw light on the situation:

'Contradictio Salomonis cum demonio nocturno.
Albericus de Mauleone delineavit.
V. Deus in adiutorium. Ps. Qui habitat.

* He died that summer; his daughter married, and settled at St. Papoul. She never understood the circumstances of her father's 'obsession'.

Sancte Bertrande, demoniorum effugator, intercede pro me miserrimo.
Primum uidi nocte 12^{mi} Dec 1694: uidebo mox ultimum.
Peccaui et passus sum, plura adhuc passurus. Dec. 29, 1701.*

I have never quite understood what was Dennistoun's view of the events I have narrated. He quoted to me once a text from Ecelesiasticus: 'Some spirits there be that are created for vengeance, and in their fury lay on sore strokes.' On another occasion he said: 'Isaiah was a very sensible man; doesn't he say something about night monsters living in the ruins of Babylon? These things are rather beyond us at present.'

Another confidence of his impressed me rather, and I sympathized with it. We had been, last year, to Comminges, to see Canon Alberic's tomb. It is a great marble erection with an effigy of the Canon in a large wig and soutane, and an elaborate eulogy of his learning below. I saw Dennistoun talking for some time with the Vicar of St. Bertrand's, and as we drove away he said to me: 'I hope it isn't wrong: you know I am a Presbyterian – but I – I believe there will be "saying of Mass and singing of dirges" for Alberic de Mauléon's rest.' Then he added, with a touch of the Northern British in his tone, 'I had no notion they came so dear.'

The book is in the Wentworth Collection at Cambridge. The drawing was photographed and then burnt by Dennistoun on the day when he left Comminges on the occasion of his first visit.

---

* *I.e.*, The Dispute of Solomon with a demon of the night. Drawn by Alberic de Mauléon. *Versicle*. O Lord, make haste to help me. *Psalm*. Whoso dwelleth (xci.) Saint Bertrand, who puttest devils to flight, pray for me most unhappy. I saw it first on the night of Dec. 12, 1694: soon I shall see it for the last time. I have sinned and suffered, and have more to suffer yet. Dec. 29, 1701. The 'Gallia Christiana' gives the date of the Canon's death as December 31, 1701, 'in bed, of a sudden seizure.' Details of this kind are not common in the great work of the Sammarthani.

AFTERWARD

EDITH WHARTON

I

"Oh, there *is* one, of course, but you'll never know it."

The assertion, laughingly flung out six months earlier in a bright June garden, came back to Mary Boyne with a sharp perception of its latent significance as she stood, in the December dusk, waiting for the lamps to be brought into the library.

The words had been spoken by their friend Alida Stair, as they sat at tea on her lawn at Pangbourne, in reference to the very house of which the library in question was the central, the pivotal "feature." Mary Boyne and her husband, in quest of a country place in one of the southern or southwestern counties, had, on their arrival in England, carried their problem straight to Alida Stair, who had successfully solved it in her own case; but it was not until they had rejected, almost capriciously, several practical and judicious suggestions that she threw it out: "Well, there's Lyng, in Dorsetshire. It belongs to Hugo's cousins, and you can get it for a song."

The reasons she gave for its being obtainable on these terms—its remoteness from a station, its lack of electric light, hot-water pipes, and other vulgar necessities—were exactly those pleading in its favor with two romantic Americans perversely in search of the economic drawbacks which were associated, in their tradition, with unusual architectural felicities.

"I should never believe I was living in an old house unless I was thoroughly uncomfortable," Ned Boyne, the more extravagant of the two, had jocosely insisted; "the least hint of 'convenience' would make me think it had been bought out of an exhibition, with the pieces numbered, and set up again." And they had proceeded to enumerate, with humorous precision, their various suspicions and exactions, refusing to believe that the house their cousin recommended was *really* Tudor till they learned it had no heating system, or that the village church was literally in the grounds till she assured them of the deplorable uncertainty of the water-supply.

"It's too uncomfortable to be true!" Edward Boyne had continued to exult as the avowal of each disadvantage was successively wrung from her; but he had cut short his rhapsody to ask, with a sudden relapse to distrust: "And the ghost? You've been concealing from us the fact that there is no ghost!"

Mary, at the moment, had laughed with him, yet almost with her laugh, being possessed of several sets of independent perceptions, had noted a sudden flatness of tone in Alida's answering hilarity.

"Oh, Dorsetshire's full of ghosts, you know."

"Yes, yes; but that won't do. I don't want to have to drive ten miles to see somebody else's ghost. I want one of my own on the premises. Is there a ghost at Lyng?"

His rejoinder had made Alida laugh again, and it was then that she had flung back tantalizingly: "Oh, there *is* one, of course, but you'll never know it."

"Never know it?" Boyne pulled her up. "But what in the world constitutes a ghost except the fact of its being known for one?"

"I can't say. But that's the story."

"That there's a ghost, but that nobody knows it's a ghost?"

"Well—not till afterward, at any rate."

"Till afterward?"

"Not till long, long afterward."

"But if it's once been identified as an unearthly visitant, why hasn't its *signalement* been handed down in the family? How has it managed to preserve its incognito?"

Alida could only shake her head. "Don't ask me. But it has."

"And then suddenly—" Mary spoke up as if from some cavernous depth of divination—"suddenly, long afterward, one says to one's self, '*That was it?*'"

She was oddly startled at the sepulchral sound with which her question fell on the banter of the other two, and she saw the shadow of the same surprise flit across Alida's clear pupils. "I suppose so. One just has to wait."

"Oh, hang waiting!" Ned broke in. "Life's too short for a ghost who can only be enjoyed in retrospect. Can't we do better than that, Mary?"

But it turned out that in the event they were not destined to, for within three months of their conversation with Mrs. Stair they were established at Lyng, and the life they had yearned for to the point of planning it out in all its daily details had actually begun for them.

It was to sit, in the thick December dusk, by just such a wide-hooded fireplace, under just such black oak rafters, with the sense that beyond the mullioned panes the downs were darkening to a deeper solitude: it was for the ultimate indulgence in such sensations that Mary Boyne had endured for nearly fourteen years the soul-deadening ugliness of the Middle West, and that Boyne had ground on doggedly at his engineering till, with a suddenness that still made her blink, the prodigious windfall of the Blue Star Mine had put them at a stroke in possession of life and the leisure to taste it. They had never for a moment meant their new state to be one of idleness; but they meant to give themselves only to harmonious activities. She had her vision of painting and gardening (against a background of gray walls), he dreamed of the production of his long-planned book on the "Economic Basis of Culture"; and with such absorbing work ahead no existence could be too sequestered; they could not get far enough from the world, or plunge deep enough into the past.

Dorsetshire had attracted them from the first by a semblance of remoteness out of all proportion to its geographical position. But to the

Boynes it was one of the ever-recurring wonders of the whole incredibly compressed island—a nest of counties, as they put it—that for the production of its effects so little of a given quality went so far: that so few miles made a distance, and so short a distance a difference.

"It's that," Ned had once enthusiastically explained, "that gives such depth to their effects, such relief to their least contrasts. They've been able to lay the butter so thick on every exquisite mouthful."

The butter had certainly been laid on thick at Lyng: the old gray house, hidden under a shoulder of the downs, had almost all the finer marks of commerce with a protracted past. The mere fact that it was neither large nor exceptional made it, to the Boynes, abound the more richly in its special sense—the sense of having been for centuries a deep, dim reservoir of life. The life had probably not been of the most vivid order: for long periods, no doubt, it had fallen as noiselessly into the past as the quiet drizzle of autumn fell, hour after hour, into the green fish-pond between the yews; but these back-waters of existence sometimes breed, in their sluggish depths, strange acuities of emotion, and Mary Boyne had felt from the first the occasional brush of an intenser memory.

The feeling had never been stronger than on the December afternoon when, waiting in the library for the belated lamps, she rose from her seat and stood among the shadows of the hearth. Her husband had gone off, after luncheon, for one of his long tramps on the downs. She had noticed of late that he preferred to be unaccompanied on these occasions; and, in the tried security of their personal relations, had been driven to conclude that his book was bothering him, and that he needed the afternoons to turn over in solitude the problems left from the morning's work. Certainly the book was not going as smoothly as she had imagined it would, and the lines of perplexity between his eyes had never been there in his engineering days. Then he had often looked fagged to the verge of illness, but the native demon of "worry" had never branded his brow. Yet the few pages he had so far read to her—the introduction, and a synopsis of the opening chapter—gave evidences of a firm possession of his subject, and a deepening confidence in his powers.

The fact threw her into deeper perplexity, since, now that he had done with "business" and its disturbing contingencies, the one other possible element of anxiety was eliminated. Unless it were his health, then? But physically he had gained since they had come to Dorsetshire, grown robuster, ruddier, and fresher-eyed. It was only within a week that she had felt in him the undefinable change that made her restless in his absence, and as tongue-tied in his presence as though it were *she* who had a secret to keep from him!

The thought that there *was* a secret somewhere between them struck her with a sudden smart rap of wonder, and she looked about her down the dim, long room.

"Can it be the house?" she mused.

The room itself might have been full of secrets. They seemed to be piling themselves up, as evening fell, like the layers and layers of velvet shadow dropping from the low ceiling, the dusky walls of books, the smoke-blurred sculpture of the hooded hearth. "Why, of course—the house is haunted!" she reflected.

The ghost—Alida's imperceptible ghost—after figuring largely in the banter of their first month or two at Lyng, had been gradually discarded as too ineffectual for imaginative use. Mary had, indeed, as became the tenant of a haunted house, made the customary inquiries among her few rural neighbors, but, beyond a vague, "They du say so, Ma'am," the villagers had nothing to impart. The elusive specter had apparently never had sufficient identity for a legend to crystallize about it, and after a time the Boynes had laughingly set the matter down to their profit-and-loss account, agreeing that Lyng was one of the few houses good enough in itself to dispense with supernatural enhancements.

"And I suppose, poor, ineffectual demon, that's why it beats its beautiful wings in vain in the void," Mary had laughingly concluded.

"Or, rather," Ned answered, in the same strain, "why, amid so much that's ghostly, it can never affirm its separate existence as *the* ghost." And thereupon their invisible housemate had finally dropped out of their references, which were numerous enough to make them promptly unaware of the loss.

Now, as she stood on the hearth, the subject of their earlier curiosity revived in her with a new sense of its meaning—a sense gradually acquired through close daily contact with the scene of the lurking mystery. It was the house itself, of course, that possessed the ghost-seeing faculty, that communed visually but secretly with its own past; and if one could only get into close enough communion with the house, one might surprise its secret, and acquire the ghost-sight on one's own account. Perhaps, in his long solitary hours in this very room, where she never trespassed till the afternoon, her husband *had* acquired it already, and was silently carrying the dread weight of whatever it had revealed to him. Mary was too well-versed in the code of the spectral world not to know that one could not talk about the ghosts one saw: to do so was almost as great a breach of good-breeding as to name a lady in a club. But this explanation did not really satisfy her. "What, after all, except for the fun of the *frisson*," she reflected, "would he really care for any of their old ghosts?" And thence she was thrown back once more on the fundamental dilemma: the fact that one's greater or less susceptibility to spectral influences had no particular bearing on the case, since, when one *did* see a ghost at Lyng, one did not know it.

"Not till long afterward," Alida Stair had said. Well, supposing Ned had seen one when they first came, and had known only within the last week what had happened to him? More and more under the spell of the hour, she threw back her searching thoughts to the early days of their tenancy, but at first only to recall a gay confusion of unpacking, settling, arranging of books, and calling to each other from remote corners of the house as treasure after treasure of their habitation revealed itself to them. It was in this particular connection that she presently recalled a certain soft afternoon of the previous October, when, passing from the first rapturous flurry of exploration to a detailed inspection of the old house, she had pressed (like a novel heroine) a panel that opened at her touch, on a narrow flight of stairs leading to an unsuspected flat ledge of the roof—the roof which, from below, seemed to slope away on all sides too abruptly for any but practised feet to scale.

The view from this hidden coign was enchanting, and she had flown down to snatch Ned from his papers and give him the freedom of her discovery. She remembered still how, standing on the narrow ledge, he had passed his arm about her while their gaze flew to the long, tossed horizon-line of the downs, and then dropped contentedly back to trace the arabesque of yew hedges about the fish-pond, and the shadow of the cedar on the lawn.

"And now the other way," he had said, gently turning her about within his arm; and closely pressed to him, she had absorbed, like some long, satisfying draft, the picture of the gray-walled court, the squat lions on the gates, and the lime-avenue reaching up to the highroad under the downs.

It was just then, while they gazed and held each other, that she had felt his arm relax, and heard a sharp "Hullo!" that made her turn to glance at him.

Distinctly, yes, she now recalled she had seen, as she glanced, a shadow of anxiety, of perplexity, rather, fall across his face; and, following his eyes, had beheld the figure of a man—a man in loose, grayish clothes, as it appeared to her—who was sauntering down the lime-avenue to the court with the tentative gait of a stranger seeking his way. Her short-sighted eyes had given her but a blurred impression of slightness and grayness, with something foreign, or at least unlocal, in the cut of the figure or its garb; but her husband had apparently seen more—seen enough to make him push past her with a sharp "Wait!" and dash down the twisting stairs without pausing to give her a hand for the descent.

A slight tendency to dizziness obliged her, after a provisional clutch at the chimney against which they had been leaning, to follow him down more cautiously; and when she had reached the attic landing she paused again for a less definite reason, leaning over the oak banister to strain her eyes through the silence of the brown, sun-flecked depths below. She lingered there till, somewhere in those depths, she heard the closing of a door; then, mechanically impelled, she went down the shallow flights of steps till she reached the lower hall.

The front door stood open on the mild sunlight of the court, and hall and court were empty. The library door was open, too, and after listening in vain for any sound of voices within, she quickly crossed the threshold, and found her husband alone, vaguely fingering the papers on his desk.

He looked up, as if surprised at her precipitate entrance, but the shadow of anxiety had passed from his face, leaving it even, as she fancied, a little brighter and clearer than usual.

"What was it? Who was it?" she asked.

"Who?" he repeated, with the surprise still all on his side.

"The man we saw coming toward the house."

He seemed honestly to reflect. "The man? Why, I thought I saw Peters; I dashed after him to say a word about the stable-drains, but he had disappeared before I could get down."

"Disappeared? Why, he seemed to be walking so slowly when we saw him."

Boyne shrugged his shoulders. "So I thought; but he must have got up steam in the interval. What do you say to our trying a scramble up Meldon Steep before sunset?"

That was all. At the time the occurrence had been less than nothing, had, indeed, been immediately obliterated by the magic of their first vision from Meldon Steep, a height which they had dreamed of climbing ever since they had first seen its bare spine heaving itself above the low roof of Lyng. Doubtless it was the mere fact of the other incident's having occurred on the very day of their ascent to Meldon that had kept it stored away in the unconscious fold of association from which it now emerged; for in itself it had no mark of the portentous. At the moment there could have been nothing more natural than that Ned should dash himself from the roof in the pursuit of dilatory tradesmen. It was the period when they were always on the watch for one or the other of the specialists employed about the place; always lying in wait for them, and dashing out at them with questions, reproaches, or reminders. And certainly in the distance the gray figure had looked like Peters.

Yet now, as she reviewed the rapid scene, she felt her husband's explanation of it to have been invalidated by the look of anxiety on his face. Why had the familiar appearance of Peters made him anxious? Why, above all, if it was of such prime necessity to confer with that authority on the subject of the stable-drains, had the failure to find him produced such a look of relief? Mary could not say that any one of these considerations had occurred to her at the time, yet, from the promptness with which they now marshaled themselves at her summons, she had a sudden sense that they must all along have been there, waiting their hour.

II

Weary with her thoughts, she moved toward the window. The library was now completely dark, and she was surprised to see how much faint light the outer world still held.

As she peered out into it across the court, a figure shaped itself in the tapering perspective of bare lines: it looked a mere blot of deeper gray in the grayness, and for an instant, as it moved toward her, her heart thumped to the thought, "It's the ghost!"

She had time, in that long instant, to feel suddenly that the man of whom, two months earlier, she had a brief distant vision from the roof was now, at his predestined hour, about to reveal himself as *not* having been Peters; and her spirit sank under the impending fear of the disclosure. But almost with the next tick of the clock the ambiguous figure, gaining substance and character, showed itself even to her weak sight as her husband's; and she turned away to meet him, as he entered, with the confession of her folly.

"It's really too absurd," she laughed out from the threshold, "but I never *can* remember!"

"Remember what?" Boyne questioned as they drew together.

"That when one sees the Lyng ghost one never knows it." Her hand was on his sleeve, and he kept it there, but with no response in his gesture or in the lines of his fagged, preoccupied face.

"Did you think you'd seen it?" he asked, after an appreciable interval.

"Why, I actually took *you* for it, my dear, in my mad determination to spot it!"

"Me—just now?" His arm dropped away, and he turned from her with a faint echo of her laugh. "Really, dearest, you'd better give it up, if that's the best you can do."

"Yes, I give it up—I give it up. Have *you*?" she asked, turning round on him abruptly.

The parlor-maid had entered with letters and a lamp, and the light struck up into Boyne's face as he bent above the tray she presented.

"Have *you*?" Mary perversely insisted, when the servant had disappeared on her errand of illumination.

"Have I what?" he rejoined absently, the light bringing out the sharp stamp of worry between his brows as he turned over the letters.

"Given up trying to see the ghost." Her heart beat a little at the experiment she was making.

Her husband, laying his letters aside, moved away into the shadow of the hearth.

"I never tried," he said, tearing open the wrapper of a newspaper.

"Well, of course," Mary persisted, "the exasperating thing is that there's no use trying, since one can't be sure till so long afterward."

He was unfolding the paper as if he had hardly heard her; but after a pause, during which the sheets rustled spasmodically between his hands, he lifted his head to say abruptly, "Have you any idea *how long*?"

Mary had sunk into a low chair beside the fireplace. From her seat she looked up, startled, at her husband's profile, which was darkly projected against the circle of lamplight.

"No; none. Have *you*?" she retorted, repeating her former phrase with an added keenness of intention.

Boyne crumpled the paper into a bunch, and then inconsequently turned back with it toward the lamp.

"Lord, no! I only meant," he explained, with a faint tinge of impatience, "is there any legend, any tradition, as to that?"

"Not that I know of," she answered; but the impulse to add, "What makes you ask?" was checked by the reappearance of the parlor-maid with tea and a second lamp.

With the dispersal of shadows, and the repetition of the daily domestic office, Mary Boyne felt herself less oppressed by that sense of something mutely imminent which had darkened her solitary afternoon. For a few moments she gave herself silently to the details of her task, and when she looked up from it she was struck to the point of bewilderment by the change in her husband's face. He had seated himself near the farther lamp, and was absorbed in the perusal of his letters; but was it something he had found in them, or merely the shifting of her own point of view, that had restored his features to their normal aspect? The longer she looked, the more definitely the change affirmed itself. The lines of painful tension had vanished, and such traces of fatigue as lingered were of the kind easily attributable to steady mental effort. He glanced up, as if drawn by her gaze, and met her eyes with a smile.

"I'm dying for my tea, you know; and here's a letter for you," he said.

She took the letter he held out in exchange for the cup she proffered him, and, returning to her seat, broke the seal with the languid gesture of the reader whose interests are all inclosed in the circle of one cherished presence.

Her next conscious motion was that of starting to her feet, the letter falling to them as she rose, while she held out to her husband a long newspaper clipping.

"Ned! What's this? What does it mean?"

He had risen at the same instant, almost as if hearing her cry before she uttered it; and for a perceptible space of time he and she studied each other, like adversaries watching for an advantage, across the space between her chair and his desk.

"What's what? You fairly made me jump!" Boyne said at length, moving toward her with a sudden, half-exasperated laugh. The shadow of apprehension was on his face again, not now a look of fixed foreboding, but a shifting vigilance of lips and eyes that gave her the sense of his feeling himself invisibly surrounded.

Her hand shook so that she could hardly give him the clipping.

"This article—from the *Waukesha Sentinel*—that a man named Elwell has brought suit against you—that there was something wrong about the Blue Star Mine. I can't understand more than half."

They continued to face each other as she spoke, and to her astonishment, she saw that her words had the almost immediate effect of dissipating the strained watchfulness of his look.

"Oh, *that*!" He glanced down the printed slip, and then folded it with the gesture of one who handles something harmless and familiar. "What's the matter with you this afternoon, Mary? I thought you'd got bad news."

She stood before him with her undefinable terror subsiding slowly under the reassuring touch of his composure.

"You knew about this, then—it's all right?"

"Certainly I knew about it; and it's all right."

"But what *is* it? I don't understand. What does this man accuse you of?"

"Oh, pretty nearly every crime in the calendar." Boyne had tossed the clipping down, and thrown himself comfortably into an arm-chair near the fire. "Do you want to hear the story? It's not particularly interesting—just a squabble over interests in the Blue Star."

"But who is this Elwell? I don't know the name."

"Oh, he's a fellow I put into it—gave him a hand up. I told you all about him at the time."

"I daresay. I must have forgotten." Vainly she strained back among her memories. "But if you helped him, why does he make this return?"

"Oh, probably some shyster lawyer got hold of him and talked him over. It's all rather technical and complicated. I thought that kind of thing bored you."

His wife felt a sting of compunction. Theoretically, she deprecated the American wife's detachment from her husband's professional interests, but in practice she had always found it difficult to fix her attention on Boyne's report of the transactions in which his varied interests involved him. Besides, she had felt from the first that, in a community where the amenities of living could be obtained only at the cost of efforts as arduous as her husband's professional labors, such brief leisure as they could command should be used as an escape from immediate preoccupations, a flight to the life they always dreamed of living. Once or twice, now that this new life had actually drawn its magic circle about them, she had asked herself if she had done right; but hitherto such conjectures had been no more than the retrospective excursions of an active fancy. Now, for the first time, it startled her a little to find how little she knew of the material foundation on which her happiness was built.

She glanced again at her husband, and was reassured by the composure of his face; yet she felt the need of more definite grounds for her reassurance.

"But doesn't this suit worry you? Why have you never spoken to me about it?"

He answered both questions at once: "I didn't speak of it at first because it *did* worry me—annoyed me, rather. But it's all ancient history now. Your correspondent must have got hold of a back number of the *Sentinel*."

She felt a quick thrill of relief. "You mean it's over? He's lost his case?"

There was a just perceptible delay in Boyne's reply. "The suit's been withdrawn—that's all."

But she persisted, as if to exonerate herself from the inward charge of being too easily put off. "Withdrawn because he saw he had no chance?"

"Oh, he had no chance," Boyne answered.

She was still struggling with a dimly felt perplexity at the back of her thoughts.

"How long ago was it withdrawn?"

He paused, as if with a slight return of his former uncertainty. "I've just had the news now; but I've been expecting it."

"Just now—in one of your letters?"

"Yes; in one of my letters."

She made no answer, and was aware only, after a short interval of waiting, that he had risen, and strolling across the room, had placed himself on the sofa at her side. She felt him, as he did so, pass an arm about her, she felt his hand seek hers and clasp it, and turning slowly, drawn by the warmth of his cheek, she met the smiling clearness of his eyes.

"It's all right—it's all right?" she questioned, through the flood of her dissolving doubts; and "I give you my word it never was righter!" he laughed back at her, holding her close.

III

One of the strangest things she was afterward to recall out of all the next day's incredible strangeness was the sudden and complete recovery of her sense of security.

It was in the air when she woke in her low-ceilinged, dusky room; it accompanied her down-stairs to the breakfast-table, flashed out at her from the fire, and re-duplicated itself brightly from the flanks of the urn and the sturdy flutings of the Georgian teapot. It was as if, in some roundabout way, all her diffused apprehensions of the previous day, with their moment of sharp concentration about the newspaper article,—as if this dim questioning of the future, and startled return upon the past,—had between them liquidated the arrears of some haunting moral obligation. If she had indeed been careless of her husband's affairs, it was, her new state seemed to prove, because her faith in him instinctively justified such carelessness; and his right to her faith had overwhelmingly affirmed itself in the very face of menace and suspicion. She had never seen him more untroubled, more naturally and unconsciously in possession of himself, than after the cross-examination to which she had subjected him: it was almost as if he had been aware of her lurking doubts, and had wanted the air cleared as much as she did.

It was as clear, thank Heaven! as the bright outer light that surprised her almost with a touch of summer when she issued from the house for her daily round of the gardens. She had left Boyne at his desk, indulging herself, as she passed the library door, by a last peep at his quiet face, where he bent, pipe in his mouth, above his papers, and now she had her own morning's task to perform. The task involved on such charmed winter days almost as much delighted loitering about the different quarters of her demesne as if spring were already at work on shrubs and borders. There were such inexhaustible possibilities still before her, such opportunities to bring out the latent graces of the old place, without a single irreverent touch of alteration, that the winter months were all too short to plan what spring and autumn executed. And her recovered sense of safety gave, on this particular morning, a peculiar zest to her progress through the sweet, still place. She went first to the kitchen-garden, where the espaliered pear-trees drew complicated patterns on the walls, and pigeons were fluttering and preening about the silvery-slated roof of their cot. There was something wrong about the piping of the hothouse, and she was expecting an authority from Dorchester, who was to drive out between trains and make a diagnosis of the boiler. But when she dipped into the damp heat of the greenhouses, among the spiced scents and waxy pinks and reds of old-fashioned exotics,—even the flora of Lyng was in the note!—she learned that the great man had not arrived, and the day being too rare to waste in an artificial atmosphere, she came out again and paced slowly along the springy turf of the bowling-green to the gardens behind the house. At their farther end rose a grass terrace, commanding, over the fish-pond and the yew hedges, a view of the long house-front, with its twisted chimney-stacks and the blue shadows of its roof angles, all drenched in the pale gold moisture of the air.

Seen thus, across the level tracery of the yews, under the suffused, mild light, it sent her, from its open windows and hospitably smoking chimneys, the look of some warm human presence, of a mind slowly ripened on a sunny wall of experience. She had never before had so deep a sense of her intimacy with it, such a conviction that its secrets were all beneficent, kept, as they said to children, "for one's good," so complete a trust in its power to gather up her life and Ned's into the harmonious pattern of the long, long story it sat there weaving in the sun.

She heard steps behind her, and turned, expecting to see the gardener, accompanied by the engineer from Dorchester. But only one figure was in sight, that of a youngish, slightly built man, who, for reasons she could not on the spot have specified, did not remotely resemble her preconceived notion of an authority on hot-house boilers. The new-comer, on seeing her, lifted his hat, and paused with the air of a gentleman —perhaps a traveler—desirous of having it immediately known that his intrusion is involuntary. The local fame of Lyng occasionally attracted the more intelligent sight-seer, and Mary half-expected to see the stranger dissemble a camera, or justify his presence by producing it. But he made no gesture of any sort, and after a moment she asked, in a tone responding to the courteous deprecation of his attitude: "Is there any one you wish to see?"

"I came to see Mr. Boyne," he replied. His intonation, rather than his accent, was faintly American, and Mary, at the familiar note, looked at him more closely. The brim of his soft felt hat cast a shade on his face, which, thus obscured, wore to her short-sighted gaze a look of seriousness, as of a person arriving "on business," and civilly but firmly aware of his rights.

Past experience had made Mary equally sensible to such claims; but she was jealous of her husband's morning hours, and doubtful of his having given any one the right to intrude on them.

"Have you an appointment with Mr. Boyne?" she asked.

He hesitated, as if unprepared for the question.

"Not exactly an appointment," he replied.

"Then I'm afraid, this being his working-time, that he can't receive you now. Will you give me a message, or come back later?"

The visitor, again lifting his hat, briefly replied that he would come back later, and walked away, as if to regain the front of the house. As his figure receded down the walk between the yew hedges, Mary saw him pause and look up an instant at the peaceful house-front bathed in faint winter sunshine; and it struck her, with a tardy touch of compunction, that it would have been more humane to ask if he had come from a distance, and to offer, in that case, to inquire if her husband could receive him. But as the thought occurred to her he passed out of sight behind a pyramidal yew, and at the same moment her attention was distracted by the approach of the gardener, attended by the bearded pepper-and-salt figure of the boiler-maker from Dorchester.

The encounter with this authority led to such far-reaching issues that they resulted in his finding it expedient to ignore his train, and beguiled Mary into spending the remainder of the morning in absorbed confabulation among the greenhouses. She was startled to find, when the colloquy ended, that it was nearly luncheon-time, and she half expected, as she hurried back to the house, to see her husband coming out to meet her. But she found no one in the court but an under-gardener raking the gravel, and the hall, when she entered it, was so silent that she guessed Boyne to be still at work behind the closed door of the library.

Not wishing to disturb him, she turned into the drawing-room, and there, at her writing-table, lost herself in renewed calculations of the outlay to which the morning's conference had committed her. The knowledge that she could permit herself such follies had not yet lost its novelty; and somehow, in contrast to the vague apprehensions of the previous days, it now seemed an element of her recovered security, of the sense that, as Ned had said, things in general had never been "righter." She was still luxuriating in a lavish play of figures when the parlor-maid, from the threshold, roused her with a dubiously worded inquiry as to the expediency of serving luncheon. It was one of their jokes that Trimmle announced luncheon as if she were divulging a state secret, and Mary, intent upon her papers, merely murmured an absent-minded assent.

She felt Trimmle wavering expressively on the threshold as if in rebuke of such offhand acquiescence; then her retreating steps sounded down the passage, and Mary, pushing away her papers, crossed the hall, and went to the library door. It was still closed, and she wavered in her turn, disliking to disturb her husband, yet anxious that he should not exceed his normal measure of work. As she stood there, balancing her impulses, the esoteric Trimmle returned with the announcement of luncheon, and Mary, thus impelled, opened the door and went into the library.

Boyne was not at his desk, and she peered about her, expecting to discover him at the book-shelves, somewhere down the length of the room; but her call brought no response, and gradually it became clear to her that he was not in the library.

She turned back to the parlor-maid.

"Mr. Boyne must be up-stairs. Please tell him that luncheon is ready."

The parlor-maid appeared to hesitate between the obvious duty of obeying orders and an equally obvious conviction of the foolishness of the injunction laid upon her. The struggle resulted in her saying doubtfully, "If you please, Madam, Mr. Boyne's not up-stairs."

"Not in his room? Are you sure?"

"I'm sure, Madam."

Mary consulted the clock. "Where is he, then?"

"He's gone out," Trimmle announced, with the superior air of one who has respectfully waited for the question that a well-ordered mind would have first propounded.

Mary's previous conjecture had been right, then. Boyne must have gone to the gardens to meet her, and since she had missed him, it was clear that he had taken the shorter way by the south door, instead of going round to the court. She crossed the hall to the glass portal opening directly on the yew garden, but the parlor-maid, after another moment of inner conflict, decided to bring out recklessly, "Please, Madam, Mr. Boyne didn't go that way."

Mary turned back. "Where *did* he go? And when?"

"He went out of the front door, up the drive, Madam." It was a matter of principle with Trimmle never to answer more than one question at a time.

"Up the drive? At this hour?" Mary went to the door herself, and glanced across the court through the long tunnel of bare limes. But its perspective was as empty as when she had scanned it on entering the house.

"Did Mr. Boyne leave no message?" she asked.

Trimmle seemed to surrender herself to a last struggle with the forces of chaos.

"No, Madam. He just went out with the gentleman."

"The gentleman? What gentleman?" Mary wheeled about, as if to front this new factor.

"The gentleman who called, Madam," said Trimmle, resignedly.

"When did a gentleman call? Do explain yourself, Trimmle!"

Only the fact that Mary was very hungry, and that she wanted to consult her husband about the greenhouses, would have caused her to lay so unusual an injunction on her attendant; and even now she was detached enough to note in Trimmle's eye the dawning defiance of the respectful subordinate who has been pressed too hard.

"I couldn't exactly say the hour, Madam, because I didn't let the gentleman in," she replied, with the air of magnanimously ignoring the irregularity of her mistress's course.

"You didn't let him in?"

"No, Madam. When the bell rang I was dressing, and Agnes—"

"Go and ask Agnes, then," Mary interjected.

Trimmle still wore her look of patient magnanimity. "Agnes would not know, Madam, for she had unfortunately burnt her hand in trying the wick of the new lamp from town—" Trimmle, as Mary was aware, had always been opposed to the new lamp— "and so Mrs. Dockett sent the kitchen-maid instead."

Mary looked again at the clock. "It's after two! Go and ask the kitchen-maid if Mr. Boyne left any word."

She went into luncheon without waiting, and Trimmle presently brought her there the kitchen-maid's statement that the gentleman had called about one o'clock, that Mr. Boyne had gone out with him without leaving any message. The kitchen-maid did not even know the caller's name, for he had written it on a slip of paper, which he had folded and handed to her, with the injunction to deliver it at once to Mr. Boyne.

Mary finished her luncheon, still wondering, and when it was over, and Trimmle had brought the coffee to the drawing-room, her wonder had deepened to a first faint tinge of disquietude. It was unlike Boyne to absent himself without explanation at so unwonted an hour, and the difficulty of identifying the visitor whose summons he had apparently obeyed made his disappearance the more unaccountable. Mary Boyne's experience as the wife of a busy engineer, subject to sudden calls and compelled to keep irregular hours, had trained her to the philosophic acceptance of surprises; but since Boyne's withdrawal from business he had adopted a Benedictine regularity of life. As if to make up for the dispersed and agitated years, with their "stand-up" lunches and dinners rattled down to the joltings of the dining-car, he cultivated the last refinements of punctuality and monotony, discouraging his wife's fancy for the unexpected; and declaring that to a delicate taste there were infinite gradations of pleasure in the fixed recurrences of habit.

Still, since no life can completely defend itself from the unforeseen, it was evident that all Boyne's precautions would sooner or later prove unavailable, and Mary concluded that he had cut short a tiresome visit by walking with his caller to the station, or at least accompanying him for part of the way.

This conclusion relieved her from farther preoccupation, and she went out herself to take up her conference with the gardener. Thence she walked to the village post-office, a mile or so away; and when she turned toward home, the early twilight was setting in.

She had taken a foot-path across the downs, and as Boyne, meanwhile, had probably returned from the station by the highroad, there was little likelihood of their meeting on the way. She felt sure, however, of his having reached the house before her; so sure that, when she entered it herself, without even pausing to inquire of Trimmle, she made directly for the library. But the library was still empty, and with an unwonted precision of visual memory she immediately observed that the papers on her husband's desk lay precisely as they had lain when she had gone in to call him to luncheon.

Then of a sudden she was seized by a vague dread of the unknown. She had closed the door behind her on entering, and as she stood alone in the long, silent, shadowy room, her dread seemed to take shape and sound, to be there audibly breathing and lurking among the shadows. Her short-sighted eyes strained through them, half-discerning an actual presence, something aloof, that watched and knew; and in the recoil from that intangible propinquity she threw herself suddenly on the bell-rope and gave it a desperate pull.

The long, quavering summons brought Trimmle in precipitately with a lamp, and Mary breathed again at this sobering reappearance of the usual.

"You may bring tea if Mr. Boyne is in," she said, to justify her ring.

"Very well, Madam. But Mr. Boyne is not in," said Trimmle, putting down the lamp.

"Not in? You mean he's come back and gone out again?"

"No, Madam. He's never been back."

The dread stirred again, and Mary knew that now it had her fast.

"Not since he went out with—the gentleman?"

"Not since he went out with the gentleman."

"But who *was* the gentleman?" Mary gasped out, with the sharp note of some one trying to be heard through a confusion of meaningless noises.

"That I couldn't say, Madam." Trimmle, standing there by the lamp, seemed suddenly to grow less round and rosy, as though eclipsed by the same creeping shade of apprehension.

"But the kitchen-maid knows—wasn't it the kitchen-maid who let him in?"

"She doesn't know either, Madam, for he wrote his name on a folded paper."

Mary, through her agitation, was aware that they were both designating the unknown visitor by a vague pronoun, instead of the conventional formula which, till then, had kept their allusions within the bounds of custom. And at the same moment her mind caught at the suggestion of the folded paper.

"But he must have a name! Where is the paper?"

She moved to the desk, and began to turn over the scattered documents that littered it. The first that caught her eye was an unfinished letter in her husband's hand, with his pen lying across it, as though dropped there at a sudden summons.

"My dear Parvis,"—who was Parvis?—"I have just received your letter announcing Elwell's death, and while I suppose there is now no farther risk of trouble, it might be safer—"

She tossed the sheet aside, and continued her search; but no folded paper was discoverable among the letters and pages of manuscript which had been swept together in a promiscuous heap, as if by a hurried or a startled gesture.

"But the kitchen-maid *saw* him. Send her here," she commanded, wondering at her dullness in not thinking sooner of so simple a solution. Trimmle, at the behest, vanished in a flash, as if thankful to be out of the room, and when she reappeared, conducting the agitated underling, Mary had regained her self-possession, and had her questions pat.

The gentleman was a stranger, yes—that she understood. But what had he said? And, above all, what had he looked like? The first question was easily enough answered, for the disconcerting reason that he had said so little—had merely asked for Mr. Boyne, and, scribbling something on a bit of paper, had requested that it should at once be carried in to him.

"Then you don't know what he wrote? You're not sure it was his name?"

The kitchen-maid was not sure, but supposed it was, since he had written it in answer to her inquiry as to whom she should announce.

"And when you carried the paper in to Mr. Boyne, what did he say?"

The kitchen-maid did not think that Mr. Boyne had said anything, but she could not be sure, for just as she had handed him the paper and he was opening it, she had become aware that the visitor had followed her into the library, and she had slipped out, leaving the two gentlemen together.

"But then, if you left them in the library, how do you know that they went out of the house?"

This question plunged the witness into momentary inarticulateness, from which she was rescued by Trimmle, who, by means of ingenious circumlocutions, elicited the statement that before she could cross the hall to the back passage she had heard the gentlemen behind her, and had seen them go out of the front door together.

"Then, if you saw the gentleman twice, you must be able to tell me what he looked like."

But with this final challenge to her powers of expression it became clear that the limit of the kitchen-maid's endurance had been reached. The obligation of going to the front door to "show in" a visitor was in itself so subversive of the fundamental disarray, and she could only stammer out, after various panting efforts at evocation, "His hat, mum, was different-like, as you might say—"

"Different? How different?" Mary flashed out at her, her own mind, in the same instant, leaping back to an image left on it that morning, but temporarily lost under layers of subsequent impressions.

"His hat had a wide brim, you mean? and his face was pale—a youngish face?" Mary pressed her, with a white-lipped intensity of interrogation. But if the kitchen-maid found any adequate answer to this challenge, it was swept away for her listener down the rushing current of her own convictions. The stranger—the stranger in the garden! Why had Mary not thought of him before? She needed no one now to tell her that it was he who had called for her husband and gone away with him. But who was he, and why had Boyne obeyed his call?

IV

It leaped out at her suddenly, like a grin out of the dark, that they had often called England so little—"such a confoundedly hard place to get lost in."

A confoundedly hard place to get lost in! That had been her husband's phrase. And now, with the whole machinery of official investigation sweeping its flash-lights from shore to shore, and across the dividing straits; now, with Boyne's name blazing from the walls of every town and village, his portrait (how that wrung her!) hawked up and down the country like the image of a hunted criminal; now the little compact, populous island, so policed, surveyed, and administered, revealed itself as a Sphinx-like guardian of abysmal mysteries, staring back into his wife's anguished eyes as if with the malicious joy of knowing something they would never know!

In the fortnight since Boyne's disappearance there had been no word of him, no trace of his movements. Even the usual misleading reports that raise expectancy in tortured bosoms had been few and fleeting. No one but the bewildered kitchen-maid had seen him leave the house, and no one else had seen "the gentleman" who accompanied him. All inquiries in the neighborhood failed to elicit the memory of a stranger's presence that day in the neighborhood of Lyng. And no one had met Edward Boyne, either alone or in company, in any of the neighboring villages, or on the road across the downs, or at either of the local railway-stations. The sunny English noon had swallowed him as completely as if he had gone out into Cimmerian night.

Mary, while every external means of investigation was working at its highest pressure, had ransacked her husband's papers for any trace of antecedent complications, of entanglements or obligations unknown to her, that might throw a faint ray into the darkness. But if any such had existed in the background of Boyne's life, they had disappeared as completely as the slip of paper on which the visitor had written his name. There remained no possible thread of guidance except—if it were indeed an exception—the letter which Boyne had apparently been in the act of writing when he received his mysterious summons. That letter, read and reread by his wife, and submitted by her to the police, yielded little enough for conjecture to feed on.

"I have just heard of Elwell's death, and while I suppose there is now no farther risk of trouble, it might be safer—" That was all. The "risk of trouble" was easily explained by the newspaper clipping which had apprised Mary of the suit brought against her husband by one of his associates in the Blue Star enterprise. The only new information conveyed in the letter was the fact of its showing Boyne, when he wrote it, to be still apprehensive of the results of the suit, though he had assured his wife that it had been withdrawn, and though the letter itself declared that the plaintiff was dead. It took several weeks of exhaustive cabling to fix the identity of the "Parvis" to whom the fragmentary communication was addressed, but even after these inquiries had shown him to be a Waukesha lawyer, no new facts concerning the Elwell suit were elicited. He appeared to have had no direct concern in it, but to have been conversant with the facts merely as an acquaintance, and possible intermediary; and he declared himself unable to divine with what object Boyne intended to seek his assistance.

This negative information, sole fruit of the first fortnight's feverish search, was not increased by a jot during the slow weeks that followed. Mary knew that the investigations were still being carried on, but she had a vague sense of their gradually slackening, as the actual march of time seemed to slacken. It was as though the days, flying horror-struck from the shrouded image of the one inscrutable day, gained assurance as the distance lengthened, till at last they fell back into their normal gait. And so with the human imaginations at work on the dark event. No doubt it occupied them still, but week by week and hour by hour it grew less absorbing, took up less space, was slowly but inevitably crowded out of the foreground of consciousness by the new problems perpetually bubbling up from the vaporous caldron of human experience.

Even Mary Boyne's consciousness gradually felt the same lowering of velocity. It still swayed with the incessant oscillations of conjecture; but they were slower, more rhythmical in their beat. There were moments of overwhelming lassitude when, like the victim of some poison which leaves the brain clear, but holds the body motionless, she saw herself domesticated with the Horror, accepting its perpetual presence as one of the fixed conditions of life.

These moments lengthened into hours and days, till she passed into a phase of stolid acquiescence. She watched the familiar routine of life with the incurious eye of a savage on whom the meaningless processes of civilization make but the faintest impression. She had come to regard herself as part of the routine, a spoke of the wheel, revolving with its motion; she felt almost like the furniture of the room in which she sat, an insensate object to be dusted and pushed about with the chairs and tables. And this deepening apathy held her fast at Lyng, in spite of the urgent entreaties of friends and the usual medical recommendation of "change." Her friends supposed that her refusal to move was inspired by the belief that her husband would one day return to the spot from which he had vanished, and a beautiful legend grew up about this imaginary state of waiting. But in reality she had no such belief: the depths of anguish inclosing her were no longer lighted by flashes of hope. She was sure that Boyne would never come back, that he had gone out of her sight as completely as if Death itself had waited that day on the threshold. She had even renounced, one by one, the various theories as to his disappearance which had been advanced by the press, the police, and her own agonized imagination. In sheer lassitude her mind turned from these alternatives of horror, and sank back into the blank fact that he was gone.

No, she would never know what had become of him—no one would ever know. But the house knew; the library in which she spent her long, lonely evenings knew. For it was here that the last scene had been enacted, here that the stranger had come, and spoken the word which had caused Boyne to rise and follow him. The floor she trod had felt his tread; the books on the shelves had seen his face; and there were moments when the intense consciousness of the old, dusky walls seemed about to break out into some audible revelation of their secret. But the revelation never came, and she knew it would never come. Lyng was not one of the garrulous old houses that betray the secrets intrusted to them. Its very legend proved that it had always been the mute accomplice, the incorruptible custodian of the mysteries it had surprised. And Mary Boyne, sitting face to face with its portentous silence, felt the futility of seeking to break it by any human means.

V

"I don't say it *wasn't* straight, yet don't say it *was* straight. It was business."

Mary, at the words, lifted her head with a start, and looked intently at the speaker.

When, half an hour before, a card with "Mr. Parvis" on it had been brought up to her, she had been immediately aware that the name had been a part of her consciousness ever since she had read it at the head of Boyne's unfinished letter. In the library she had found awaiting her a small neutral-tinted man with a bald head and gold eye-glasses, and it sent a strange tremor through her to know that this was the person to whom her husband's last known thought had been directed.

Parvis, civilly, but without vain preamble,—in the manner of a man who has his watch in his hand, — had set forth the object of his visit. He had "run over" to England on business, and finding himself in the neighborhood of Dorchester, had not wished to leave it without paying his respects to Mrs. Boyne; without asking her, if the occasion offered, what she meant to do about Bob Elwell's family.

The words touched the spring of some obscure dread in Mary's bosom. Did her visitor, after all, know what Boyne had meant by his unfinished phrase? She asked for an elucidation of his question, and noticed at once that he seemed surprised at her continued ignorance of the subject. Was it possible that she really knew as little as she said?

"I know nothing—you must tell me," she faltered out; and her visitor thereupon proceeded to unfold his story. It threw, even to her confused perceptions, and imperfectly initiated vision, a lurid glare on the whole hazy episode of the Blue Star Mine. Her husband had made his money in that brilliant speculation at the cost of "getting ahead" of some one less alert to seize the chance; the victim of his ingenuity was young Robert Elwell, who had "put him on" to the Blue Star scheme.

Parvis, at Mary's first startled cry, had thrown her a sobering glance through his impartial glasses.

"Bob Elwell wasn't smart enough, that's all; if he had been, he might have turned round and served Boyne the same way. It's the kind of thing that happens every day in business. I guess it's what the scientists call the survival of the fittest," said Mr. Parvis, evidently pleased with the aptness of his analogy.

Mary felt a physical shrinking from the next question she tried to frame; it was as though the words on her lips had a taste that nauseated her.

"But then—you accuse my husband of doing something dishonorable?"

Mr. Parvis surveyed the question dispassionately. "Oh, no, I don't. I don't even say it wasn't straight." He glanced up and down the long lines of books, as if one of them might have supplied him with the definition he sought. "I don't say it *wasn't* straight, and yet I don't say it *was* straight. It was business." After all, no definition in his category could be more comprehensive than that.

Mary sat staring at him with a look of terror. He seemed to her like the indifferent, implacable emissary of some dark, formless power.

"But Mr. Elwell's lawyers apparently did not take your view, since I suppose the suit was withdrawn by their advice."

"Oh, yes, they knew he hadn't a leg to stand on, technically. It was when they advised him to withdraw the suit that he got desperate. You see, he'd borrowed most of the money he lost in the Blue Star, and he was up a tree. That's why he shot himself when they told him he had no show."

The horror was sweeping over Mary in great, deafening waves.

"He shot himself? He killed himself because of *that*?"

"Well, he didn't kill himself, exactly. He dragged on two months before he died." Parvis emitted the statement as unemotionally as a gramophone grinding out its "record."

"You mean that he tried to kill himself, and failed? And tried again?"

"Oh, he didn't have to *try* again," said Parvis, grimly.

They sat opposite each other in silence, he swinging his eye-glass thoughtfully about his finger, she, motionless, her arms stretched along her knees in an attitude of rigid tension.

"But if you knew all this," she began at length, hardly able to force her voice above a whisper, "how is it that when I wrote you at the time of my husband's disappearance you said you didn't understand his letter?"

Parvis received this without perceptible discomfiture. "Why, I didn't understand it—strictly speaking. And it wasn't the time to talk about it, if I had. The Elwell business was settled when the suit was withdrawn. Nothing I could have told you would have helped you to find your husband."

Mary continued to scrutinize him. "Then why are you telling me now?"

Still Parvis did not hesitate. "Well, to begin with, I supposed you knew more than you appear to—I mean about the circumstances of Elwell's death. And then people are talking of it now; the whole matter's been raked up again. And I thought, if you didn't know, you ought to."

She remained silent, and he continued: "You see, it's only come out lately what a bad state Elwell's affairs were in. His wife's a proud woman, and she fought on as long as she could, going out to work, and taking sewing at home, when she got too sick—something with the heart, I believe. But she had his bedridden mother to look after, and the children, and she broke down under it, and finally had to ask for help. That attracted attention to the case, and the papers took it up, and a subscription was started. Everybody out there liked Bob Elwell, and most of the prominent names in the place are down on the list, and people began to wonder why—"

Parvis broke off to fumble in an inner pocket. "Here," he continued, "here's an account of the whole thing from the *Sentinel*—a little sensational, of course. But I guess you'd better look it over."

He held out a newspaper to Mary, who unfolded it slowly, remembering, as she did so, the evening when, in that same room, the perusal of a clipping from the *Sentinel* had first shaken the depths of her security.

As she opened the paper, her eyes, shrinking from the glaring head-lines, "Widow of Boyne's Victim Forced to Appeal for Aid," ran down the column of text to two portraits inserted in it. The first was her husband's, taken from a photograph made the year they had come to England. It was the picture of him that she liked best, the one that stood on the writing-table up-stairs in her bedroom. As the eyes in the photograph met hers, she felt it would be impossible to read what was said of him, and closed her lids with the sharpness of the pain.

"I thought if you felt disposed to put your name down—" she heard Parvis continue.

She opened her eyes with an effort, and they fell on the other portrait. It was that of a youngish man, slightly built, in rough clothes, with features somewhat blurred by the shadow of a projecting hat-brim. Where had she seen that outline before? She stared at it confusedly, her heart hammering in her throat and ears. Then she gave a cry.

"This is the man—the man who came for my husband!"

She heard Parvis start to his feet, and was dimly aware that she had slipped backward into the corner of the sofa, and that he was bending above her in alarm. With an intense effort she straightened herself, and reached out for the paper, which she had dropped.

"It's the man! I should know him anywhere!" she cried in a voice that sounded in her own ears like a scream.

Parvis's voice seemed to come to her from far off, down endless, fog-muffled windings.

"Mrs. Boyne, you're not very well. Shall I call somebody? Shall I get a glass of water?"

"No, no, no!" She threw herself toward him, her hand frantically clenching the newspaper. "I tell you, it's the man! I know him! He spoke to me in the garden!"

Parvis took the journal from her, directing his glasses to the portrait. "It can't be, Mrs. Boyne. It's Robert Elwell."

"Robert Elwell?" Her white stare seemed to travel into space. "Then it was Robert Elwell who came for him."

"Came for Boyne? The day he went away?" Parvis's voice dropped as hers rose. He bent over, laying a fraternal hand on her, as if to coax her gently back into her seat. "Why, Elwell was dead! Don't you remember?"

Mary sat with her eyes fixed on the picture, unconscious of what he was saying.

"Don't you remember Boyne's unfinished letter to me—the one you found on his desk that day? It was written just after he'd heard of Elwell's death." She noticed an odd shake in Parvis's unemotional voice. "Surely you remember that!" he urged her.

Yes, she remembered: that was the profoundest horror of it. Elwell had died the day before her husband's disappearance; and this was Elwell's portrait; and it was the portrait of the man who had spoken to her in the garden. She lifted her head and looked slowly about the library. The library could have borne witness that it was also the portrait of the man who had come in that day to call Boyne from his unfinished letter. Through the misty surgings of her brain she heard the faint boom of half-forgotten words—words spoken by Alida Stair on the lawn at Pangbourne before Boyne and his wife had ever seen the house at Lyng, or had imagined that they might one day live there.

"This was the man who spoke to me," she repeated.

She looked again at Parvis. He was trying to conceal his disturbance under what he imagined to be an expression of indulgent commiseration; but the edges of his lips were blue. "He thinks me mad; but I'm not mad," she reflected; and suddenly there flashed upon her a way of justifying her strange affirmation.

She sat quiet, controlling the quiver of her lips, and waiting till she could trust her voice to keep its habitual level; then she said, looking straight at Parvis: "Will you answer me one question, please? When was it that Robert Elwell tried to kill himself?"

"When—when?" Parvis stammered.

"Yes; the date. Please try to remember."

She saw that he was growing still more afraid of her. "I have a reason," she insisted gently.

"Yes, yes. Only I can't remember. About two months before, I should say."

"I want the date," she repeated.

Parvis picked up the newspaper. "We might see here," he said, still humoring her. He ran his eyes down the page. "Here it is. Last October—the—"

She caught the words from him. "The 20th, wasn't it?" With a sharp look at her, he verified. "Yes, the 20th. Then you *did* know?"

"I know now." Her white stare continued to travel past him. "Sunday, the 20th—that was the day he came first."

Parvis's voice was almost inaudible. "Came here first?"

"Yes."

"You saw him twice, then?"

"Yes, twice." She breathed it at him with dilated eyes. "He came first on the 20th of October. I remember the date because it was the day we went up Meldon Steep for the first time." She felt a faint gasp of inward laughter at the thought that but for that she might have forgotten.

Parvis continued to scrutinize her, as if trying to intercept her gaze.

"We saw him from the roof," she went on. "He came down the lime-avenue toward the house. He was dressed just as he is in that picture. My husband saw him first. He was frightened, and ran down ahead of me; but there was no one there. He had vanished."

"Elwell had vanished?" Parvis faltered.

"Yes." Their two whispers seemed to grope for each other. "I couldn't think what had happened. I see now. He *tried* to come then; but he wasn't dead enough—he couldn't reach us. He had to wait for two months; and then he came back again—and Ned went with him."

She nodded at Parvis with the look of triumph of a child who has successfully worked out a difficult puzzle. But suddenly she lifted her hands with a desperate gesture, pressing them to her bursting temples.

"Oh, my God! I sent him to Ned—I told him where to go! I sent him to this room!" she screamed out.

She felt the walls of the room rush toward her, like inward falling ruins; and she heard Parvis, a long way off, as if through the ruins, crying to her, and struggling to get at her. But she was numb to his touch, she did not know what he was saying. Through the tumult she heard but one clear note, the voice of Alida Stair, speaking on the lawn at Pangbourne.

"You won't know till afterward," it said. "You won't know till long, long afterward."

THE BUS-CONDUCTOR

EDWARD FREDERIC BENSON

My friend, Hugh Grainger, and I had just returned from a two days' visit in the country, where we had been staying in a house of sinister repute which was supposed to be haunted by ghosts of a peculiarly fearsome and truculent sort. The house itself was all that such a house should be, Jacobean and oak-panelled, with long dark passages and high vaulted rooms. It stood, also, very remote, and was encompassed by a wood of sombre pines that muttered and whispered in the dark, and all the time that we were there a southwesterly gale with torrents of scolding rain had prevailed, so that by day and night weird voices moaned and fluted in the chimneys, a company of uneasy spirits held colloquy among the trees, and sudden tattoos and tappings beckoned from the window-panes. But in spite of these surroundings, which were sufficient in themselves, one would almost say, to spontaneously generate occult phenomena, nothing of any description had occurred. I am bound to add, also, that my own state of mind was peculiarly well adapted to receive or even to invent the sights and sounds we had gone to seek, for I was, I confess, during the whole time that we were there, in a state of abject apprehension, and lay awake both nights through hours of terrified unrest, afraid of the dark, yet more afraid of what a lighted candle might show me.

Hugh Grainger, on the evening after our return to town, had dined with me, and after dinner our conversation, as was natural, soon came back to these entrancing topics.

'But why you go ghost-seeking I cannot imagine,' he said, 'because your teeth were chattering and your eyes starting out of your head all the time you were there, from sheer fright. Or do you like being frightened?'

Hugh, though generally intelligent, is dense in certain ways; this is one of them.

'Why, of course, I like being frightened,' I said. 'I want to be made to creep and creep and creep. Fear is the most absorbing and luxurious of emotions. One forgets all else if one is afraid.'

'Well, the fact that neither of us saw anything,' he said, 'confirms what I have always believed.'

'And what have you always believed?'

'That these phenomena are purely objective, not subjective, and that one's state of mind has nothing to do with the perception that perceives them, nor have circumstances or surroundings anything to do with them either. Look at Osburton. It has had the reputation of being a haunted house for years, and it certainly has all the accessories of one. Look at yourself, too, with all your nerves on edge, afraid to look round or light a candle for fear of seeing something! Surely there was the right man in the right place then, if ghosts are subjective.'

He got up and lit a cigarette, and looking at him – Hugh is about six feet high, and as broad as he is long – I felt a retort on my lips, for I could not help my mind going back to a certain period in his life, when, from some cause which, as far as I knew, he had never told anybody, he had become a mere quivering mass of disordered nerves. Oddly enough, at the same moment and for the first time, he began to speak of it himself.

'You may reply that it was not worth my while to go either,' he said, 'because I was so clearly the wrong man in the wrong place. But I wasn't. You for all your apprehensions and expectancy have never seen a ghost. But I have, though I am the last person in the world you would have thought likely to do so, and, though my nerves are steady enough again now, it knocked me all to bits.'

He sat down again in his chair.

'No doubt you remember my going to bits,' he said, 'and since I believe that I am sound again now, I should rather like to tell you about it. But before I couldn't; I couldn't speak of it at all to anybody. Yet there ought to have been nothing frightening about it; what I saw was certainly a most useful and friendly ghost. But it came from the shaded side of things; it looked suddenly out of the night and the mystery with which life is surrounded.

'I want first to tell you quite shortly my theory about ghost-seeing,' he continued, 'and I can explain it best by a simile, an image. Imagine then that you and I and everybody in the world are like people whose eye is directly opposite a little tiny hole in a sheet of cardboard which is continually shifting and revolving and moving about. Back to back with that sheet of cardboard is another, which also, by laws of its own, is in perpetual but independent motion. In it too there is another hole, and when, fortuitously it would seem, these two holes, the one through which we are always looking, and the other in the spiritual plane, come opposite one another, we see through, and then only do the sights and sounds of the spiritual world become visible or audible to us. With most people these holes never come opposite each other during their life. But at the hour of death they do, and then they remain stationary. That, I fancy, is how we "pass over".

'Now, in some natures, these holes are comparatively large, and are constantly coming into opposition. Clairvoyants, mediums are like that. But, as far as I knew, I had no clairvoyant or mediumistic powers at all. I therefore am the sort of person who long ago made up his mind that he never would see a ghost. It was, so to speak, an incalculable chance that my minute spy-hole should come into opposition with the other. But it did: and it knocked me out of time.'

I had heard some such theory before, and though Hugh put it rather picturesquely, there was nothing in the least convincing or practical about it. It might be so, or again it might not.

'I hope your ghost was more original than your theory,' said I, in order to bring him to the point.

'Yes, I think it was. You shall judge.'

I put on more coal and poked up the fire. Hugh has got, so I have always considered, a great talent for telling stories, and that sense of drama which is so necessary for the narrator. Indeed, before now, I have suggested to him that he should take this up as a profession, sit by the fountain in Piccadilly Circus, when times are, as usual, bad, and tell stories to the passers-by in the street, Arabian fashion, for reward. The most part of mankind, I am aware, do not like long stories, but to the few, among whom I number myself, who really like to listen to lengthy accounts of experiences, Hugh is an ideal narrator. I do not care for his theories, or for his similes, but when it comes to facts, to things that happened, I like him to be lengthy.

'Go on, please, and slowly,' I said. 'Brevity may be the soul of wit, but it is the ruin of story-telling. I want to hear when and where and how it all was, and what you had for lunch and where you had dined and what—'

Hugh began:

'It was the 24th of June, just eighteen months ago,' he said. 'I had let my flat, you may remember, and came up from the country to stay with you for a week. We had dined alone here—'

I could not help interrupting.

'Did you see the ghost here?' I asked. 'In this square little box of a house in a modern street?'

'I was in the house when I saw it.'

I hugged myself in silence.

'We had dined alone here in Graeme Street,' he said, 'and after dinner I went out to some party, and you stopped at home. At dinner your man did not wait, and when I asked where he was, you told me he was ill, and, I thought, changed the subject rather abruptly. You gave me your latch-key when I went out, and on coming back, I found you had gone to bed. There were, however, several letters for me, which required answers. I wrote them there and then, and posted them at the pillar-box opposite. So I suppose it was rather late when I went upstairs.

'You had put me in the front room, on the third floor, overlooking the street, a room which I thought you generally occupied yourself. It was a very hot night, and though there had been a moon when I started to my party, on my return the whole sky was cloud-covered, and it both looked and felt as if we might have a thunderstorm before morning. I was feeling very sleepy and heavy, and it was not till after I had got into bed that I noticed by the shadows of the window-frames on the blind that only one of the windows was open. But it did not seem worth while to get out of bed in order to open it, though I felt rather airless and uncomfortable, and I went to sleep.

'What time it was when I awoke I do not know, but it was certainly not yet dawn, and I never remember being conscious of such an extraordinary stillness as prevailed. There was no sound either of foot-passengers or wheeled traffic; the music of life appeared to be absolutely mute. But now, instead of being sleepy and heavy, I felt, though I must have slept an hour or two at most, since it was not yet dawn, perfectly fresh and wide-awake, and the effort which had seemed not worth making before, that of getting out of bed and opening the other window, was quite easy now and I pulled up the blind, threw it wide open, and leaned out, for somehow I parched and pined for air. Even outside the oppression was very noticeable, and though, as you know, I am not easily given to feel the mental effects of climate, I was aware of an awful creepiness coming over me. I tried to analyse it away, but without success; the past day had been pleasant, I looked forward to another pleasant day to-morrow, and yet I was full of some nameless apprehension. I felt, too, dreadfully lonely in this stillness before the dawn.

'Then I heard suddenly and not very far away the sound of some approaching vehicle; I could distinguish the tread of two horses walking at a slow foot's pace. They were, though not yet visible, coming up the street, and yet this indication of life did not abate that dreadful sense of loneliness which I have spoken of. Also in some dim unformulated way that which was coming seemed to me to have something to do with the cause of my oppression.

'Then the vehicle came into sight. At first I could not distinguish what it was. Then I saw that the horses were black and had long tails, and that what they dragged was made of glass, but had a black frame. It was a hearse. Empty.

'It was moving up this side of the street. It stopped at your door.

'Then the obvious solution struck me. You had said at dinner that your man was ill, and you were, I thought, unwilling to speak more about his illness. No doubt, so I imagined now, he was dead, and for some reason, perhaps because you did not want me to know anything about it, you were having the body removed at night. This, I must tell you, passed through my mind quite instantaneously, and it did not occur to me how unlikely it really was, before the next thing happened.

'I was still leaning out of the window, and I remember also wondering, yet only momentarily, how odd it was that I saw things – or rather the one thing I was looking at – so very distinctly. Of course, there was a moon behind the clouds, but it was curious how every detail of the hearse and the horses was visible. There was only one man, the driver, with it, and the street was otherwise absolutely empty. It was at him I was looking now. I could see every detail of his clothes, but from where I was, so high above him, I could not see his face. He had on grey trousers, brown boots, a black coat buttoned all the way up, and a straw hat. Over his shoulder there was a strap, which seemed to support some sort of little bag. He looked exactly like – well, from my description what did he look exactly like?'

'Why – a bus-conductor,' I said instantly.

'So I thought, and even while I was thinking this, he looked up at me. He had a rather long thin face, and on his left cheek there was a mole with a growth of dark hair on it. All this was as distinct as if it had been noonday, and as if I was within a yard of him. But – so instantaneous was all that takes so long in the telling – I had not time to think it strange that the driver of a hearse should be so unfunereally dressed.

'Then he touched his hat to me, and jerked his thumb over his shoulder.

'"Just room for one inside, sir," he said.

'There was something so odious, so coarse, so unfeeling about this that I instantly drew my head in, pulled the blind down again, and then, for what reason I do not know, turned on the electric light in order to see what time it was. The hands of my watch pointed to half-past eleven.

'It was then for the first time, I think, that a doubt crossed my mind as to the nature of what I had just seen. But I put out the light again, got into bed, and began to think. We had dined; I had gone to a party, I had come back and written letters, had gone to bed and had slept. So how could it be half-past eleven? ... Or – what half-past eleven was it?

'Then another easy solution struck me; my watch must have stopped. But it had not; I could hear it ticking.

'There was stillness and silence again. I expected every moment to hear muffled footsteps on the stairs, footsteps moving slowly and smally under the weight of a heavy burden, but from inside the house there was no sound whatever. Outside, too, there was the same dead silence, while the hearse waited at the door. And the minutes ticked on and ticked on, and at length I began to see a difference in the light in the room, and knew that the dawn was beginning to break outside. But how had it happened, then, that if the corpse was to be removed at night it had not gone, and that the hearse still waited, when morning was already coming?

'Presently I got out of bed again, and with the sense of strong physical shrinking I went to the window and pulled back the blind. The dawn was coming fast; the whole street was lit by that silver hueless light of morning. But there was no hearse there.

'Once again I looked at my watch. It was just a quarter-past four. But I would swear that not half an hour had passed since it had told me that it was half-past eleven.

'Then a curious double sense, as if I was living in the present and at the same moment had been living in some other time, came over me. It was dawn on June 25th, and the street, as natural, was empty. But a little while ago the driver of a hearse had spoken to me, and it was half-past eleven. What was that driver, to what plane did he belong? And again what half-past eleven was it that I had seen recorded on the dial of my watch?

'And then I told myself that the whole thing had been a dream. But if you ask me whether I believed what I told myself, I must confess that I did not.

'Your man did not appear at breakfast next morning, nor did I see him again before I left that afternoon. I think if I had, I should have told you about all this, but it was still possible, you see, that what I had seen was a real hearse, driven by a real driver, for all the ghastly gaiety of the face that had looked up to mine, and the levity of his pointing hand. I might possibly have fallen asleep soon after seeing him, and slumbered through the removal of the body and the departure of the hearse. So I did not speak of it to you.'

There was something wonderfully straight-forward and prosaic in all this; here were no Jacobean houses oak-panelled and surrounded by weeping pine-trees, and somehow the very absence of suitable surroundings made the story more impressive. But for a moment a doubt assailed me.

'Don't tell me it was all a dream,' I said.

'I don't know whether it was or not. I can only say that I believe myself to have been wide awake. In any case the rest of the story is – odd.

'I went out of town again that afternoon,' he continued, 'and I may say that I don't think that even for a moment did I get the haunting sense of what I had seen or dreamed that night out of my mind. It was present to me always as some vision unfulfilled. It was as if some clock had struck the four quarters, and I was still waiting to hear what the hour would be.

'Exactly a month afterwards I was in London again, but only for the day. I arrived at Victoria about eleven, and took the underground to Sloane Square in order to see if you were in town and would give me lunch. It was a baking hot morning, and I intended to take a bus from the King's Road as far as Graeme Street. There was one standing at the corner just as I came out of the station, but I saw that the top was full, and the inside appeared to be full also. Just as I came up to it the conductor, who, I suppose, had been inside, collecting fares or what not, came out on to the step within a few feet of me. He wore grey trousers, brown boots, a black coat buttoned, a straw hat, and over his shoulder was a strap on which hung his little machine for punching tickets. I saw his face, too; it was the face of the driver of the hearse, with a mole on the left cheek. Then he spoke to me, jerking his thumb over his shoulder.

'"Just room for one inside, sir," he said.

'At that a sort of panic-terror took possession of me, and I knew I gesticulated wildly with my arms, and cried, "No, no!" But at that moment I was living not in the hour that was then passing, but in that hour which had passed a month ago, when I leaned from the window of your bedroom here just before the dawn broke. At this moment too I knew that my spy-hole had been opposite the spy-hole into the spiritual world. What I had seen there had some significance, now being fulfilled, beyond the significance of the trivial happenings of to-day and to-morrow. The Powers of which we know so little were visibly working before me. And I stood there on the pavement shaking and trembling.

'I was opposite the post-office at the corner, and just as the bus started my eye fell on the clock in the window there. I need not tell you what the time was.

'Perhaps I need not tell you the rest, for you probably conjecture it, since you will not have forgotten what happened at the corner of Sloane Square at the end of July, the summer before last. The bus pulled out from the pavement into the street in order to get round a van that was standing in front of it. At the moment there came down the King's Road a big motor going at a hideously dangerous pace. It crashed full into the bus, burrowing into it as a gimlet burrows into a board.'

He paused.

'And that's my story,' he said.

THE WHITE VILLA

RALPH ADAMS CRAM

When we left Naples on the 8.10 train for Pæstum, Tom and I, we fully intended returning by the 2.46. Not because two hours time seemed enough wherein to exhaust the interests of those deathless ruins of a dead civilization, but simply for the reason that, as our *Indicatore* informed us, there was but one other train, and that at 6.11, which would land us in Naples too late for the dinner at the Turners and the San Carlo afterwards. Not that I cared in the least for the dinner or the theatre; but then, I was not so obviously in Miss Turner's good graces as Tom Rendel was, which made a difference.

However, we had promised, so that was an end of it.

This was in the spring of '88, and at that time the railroad, which was being pushed onward to Reggio, whereby travellers to Sicily might be spared the agonies of a night on the fickle Mediterranean, reached no farther than Agropoli, some twenty miles beyond Pæstum; but although the trains were as yet few and slow, we accepted the half-finished road with gratitude, for it penetrated the very centre of Campanian brigandage, and made it possible for us to see the matchless temples in safety, while a few years before it was necessary for intending visitors to obtain a military escort from the Government; and military escorts are not for young architects.

So we set off contentedly, that white May morning, determined to make the best of our few hours, little thinking that before we saw Naples again we were to witness things that perhaps no American had ever seen before.

For a moment, when we left the train at "Pesto," and started to walk up the flowery lane leading to the temples, we were almost inclined to curse this same railroad. We had thought, in our innocence, that we should be alone, that no one else would think of enduring the long four hours' ride from Naples just to spend two hours in the ruins of these temples; but the event proved our unwisdom. We were *not* alone. It was a compact little party of conventional sight-seers that accompanied us. The inevitable English family with the three daughters, prominent of teeth, flowing of hair, aggressive of scarlet Murrays and Baedekers; the two blond and untidy Germans; a French couple from the pages of *La Vie Parisienne*; and our "old man of the sea," the white-bearded Presbyterian minister from Pennsylvania who had made our life miserable in Rome at the time of the Pope's Jubilee. Fortunately for us, this terrible old man had fastened himself upon a party of American school-teachers travelling *en Cook*, and for the time we were safe; but our vision of two hours of dreamy solitude faded lamentably away.

Yet how beautiful it was! this golden meadow walled with far, violet mountains, breathless under a May sun; and in the midst, rising from tangles of asphodel and acanthus, vast in the vacant plain, three temples, one silver gray, one golden gray, and one flushed with intangible rose. And all around nothing but velvet meadows stretching from the dim mountains behind, away to the sea, that showed only as a thin line of silver just over the edge of the still grass.

The tide of tourists swept noisily through the Basilica and the temple of Poseidon across the meadow to the distant temple of Ceres, and Tom and I were left alone to drink in all the fine wine of dreams that was possible in the time left us. We gave but little space to examining the temples the tourists had left, but in a few moments found ourselves lying in the grass to the east of Poseidon, looking dimly out towards the sea, heard now, but not seen,—a vague and pulsating murmur that blended with the humming of bees all about us.

A small shepherd boy, with a woolly dog, made shy advances of friendship, and in a little time we had set him to gathering flowers for us: asphodels and bee-orchids, anemones, and the little thin green iris so fairylike and frail. The murmur of the tourist crowd had merged itself in the moan of the sea, and it was very still; suddenly I heard the words I had been waiting for,—the suggestion I had refrained from making myself, for I knew Thomas.

"I say, old man, shall we let the 2.46 go to thunder?"

I chuckled to myself. "But the Turners?"

"They be blowed, we can tell them we missed the train."

"That is just exactly what we shall do," I said, pulling out my watch, "unless we start for the station right now."

But Tom drew an acanthus leaf across his face and showed no signs of moving; so I filled my pipe again, and we missed the train.

As the sun dropped lower towards the sea, changing its silver line to gold, we pulled ourselves together, and for an hour or more sketched vigorously; but the mood was not on us. It was "too jolly fine to waste time working," as Tom said; so we started off to explore the single street of the squalid town of Pesto that was lost within the walls of dead Poseidonia. It was not a pretty village,—if you can call a rut-riven lane and a dozen houses a village,—nor were the inhabitants thereof reassuring in appearance. There was no sign of a church,—nothing but dirty huts, and in the midst, one of two stories, rejoicing in the name of *Albergo del Sole*, the first story of which was a black and cavernous smithy, where certain swarthy knaves, looking like banditti out of a job, sat smoking sulkily.

"We might stay here all night," said Tom, grinning askance at this choice company; but his suggestion was not received with enthusiasm.

Down where the lane from the station joined the main road stood the only sign of modern civilization,—a great square structure, half villa, half fortress, with round turrets on its four corners, and a ten-foot wall surrounding it. There were no windows in its first story, so far as we could see, and it had evidently been at one time the fortified villa of some Campanian noble. Now, however, whether because brigandage had been stamped out, or because the villa was empty and deserted, it was no longer formidable; the gates of the great wall hung sagging on their hinges, brambles growing all over them, and many of the windows in the upper story were broken and black. It was a strange place, weird and mysterious, and we looked at it curiously. "There is a story about that place," said Tom, with conviction.

It was growing late: the sun was near the edge of the sea as we walked down the ivy-grown walls of the vanished city for the last time, and as we turned back, a red flush poured from the west, and painted the Doric temples in pallid rose against the evanescent purple of the Apennines. Already a thin mist was rising from the meadows, and the temples hung pink in the misty grayness.

It was a sorrow to leave the beautiful things, but we could run no risk of missing this last train, so we walked slowly back towards the temples.

"What is that Johnny waving his arm at us for?" asked Tom, suddenly.

"How should I know? We are not on his land, and the walls don't matter."

We pulled out our watches simultaneously.

"What time are you?" I said.

"Six minutes before six."

"And I am seven minutes. It can't take us all that time to walk to the station."

"Are you sure the train goes at 6.11?"

"Dead sure," I answered; and showed him the *Indicatore*.

By this time a woman and two children were shrieking at us hysterically; but what they said I had no idea, their Italian being of a strange and awful nature.

"Look here," I said, "let's run; perhaps our watches are both slow."

"Or—perhaps the time-table is changed."

Then we ran, and the populace cheered and shouted with enthusiasm; our dignified run became a panic-stricken rout, for as we turned into the lane, smoke was rising from beyond the bank that hid the railroad; a bell rang; we were so near that we could hear the interrogative *Pronte?* the impatient *Partenza!* and the definitive *Andiamo!* But the train was five hundred yards away, steaming towards Naples, when we plunged into the station as the clock struck six, and yelled for the station-master.

He came, and we indulged in crimination and recrimination.

When we could regard the situation calmly, it became apparent that the time-table *had* been changed two days before, the 6.11 now leaving at 5.58. A *facchino* came in, and we four sat down and regarded the situation judicially.

"Was there any other train?"

"No."

"Could we stay at the Albergo del Sole?"

A forefinger drawn across the throat by the Capo Stazione with a significant "cluck" closed that question.

"Then we must stay with you here at the station."

"But, Signori, I am not married. I live here only with the *facchini*. I have only one room to sleep in. It is impossible!"

"But we must sleep somewhere, likewise eat. What can we do?" and we shifted the responsibility deftly on the shoulders of the poor old man, who was growing excited again.

He trotted nervously up and down the station for a minute, then he called the *facchino*. "Giuseppe, go up to the villa and ask if two *forestieri* who have missed the last train can stay there all night!"

Protests were useless. The *facchino* was gone, and we waited anxiously for his return. It seemed as though he would never come. Darkness had fallen, and the moon was rising over the mountains. At last he appeared.

"The Signori may stay all night, and welcome; but they cannot come to dinner, for there is nothing in the house to eat!"

This was not reassuring, and again the old station-master lost himself in meditation. The results were admirable, for in a little time the table in the waiting-room had been transformed into a dining-table, and Tom and I were ravenously devouring a big omelette, and bread and cheese, and drinking a most shocking sour wine as though it were Château Yquem. A *facchino* served us, with clumsy good-will; and when we had induced our nervous old host to sit down with us and partake of his own hospitality, we succeeded in forming a passably jolly dinner-party, forgetting over our sour wine and cigarettes the coming hours from ten until sunrise, which lay before us in a dubious mist.

It was with crowding apprehensions which we strove in vain to joke away that we set out at last to retrace our steps to the mysterious villa, the *facchino* Giuseppe leading the way. By this time the moon was well overhead, and just behind us as we tramped up the dewy lane, white in the moonlight between the ink-black hedgerows on either side. How still it was! Not a breath of air, not a sound of life; only the awful silence that had lain almost unbroken for two thousand years over this vast graveyard of a dead world.

As we passed between the shattered gates and wound our way in the moonlight through the maze of gnarled fruit-trees, decaying farm implements and piles of lumber, towards the small door that formed the only opening in the first story of this deserted fortress, the cold silence was shattered by the harsh baying of dogs somewhere in the distance to the right, beyond the barns that formed one side of the court. From the villa came neither light nor sound. Giuseppe knocked at the weather-worn door, and the sound echoed cavernously within; but there was no other reply. He knocked again and again, and at length we heard the rasping jar of sliding bolts, and the door opened a little, showing an old, old man, bent with age and gaunt with malaria. Over his head he held a big Roman lamp, with three wicks, that cast strange shadows on his face,—a face that was harmless in its senility, but intolerably sad. He made no reply to our timid salutations, but motioned tremblingly to us to enter; and with a last "good-night" to Giuseppe we obeyed, and stood half-way up the stone stairs that led directly from the door, while the old man tediously shot every bolt and adjusted the heavy bar.

Then we followed him in the semi-darkness up the steps into what had been the great hall of the villa. A fire was burning in a great fireplace so beautiful in design that Tom and I looked at each other with interest. By its fitful light we could see that we were in a huge circular room covered by a flat, saucer-shaped dome,—a room that must once have been superb and splendid, but that now was a lamentable wreck. The frescoes on the dome were stained and mildewed, and here and there the plaster was gone altogether; the carved doorways that led out on all sides had lost half the gold with which they had once been covered, and the floor was of brick, sunken into treacherous valleys. Rough chests, piles of old newspapers, fragments of harnesses, farm implements, a heap of rusty carbines and cutlasses, nameless litter of every possible kind, made the room into a wilderness which under the firelight seemed even more picturesque than it really was. And on this inexpressible confusion of lumber the pale shapes of the seventeenth-century nymphs, startling in their weather-stained nudity, looked down with vacant smiles.

For a few moments we warmed ourselves before the fire; and then, in the same dejected silence, the old man led the way to one of the many doors, handed us a brass lamp, and with a stiff bow turned his back on us.

Once in our room alone, Tom and I looked at each other with faces that expressed the most complex emotions.

"Well, of all the rum goes," said Tom, "this is the rummiest go I ever experienced!"

"Right, my boy; as you very justly remark, we are in for it. Help me shut this door, and then we will reconnoitre, take account of stock, and size up our chances."

But the door showed no sign of closing; it grated on the brick floor and stuck in the warped casing, and it took our united efforts to jam the two inches of oak into its place, and turn the enormous old key in its rusty lock.

"Better now, much better now," said Tom; "now let us see where we are."

The room was easily twenty-five feet square, and high in proportion; evidently it had been a state apartment, for the walls were covered with carved panelling that had once been white and gold, with mirrors in the panels, the wood now stained every imaginable color, the mirrors cracked and broken, and dull with mildew. A big fire had just been lighted in the fireplace, the shutters were closed, and although the only furniture consisted of two massive bedsteads, and a chair with one leg shorter than the others, the room seemed almost comfortable.

I opened one of the shutters, that closed the great windows that ran from the floor almost to the ceiling, and nearly fell through the cracked glass into the floorless balcony. "Tom, come here, quick," I cried; and for a few minutes neither of us thought about our dubious surroundings, for we were looking at Pæstum by moonlight.

A flat, white mist, like water, lay over the entire meadow; from the midst rose against the blue-black sky the three ghostly temples, black and silver in the vivid moonlight, floating, it seemed, in the fog; and behind them, seen in broken glints between the pallid shafts, stretched the line of the silver sea.

Perfect silence,—the silence of implacable death.

We watched the white tide of mist rise around the temples, until we were chilled through, and so presently went to bed. There was but one door in the room, and that was securely locked; the great windows were twenty feet from the ground, so we felt reasonably safe from all possible attack.

In a few minutes Tom was asleep and breathing audibly; but my constitution is more nervous than his, and I lay awake for some little time, thinking of our curious adventure and of its possible outcome. Finally, I fell asleep,—for how long I do not know: but I woke with the feeling that some one had tried the handle of the door. The fire had fallen into a heap of coals which cast a red glow in the room, whereby I could see dimly the outline of Tom's bed, the broken-legged chair in front of the fireplace, and the door in its deep casing by the chimney, directly in front of my bed. I sat up, nervous from my sudden awakening under these strange circumstances, and stared at the door. The latch rattled, and the door swung smoothly open. I began to shiver coldly. That door was locked; Tom and I had all we could do to jam it together and lock it. But we *did* lock it; and now it was opening silently. In a minute more it as silently closed.

Then I heard a footstep,—I swear I heard a footstep *in the room*, and with it the *frou-frou* of trailing skirts; my breath stopped and my teeth grated against each other as I heard the soft footfalls and the feminine rustle pass along the room towards the fireplace. My eyes saw nothing; yet there was enough light in the room for me to distinguish the pattern on the carved panels of the door. The steps stopped by the fire, and I saw the broken-legged chair lean to the left, with a little jar as its short leg touched the floor.

I sat still, frozen, motionless, staring at the vacancy that was filled with such terror for me; and as I looked, the seat of the chair creaked, and it came back to its upright position again.

And then the footsteps came down the room lightly, towards the window; there was a pause, and then the great shutters swung back, and the white moonlight poured in. Its brilliancy was unbroken by any shadow, by any sign of material substance.

I tried to cry out, to make some sound, to awaken Tom; this sense of utter loneliness in the presence of the Inexplicable was maddening. I don't know whether my lips obeyed my will or no; at all events, Tom lay motionless, with his deaf ear up, and gave no sign.

The shutters closed as silently as they had opened; the moonlight was gone, the firelight also, and in utter darkness I waited. If I could only *see*! If something were visible, I should not mind it so much; but this ghastly hearing of every little sound, every rustle of a gown, every breath, yet seeing nothing, was soul-destroying. I think in my abject terror I prayed that I might see, only see; but the darkness was unbroken.

Then the footsteps began to waver fitfully, and I heard the rustle of garments sliding to the floor, the clatter of little shoes flung down, the rattle of buttons, and of metal against wood.

Rigors shot over me, and my whole body shivered with collapse as I sank back on the pillow, waiting with every nerve tense, listening with all my life.

The coverlid was turned back beside me, and in another moment the great bed sank a little as something slipped between the sheets with an audible sigh.

I called to my aid every atom of remaining strength, and, with a cry that shivered between my clattering teeth, I hurled myself headlong from the bed on to the floor.

I must have lain for some time stunned and unconscious, for when I finally came to myself it was cold in the room, there was no last glow of lingering coals in the fireplace, and I was stiff with chill.

It all flashed over me like the haunting of a heavy dream. I laughed a little at the dim memory, with the thought, "I must try to recollect all the details; they will do to tell Tom," and rose stiffly to return to bed, when—there it was again, and my heart stopped,—the hand on the door.

I paused and listened. The door opened with a muffled creak, closed again, and I heard the lock turn rustily. I would have died now before getting into that bed again; but there was terror equally without; so I stood trembling and listened,—listened to heavy, stealthy steps creeping along on the other side of the bed. I clutched the coverlid, staring across into the dark.

There was a rush in the air by my face, the sound of a blow, and simultaneously a shriek, so awful, so despairing, so blood-curdling that I felt my senses leaving me again as I sank crouching on the floor by the bed.

And then began the awful duel, the duel of invisible, audible shapes; of things that shrieked and raved, mingling thin, feminine cries with low, stifled curses and indistinguishable words. Round and round the room, footsteps chasing footsteps in the ghastly night, now away by Tom's bed, now rushing swiftly down the great room until I felt the flash of swirling drapery on my hard lips. Round and round, turning and twisting till my brain whirled with the mad cries.

They were coming nearer. I felt the jar of their feet on the floor beside me. Came one long, gurgling moan close over my head, and then, crushing down upon me, the weight of a collapsing body; there was long hair over my face, and in my staring eyes; and as awful silence succeeded the less awful tumult, life went out, and I fell unfathomable miles into nothingness.

The gray dawn was sifting through the chinks in the shutters when I opened my eyes again. I lay stunned and faint, staring up at the mouldy frescoes on the ceiling, struggling to gather together my wandering senses and knit them into something like consciousness. But now as I pulled myself little by little together there was no thought of dreams before me. One after another the awful incidents of that unspeakable night came back, and I lay incapable of movement, of action, trying to piece together the whirling fragments of memory that circled dizzily around me.

Little by little it grew lighter in the room. I could see the pallid lines struggling through the shutters behind me, grow stronger along the broken and dusty floor. The tarnished mirrors reflected dirtily the growing daylight; a door closed, far away, and I heard the crowing of a cock; then by and by the whistle of a passing train.

Years seemed to have passed since I first came into this terrible room. I had lost the use of my tongue, my voice refused to obey my panic-stricken desire to cry out; once or twice I tried in vain to force an articulate sound through my rigid lips; and when at last a broken whisper rewarded my feverish struggles, I felt a strange sense of great victory. How soundly he slept! Ordinarily, rousing him was no easy task, and now he revolted steadily against being awakened at this untimely hour. It seemed to me that I had called him for ages almost, before I heard him grunt sleepily and turn in bed.

"Tom," I cried weakly, "Tom, come and help me!"

"What do you want? what is the matter with you?"

"Don't ask, come and help me!"

"Fallen out of bed I guess;" and he laughed drowsily.

My abject terror lest he should go to sleep again gave me new strength. Was it the actual physical paralysis born of killing fear that held me down? I could not have raised my head from the floor on my life; I could only cry out in deadly fear for Tom to come and help me.

"Why don't you get up and get into bed?" he answered, when I implored him to come to me. "You have got a bad nightmare; wake up!"

But something in my voice roused him at last, and he came chuckling across the room, stopping to throw open two of the great shutters and let a burst of white light into the room. He climbed up on the bed and peered over jeeringly. With the first glance the laugh died, and he leaped the bed and bent over me.

"My God, man, what is the matter with you? You are hurt!"

"I don't know what is the matter; lift me up, get me away from here, and I'll tell you all I know."

"But, old chap, you must be hurt awfully; the floor is covered with blood!"

He lifted my head and held me in his powerful arms. I looked down: a great red stain blotted the floor beside me.

But, apart from the black bruise on my head, there was no sign of a wound on my body, nor stain of blood on my lips. In as few words as possible I told him the whole story.

"Let's get out of this," he said when I had finished; "this is no place for us. Brigands I can stand, but—"

He helped me to dress, and as soon as possible we forced open the heavy door, the door I had seen turn so softly on its hinges only a few hours before, and came out into the great circular hall, no less strange and mysterious now in the half light of dawn than it had been by firelight. The room was empty, for it must have been very early, although a fire already blazed in the fireplace. We sat by the fire some time, seeing no one. Presently slow footsteps sounded in the stairway, and the old man entered, silent as the night before, nodding to us civilly, but showing by no sign any surprise which he may have felt at our early rising. In absolute silence he moved around, preparing coffee for us; and when at last the frugal breakfast was ready, and we sat around the rough table munching coarse bread and sipping the black coffee, he would reply to our overtures only by monosyllables.

Any attempt at drawing from him some facts as to the history of the villa was received with a grave and frigid repellence that baffled us; and we were forced to say *addio* with our hunger for some explanation of the events of the night still unsatisfied.

But we saw the temples by sunrise, when the mistlike lambent opals bathed the bases of the tall columns salmon in the morning light! It was a rhapsody in the pale and unearthly colors of Puvis de Chavannes vitalized and made glorious with splendid sunlight; the apotheosis of mist; a vision never before seen, never to be forgotten. It was so beautiful that the memory of my ghastly night paled and faded, and it was Tom who assailed the station-master with questions while we waited for the train from Agropoli.

Luckily he was more than loquacious, he was voluble under the ameliorating influence of the money we forced upon him; and this, in few words, was the story he told us while we sat on the platform smoking, marvelling at the mists that rose to the east, now veiling, now revealing the lavender Apennines.

"Is there a story of *La Villa Bianca*?"

"Ah, Signori, certainly; and a story very strange and very terrible. It was much time ago, a hundred,—two hundred years; I do not know. Well, the Duca di San Damiano married a lady so fair, so most beautiful that she was called *La Luna di Pesto*; but she was of the people,—more, she was of the banditti: her father was of Calabria, and a terror of the Campagna. But the Duke was young, and he married her, and for her built the white villa; and it was a wonder throughout Campania,—you have seen? It is splendid now, even if a ruin. Well, it was less than a year after they came to the villa before the Duke grew jealous,—jealous of the new captain of the banditti who took the place of the father of *La Luna*, himself killed in a great battle up there in the mountains. Was there cause? Who shall know? But there were stories among the people of terrible things in the villa, and how *La Luna* was seen almost never outside the walls. Then the Duke would go for many days to Napoli, coming home only now and then to the villa that was become a fortress, so many men guarded its never-opening gates. And once—it was in the spring—the Duke came silently down from Napoli, and there, by the three poplars you see away towards the north, his carriage was set upon by armed men, and he was almost killed; but he had with him many guards, and after a terrible fight the brigands were beaten off; but before him, wounded, lay the captain,—the man whom he feared and hated. He looked at him, lying there under the torchlight, and in his hand saw *his own sword*. Then he became a devil: with the same sword he ran the brigand through, leaped in the carriage, and, entering the villa, crept to the chamber of *La Luna*, and killed her with the sword she had given to her lover.

"This is all the story of the White Villa, except that the Duke came never again to Pesto. He went back to the king at Napoli, and for many years he was the scourge of the banditti of Campania; for the King made him a general, and San Damiano was a name feared by the lawless and loved by the peaceful, until he was killed in a battle down by Mormanno.

"And *La Luna*? Some say she comes back to the villa, once a year, when the moon is full, in the month when she was slain; for the Duke buried her, they say, with his own hands, in the garden that was once under the window of her chamber; and as she died unshriven, so was she buried without the pale of the Church. Therefore she cannot sleep in peace,—*non è vero*? I do not know if the story is true, but this is the story, Signori, and there is the train for Napoli. *Ah, grazie! Signori, grazie tanto! A rivederci! Signori, a rivederci!*"

AN ITINERANT HOUSE

EMMA FRANCES DAWSON

"Eternal longing with eternal pain,
Want without hope, and memory saddening all,
All congregated failure and despair
Shall wander there through some old maze of wrong."

"His *wife*?" cried Felipa.

"Yes," I answered, unwillingly; for until the steamer brought Mrs. Anson I believed in this Mexican woman's right to that name. I felt sorry for the bright eyes and kind heart that had cheered Anson's lodgers through weary months of early days in San Francisco.

She burst into tears. None of us knew how to comfort her. Dering spoke first: "Beauty always wins friends." Between her sobs she repeated one of the pithy sayings of her language: "It is as easy to find a lover as to keep a friend, but as hard to find a friend as to keep a lover."

"Yes," said Volz, "a new friendship is like a new string to your guitar—you are not sure what its tone may prove, nor how soon it may break."

"But at least its falsity is learned at once," she sobbed.

"Is it possible," I asked, "that you had no suspicion?"

"None. He told me—" She ended in a fresh gust of tears.

"The old story," muttered Dering. "Marryatt's skipper was right in thinking everything that once happened would come again somewhere."

Anson came. He had left the new-comer at the Niantic, on pretense of putting his house in order. Felipa turned on him before we could go.

"Is this true?" she cried.

Without reply he went to the window and stood looking out. She sprang toward him, with rage distorting her face.

"Coward!" she screamed, in fierce scorn.

Then she fell senseless. Two doctors were called. One said she was dead. The other, at first doubtful, vainly tried hot sealing-wax and other tests. After thirty-six hours her funeral was planned. Yet Dering, once medical student, had seen an electric current used in such a case in Vienna, and wanted to try it. That night, he, Volz, and I offered to watch. When all was still, Dering, who had smuggled in the simple things needed, began his weird work.

"Is it not too late?" I asked.

"Every corpse," said he, "can be thus excited soon after death, for a brief time only, and but once. If the body is not lifeless, the electric current has power at any time." Volz, too nervous to stay near, stood in the door open to the dark hall. It was a dreadful sight. The dead woman's breast rose and fell; smiles and frowns flitted across her face. "The body begins to react finely," cried Dering, making Volz open the windows, while I wrapped hot blankets round Felipa, and he instilled clear coffee and brandy.

"It seems like sacrilege! Let her alone!" I exclaimed. "Better dead than alive!"

"My God! say not that!" cried Volz; "the nerve which hears is last to die. She may know all we say."

"Musical bosh!" I muttered.

"Perhaps not," said Dering; "in magnetic sleep that nerve can be roused."

The night seemed endless. The room gained an uncanny look, the macaws on the gaudy, old-fashioned wall-paper seemed fluttering and changing places. Volz crouched in a heap near the door. Dering stood by Felipa, watching closely. I paced the shadowy room, looked at the gleam of the moon on the bay, listened to the soughing wind in the gum-trees mocking the sea, and tried to recall more cheerful scenes, but always bent under the weight of that fearful test going on beside me. Where was her soul? Beyond the stars, in the room with us, or "like trodden snowdrift melting in the dark?" Volz came behind, startling me by grasping my elbow.

"Shall I not play?" he whispered. "Familiar music is remembrance changed to sound—it brings the past as perfume does. Gypsy music in her ear would be like holding wild flowers to her nostrils."

"Ask Dering," I said; "he will know best."

I heard him urging Dering.

"She has gypsy blood," he said; "their music will rouse her." Dering unwillingly agreed. "But nothing abrupt—begin low," said he.

Vaguely uneasy, I turned to object; but Volz had gone for his violin. Far off arose a soft, wavering, sleepy strain, like a wind blowing over a field of poppies. He passed, in slow, dramatic style, through the hall, playing on the way. As he came in, oddly sustained notes trembled like sighs and sobs; these were by degrees subdued, though with spasmodic outbursts, amid a grand movement as of phantom shapes through cloud-land. One heart-rending phrase recurring as of one of the shadowy host striving to break loose, but beaten back by impalpable throngs, numberless grace-notes trailing their sparks like fire-works. No music of our intervals and our rhythms, but perplexing in its charm like a draught that maddens. Time, space, our very identities, were consumed in this white heat of sound. I held my breath. I caught his arm.

"It is too bold and distracting," I cried. "It is enough to kill us! Do you expect to torment her back? How can it affect us so?"

"Because," he answered, laying down his violin and wiping his brow, "in the gypsy minor scale the fourth and seventh are augmented. The sixth is diminished. The frequent augmentation of the fourth makes that sense of unrest."

"Bah! Technical terms make it no plainer," I said, returning to the window.

He played a whispered, merry discordance, resolving into click of castanets, laugh, and dance of a gypsy camp. Out of the whirl of flying steps and tremolo of tambourines rose a tender voice, asking, denying, sighing, imploring, passing into an over-ruling, long-drawn call that vibrated in widening rings to reach the farthest horizon—nay, beyond land or sea, "east of the sun, west of the moon." With a rush returned the wild jollity of men's bass laughter, women's shrill reply, the stir of the gypsy camp. This dropped behind vague, rolling measures of clouds and chaos, where to and fro floated grotesque goblins of grace-notes like the fancies of a madman; struggling, rising, falling, vain-reaching strains; fierce cries like commands. The music seemed another vital essence thrilling us with its own emotion.

"No more, no more!" I cried, half gasping, and grasping Volz's arm. "What is it, Dering?"

He had staggered from the bed and was trying to see his watch. "It is just forty-four hours!" he said, pointing to Felipa.

Her eyes were open! We were alarmed as if doing wrong and silently watched her. Fifteen minutes later her lips formed one word:

"Idiots!"

Half an hour after she flung the violin from bed to floor, but would not speak. People began to stir about the house. The prosaic sounds jarred on our strained nerves. We felt brought from another sphere. Volz and I were going, but Felipa's upraised hand kept us. She sat up, looking a ghastly vision. Turning first toward me she quoted my words:

"'Better dead than alive!' True. You knew I would be glad to die. What right had you to bring me back? God's curses on you! I was dead. Then came agony. I heard your voices. I thought we were all in hell. Then I found how by your evil cunning I was to be forced to live. It was like an awful nightmare. I shall not forget you, nor you me. These very walls shall remember—here, where I have been so tortured no one shall have peace! Fools! Leave me! Never come in this room again!"

We went, all talking at once, Dering angry at her mood; Volz, sorry he had not reached a soothing *pianissimo* passage; I, owning we had no right to make the test. We saw her but once more, when with a threatening nod toward us she left the house.

From that time a gloom settled over the place. Mrs. Anson proved a hard-faced, cold-hearted, Cape Cod woman, a scold and drudge, who hated us as much as we disliked her. Homesick and unhappy, she soon went East and died. Within a year, Anson was found dead where he had gone hunting in the Saucelito woods, supposed a suicide; Dering was hung by the Vigilantes, and the rest were scattered on the four winds. Volz and I were last to go. The night before we sailed, he for Australia, I for New York, he said:

"I am sorry for those who come after us in this house."

"Not knowing of any tragedy here," I said, "they will not feel its influence."

"They must feel it," he insisted; "it is written in the Proverbs, 'Evil shall not depart from his house.'"

Some years later, I was among passengers embarking at New York for California, when there was a cry of "Man overboard!" In the confusion of his rescue, among heartless and pitiful talk, I overheard one man declare that the drowned might be revived.

"Oh, yes!" cried a well-known voice behind me. "But they might not thank you."

I turned—to find Volz! He was coming out with Wynne, the actor. Enjoying our comradeship on the voyage, on reaching San Francisco we took rooms together, on Bush Street, in an old house with a large garden. Volz became leader of the orchestra, and Wynne, leading man at the same theatre. Lest my folks, a Maine deacon's family, should think I was on the road to ruin, I told in letters home only of the city missionary in the house.

Volz was hard worked. Wynne was not much liked. My business went wrong. It rained for many weeks; to this we laid the discomfort that grew to weigh on us. Volz wreaked his sense of it on his violin, adding to the torment of Wynne and myself, for to lonesome anxious souls "the demon in music" shows horns and cloven foot in the trying sounds of practice. One Sunday Volz played the "Witches Dance," the "Dream," and "The long, long weary day."

"I can bear it no longer!" said Wynne. "I feel like the haunted Matthias in 'The Bells.' If I could feel so when acting such parts, it would make my fortune. But I feel it only here."

"I think," said Volz, "it is the *gloria fonda* bush near the window; the scent is too strong." He dashed off Strauss' fretful, conflicting "Hurry and Delay."

"There, there! It is too much," said I. "You express my feelings."

He looked doubtful. "Put it in words," said he.

"How can I?" I said. "When our firm sent me abroad, I went sight-seeing among old palaces, whose Gobelin tapestries framed in their walls were faded to gray phantoms of pictures, but out of some the thrilling eyes followed me till I could not stay in their range. My feeling here is the uneasy one of being watched."

"Ha!" said Volz. "You remind me of Heine, when he wrote from Livorno. He knew no Italian, but the old palaces whispered secrets unheard by day. The moon was interpreter, knew the lapidary style, translated to dialect of his heart."

"'Strange effects after the moon,'" mused Wynne. "That gives new meaning to Kent's threat: 'I'll make a sop o' the moonshine of you!'"

Volz went on: "Heine wrote: 'The stones here speak to me, and I know their mute language. Also, they seem deeply to feel what I think. So a broken column of the old Roman times, an old tower of Lombardy, a weather-beaten Gothic piece of a pillar understands me well. But I am a ruin myself, wandering among ruins.'"

"Perhaps, like Poe's hero," said I, "'I have imbibed shadows of fallen columns at Balbec, and Tadmor, and Persepolis, until my very soul has become a ruin.'"

"But I, too," said Wynne, "feel the unrest of Tannhauser:

'Alas! what seek I here, or anywhere,
Whose way of life is like the crumbled stair
That winds and winds about a ruined tower,
And leads no whither.'"

"I am oppressed," Volz owned, "as if some one in my presence was suffering deeply."

"I feel," said Wynne, "as if the scene was not set right for the performance now going on. There is a hitch and drag somewhere—scene-shifters on a strike. Happy are you poets and musicians, who can express what is vague."

Volz laughed. "As in Liszt's oratorio of 'Christus,'" said he, "where a sharp, ear-piercing *sostenuto* on the piccolo-flute shows the shining of the star of Bethlehem." He turned to me. "Schubert's 'Wanderer' always recalls to me a house you and I know to be under a ban."

"Haunted?" asked Wynne. "Of all speculative theories, St. Martin's sends the most cold thrills up one's back. He said none of the dead come back, but some stay."

"What we Germans call *gebannt*—tied to one spot," said Volz. "But this is no ghost, only a proof of what a German psychologist holds, that the magnetic man is a spirit."

"Go on, 'and tell quaint lies'—I like them," said Wynne.

I told in brief outline, with no names, the tale Volz and I knew, while we strolled to Telegraph Hill, passing five streets blocked by the roving houses common to San Francisco. Wynne said: "They seem to have minds of their own, with their entrances and exits in a *moving* drama."

"Sort of 'Poor Jo's,'" said I.

"Castles in chess," said Volz.

"Io-like," said Wynne, "with a gad in their hearts that forever drives them on."

A few foreign sailors lounged on the hill top, looking at the view. The wind blew such a gale we did not stay. The steps we had known, cut in the side, were gone. Where the old house used to be, goats were browsing.

"Perchance we do inhabit it but now," mockingly cried Wynne; "methinks it must be so."

"Then," said Volz, thoughtfully, "it might be what Germans call 'far-working'—acted in distance—that affects us."

"What do you mean?" I asked. "Do you know anything of her now?"

"I know she went to Mexico," said he; "that is all."

"What is 'far-working?'" asked Wynne. "If I could act in the distance, and here too—'what larks!'"

"Yes—'if,'" said I. "Think how all our lives turn on that pivot. Suppose Hawthorne's offer to join Wilkes' exploring expedition had been taken!"

"Only to wills that know no 'if' is 'far-working' possible," said Volz. "Substance or space can no more hinder this force than the one of mineral magnetism. Passavent joins it with pictures falling, or watches stopping at the time of a death. In sleep-walking, some kinds of illness, or nearness of death, the nervous ether is not so closely allied to its material conductors, the nerves, and may be loosened to act from afar, the surest where blood or feeling makes attraction or repulsion."

Wynne in the two voices of the play repeated:

"Victor.—Where is the gentleman?
Chispe.—As the old song says:

'His body is in Segovia,
His soul is in Madrid.'"

We could learn about the house we were in only that five families had moved in and out during the last year. Wynne resolved to shake off the gloom that wrapped us. In struggles to defy it, he on the strength of a thousand-dollar benefit, made one payment on the house and began repairs.

On an off-night he was vainly trying to study a new part. Volz advised the relief to his nerves of reciting the dream scene from "The Bells," reminding him he had compared it with his restlessness there. Wynne denied it.

"Yes," said Volz, "where the mesmerizer forces Matthias to confess."

But Wynne refused, as if vexed, till Volz offered to show in music his own mood, and I agreed to read some rhymes about mine. Volz was long tuning his violin.

"I feel," he said, "as if the passers-by would hear a secret. Music is such a subtle expression of emotion—like flower-odor rolls far and affects the stranger. Hearken! In Heine's 'Reisebilder,' as the cross was thrown ringing on the banquet table of the gods, they grew dumb and pale, and even paler till they melted in mist. So shall you at the long-drawn wail of my violin grow breathless, and fade from each other's sight."

The music closed round us, and we waited in its deep solitude. One brief, sad phrase fell from airy heights to lowest depths into a sea of sound, whose harmonious eddies as they widened breathed of passion and pain, now swooning, now reviving, with odd pauses and sighs that rose to cries of despair, but the tormenting first strain recurring fainter and fainter, as if drowning, drowning, drowned—yet floating back for repeated last plaint, as if not to be quelled, and closing, as it began, the whole.

As I read the name of my verses, Volz murmured: "Les Nuits Blanches. No. 4. Stephen Heller."

SLEEPLESS NIGHTS.

Against the garden's mossy paling
I lean, and wish the night away,
Whose faint, unequal shadows trailing
Seem but a dream of those of day.

Sleep burdens blossom, bud, and leaf,
My soul alone aspires, dilates,
Yearns to forget its care and grief—
No bath of sleep its pain abates.

How dread these dreams of wide-eyed nights!
What is, and is not, both I rue,
My wild thoughts fly like wand'ring kites,
No peace falls with this balmy dew.

Through slumb'rous stillness, scarcely stirred
By sudden trembles, as when shifts
O'er placid pool some skimming bird,
Its Lethean bowl a poppy lifts.

If one deep draught my doubts could solve,
The world might bubble down its brim,
Like Cleopatra's pearl dissolve,
With all my dreams within its rim.

What should I know but calm repose?
How feel, recalling this lost sphere?
Alas! the fabled poppy shows
Upon its bleeding heart—a tear!

Wynne unwillingly began to recite: "'I fear nothing, but dreams are dreams—'" He stammered, could not go on, and fell to the floor. We got him to bed. He never spoke sanely after. His wild fancies appalled us watching him all night.

"Avaunt Sathanas! That's not my cue," he muttered. "A full house to-night. How could Talma forget how the crowd looked, and fancy it a pack of skeletons? Tell Volz to keep the violins playing through this scene, it works me up as well as thrills the audience. Oh, what tiresome nights I have lately, always dreaming of scenes where rival women move, as in 'Court and Stage,' where, all masked, the king makes love to Frances Stewart before the queen's face! How do I try to cure it? 'And being thus frighted, swear a prayer or two and sleep again.' Madame, you're late; you've too little rouge; you'll look ghastly. We're not called yet; let's rehearse our scene. Now, then, I enter left, pass to the window. You cry 'is this true?' and faint. All crowd about. Quick curtain."

Volz and I looked at each other.

"Can our magnetism make his senses so sharp that he knows what is in our minds?" he asked me.

"Nonsense!" I said. "Memory, laudanum, and whisky."

"There," Wynne went on, "the orchestra is stopping. They've rung up the curtain. Don't hold me. The stage waits, yet how can I go outside my door to step on dead bodies? Street and sidewalk are knee-deep with them. They rise and curse me for disturbing them. I lift my cane to strike. It turns to a snake, whose slimy body writhes in my hand. Trying to hold it from biting me, my nails cut my palm till blood streams to drown the snake."

He awed us not alone from having no control of his thoughts, but because there came now and then a strange influx of emotion as if other souls passed in and out of his body.

"Is this hell?" he groaned. "What blank darkness! Where am I? What is that infernal music haunting me through all space? If I could only escape it I need not go back to earth—to that room where I feel choked, where the very wall paper frets me with its flaunting birds flying to and fro, mocking my fettered state. 'Here, here in the very den of the wolf!' Hallo, Benvolio, call-boy's hunting you. Romeo's gone on.

'See where he steals—
Locked in some gloomy covert under key
Of cautionary silence, with his arms
Threaded, like these cross-boughs, in sorrow's knot.'

What is this dread that weighs like a nightmare? 'I do not fear; like Macbeth, I only inhabit trembling.' 'For one of them—she is in hell already, and burns, poor soul! For the other'—Ah! must I die here, alone in the woods, felled by a coward, Indian-like, from behind a tree? None of the boys will know. 'I just now come from a whole world of mad women that had almost—what, is she dead?' Poor Felipa!"

"Did you tell him her name?" I asked Volz.

"No," said he. "Can one man's madness be another's real life?"

"Blood was spilt—the avenger's wing hovered above my house," raved Wynne. "What are these lights, hundreds of them—serpent's eyes? Is it the audience—coiled, many-headed monster, following me round the world? Why do they hiss? I've played this part a hundred times. 'Taught by Rage, and Hunger, and Despair?' Do they, full-fed, well-clothed, light-hearted, know how to judge me? 'A plague on both your houses!' What is that flame? Fire that consumes my vitals—spontaneous combustion! It is then possible. Water! water!"

The doctor said there had been some great strain on Wynne's mind. He sank fast, though we did all we could.

Toward morning I turned to Volz with the words:

"He is dead."

The city missionary was passing the open door. He grimly muttered:

"Better dead than alive!"

"My God! say not that!" cried Volz. "The nerve which hears is last to die. He may know—"

He faltered. We stood aghast. The room grew suddenly familiar. I tore off a strip of the gray tint on the walls. Under it we found the old paper with its bright macaws.

"Ah, ha!" Volz said; "will you now deny my theory of 'far-working?'"

Dazed, I could barely murmur: "Then people *can* be affected by it!"

"Certainly," said he, "as rubbed glasses gain electric power."

Within a week we sailed—he for Brazil, I for New York.

Several years after, at Sacramento, Arne, an artist I had known abroad, found me on the overland train, and on reaching San Francisco urged me to go where he lodged.

"I am low-spirited here," he said; "I don't know why."

I stopped short on the crowded wharf. "Where do you live?" I asked.

"Far up Market Street," said he.

"What sort of a house?" I insisted.

"Oh—nothing modern—over a store," he answered. Reassured, I went with him. He lived in a jumble of easels, portfolios, paint, canvas, bits of statuary, casts, carvings, foils, red curtains, Chinese goatskins, woodcuts, photographs, sketches, and unfinished pictures. On the wall hung a scene from "The Wandering Jew," as we saw it at the Adelphi, in London, where in the Arctic regions he sees visions foreshadowing the future of his race. Under it was quoted:

"All in my mind is confused, nor can I dissever
The mould of the visible world from the shape of my thought in me—
The Inward and Outward are fused, and through them murmur forever
The sorrow whose sound is the wind and the roar of the limitless sea."

"Do you remember," Arne asked, "when we saw that play? Both younger and more hopeful. How has the world used you? As for me, I have done nothing since I came here but that sketch, finished months ago. I have not lost ambition, but I feel fettered."

"Absinthe?—opium?—tobacco?" I hinted.

"Neither," he answered. "I try to work, but visions, widely different from what I will, crowd on me, as on the Jew in the play. Not the unconscious brain action all thinkers know, but a dictation from without. No rush of creative impulses, but a dragging sense of something else I ought to paint."

"Briefly," I said, "you are a 'Haunted Man.'"

"Haunted by a willful design," said he. "I feel as if something had happened somewhere which I *must* show."

"What is it like?" I asked.

"I wish I could tell you," he replied. "But only odd bits change places, like looking in a kaleidoscope; yet all cluster around one centre."

One day, looking over his portfolios, I found an old *Temple Bar*, which he said he kept for this passage—which he read to me—from T. A. Trollope's "Artist's Tragedy:"

"The old walls and ceilings and floors must be saturated with the exhalations of human emotions! These lintels, doorways, and stairs have become, by long use and homeliness, dear to human hearts, and have become so intimately blended a portion of the mental furniture of human lives, that they have contributed their part to the formation of human characters. Such facts and considerations have gone to the fashioning of the mental habitudes of all of us. If all could have been recorded! If emotion had the property of photographing itself on the surfaces of the walls which had witnessed it! Even if only passion, when translated into acts, could have done so! Ah, what palimpsests! What deciphering of tangled records! What skillful separation of successive layers of 'passionography!'"

"I know a room," said Arne, "thronged with acts that elbow me from my work and fill me with unrest."

I looked at him in mute surprise.

"I suppose," he went on, "such things do not interest you."

"No—yes," I stammered. "I have marked in traveling how lonely houses change their expression as you come near, pass, and leave them. Some frown, others smile. The Bible buildings had life of their own and human diseases; the priests cursed or blessed them as men."

"Houses seem to remember," said he. "Some rooms oppress us with a sense of lives that have been lived in them."

"That," I said, "is like Draper's theory of shadows on walls always staying. He shows how after a breath passes over a coin or key, its spectral outline remains for months after the substance is removed. But can the mist of circumstance sweeping over us make our vacant places hold any trace of us?"

"Why not? Who can deny it? Why do you look at me so?" he asked.

I could not tell him the sad tale. I hesitated; then said: "I was thinking of Volz, a friend I had, who not only believed in what Bulwer calls 'a power akin to mesmerism and superior to it, once called Magic, and that it might reach over the dead, so far as their experience on earth,' but also in animal magnetism from any distance."

Arne grew queerly excited. "If Time and Space exist but in our thoughts, why should it not be true?" said he. "Macdonald's lover cries, 'That which has been is, and the Past can never cease. She is mine, and I shall find her—what matters it when, or where, or how?'" He sighed. "In Acapulco, a year ago, I saw a woman who has been before me ever since—the centre of the circling, changing, crude fancies that trouble me."

"Did you know her?" I asked.

"No, nor anything about her, not even her name. It is like a spell. I must paint her before anything else, but I cannot yet decide how. I feel sure she has played a tragic part in some life-drama."

"Swinburne's queen of panthers," I hinted.

"Yes. But I was not in love. Love I must forego. I am not a man with an income."

"I know you are not a nincompoop!" I said, always trying to change such themes by a jest. I could not tell him I knew a place which had the influence he talked of. I could not re-visit that house.

Soon after he told me he had begun his picture, but would not show it. He complained that one figure kept its back toward him. He worked on it till he fell ill. Even then he hid it. "Only a layer of passionography," he said.

I grew restless. I thought his mood affected mine. It was a torment as well as a puzzle to me that his whole talk should be of the influence of houses, rooms, even personal property that had known other owners.

Once I asked him if he had anything like the brown coat Sheridan swore drew ill-luck to him.

"Sometimes I think," he answered, "it is this special brown paint artists prize which affects me. It is made from the best asphaltum, and that can be got only from Egyptian mummycloths. Very likely dust of the mummies is ground in it. I ought to feel their ill-will."

One day I went to Saucelito. In the still woods I forgot my unrest till coming to the stream where, as I suddenly remembered, Anson was found dead, a dread took me which I tried to lose by putting into rhyme. Turning my pockets at night, I crumpled the page I had written on, and threw it on the floor.

In uneasy sleep I dreamed I was again in Paris, not where I liked to recall being, but at "Bullier's," and in war-time. The bald, spectacled leader of the orchestra, leaning back, shamming sleep, while a dancing, stamping, screaming crowd wave tri-colored flags, and call for the "Chant du Depart." Three thousand voices in a rushing roar that makes the twenty thousand lights waver, in spasmodic but steady chorus:

"Les departs—parts—parts!
Les departs—parts—parts!
Les departs—parts—parts!"

Roused, I supposed by passing rioters, I did not try to sleep again, but rose to write a letter for the early mail. As I struck a light I saw, smoothed out on the table, the wrinkled page I had cast aside. The ink was yet wet on two lines added to each verse. A chill crept over me as I read:

FOREST MURMURS.

Across the woodland bridge I pass,
And sway its three long, narrow planks,
To mark how gliding waters glass
Bright blossoms doubled ranks on ranks;

And how through tangle of the ferns
Floats incense from veiled flower-urns,
What would the babbling brook reveal?
What may these trembling depths conceal?
Dread secret of the dense woods, held
With restless shudders horror-spelled!

How shift the shadows of the wood,
As if it tossed in troubled sleep!
Strange whispers, vaguely understood,
Above, below, around me creep;
While in the sombre-shadowed stream
Great scarlet splashes far down gleam,
The odd-reflected, stately shapes
Of cardinals in crimson capes;
Not those—but spectral pools of blood
That stain these sands through strongest flood!

Like blare of trumpets through black nights—
Or sunset clouds before a storm—
Are these red phantom water-sprites
That mock me with fantastic form;
With flitting of the last year's bird
Fled ripples that its low flight stirred—
How should these rushing waters learn
Aught but the bend of this year's fern?
The lonesome wood, with bated breath,
Hints of a hidden blow—and death!

I could not stay alone. I ran to Arne's room. As I knocked, the falling of some light thing within made me think he was stirring. I went in. He sat in the moonlight, back to me before his easel. The picture on it might be the one he kept secret. I would not look. I went to his side and touched him. He had been dead for hours! I turned the unseen canvas to the wall.

Next day I packed and planned to go East. I paid the landlady not to send Arne's body to the morgue, and watched it that night, when a sudden memory swept over me like a tidal wave. There was a likeness in the room to one where I had before watched the dead. Yes—there were the windows, there the doors—just here stood the bed, in the same spot I sat. What wildness was in the air of San Francisco!

To put such crazy thoughts to flight I would look at Arne's last work. Yet I wavered, and more than once turned away after laying my hand on it. At last I snatched it, placed it on the easel and lighted the nearest gas-burner before looking at it.

Then—great heavens! How had this vision come to Arne? It was the scene where Felipa cursed us. Every detail of the room reproduced, even the gay birds on the wall-paper, and her flower-pots. The figures and faces of Dering and Volz were true as hers, and in the figure with averted face which Arne had said kept its back to him, I knew—myself! What strange insight had he gained by looking at Felipa? It was like the man who trembled before the unknown portrait of the Marquise de Brinvilliers.

How long I gazed at the picture I do not know. I heard, without heeding, the doorbell ring and steps along the hall. Voices. Some one looking at rooms. The landlady, saying this room was to let, but unwilling to show it, forced to own its last tenant lay there dead. This seemed no shock to the stranger. "Well," said her shrill tones, "poor as he was he's better dead than alive!"

The door opened as a well-known voice cried: "My God! say not that! The nerve which hears is last to die—"

Volz stood before me! Awe-struck, we looked at each other in silence. Then he waved his hand to and fro before his eyes.

"Is this a dream?" he said. "There," pointing to the bed; "you"—to me; "the same words—the very room! Is it our fate?"

I pointed to the picture and to Arne. "The last work of this man, who thought it a fancy sketch?"

While Volz stood dumb and motionless before it, the landlady spoke:

"Then you know the place. Can you tell what ails it? There have been suicides in this room. No one prospers in the house. My cousin, who is a house-mover, warned me against taking it. He says before the store was put under it here it stood on Bush Street, and before that on Telegraph Hill."

Volz clutched my arm. "It is 'The Flying Dutchman' of a house!" he cried, and drew me fast down stairs and out into a dense fog which made the world seem a tale that was told, blotting out all but our two slanting forms, bent as by what poor Wynne would have called "a blast from hell," hurrying blindly away. I heard the voice of Volz as if from afar: "The magnetic man *is* a spirit!"

The Mezzotint

MONTAGUE RHODES JAMES

Some time ago I believe I had the pleasure of telling you the story of an adventure which happened to a friend of mine by the name of Dennistoun, during his pursuit of objects of art for the museum at Cambridge.

He did not publish his experiences very widely upon his return to England; but they could not fail to become known to a good many of his friends, and among others to the gentleman who at that time presided over an art museum at another University. It was to be expected that the story should make a considerable impression on the mind of a man whose vocation lay in lines similar to Dennistoun's, and that he should be eager to catch at any explanation of the matter which tended to make it seem improbable that he should ever be called upon to deal with so agitating an emergency. It was, indeed, somewhat consoling to him to reflect that he was not expected to acquire ancient MSS. for his institution; that was the business of the Shelburnian Library. The authorities of that institution might, if they pleased, ransack obscure corners of the Continent for such matters. He was glad to be obliged at the moment to confine his attention to enlarging the already unsurpassed collection of English topographical drawings and engravings possessed by his museum. Yet, as it turned out, even a department so homely and familiar as this may have its dark corners and to one of these Mr. Williams was expectedly introduced.

Those who have taken even the most limited interest in the acquisition of topographical pictures are aware that there is one London dealer whose aid is indispensable to their researches. Mr. J. W. Britnell publishes at short intervals very admirable catalogues of a large and constantly changing stock of engravings, plans, and old sketches of mansions, churches, and towns in England and Wales. These catalogues were, of course, the ABC of his subject to Mr. Williams: but as his museum already contained an enormous accumulation of topographical pictures, he was a regular, rather than a copious, buyer; and he rather looked to Mr. Britnell to fill up gaps in the rank and file of his collection than to supply him with rarities.

Now, in February of last year there appeared upon Mr. Williams' desk at the museum a catalogue in Mr. Britnell's emporium, and accompanying it was a typewritten communication from the dealer himself. This latter ran as follows:

'Dear Sir,

We beg to call your attention to No. 978 in our accompanying catalogue, which we shall be glad to send on approval.

Yours faithfully,
J. W. Britnell.'

To turn to No. 978 in the accompanying catalogue was with Mr. Williams (as he observed to himself) the work of a moment, and in the place indicated he found the following entry:

'978. – *Unknown*. Interesting mezzotint: View of a manor-house, early part of the century. 15 by 10 inches; black frame. £2 2s.'

It was not specially exciting, and the price seemed high. However, as Mr. Britnell, who knew his business and his customer, seemed to set store by it, Mr. Williams wrote a postcard asking for the article to be sent on approval, along with some other engravings and sketches which appeared in the same catalogue. And so he passed without much excitement of anticipation to the ordinary labours of the day.

A parcel of any kind always arrives a day later than you expect it, and that of Mr. Britnell proved, as I believe the right phrase goes, no exception to the rule. It was delivered at the museum by the afternoon post of Saturday, after Mr. Williams had left his work, and it was accordingly brought to round his rooms in college by the attendant, in order that he might not have to wait over Sunday before looking through it and returning such of the contents as he did not propose to keep. And here he found it when he came in to tea, with a friend.

The only item with which I am concerned was the rather large, black-framed mezzotint of which I have already quoted the short description given in Mr. Britnell's catalogue. Some more details of it will have to be given, though I cannot hope to put before you the look of the picture as clearly as it is present to my own eye. Very nearly the exact duplicate of it may be seen in a good many old inn parlours, or in the passages of undisturbed country mansions at the present moment. It was a rather indifferent mezzotint, and an indifferent mezzotint is, perhaps, the worst form of engraving known. It presented a full-face view of a not very large manor-house of the last century, with three rows of plain sashed windows with rusticated masonry about them, a parapet with balls or vases at the angles, and a small portico in the centre. On either side were trees, and in front a considerable expanse of lawn. The legend 'A. W. F. sculpsit' was engraved on the narrow margin; and there was no further inscription. The whole thing gave the impression that it was the work of an amateur. What in the world Mr. Britnell could mean by affixing the price of £2 2s. to such an object was more than Mr. Williams could imagine. He turned it over with a good deal of contempt; upon the back was a paper label, the left-hand half of which had been torn off. All that remained were the ends of two lines of writing: the first had the letters *—ngley Hall;* the second, *—ssex.*

It would, perhaps, be just worth while to identify the place represented, which he could easily do with the help of a gazetteer, and then he would send it back to Mr. Britnell, with some remarks reflecting upon the judgment of that gentleman.

He lighted the candles, for it was now dark, made the tea, and supplied the friend with whom he had been playing golf (for I believe the authorities of the University I write of indulge in that pursuit by way of relaxation); and tea was taken to the accompaniment of a discussion which golfing persons can imagine for themselves, but which the conscientious writer has no right to inflict upon any non-golfing persons.

The conclusion arrived at was that certain strokes might have been better, and that in certain emergencies neither player had experienced that amount of luck which a human being has a right to expect. It was now that the friend – let us call him Professor Binks – took up the framed engraving, and said:

'What's this place, Williams?'

'Just what I am going to try to find out,' said Williams, going to the shelf for a gazetteer. 'Look at the back. Somethingley Hall, either in Sussex or Essex. Half the name's gone, you see. You don't happen to know it, I suppose?'

'It's from that man Britnell, I suppose, isn't it?' said Binks. 'Is it for the museum?'

'Well, I think I should buy it if the price was five shillings,' said Williams; 'but for some unearthly reason he wants two guineas for it. I can't conceive why. It's a wretched engraving, and there aren't even any figures to give it life.'

'It's not worth two guineas, I should think,' said Binks; 'but I don't think it's so badly done. The moonlight seems rather good to me; and I should have thought there *were* figures, or at least a figure, just on the edge in front.'

'Let's look,' said Williams. 'Well, it's true the light is rather cleverly given. Where's your figure? Oh yes! Just the head, in the very front of the picture.'

And indeed there was – hardly more than a black blot on the extreme edge of the engraving – the head of a man or woman, a good deal muffled up, the back turned to the spectator, and looking towards the house.

Williams had not noticed it before.

'Still,' he said, 'though it's a cleverer thing than I thought, I can't spend two guineas of museum money on a picture of a place I don't know.'

Professor Binks had his work to do, and soon went; and very nearly up to Hall time Williams was engaged in a vain attempt to identify the subject of his picture. 'If the vowel before the *ng* had only been left, it would have been easy enough,' he thought; 'but as it is, the name may be anything from Guestingley to Langley, and there are many more names ending like this than I thought; and this rotten book has no index of terminations.'

Hall in Mr. Williams's college was at seven. It need not be dwelt upon; the less so as he met there colleagues who had been playing golf during the afternoon, and words with which we have no concern were freely bandied across the table – merely golfing words, I would hasten to explain.

I suppose an hour or more to have been spent in what is called common-room after dinner. Later in the evening some few retired to Williams's room, and I have little doubt that whist was played and tobacco smoked. During a lull in these operations Williams picked up the mezzotint from the table without looking at it, and handed it to a person mildly interested in art, telling him where it had come from, and the other particulars which we already know.

The gentleman took it carelessly, looked at it, then said, in a tone of some interest:

'It's really a very good piece of work, Williams; it has quite a feeling of the romantic period. The light is admirably managed, it seems to me, and the figure, though it's rather too grotesque, is somehow very impressive.'

'Yes, isn't it?' said Williams, who was just then busy giving whisky-and-soda to others of the company, and was unable to come across the room to look at the view again.

It was by this time rather late in the evening, and the visitors were on the move. After they went Williams was obliged to write a letter or two and clear up some odd bits of work. At last, some time past midnight, he was disposed to turn in, and he put out his lamp after lighting his bedroom candle. The picture lay face upwards on the table where the last man who looked at it had put it, and it caught his eye as he turned the lamp down. What he saw made him very nearly drop the candle on the floor, and he declares now that if he had been left in the dark at that moment he would have had a fit. But, as that did not happen, he was able to put down the light on the table and take a good look at the picture. It was indubitable – rankly impossible, no doubt, but absolutely certain. In the middle of the lawn in front of the unknown house there was a figure where no figure had been at five o'clock that afternoon. It was crawling on all-fours towards the house, and it was muffled in a strange black garment with a white cross on the back.

I do not know what is the ideal course to pursue in a situation of this kind. I can only tell you what Mr. Williams did. He took the picture by one corner and carried it across the passage to a second set of rooms which he possessed. There he locked it up in a drawer, sported the doors of both sets of rooms, and retired to bed; but first he wrote out and signed an account of the extraordinary change which the picture had undergone since it had come into his possession.

Sleep visited him rather late; but it was consoling to reflect that the behaviour of the picture did not depend upon his own unsupported testimony. Evidently the man who had looked at it the night before had seen something of the same kind as he had, otherwise he might have been tempted to think that something gravely wrong was happening either to his eyes or his mind. This possibility being fortunately precluded, two matters awaited him on the morrow. He must take stock of the picture very carefully, and call in a witness for the purpose, and he must make a determined effort to ascertain what house it was that was represented. He would therefore ask his neighbour Nisbet to breakfast with him, and he would subsequently spend a morning over the gazetteer.

Nisbet was disengaged, and arrived about 9.30. His host was not quite dressed, I am sorry to say, even at this late hour. During breakfast nothing was said about the mezzo-tint by Williams, save that he had a picture on which he wished for Nisbet's opinion. But those who are familiar with University life can picture for themselves the wide and delightful range of subjects over which the conversation of two Fellows of Canterbury College is likely to extend during a Sunday morning breakfast. Hardly a topic was left unchallenged, from golf to lawn-tennis. Yet I am bound to say that Williams was rather distraught; for his interest naturally centred in that very strange picture which was now reposing, face downwards, in the drawer in the room opposite.

The morning pipe was at last lighted, and the moment had arrived for which he looked. With very considerable – almost tremulous – excitement, he ran across, unlocked the drawer, and, extracting the picture – still face downwards – ran back, and put it into Nisbet's hands.

'Now,' he said, 'Nisbet, I want you to tell me exactly what you see in that picture. Describe it, if you don't mind, rather minutely. I'll tell you why afterwards.'

'Well,' said Nisbet, 'I have here a view of a country-house – English, I presume – by moonlight.'

'Moonlight? You're sure of that?'

'Certainly. The moon appears to be on the wane, if you wish for details, and there are clouds in the sky.'

'All right. Go on. I'll swear,' added Williams in an aside, 'there was no moon when I saw it first.'

'Well, there's not much more to be said,' Nisbet continued. 'The house has one – two – three rows of windows, five in each row, except at the bottom, where there's a porch instead of the middle one, and—'

'But what about figures?' said Williams, with marked interest.

'There aren't any,' said Nisbet; 'but—'

'What! No figure on the grass in front?'

'Not a thing.'

'You'll swear to that?'

'Certainly I will. But there's just one other thing.'

'What?'

'Why, one of the windows on the ground-floor – left of the door – is open.'

'Is it really so? My goodness! he must have got in,' said Williams, with great excitement; and he hurried to the back of the sofa on which Nisbet was sitting, and, catching the picture from him, verified the matter for himself.

It was quite true. There was no figure, and there was the open window. Williams, after a moment of speechless surprise, went to the writing-table and scribbled for a short time. Then he brought two papers to Nisbet, and asked him first to sign one – it was his own description of the picture, which you have just heard – and then to read the other, which was Williams's statement written the night before.

'What can it all mean?' said Nisbet.

'Exactly,' said Williams. 'Well, one thing I must do – or three things, now I think of it. I must find out from Garwood' – this was his last night's visitor – 'what he saw, and then I must get the thing photographed before it goes further, and then I must find out what the place is.'

'I can do the photographing myself,' said Nisbet, 'and I will. But, you know, it looks very much as if we were assisting at the working out of a tragedy somewhere. The question is, Has it happened already, or is it going to come off? You must find out what the place is. Yes,' he said, looking at the picture again, 'I expect you're right: he has got in. And if I don't mistake there'll be the devil to pay in one of the rooms upstairs.'

'I'll tell you what,' said Williams: 'I'll take the picture across to old Green' (this was the senior Fellow of the College, who had been Bursar for many years). 'It's quite likely he'll know it. We have property in Essex and Sussex, and he must have been over the two counties a lot in his time.'

'Quite likely he will,' said Nisbet; 'but just let me take my photograph first. But look here, I rather think Green isn't up to-day. He wasn't in Hall last night, and I think I heard him say he was going down for the Sunday.'

'That's true, too,' said Williams; 'I know he's gone to Brighton. Well, if you'll photograph it now, I'll go across to Garwood and get his statement, and you keep an eye on it while I'm gone. I'm beginning to think two guineas is not a very exorbitant price for it now.'

In a short time he had returned, and brought Mr. Garwood with him. Garwood's statement was to the effect that the figure, when he had seen it, was clear of the edge of the picture, but had not got far across the lawn. He remembered a white mark on the back of its drapery, but could not have been sure it was a cross. A document to this effect was then drawn up and signed, and Nisbet proceeded to photograph the picture.

'Now what do you mean to do?' he said. 'Are you going to sit and watch it all day?'

'Well, no, I think not,' said Williams. 'I rather imagine we're meant to see the whole thing. You see, between the time I saw it last night and this morning there was time for lots of things to happen, but the creature only got into the house. It could easily have got through its business in the time and gone to its own place again; but the fact of the window being open, I think, must mean that it's in there now. So I feel quite easy about leaving it. And, besides, I have a kind of idea that it wouldn't change much, if at all, in the daytime. We might go out for a walk this afternoon, and come in to tea, or whenever it gets dark. I shall leave it out on the table here, and sport the door. My skip can get in, but no one else.'

The three agreed that this would be a good plan; and, further, that if they spent the afternoon together they would be less likely to talk about the business to other people; for any rumour of such a transaction as was going on would bring the whole of the Phasmatological Society about their ears.

We may give them a respite until five o'clock.

At or near that hour the three were entering Williams's staircase. They were at first slightly annoyed to see that the door of his rooms was unsported; but in a moment it was remembered that on Sunday the skips came for orders an hour or so earlier than on weekdays. However, a surprise was awaiting them. The first thing they saw was the picture leaning up against a pile of books on the table, as it had been left, and the next thing was Williams's skip, seated on a chair opposite, gazing at it with undisguised horror. How was this? Mr. Filcher (the name is not my own invention) was a servant of considerable standing, and set the standard of etiquette to all his own college and to several neighbouring ones, and nothing could be more alien to his practice than to be found sitting on his master's chair, or appearing to take any particular notice of his master's furniture or pictures. Indeed, he seemed to feel this himself. He started violently when the three men were in the room, and got up with a marked effort. Then he said:

'I ask your pardon, sir, for taking such a freedom as to set down.'

'Not at all, Robert,' interposed Mr. Williams. 'I was meaning to ask you some time what you thought of that picture.'

'Well, sir, of course I don't set up my opinion again yours, but it ain't the pictur I should 'ang where my little girl could see it, sir.'

'Wouldn't you, Robert? Why not?'

'No, sir. Why, the pore child, I recollect once she see a Door Bible, with pictures not 'alf what that is, and we 'ad to set up with her three or four nights afterwards, if you'll believe me; and if she was to ketch a sight of this skelinton here, or whatever it is, carrying off the pore baby, she would be in a taking. You know 'ow it is with children; 'ow nervish they git with a little thing and all. But what I should say, it don't seem a right pictur to be laying about, sir, not where anyone that's liable to be startled could come on it. Should you be wanting anything this evening, sir? Thank you, sir.'

With these words the excellent man went to continue the round of his masters and you may be sure the gentleman whom he left lost no time in gathering round the engraving. There was the house, as before under the waning moon and the drifting clouds The window that had been open was shut, and the figure was once more on the lawn: but not this time crawling cautiously on hands and knees. Now it was erect and stepping swiftly, with long strides, towards the front of the picture. The moon was behind it, and the black drapery hung down over its face so that only hints of that could be seen, and what was visible made the spectators profoundly thankful that they could see no more than a white dome-like forehead and a few straggling hairs. The head was bent down, and the arms were tightly clasped over an object which could be dimly seen and identified as a child, whether dead or living it was not possible to say. The legs of the appearance alone could be plainly discerned, and they were horribly thin.

From five to seven the three companions sat and watched the picture by turns. But it never changed. They agreed at last that it would be safe to leave it, and that they would return after Hall and await further developments.

When they assembled again, at the earliest possible moment, the engraving was there, but the figure was gone, and the house was quiet under the moonbeams. There was nothing for it but to spend the evening over gazetteers and guide-books. Williams was the lucky one at last, and perhaps he deserved it. At 11.30 p.m. he read from Murray's *Guide to Essex* the following lines:

'16½ miles, *Anningley*. The church has been an interesting building of Norman date, but was extensively classicized in the last century. It contains the tomb of the family of Francis, whose mansion, Anningley Hall, a solid Queen Anne house, stands immediately beyond the churchyard in a park of about 80 acres. The family is now extinct, the last heir having disappeared mysteriously in infancy in the year 1802. The father, Mr. Arthur Francis, was locally known as a talented amateur engraver in mezzotint. After his son's disappearance he lived in complete retirement at the Hall, and was found dead in his studio on the third anniversary of the disaster, having just completed an engraving of the house, impressions of which are of considerable rarity.'

This looked like business, and, indeed, Mr. Green on his return at once identified the house as Anningley Hall.

'Is there any kind of explanation of the figure, Green?' was the question which Williams naturally asked.

'I don't know, I'm sure, Williams. What used to be said in the place when I first knew it, which was before I came up here, was just this: old Francis was always very much down on these poaching fellows, and whenever he got a chance he used to get a man whom he suspected of it turned off the estate, and by degrees he got rid of them all but one. Squires could do a lot of things then that they daren't think of now. Well, this man that was left was what you find pretty often in that country – the last remains of a very old family. I believe they were Lords of the Manor at one time. I recollect just the same thing in my own parish.'

'What, like the man in *Tess of the d'Urbervilles?*' Williams put in.

'Yes, I dare say; it's not a book I could ever read myself. But this fellow could show a row of tombs in the church there that belonged to his ancestors, and all that went to sour him a bit; but Francis, they said, could never get at him – he always kept just on the right side of the law – until one night the keepers found him at it in a wood right at the end of the estate. I could show you the place now; it marches with some land that used to belong to an uncle of mine. And you can imagine there was a row; and this man Gawdy (that was the name, to be sure – Gawdy; I thought I should get it – Gawdy), he was unlucky enough, poor chap! to shoot a keeper. Well, that was what Francis wanted, and grand juries – you know what they would have been then – and poor Gawdy was strung up in double-quick time; and I've been shown the place he was buried in, on the north side of the church – you know the way in that part of the world: anyone that's been hanged or made away with themselves, they bury them that side. And the idea that there was some friend of Gawdy's – not a relation, because he had none, poor devil! he was the last of his line: kind of *spes ultima gentis* – must have planned to get hold of Francis's boy and put an end to *his* line, too. I don't know – it's rather an out-of-the-way thing for an Essex poacher to think of – but, you know, I should say now it looks more as if old Gawdy had managed the job himself. Booh! I hate to think of it! have some whisky, Williams!'

The facts were communicated by Williams to Dennistoun, and by him to a mixed company, of which I was one, and the Sadducean Professor of Ophiology another. I am sorry to say that the latter, when asked what he thought of it, only remarked: 'Oh, those Bridgeford people will say anything' – a sentiment which met with the reception it deserved.

I have only to add that the picture is now in the Ashleian Museum; that it has been treated with a view to discovering whether sympathetic ink has been used in it, but without effect; that Mr. Britnell knew nothing of it save that he was sure it was uncommon; and that, though carefully watched, it has never been known to change again.

Madam Crowl's Ghost

SHERIDAN LE FANU

I'm an old woman now; and I was but thirteen, my last birthday, the night I came to Applewale House. My aunt was the housekeeper there, and a sort o' one-horse carriage was down at Lexhoe to take me and my box up to Applewale.

I was a bit frightened by the time I got to Lexhoe, and when I saw the carriage and horse, I wished myself back again with my mother at Hazelden. I was crying when I got into the 'shay' – that's what we used to call it – and old John Mulbery that drove it, and was a good-natured fellow, bought me a handful of apples at the Golden Lion, to cheer me up a bit; and he told me that there was a currant-cake, and tea, and pork-chops, waiting for me, all hot, in my aunt's room at the great house. It was a fine moonlight night and I eat the apples, lookin' out o' the shay winda.

It is a shame for gentlemen to frighten a poor foolish child like I was. I sometimes think it might be tricks. There was two on 'em on the tap o' the coach beside me. And they began to question me after nightfall, when the moon rose, where I was going to. Well, I told them it was to wait on Dame Arabella Crowl, of Applewale House, near by Lexhoe.

'Ho, then,' says one of them, 'you'll not be long there!'

And I looked at him as much as to say, 'Why not?' for I had spoke out when I told them where I was goin', as if 'twas something clever I had to say.

'Because,' says he – 'and don't you for your life tell no one, only watch her and see – she's possessed by the devil, and more an half a ghost. Have you got a Bible?'

'Yes, sir,' says I. For my mother put my little Bible in my box, and I knew it was there: and by the same token, though the print's too small for my ald eyes, I have it in my press to this hour.

As I looked up at him, saying 'Yes, sir,' I thought I saw him winkin' at his friend; but I could not be sure.

'Well,' says he, 'be sure you put it under your bolster every night, it will keep the ald girl's claws aff ye.'

And I got such a fright when he said that, you wouldn't fancy! And I'd a liked to ask him a lot about the ald lady, but I was too shy, and he and his friend began talkin' together about their own consarns, and dowly enough I got down, as I told ye, at Lexhoe. My heart sank as I drove into the dark avenue. The trees stands very thick and big, as ald as the ald house almost, and four people, with their arms out and finger-tips touchin', barely girds round some of them.

Well, my neck was stretched out o' the winda, looking for the first view o' the great house; and, all at once we pulled up in front of it.

A great white-and-black house it is, wi' great black beams across and right up it, and gables lookin' out, as white as a sheet, to the moon, and the shadows o' the trees, two or three up and down upon the front, you could count the leaves on them, and all the little diamond-shaped winda-panes, glimmering on the great hall winda, and great shutters, in the old fashion, hinged on the wall outside, boulted across all the rest o' the windas in front, for there was but three or four servants, and the old lady in the house, and most o' t'rooms was locked up.

My heart was in my mouth when I sid the journey was over, and this, the great house afore me, and I sa near my aunt that I never sid till noo, and Dame Crowl, that I was come to wait upon, and was afeard on already.

My aunt kissed me in the hall, and brought me to her room. She was tall and thin, wi' a pale face and black eyes, and long thin hands wi' black mittins on. She was past fifty, and her word was short; but her word was law. I hev no complaints to make of her; but she was a hard woman, and

I think she would hev bin kinder to me if I had bin her sister's child in place of her brother's. But all that's o' no consequence noo.

The squire – his name was Mr. Chevenix Crowl, he was Dame Crowl's grandson – came down there, by way of seeing that the old lady was well treated, about twice or thrice in the year. I sid him but twice all the time I was at Applewale House.

I can't say but she was well taken care of, notwithstanding, but that was because my aunt and Meg Wyvern, that was her maid, had a conscience, and did their duty by her.

Mrs. Wyvern – Meg Wyvern my aunt called her to herself, and Mrs. Wyvern to me – was a fat, jolly lass of fifty, a good height and a good breadth, always good-humoured, and walked slow. She had fine wages, but she was a bit stingy, and kept all her fine clothes under lock and key, and wore, mostly, a twilled chocolate cotton, wi' red, and yellow, and green sprigs and balls on it, and it lasted wonderful.

She never gave me nout, not the vally o' a brass thimble, all the time I was there; but she was good-humoured, and always laughin', and she talked no end o' proas over her tea; and, seeing me sa sackless and dowly, she roused me up wi' her laughin' and stories; and I think I liked her better than my aunt – children is so taken wi' a bit o' fun or a story – though my aunt was very good to me, but a hard woman about some things, and silent always.

My aunt took me into her bed-chamber, that I might rest myself a bit while she was settin' the tea in her room. But first she patted me on the shouther, and said I was a tall lass o' my years, and had spired up well, and asked me if I could do plain work and stitchin'; and she looked in my face, and said I was like my father, her brother, that was dead and gone, and she hoped I was a better Christian, and wad na du a' that lids.

It was a hard sayin' the first time I set my foot in her room, I thought.

When I went into the next room, the housekeeper's room – very comfortable, yak (oak) all round – there was a fine fire blazin' away, wi' coal, and peat, and wood, all in a low together, and tea on the table, and hot cake, and smokin' meat; and there was Mrs. Wyvern, fat, jolly, and talkin' away, more in an hour than my aunt would in a year.

While I was still at my tea my aunt went up-stairs to see Madam Crowl.

'She's agone up to see that old Judith Squailes is awake,' says Mrs. Wyvern. 'Judith sits with Madam Crowl when me and Mrs. Shutters' – that was my aunt's name – 'is away. She's a troublesome old lady. Ye'll hev to be sharp wi' her, or she'll be into the fire, or out o' t' winda. She goes on wires, she does, old though she be.'

'How old, ma'am?' says I.

'Ninety-three her last birthday, and that's eight months gone,' says she; and she laughed. 'And don't be askin' questions about her before your aunt – mind, I tell ye; just take her as you find her, and that's all.'

'And what's to be my business about her, please ma'am?' says I.

'About the old lady? Well,' says she, 'your aunt, Mrs. Shutters, will tell you that; but I suppose you'll hev to sit in the room with your work, and see she's at no mischief, and let her amuse herself with her things on the table, and get her her food or drink as she calls for it, and keep her out o' mischief, and ring the bell hard if she's troublesome.'

'Is she deaf, ma'am?'

'No, nor blind,' says she; 'as sharp as a needle, but she's gone quite aupy, and can't remember nout rightly; and Jack the Giant Killer, or Goody Twoshoes will please her as well as the King's court, or the affairs of the nation.'

'And what did the little girl go away for, ma'am, that went on Friday last? My aunt wrote to my mother she was to go.'

'Yes; she's gone.'

'What for?' says I again.

'She didn't answer Mrs. Shutters, I do suppose,' says she. 'I don't know. Don't be talkin'; your aunt can't abide a talkin' child.'

'And please, ma'am, is the old lady well in health?' says I.

'It ain't no harm to ask that,' says she. 'She's torflin' a bit lately, but better this week past, and I dare say she'll last out her hundred years yet. Hish! Here's your aunt coming down the passage.'

In comes my aunt, and begins talkin' to Mrs. Wyvern, and I, beginnin' to feel more comfortable and at home like, was walkin' about the room lookin' at this thing and at that. There was pretty old china things on the cupboard, and pictures again the wall; and there was a door open in the wainscot, and I sees a queer old leathern jacket, wi' straps and buckles to it, and sleeves as long as the bed-post, hangin' up inside.

'What's that you're at, child?' says my aunt, sharp enough, turning about when I thought she least minded. 'What's that in your hand?'

'This, ma'am?' says I, turning about with the leathern jacket. 'I don't know what it is, ma'am.'

Pale as she was, the red came up in her cheeks, and her eyes flashed wi' anger, and I think only she had half a dozen steps to take, between her and me, she'd a gov me a sizzup. But she did give me a shake by the shouther, and she plucked the thing out o' my hand, and says she, 'While ever you stay here, don't ye meddle wi' nout that don't belong to ye,' and she hung it up on the pin that was there, and shut the door wi' a bang and locked it fast.

Mrs. Wyvern was liftin' up her hands and laughin' all this time, quietly in her chair, rolling herself a bit in it, as she used when she was kinkin'.

The tears was in my eyes, and she winked at my aunt, and says she, dryin' her own eyes that was wet wi' the laughin', 'Tut, the child meant no harm – come here to me, child. It's only a pair o' crutches for lame ducks, and ask us no questions mind, and we'll tell ye no lies; and come here and sit down, and drink a mug o' beer before ye go to your bed.'

My room, mind ye, was up-stairs, next to the old lady's, and Mrs. Wyvern's bed was near hers in her room and I was to be ready at call, if need should be.

The old lady was in one of her tantrums that night and part of the day before. She used to take fits o' the sulks. Sometimes she would not let them dress her, and other times she would not let them take her clothes off. She was a great beauty, they said, in her day. But there was no one about Applewale that remembered her in her prime. And she was dreadful fond o' dress, and had thick silks, and stiff satins, and velvets, and laces, and all sorts, enough to set up seven shops at the least. All her dresses was old-fashioned and queer, but worth a fortune.

Well, I went to my bed. I lay for a while awake; for a' things was new to me; and I think the tea was in my nerves, too, for I wasn't used to it, except now and then on a holiday, or the like. And I heard Mrs. Wyvern talkin', and I listened with my hand to my ear; but I could not hear Mrs. Crowl, and I don't think she said a word.

There was great care took of her. The people at Applewale knew that when she died they would every one get the sack; and their situations was well paid and easy.

The doctor come twice a week to see the old lady, and you may be sure they all did as he bid them. One thing was the same every time; they were never to cross or frump her, any way, but to humour and please her in everything.

So she lay in her clothes all that night, and next day, not a word she said, and I was at my needlework all that day, in my own room, except when I went down to my dinner.

I would a liked to see the ald lady, and even to hear her speak. But she might as well a'bin in Lunnon a' the time for me.

When I had my dinner my aunt sent me out for a walk for an hour. I was glad when I came back, the trees was so big, and the place so dark and lonesome, and 'twas a cloudy day, and I cried a deal, thinkin' of home, while I was walkin' alone there. That evening, the candles bein' alight, I was sittin' in my room, and the door was open into Madam Crowl's chamber, where my aunt was. It was, then, for the first time I heard what I suppose was the ald lady talking.

It was a queer noise like, I couldn't well say which, a bird, or a beast, only it had a bleatin' sound in it, and was very small.

I pricked my ears to hear all I could. But I could not make out one word she said. And my aunt answered:

'The evil one can't hurt no one, ma'am, bout the Lord permits.'

Then the same queer voice from the bed says something more that I couldn't make head nor tail on.

And my aunt med answer again: 'Let them pull faces, ma'am, and say what they will; if the Lord be for us, who can be against us?'

I kept listenin' with my ear turned to the door, holdin' my breath, but not another word or sound came in from the room. In about twenty minutes, as I was sittin' by the table, lookin' at the pictures in the old Æsop's Fables, I was aware o' something moving at the door, and lookin' up I sid my aunt's face lookin' in at the door, and her hand raised.

'Hish!' says she, very soft, and comes over to me on tiptoe, and she says in a whisper: 'Thank God, she's asleep at last, and don't ye make no noise till I come back, for I'm goin' down to take my cup o' tea, and I'll be back i' noo – me and Mrs. Wyvern, and she'll be sleepin' in the room, and you can run down when we come up, and Judith will gie ye yaur supper in my room.'

And with that away she goes.

I kep' looking at the picture-book, as before, listenin' every noo and then, but there was no sound, not a breath, that I could hear; an' I began whisperin' to the pictures and talkin' to myself to keep my heart up, for I was growin' feared in that big room.

And at last up I got, and began walkin' about the room, lookin' at this and peepin' at that, to amuse my mind, ye'll understand. And at last what sud I do but peeps into Madame Crowl's bed-chamber.

A grand chamber it was, wi' a great four-poster, wi' flowered silk curtains as tall as the ceilin', and foldin' down on the floor, and drawn close all round. There was a lookin'-glass, the biggest I ever sid before, and the room was a blaze o' light. I counted twenty-two wax-candles, all alight. Such was her fancy, and no one dared say her nay.

I listened at the door, and gaped and wondered all round. When I heard there was not a breath, and did not see so much as a stir in the curtains, I took heart, and I walked into the room on tiptoe, and looked round again. Then I takes a keek at myself in the big glass; and at last it came in my head, 'Why couldn't I ha' a keek at the ald lady herself in the bed?'

Ye'd think me a fule if ye knew half how I longed to see Dame Crowl, and I thought to myself if I didn't peep now I might wait many a day before I got so gude a chance again.

Well, my dear, I came to the side o' the bed, the curtains bein' close, and my heart a'most failed me. But I took courage, and I slips my finger in between the thick curtains, and then my hand. So I waits a bit, but all was still as death. So, softly, softly I draws the curtain, and there, sure enough, I sid before me, stretched out like the painted lady on the tomb-stean in Lexhoe Church, the famous Dame Crowl, of Applewale House. There she was, dressed out. You never sid the like in they days. Satin and silk, and scarlet and green, and gold and pint lace; by Jen! 'twas a sight! A big powdered wig, half as high as herself, was a-top o' her head, and, wow! – was ever such wrinkles? – and her old baggy throat all powdered white, and her cheeks rouged, and mouse-skin eyebrows, that Mrs. Wyvern used to stick on, and there she lay grand and stark, wi' a pair o' clocked silk hose on, and heels to her shoon as tall as nine-pins. Lawk! But her nose was crooked and thin, and half the whites o' her eyes was open. She used to stand, dressed as she was, gigglin' and dribblin' before the lookin'-glass, wi' a fan in her hand, and a big nosegay in her bodice. Her wrinkled little hands was stretched down by her sides, and such long nails, all cut into points, I never sid in my days. Could it ever a bin the fashion for grit fowk to wear their finger-nails so?

Well, I think ye'd a bin frightened yourself if ye'd a sid such a sight. I couldn't let go the curtain, nor move an inch, not take my eyes off her; my very heart stood still. And in an instant she opens her eyes, and up she sits, and spins herself round, and down wi' her, wi' a clack on her two tall heels on the floor, facin' me, ogglin' in my face wi' her two great glassy eyes, and a wicked simper wi' her old wrinkled lips, and lang fause teeth.

Well, a corpse is a natural thing; but this was the dreadfullest sight I ever sid. She had her fingers straight out pointin' at me, and her back was crooked, round again wi' age. Says she:

'Ye little limb! what for did ye say I killed the boy? I'll tickle ye till ye're stiff!'

If I'd a thought an instant, I'd a turned about and run. But I couldn't take my eyes off her, and I backed from her as soon as I could; and she came clatterin' after, like a thing on wires, with her fingers pointing to my throat, and she makin' all the time a sound with her tongue like zizz-zizz-zizz.

I kept backin' and backin' as quick as I could, and her fingers was only a few inches away from my throat, and I felt I'd lose my wits if she touched me.

I went back this way, right into the corner, and I gev a yellock, ye'd think saul and body was partin', and that minute my aunt, from the door, calls out wi' a blare, and the ald lady turns round on her, and I turns about, and ran through my room, and down the back stairs, as hard as my legs could carry me.

I cried hearty, I can tell you, when I got down to the housekeeper's room. Mrs. Wyvern laughed a deal when I told her what happened. But she changed her key when she heard the ald lady's words.

'Say them again,' says she.

So I told her.

'Ye little limb! What for did ye say I killed the boy? I'll tickle ye till ye're stiff.'

'And did ye say she killed a boy?' says she.

'Not I, ma'am,' says I.

Judith was always up with me, after that, when the two elder women was away from her. I would a jumped out at winda, rather than stay alone in the same room wi' her.

It was about a week after, as well as I can remember, Mrs. Wyvern, one day when me and her was alone, told me a thing about Madam Crowl that I did not know before.

She being young, and a great beauty, full seventy years before, had married Squire Crowl of Applewale. But he was a widower, and had a son about nine year old.

There never was tale or tidings of this boy after one mornin'. No one could say where he went to. He was allowed too much liberty, and used to be off in the morning, one day, to the keeper's cottage, and breakfast wi' him, and away to the warren, and not home, mayhap, till evening, and another time down to the lake, and bathe there, and spend the day fishin' there, or paddlin' about in the boat. Well, no one could say what was gone wi' him; only this, that his hat was found by the lake, under a haathorn that grows thar to this day, and 'twas thought he was drowned bathin'. And the squire's son, by his second marriage, by this Madam Crowl that lived sa dreadful lang, came in for the estates. It was his son, the ald lady's grandson, Squire Chevenix Crowl, that owned the estates at the time I came to Applewale.

There was a deal o' talk lang before my aunt's time about it; and 'twas said the step-mother knew more than she was like to let out. And she managed her husband, the ald squire, wi' her whiteheft and flatteries. And as the boy was never seen more, in course of time the thing died out of fowks' minds.

I'm goin' to tell ye noo about what I sid wi' my own een.

I was not there six months, and it was winter time, when the ald lady took her last sickness.

The doctor was afeard she might a took a fit o' madness, as she did, fifteen years befoore, and was buckled up, many a time, in a strait-waistcoat, which was the very leathern jerkin' I sid in the closet, off my aunt's room.

Well, she didn't. She pined, and windered, and went off, torflin', torflin', quiet enough, till a day or two before her flittin', and then she took to rabblin', and sometimes skirlin' in the bed, ye'd think a robber had a knife to her throat, and she used to work out o' the bed, and not being strong enough, then, to walk or stand, she'd fall on the flure, wi' her ald wizened hands stretched before her face, and skirlin' still for mercy.

Ye may guess I didn't go into the room, and I used to be shiverin' in my bed wi' fear, at her skirlin' and scrafflin' on the flure, and blarin' out words that id make your skin turn blue.

My aunt, and Mrs. Wyvern, and Judith Squailes, and a woman from Lexhoe, was always about her. At last she took fits, and they wore her out.

T'sir (parson) was there, and prayed for her; but she was past praying with. I suppose it was right, but none could think there was much good in it, and sa at lang last she made her flittin', and a' was over, and old Dame Crowl was shrouded and coffined and Squire Chevenix was wrote for. But he was away in France, and the delay was sa lang, that t'sir and doctor both agreed it would not du to keep her langer out o' her place, and no one cared but just them two, and my aunt and the rest o' us, from Applewale, to go to the buryin'. So the old lady of Applewale was laid in the vault under Lexhoe Church; and we lived up at the great house till such time as the squire should come to tell his will about us, and pay off such as he chose to discharge.

I was put into another room, two doors away from what was Dame Crowl's chamber, after her death, and this thing happened the night before Squire Chevenix came to Applewale.

The room I was in now was a large square chamber, covered wi' yak pannels, but unfurnished except for my bed, which had no curtains to it, and a chair and a table, or so, that looked nothing at all in such a big room. And the big looking-glass, that the old lady used to keek into and admire herself from head to heel, now that there was na mair o' that wark, was put out of the way, and stood against the wall in my room, for there was shiftin' o' many things in her chambers ye may suppose, when she came to be coffined.

The news had come that day that the squire was to be down next morning at Applewale; and not sorry was I, for I thought I was sure to be sent home again to my mother. And right glad was I, and I was thinkin' of a' at hame, and my sister, Janet, and the kitten and the pymag, and Trimmer the tike, and all the rest, and I got sa fidgetty, I couldn't sleep, and the clock struck twelve, and me wide awake, and the room as dark as pick. My back was turned to the door, and my eyes toward the wall opposite.

Well, it could na be a full quarter past twelve, when I sees a lightin' on the wall befoore me, as if something took fire behind, and the shadas o' the bed, and the chair, and my gown, that was hangin' from the wall, was dancin' up and down, on the ceilin' beams and the yak pannels; and I turns my head ower my shouther quick, thinkin' something must a gone a' fire.

And what sud I see, by Jen! but the likeness o' the ald beldame, bedizened out in her satins and velvets, on her dead body, simperin', wi' her eyes as wide as saucers, and her face like the fiend himself. 'Twas a red light that rose about her in a fuffin low, as if her dress round her feet was blazin'. She was drivin' on right for me, wi' her ald shrivelled hands crooked as if she was goin' to claw me. I could not stir, but she passed me straight by, wi' a blast o' cald air, and I sid her, at the wall, in the alcove as my aunt used to call it, which was a recess where the state bed used to stand in ald times, wi' a door open wide, and her hands gropin' in at somethin' was there. I never sid that door befoore. And she turned round to me, like a thing on a pivot, flyrin' (grinning), and all at once the room was dark, and I standin' at the far side o' the bed; I don't know how I got there, and I found my tongue at last, and if I did na blare a yellock, rennin' down the gallery and almost pulled Mrs. Wyvern's door, off t'hooks, and frightened her half out o' her wits.

Ye may guess I did na sleep that night; and wi' the first light, down wi' me to my aunt, as fast as my two legs cud carry me.

Well, my aunt did na frump or flite me, as I thought she would, but she held me by the hand, and looked hard in my face all the time. And she telt me not to be feared; and says she:

'Hed the appearance a key in its hand?'

'Yes,' says I, bringin' it to mind, 'a big key in a queer brass handle.'

'Stop a bit,' says she, lettin' go ma hand, and openin' the cupboard-door. 'Was it like this?' says she, takin' one out in her fingers and showing it to me, with a dark look in my face.

'That was it,' says I, quick enough.

'Are ye sure?' she says, turnin' it round.

'Sart,' says I, and I felt like I was gain' to faint when I sid it.

'Well, that will do, child,' says she, saftly thinkin', and she locked it up again.

'The squire himself will be here to-day, before twelve o'clock, and ye must tell him all about it,' says she, thinkin', 'and I suppose I'll be leavin' soon, and so the best thing for the present is, that ye should go home this afternoon, and I'll look out another place for you when I can.'

Fain was I, ye may guess, at that word.

My aunt packed up my things for me, and the three pounds that was due to me, to bring home, and Squire Crowl himself came down to Applewale that day, a handsome man, about thirty years ald. It was the second time I sid him. But this was the first time he spoke to me.

My aunt talked wi' him in the housekeeper's room, and I don't know what they said. I was a bit feared on the squire, he bein' a great gentleman down in Lexhoe, and I darn't go near till I was called. And says he, smilin':

'What's a' this ye a sen, child? it mun be a dream, for ye know there's na sic a thing as a bo or a freet in a' the world. But whatever it was, ma little maid, sit ye down and tell us all about it from first to last.'

Well, so soon as I med an end, he thought a bit, and says he to my aunt:

'I mind the place well. In old Sir Oliver's time lame Wyndel told me there was a door in that recess, to the left, where the lassie dreamed she saw my grandmother open it. He was past eighty when he telt me that, and I but a boy. It's twenty year sen. The plate and jewels used to be kept there, long ago, before the iron closet was made in the arras chamber, and he told me the key had a brass handle, and this ye say was found in the bottom o' the kist where she kept her old fans. Now, would not it be a queer thing if we found some spoons or diamonds forgot there? Ye mun come up wi' us, lassie, and point to the very spot.'

Loth was I, and my heart in my mouth, and fast I held by my aunt's hand as I stept into that awsome room, and showed them both how she came and passed me by, and the spot where she stood, and where the door seemed to open.

There was an ald empty press against the wall then, and shoving it aside, sure enough there was the tracing of a door in the wainscot, and a keyhole stopped with wood, and planed across as smooth as the rest, and the joining of the door all stopped wi' putty the colour o' yak, and, but for the hinges that showed a bit when the press was shoved aside, ye would not consayt there was a door there at all.

'Ha!' says he, wi' a queer smile, 'this looks like it.'

It took some minutes wi' a small chisel and hammer to pick the bit o' wood out o' the keyhole. The key fitted, sure enough, and, wi' a strang twist and a lang skreeak, the boult went back and he pulled the door open.

There was another door inside, stranger than the first, but the lacks was gone, and it opened easy. Inside was a narrow floor and walls and vault o' brick; we could not see what was in it, for 'twas dark as pick.

When my aunt had lighted the candle the squire held it up and stept in.

My aunt stood on tiptoe tryin' to look over his shouther, and I did na see nout.

'Ha! ha!' says the squire, steppin' backward. 'What's that? Gi'ma the poker – quick!' says he to my aunt. And as she went to the hearth I peeps beside his arm, and I sid squat down in the far corner a monkey or a flayin' on the chest, or else the maist shrivelled up, wizzened ald wife that ever was sen on yearth.

'By Jen!' says my aunt, as, puttin' the poker in his hand, she keeked by his shouther, and sid the ill-favoured thing, 'hae a care sir, what ye're doin'. Back wi' ye, and shut to the door!'

But in place o' that he steps in saftly, wi' the poker pointed like a swoord, and he gies it a poke, and down it a' tumbles together, head and a', in a heap o' bayans and dust, little meyar an' a hatful.

'Twas the bayans o' a child; a' the rest went to dust at a touch. They said nout for a while, but he turns round the skull as it lay on the floor.

Young as I was I consayted I knew well enough what they was thinkin' on.

'A dead cat!' says he, pushin' back and blowin' out the can'le, and shuttin' to the door. 'We'll come back, you and me, Mrs. Shutters, and look on the shelves by-and-bye. I've other matters first to speak to ye about; and this little girl's goin' hame, ye say. She has her wages, and I mun mak' her a present,' says he, pattin' my shoulder wi' his hand.

And he did gimma a goud pound, and I went aff to Lexhoe about an hour after, and sa hame by the stagecoach, and fain was I to be at hame again; and I never saa ald Dame Crowl o' Applewale, God be thanked, either in appearance or in dream, at-efter. But when I was grown to be a woman my aunt spent a day and night wi' me at Littleham, and she telt me there was na doubt it was the poor little boy that was missing sa lang sen that was shut up to die thar in the dark by that wicked beldame, whar his skirls, or his prayers, or his thumpin' cud na be heard, and his hat was left by the water's edge, whoever did it, to mak' belief he was drowned. The clothes, at the first touch, a' ran into a snuff o' dust in the cell whar the bayans was found. But there was a handful o' jet buttons, and a knife with a green handle, together wi' a couple o' pennies the poor little fella had in his pocket, I suppose, when he was decoyed in thar, and sid his last o' the light. And there was, amang the squire's papers, a copy o' the notice that was prented after he was lost, when the old squire thought he might 'a run away, or bin took by gipsies, and it said he had a green-hefted knife wi' him, and that his buttons were o' cut jet. Sa that is a' I hev to say consarnin' ald Dame Crowl, o' Applewale House.

The Doll's Ghost

Francis Marion Crawford

It was a terrible accident, and for one moment the splendid machinery of Cranston House got out of gear and stood still. The butler emerged from the retirement in which he spent his elegant leisure, two grooms of the chambers appeared simultaneously from opposite directions, there were actually housemaids on the grand staircase, and those who remember the facts most exactly assert that Mrs. Pringle herself positively stood upon the landing. Mrs. Pringle was the housekeeper. As for the head nurse, the under nurse, and the nursery maid, their feelings cannot be described. The head nurse laid one hand upon the polished marble balustrade and stared stupidly before her, the under nurse stood rigid and pale, leaning against the polished marble wall, and the nursery-maid collapsed and sat down upon the polished marble step, just beyond the limits of the velvet carpet, and frankly burst into tears.

The Lady Gwendolen Lancaster-Douglas-Scroop, youngest daughter of the ninth Duke of Cranston, and aged six years and three months, picked herself up quite alone, and sat down on the third step from the foot of the grand staircase in Cranston House.

"Oh!" ejaculated the butler, and he disappeared again.

"Ah!" responded the grooms of the chambers, as they also went away.

"It's only that doll," Mrs. Pringle was distinctly heard to say, in a tone of contempt.

The under nurse heard her say it. Then the three nurses gathered round Lady Gwendolen and patted her, and gave her unhealthy things out of their pockets, and hurried her out of Cranston House as fast as they could, lest it should be found out upstairs that they had allowed the Lady Gwendolen Lancaster-Douglas-Scroop to tumble down the grand staircase with her doll in her arms. And as the doll was badly broken, the nursery-maid carried it, with the pieces, wrapped up in Lady Gwendolen's little cloak. It was not far to Hyde Park, and when they had reached a quiet place they took means to find out that Lady Gwendolen had no bruises. For the carpet was very thick and soft, and there was thick stuff under it to make it softer.

Lady Gwendolen Douglas-Scroop sometimes yelled, but she never cried. It was because she had yelled that the nurse had allowed her to go downstairs alone with Nina, the doll, under one arm, while she steadied herself with her other hand on the balustrade, and trod upon the polished marble steps beyond the edge of the carpet. So she had fallen, and Nina had come to grief.

When the nurses were quite sure that she was not hurt, they unwrapped the doll and looked at her in her turn. She had been a very beautiful doll, very large, and fair, and healthy, with real yellow hair, and eyelids that would open and shut over very grown-up dark eyes. Moreover, when you moved her right arm up and down she said "Pa-pa," and when you moved the left she said "Ma-ma," very distinctly.

"I heard her say 'Pa' when she fell," said the under nurse, who heard everything. "But she ought to have said 'Pa-pa.'"

"That's because her arm went up when she hit the step," said the head nurse. "She'll say the other 'Pa' when I put it down again."

"Pa," said Nina, as her right arm was pushed down, and speaking through her broken face. It was cracked right across, from the upper corner of the forehead, with a hideous gash, through the nose and down to the little frilled collar of the pale green silk Mother Hubbard frock, and two little three-cornered pieces of porcelain had fallen out.

"I'm sure it's a wonder she can speak at all, being all smashed," said the under nurse.

"You'll have to take her to Mr. Puckler," said her superior. "It's not far, and you'd better go at once."

Lady Gwendolen was occupied in digging a hole in the ground with a little spade, and paid no attention to the nurses.

"What are you doing?" enquired the nursery-maid, looking on.

"Nina's dead, and I'm diggin' her a grave," replied her ladyship thoughtfully.

"Oh, she'll come to life again all right," said the nursery-maid.

The under nurse wrapped Nina up again and departed. Fortunately a kind soldier, with very long legs and a very small cap, happened to be there; and as he had nothing to do, he offered to see the under nurse safely to Mr. Puckler's and back.

Mr. Bernard Puckler and his little daughter lived in a little house in a little alley, which led out off a quiet little street not very far from Belgrave Square. He was the great doll doctor, and his extensive practice lay in the most aristocratic quarter. He mended dolls of all sizes and ages, boy dolls and girl dolls, baby dolls in long clothes, and grown-up dolls in fashionable gowns, talking dolls and dumb dolls, those that shut their eyes when they lay down, and those whose eyes had to be shut for them by means of a mysterious wire. His daughter Else was only just over twelve years old, but she was already very clever at mending dolls' clothes, and at doing their hair, which is harder than you might think, though the dolls sit quite still while it is being done.

Mr. Puckler had originally been a German, but he had dissolved his nationality in the ocean of London many years ago, like a great many foreigners. He still had one or two German friends, however, who came on Saturday evenings, and smoked with him and played picquet or "skat" with him for farthing points, and called him "Herr Doctor," which seemed to please Mr. Puckler very much.

He looked older than he was, for his beard was rather long and ragged, his hair was grizzled and thin, and he wore horn-rimmed spectacles. As for Else, she was a thin, pale child, very quiet and neat, with dark eyes and brown hair that was plaited down her back and tied with a bit of black ribbon. She mended the dolls' clothes and took the dolls back to their homes when they were quite strong again.

The house was a little one, but too big for the two people who lived in it. There was a small sitting-room on the street, and the workshop was at the back, and there were three rooms upstairs. But the father and daughter lived most of their time in the workshop, because they were generally at work, even in the evenings.

Mr. Puckler laid Nina on the table and looked at her a long time, till the tears began to fill his eyes behind the horn-rimmed spectacles. He was a very susceptible man, and he often fell in love with the dolls he mended, and found it hard to part with them when they had smiled at him for a few days. They were real little people to him, with characters and thoughts and feelings of their own, and he was very tender with them all. But some attracted him especially from the first, and when they were brought to him maimed and injured, their state seemed so pitiful to him that the tears came easily. You must remember that he had lived among dolls during a great part of his life, and understood them.

"How do you know that they feel nothing?" he went on to say to Else. "You must be gentle with them. It costs nothing to be kind to the little beings, and perhaps it makes a difference to them."

And Else understood him, because she was a child, and she knew that she was more to him than all the dolls.

He fell in love with Nina at first sight, perhaps because her beautiful brown glass eyes were something like Else's own, and he loved Else first and best, with all his heart. And, besides, it was a very sorrowful case. Nina had evidently not been long in the world, for her complexion was perfect, her hair was smooth where it should be smooth, and curly where it should be curly, and her silk clothes were perfectly new. But across her face was that frightful gash, like a sabre-cut, deep and shadowy within, but clean and sharp at the edges. When he tenderly pressed her head to close the gaping wound, the edges made a fine grating sound, that was painful to hear, and the lids of the dark eyes quivered and trembled as though Nina were suffering dreadfully.

"Poor Nina!" he exclaimed sorrowfully. "But I shall not hurt you much, though you will take a long time to get strong."

He always asked the names of the broken dolls when they were brought to him, and sometimes the people knew what the children called them, and told him. He liked "Nina" for a name. Altogether and in every way she pleased him more than any doll he had seen for many years, and he felt drawn to her, and made up his mind to make her perfectly strong and sound, no matter how much labour it might cost him.

Mr. Puckler worked patiently a little at a time, and Else watched him. She could do nothing for poor Nina, whose clothes needed no mending. The longer the doll doctor worked, the more fond he became of the yellow hair and the beautiful brown glass eyes. He sometimes forgot all the other dolls that were waiting to be mended, lying side by side on a shelf, and sat for an hour gazing at Nina's face, while he racked his ingenuity for some new invention by which to hide even the smallest trace of the terrible accident.

She was wonderfully mended. Even he was obliged to admit that; but the scar was still visible to his keen eyes, a very fine line right across the face, downwards from right to left. Yet all the conditions had been most favourable for a cure, since the cement had set quite hard at the first attempt and the weather had been fine and dry, which makes a great difference in a dolls' hospital.

At last he knew that he could do no more, and the under nurse had already come twice to see whether the job was finished, as she coarsely expressed it.

"Nina is not quite strong yet," Mr. Puckler had answered each time, for he could not make up his mind to face the parting.

And now he sat before the square deal table at which he worked, and Nina lay before him for the last time with a big brown paper box beside her. It stood there like her coffin, waiting for her, he thought. He must put her into it, and lay tissue paper over her dear face, and then put on the lid, and at the thought of tying the string his sight was dim with tears again. He was never to look into the glassy depths of the beautiful brown eyes any more, nor to hear the little wooden voice say "Pa-pa" and "Ma-ma." It was a very painful moment.

In the vain hope of gaining time before the separation, he took up the little sticky bottles of cement and glue and gum and colour, looking at each one in turn, and then at Nina's face. And all his small tools lay there, neatly arranged in a row, but he knew that he could not use them again for Nina. She was quite strong at last, and in a country where there should be no cruel children to hurt her she might live a hundred years, with only that almost imperceptible line across her face to tell of the fearful thing that had befallen her on the marble steps of Cranston House.

Suddenly Mr. Puckler's heart was quite full, and he rose abruptly from his seat and turned away.

"Else," he said unsteadily, "you must do it for me. I cannot bear to see her go into the box."

So he went and stood at the window with his back turned, while Else did what he had not the heart to do.

"Is it done?" he asked, not turning round. "Then take her away, my dear. Put on your hat, and take her to Cranston House quickly, and when you are gone I will turn round."

Else was used to her father's queer ways with the dolls, and though she had never seen him so much moved by a parting, she was not much surprised.

"Come back quickly," he said, when he heard her hand on the latch. "It is growing late, and I should not send you at this hour. But I cannot bear to look forward to it any more."

When Else was gone, he left the window and sat down in his place before the table again, to wait for the child to come back. He touched the place where Nina had lain, very gently, and he recalled the softly tinted pink face, and the glass eyes, and the ringlets of yellow hair, till he could almost see them.

The evenings were long, for it was late in the spring. But it began to grow dark soon, and Mr. Puckler wondered why Else did not come back. She had been gone an hour and a half, and that was much longer than he had expected, for it was barely half a mile from Belgrave Square to Cranston House. He reflected that the child might have been kept waiting, but as the twilight deepened he grew anxious, and walked up and down in the dim workshop, no longer thinking of Nina, but of Else, his own living child, whom he loved.

An undefinable, disquieting sensation came upon him by fine degrees, a chilliness and a faint stirring of his thin hair, joined with a wish to be in any company rather than to be alone much longer. It was the beginning of fear.

He told himself in strong German-English that he was a foolish old man, and he began to feel about for the matches in the dusk. He knew just where they should be, for he always kept them in the same place, close to the little tin box that held bits of sealing-wax of various colours, for some kinds of mending. But somehow he could not find the matches in the gloom.

Something had happened to Else, he was sure, and as his fear increased, he felt as though it might be allayed if he could get a light and see what time it was. Then he called himself a foolish old man again, and the sound of his own voice startled him in the dark. He could not find the matches.

The window was grey still; he might see what time it was if he went close to it, and he could go and get matches out of the cupboard afterwards. He stood back from the table, to get out of the way of the chair, and began to cross the board floor.

Something was following him in the dark. There was a small pattering, as of tiny feet upon the boards. He stopped and listened, and the roots of his hair tingled. It was nothing, and he was a foolish old man. He made two steps more, and he was sure that he heard the little pattering again. He turned his back to the window, leaning against the sash so that the panes began to crack, and he faced the dark. Everything was quite still, and it smelt of paste and cement and wood-filings as usual.

"Is that you, Else?" he asked, and he was surprised by the fear in his voice.

There was no answer in the room, and he held up his watch and tried to make out what time it was by the grey dusk that was just not darkness. So far as he could see, it was within two or three minutes of ten o'clock. He had been a long time alone. He was shocked, and frightened for Else, out in London, so late, and he almost ran across the room to the door. As he fumbled for the latch, he distinctly heard the running of the little feet after him.

"Mice!" he exclaimed feebly, just as he got the door open.

He shut it quickly behind him, and felt as though some cold thing had settled on his back and were writhing upon him. The passage was quite dark, but he found his hat and was out in the alley in a moment, breathing more freely, and surprised to find how much light there still was in the open air. He could see the pavement clearly under his feet, and far off in the street to which the alley led he could hear the laughter and calls of children, playing some game out of doors. He wondered how he could have been so nervous, and for an instant he thought of going back into the house to wait quietly for Else. But instantly he felt that nervous fright of something stealing over him again. In any case it was better to walk up to Cranston House and ask the servants about the child. One of the women had perhaps taken a fancy to her, and was even now giving her tea and cake.

He walked quickly to Belgrave Square, and then up the broad streets, listening as he went, whenever there was no other sound, for the tiny footsteps. But he heard nothing, and was laughing at himself when he rang the servants' bell at the big house. Of course, the child must be there.

The person who opened the door was quite an inferior person, for it was a back door, but affected the manners of the front, and stared at Mr. Puckler superciliously under the strong light.

No little girl had been seen, and he knew "nothing about no dolls."

"She is my little girl," said Mr. Puckler tremulously, for all his anxiety was returning tenfold, "and I am afraid something has happened."

The inferior person said rudely that "nothing could have happened to her in that house, because she had not been there, which was a jolly good reason why;" and Mr. Puckler was obliged to admit that the man ought to know, as it was his business to keep the door and let people in. He wished to be allowed to speak to the under nurse, who knew him; but the man was ruder than ever, and finally shut the door in his face.

When the doll doctor was alone in the street, he steadied himself by the railing, for he felt as though he were breaking in two, just as some dolls break, in the middle of the backbone.

Presently he knew that he must be doing something to find Else, and that gave him strength. He began to walk as quickly as he could through the streets, following every highway and byway which his little girl might have taken on her errand. He also asked several policemen in vain if they had seen her, and most of them answered him kindly, for they saw that he was a sober man and in his right senses, and some of them had little girls of their own.

It was one o'clock in the morning when he went up to his own door again, worn out and hopeless and broken-hearted. As he turned the key in the lock, his heart stood still, for he knew that he was awake and not dreaming, and that he really heard those tiny footsteps pattering to meet him inside the house along the passage.

But he was too unhappy to be much frightened any more, and his heart went on again with a dull regular pain, that found its way all through him with every pulse. So he went in, and hung up his hat in the dark, and found the matches in the cupboard and the candlestick in its place in the corner.

Mr. Puckler was so much overcome and so completely worn out that he sat down in his chair before the work-table and almost fainted, as his face dropped forward upon his folded hands. Beside him the solitary candle burned steadily with a low flame in the still warm air.

"Else! Else!" he moaned against his yellow knuckles. And that was all he could say, and it was no relief to him. On the contrary, the very sound of the name was a new and sharp pain that pierced his ears and his head and his very soul. For every time he repeated the name it meant that little Else was dead, somewhere out in the streets of London in the dark.

He was so terribly hurt that he did not even feel something pulling gently at the skirt of his old coat, so gently that it was like the nibbling of a tiny mouse. He might have thought that it was really a mouse if he had noticed it.

"Else! Else!" he groaned right against his hands.

Then a cool breath stirred his thin hair, and the low flame of the one candle dropped down almost to a mere spark, not flickering as though a draught were going to blow it out, but just dropping down as if it were tired out. Mr. Puckler felt his hands stiffening with fright under his face; and there was a faint rustling sound, like some small silk thing blown in a gentle breeze. He sat up straight, stark and scared, and a small wooden voice spoke in the stillness.

"Pa-pa," it said, with a break between the syllables.

Mr. Puckler stood up in a single jump, and his chair fell over backwards with a smashing noise upon the wooden floor. The candle had almost gone out.

It was Nina's doll voice that had spoken, and he should have known it among the voices of a hundred other dolls. And yet there was something more in it, a little human ring, with a pitiful cry and a call for help, and the wail of a hurt child. Mr. Puckler stood up, stark and stiff, and tried to look round, but at first he could not, for he seemed to be frozen from head to foot.

Then he made a great effort, and he raised one hand to each of his temples, and pressed his own head round as he would have turned a doll's. The candle was burning so low that it might as well have been out altogether, for any light it gave, and the room seemed quite dark at first. Then he saw something. He would not have believed that he could be more frightened than he had been just before that. But he was, and his knees shook, for he saw the doll standing in the middle of the floor, shining with a faint and ghostly radiance, her beautiful glassy brown eyes fixed on his. And across her face the very thin line of the break he had mended shone as though it were drawn in light with a fine point of white flame.

Yet there was something more in the eyes, too; there was something human, like Else's own, but as if only the doll saw him through them, and not Else. And there was enough of Else to bring back all his pain and to make him forget his fear.

"Else! my little Else!" he cried aloud.

The small ghost moved, and its doll-arm slowly rose and fell with a stiff, mechanical motion.

"Pa-pa," it said.

It seemed this time that there was even more of Else's tone echoing somewhere between the wooden notes that reached his ears so distinctly, and yet so far away. Else was calling him, he was sure.

His face was perfectly white in the gloom, but his knees did not shake any more, and he felt that he was less frightened.

"Yes, child! But where? Where?" he asked. "Where are you, Else?"

"Pa-pa!"

The syllables died away in the quiet room. There was a low rustling of silk, the glassy brown eyes turned slowly away, and Mr. Puckler heard the pitter-patter of the small feet in the bronze kid slippers as the figure ran straight to the door. Then the candle burned high again, the room was full of light, and he was alone.

Mr. Puckler passed his hand over his eyes and looked about him. He could see everything quite clearly, and he felt that he must have been dreaming, though he was standing instead of sitting down, as he should have been if he had just waked up. The candle burned brightly now. There were the dolls to be mended, lying in a row with their toes up. The third one had lost her right shoe, and Else was making one. He knew that, and he was certainly not dreaming now. He had not been dreaming when he had come in from his fruitless search and had heard the doll's footsteps running to the door. He had not fallen asleep in his chair. How could he possibly have fallen asleep when his heart was breaking? He had been awake all the time.

He steadied himself, set the fallen chair upon its legs, and said to himself again very emphatically that he was a foolish old man. He ought to be out in the streets looking for his child, asking questions, and enquiring at the police stations, where all accidents were reported as soon as they were known, or at the hospitals.

"Pa-pa!"

The longing, wailing, pitiful little wooden cry rang from the passage, outside the door, and Mr. Puckler stood for an instant with white face, transfixed and rooted to the spot. A moment later his hand was on the latch. Then he was in the passage, with the light streaming from the open door behind him.

Quite at the other end he saw the little phantom shining clearly in the shadow, and the right hand seemed to beckon to him as the arm rose and fell once more. He knew all at once that it had not come to frighten him but to lead him, and when it disappeared, and he walked boldly towards the door, he knew that it was in the street outside, waiting for him. He forgot that he was tired and had eaten no supper, and had walked many miles, for a sudden hope ran through and through him, like a golden stream of life.

And sure enough, at the corner of the alley, and at the corner of the street, and out in Belgrave Square, he saw the small ghost flitting before him. Sometimes it was only a shadow, where there was other light, but then the glare of the lamps made a pale green sheen on its little Mother Hubbard frock of silk; and sometimes, where the streets were dark and silent, the whole figure shone out brightly, with its yellow curls and rosy neck. It seemed to trot along like a tiny child, and Mr. Puckler could almost hear the pattering of the bronze kid slippers on the pavement as it ran. But it went very fast, and he could only just keep up with it, tearing along with his hat on the back of his head and his thin hair blown by the night breeze, and his horn-rimmed spectacles firmly set upon his broad nose.

On and on he went, and he had no idea where he was. He did not even care, for he knew certainly that he was going the right way.

Then at last, in a wide, quiet street, he was standing before a big, sober-looking door that had two lamps on each side of it, and a polished brass bell-handle, which he pulled.

And just inside, when the door was opened, in the bright light, there was the little shadow, and the pale green sheen of the little silk dress, and once more the small cry came to his ears, less pitiful, more longing.

"Pa-pa!"

The shadow turned suddenly bright, and out of the brightness the beautiful brown glass eyes were turned up happily to his, while the rosy mouth smiled so divinely that the phantom doll looked almost like a little angel just then.

"A little girl was brought in soon after ten o'clock," said the quiet voice of the hospital doorkeeper. "I think they thought she was only stunned. She was holding a big brown-paper box against her, and they could not get it out of her arms. She had a long plait of brown hair that hung down as they carried her."

"She is my little girl," said Mr. Puckler, but he hardly heard his own voice.

He leaned over Else's face in the gentle light of the children's ward, and when he had stood there a minute the beautiful brown eyes opened and looked up to his.

"Pa-pa!" cried Else, softly, "I knew you would come!"

Then Mr. Puckler did not know what he did or said for a moment, and what he felt was worth all the fear and terror and despair that had almost killed him that night. But by and by Else was telling her story, and the nurse let her speak, for there were only two other children in the room, who were getting well and were sound asleep.

"They were big boys with bad faces," said Else, "and they tried to get Nina away from me, but I held on and fought as well as I could till one of them hit me with something, and I don't remember any more, for I tumbled down, and I suppose the boys ran away, and somebody found me there. But I'm afraid Nina is all smashed."

"Here is the box," said the nurse. "We could not take it out of her arms till she came to herself. Should you like to see if the doll is broken?"

And she undid the string cleverly, but Nina was all smashed to pieces. Only the gentle light of the children's ward made a pale green sheen in the folds of the little Mother Hubbard frock.

SISTER MADDELENA

RALPH ADAMS CRAM

Across the valley of the Oreto from Monreale, on the slopes of the mountains just above the little village of Parco, lies the old convent of Sta. Catarina. From the cloister terrace at Monreale you can see its pale walls and the slim campanile of its chapel rising from the crowded citron and mulberry orchards that flourish, rank and wild, no longer cared for by pious and loving hands. From the rough road that climbs the mountains to Assunto, the convent is invisible, a gnarled and ragged olive grove intervening, and a spur of cliffs as well, while from Palermo one sees only the speck of white, flashing in the sun, indistinguishable from the many similar gleams of desert monastery or pauper village.

Partly because of this seclusion, partly by reason of its extreme beauty, partly, it may be, because the present owners are more than charming and gracious in their pressing hospitality, Sta. Catarina seems to preserve an element of the poetic, almost magical; and as I drove with the Cavaliere Valguanera one evening in March out of Palermo, along the garden valley of the Oreto, then up the mountain side where the warm light of the spring sunset swept across from Monreale, lying golden and mellow on the luxuriant growth of figs, and olives, and orange-trees, and fantastic cacti, and so up to where the path of the convent swung off to the right round a dizzy point of cliff that reached out gaunt and gray from the olives below,—as I drove thus in the balmy air, and saw of a sudden a vision of creamy walls and orange roofs, draped in fantastic festoons of roses, with a single curving palm-tree stuck black and feathery against the gold sunset, it is hardly to be wondered at that I should slip into a mood of visionary enjoyment, looking for a time on the whole thing as the misty phantasm of a summer dream.

The Cavaliere had introduced himself to us,—Tom Rendel and me,—one morning soon after we reached Palermo, when, in the first bewilderment of architects in this paradise of art and color, we were working nobly at our sketches in that dream of delight, the Capella Palatina. He was himself an amateur archæologist, he told us, and passionately devoted to his island; so he felt impelled to speak to any one whom he saw appreciating the almost—and in a way fortunately—unknown beauties of Palermo. In a little time we were fully acquainted, and talking like the oldest friends. Of course he knew acquaintances of Rendel's,—some one always does: this time they were officers on the tubby U. S. S. "Quinebaug," that, during the summer of 1888, was trying to uphold the maritime honor of the United States in European waters. Luckily for us, one of the officers was a kind of cousin of Rendel's, and came from Baltimore as well, so, as he had visited at the Cavaliere's place, we were soon invited to do the same. It was in this way that, with the luck that attends Rendel wherever he goes, we came to see something of domestic life in Italy, and that I found myself involved in another of those adventures for which I naturally sought so little.

I wonder if there is any other place in Sicily so faultless as Sta. Catarina? Taormina is a paradise, an epitome of all that is beautiful in Italy,—Venice excepted. Girgenti is a solemn epic, with its golden temples between the sea and hills. Cefalù is wild and strange, and Monreale a vision out of a fairy tale; but Sta. Catarina!—

Fancy a convent of creamy stone and rose-red brick perched on a ledge of rock midway between earth and heaven, the cliff falling almost sheer to the valley two hundred feet and more, the mountain rising behind straight towards the sky; all the rocks covered with cactus and dwarf fig-trees, the convent draped in smothering roses, and in front a terrace with a fountain in the midst; and then—nothing—between you and the sapphire sea, six miles away. Below stretches the Eden valley, the Concha d'Oro, gold-green fig orchards alternating with smoke-blue olives, the mountains rising on either hand and sinking undulously away towards the bay where, like a magic city of ivory and nacre, Palermo lies guarded by the twin mountains, Monte Pellegrino and Capo Zafferano, arid rocks like dull amethysts, rose in sunlight, violet in shadow: lions couchant, guarding the sleeping town.

Seen as we saw it for the first time that hot evening in March, with the golden lambent light pouring down through the valley, making it in verity a "shell of gold," sitting in Indian chairs on the terrace, with the perfume of roses and jasmines all around us, the valley of the Oreto, Palermo, Sta. Catarina, Monreale,—all were but parts of a dreamy vision, like the heavenly city of Sir Percivale, to attain which he passed across the golden bridge that burned after him as he vanished in the intolerable light of the Beatific Vision.

It was all so unreal, so phantasmal, that I was not surprised in the least when, late in the evening after the ladies had gone to their rooms, and the Cavaliere, Tom, and I were stretched out in chairs on the terrace, smoking lazily under the multitudinous stars, the Cavaliere said, "There is something I really must tell you both before you go to bed, so that you may be spared any unnecessary alarm."

"You are going to say that the place is haunted," said Rendel, feeling vaguely on the floor beside him for his glass of Amaro: "thank you; it is all it needs."

The Cavaliere smiled a little: "Yes, that is just it. Sta. Catarina is really haunted; and much as my reason revolts against the idea as superstitious and savoring of priestcraft, yet I must acknowledge I see no way of avoiding the admission. I do not presume to offer any explanations, I only state the fact; and the fact is that to-night one or other of you will, in all human—or unhuman—probability, receive a visit from Sister Maddelena. You need not be in the least afraid, the apparition is perfectly gentle and harmless; and, moreover, having seen it once, you will never see it again. No one sees the ghost, or whatever it is, but once, and that usually the first night he spends in the house. I myself saw the thing eight—nine years ago, when I first bought the place from the Marchese di Muxaro; all my people have seen it, nearly all my guests, so I think you may as well be prepared."

"Then tell us what to expect," I said; "what kind of a ghost is this nocturnal visitor?"

"It is simple enough. Some time to-night you will suddenly awake and see before you a Carmelite nun who will look fixedly at you, say distinctly and very sadly, 'I cannot sleep,' and then vanish. That is all, it is hardly worth speaking of, only some people are terribly frightened if they are visited unwarned by strange apparitions; so I tell you this that you may be prepared."

"This was a Carmelite convent, then?" I said.

"Yes; it was suppressed after the unification of Italy, and given to the House of Muxaro; but the family died out, and I bought it. There is a story about the ghostly nun, who was only a novice, and even that unwillingly, which gives an interest to an otherwise very commonplace and uninteresting ghost."

"I beg that you will tell it us," cried Rendel.

"There is a storm coming," I added. "See, the lightning is flashing already up among the mountains at the head of the valley; if the story is tragic, as it must be, now is just the time for it. You will tell it, will you not?"

The Cavaliere smiled that slow, cryptic smile of his that was so unfathomable.

"As you say, there is a shower coming, and as we have fierce tempests here, we might not sleep; so perhaps we may as well sit up a little longer, and I will tell you the story."

The air was utterly still, hot and oppressive; the rich, sick odor of the oranges just bursting into bloom came up from the valley in a gently rising tide. The sky, thick with stars, seemed mirrored in the rich foliage below, so numerous were the glow-worms under the still trees, and the fireflies that gleamed in the hot air. Lightning flashed fitfully from the darkening west; but as yet no thunder broke the heavy silence.

The Cavaliere lighted another cigar, and pulled a cushion under his head so that he could look down to the distant lights of the city. "This is the story," he said.

"Once upon a time, late in the last century, the Duca di Castiglione was attached to the court of Charles III, King of the Two Sicilies, down at Palermo. They tell me he was very ambitious, and, not content with marrying his son to one of the ladies of the House of Tuscany, had betrothed his only daughter, Rosalia, to Prince Antonio, a cousin of the king. His whole life was wrapped up in the fame of his family, and he quite forgot all domestic affection in his madness for dynastic glory. His son was a worthy scion, cold and proud; but Rosalia was, according to legend, utterly the reverse,—a passionate, beautiful girl, wilful and head-strong, and careless of her family and the world.

"The time had nearly come for her to marry Prince Antonio, a typical *roué* of the Spanish court, when, through the treachery of a servant, the Duke discovered that his daughter was in love with a young military officer whose name I don't remember, and that an elopement had been planned to take place the next night. The fury and dismay of the old autocrat passed belief; he saw in a flash the downfall of all his hopes of family aggrandizement through union with the royal house, and, knowing well the spirit of his daughter, despaired of ever bringing her to subjection. Nevertheless, he attacked her unmercifully, and, by bullying and threats, by imprisonment, and even bodily chastisement, he tried to break her spirit and bend her to his indomitable will. Through his power at court he had the lover sent away to the mainland, and for more than a year he held his daughter closely imprisoned in his palace on the Toledo,—that one, you may remember, on the right, just beyond the Via del Collegio dei Gesuiti, with the beautiful iron-work grilles at all the windows, and the painted frieze. But nothing could move her, nothing bend her stubborn will; and at last, furious at the girl he could not govern, Castiglione sent her to this convent, then one of the few houses of barefoot Carmelite nuns in Italy. He stipulated that she should take the name of Maddelena, that he should never hear of her again, and that she should be held an absolute prisoner in this conventual castle.

"Rosalia—or Sister Maddelena, as she was now—believed her lover dead, for her father had given her good proofs of this, and she believed him; nevertheless she refused to marry another, and seized upon the convent life as a blessed relief from the tyranny of her maniacal father.

"She lived here for four or five years; her name was forgotten at court and in her father's palace. Rosalia di Castiglione was dead, and only Sister Maddelena lived, a Carmelite nun, in her place.

"In 1798 Ferdinand IV found himself driven from his throne on the mainland, his kingdom divided, and he himself forced to flee to Sicily. With him came the lover of the dead Rosalia, now high in military honor. He on his part had thought Rosalia dead, and it was only by accident that he found that she still lived, a Carmelite nun. Then began the second act of the romance that until then had been only sadly commonplace, but now became dark and tragic. Michele—Michele Biscari,—that was his name; I remember now—haunted the region of the convent, striving to communicate with Sister Maddelena; and at last, from the cliffs over us, up there among the citrons—you will see by the next flash of lightning—he saw her in the great cloister, recognized her in her white habit, found her the same dark and splendid beauty of six years before, only made more beautiful by her white habit and her rigid life. By and by he found a day when she was alone, and tossed a ring to her as she stood in the midst of the cloister. She looked up, saw him, and from that moment lived only to love him in life as she had loved his memory in the death she had thought had overtaken him.

"With the utmost craft they arranged their plans together. They could not speak, for a word would have aroused the other inmates of the convent. They could make signs only when Sister Maddelena was alone. Michele could throw notes to her from the cliff,—a feat demanding a strong arm, as you will see, if you measure the distance with your eye,—and she could drop replies from the window over the cliff, which he picked up at the bottom. Finally he succeeded in casting into the cloister a coil of light rope. The girl fastened it to the bars of one of the windows, and—so great is the madness of love—Biscari actually climbed the rope from the valley to the window of the cell, a distance of almost two hundred feet, with but three little craggy resting-places in all that height. For nearly a month these nocturnal visits were undiscovered, and Michele had almost completed his arrangements for carrying the girl from Sta. Catarina and away to Spain, when unfortunately one of the sisters, suspecting some mystery, from the changed face of Sister Maddelena, began investigating, and at length discovered the rope neatly coiled up by the nun's window, and hidden under some clinging vines. She instantly told the Mother Superior; and together they watched from a window in the crypt of the chapel,—the only place, as you will see to-morrow, from which one could see the window of Sister Maddelena's cell. They saw the figure of Michele daringly ascending the slim rope; watched hour after hour, the Sister remaining while the Superior went to say the hours in the chapel, at each of which Sister Maddelena was present; and at last, at prime, just as the sun was rising, they saw the figure slip down the rope, watched the rope drawn up and concealed, and knew that Sister Maddelena was in their hands for vengeance and punishment,—a criminal.

"The next day, by the order of the Mother Superior, Sister Maddelena was imprisoned in one of the cells under the chapel, charged with her guilt, and commanded to make full and complete confession. But not a word would she say, although they offered her forgiveness if she would tell the name of her lover. At last the Superior told her that after this fashion would they act the coming night: she herself would be placed in the crypt, tied in front of the window, her mouth gagged; that the rope would be lowered, and the lover allowed to approach even to the sill of her window, and at that moment the rope would be cut, and before her eyes her lover would be dashed to death on the ragged cliffs. The plan was feasible, and Sister Maddelena knew that the Mother was perfectly capable of carrying it out. Her stubborn spirit was broken, and in the only way possible; she begged for mercy, for the sparing of her lover. The Mother Superior was deaf at first; at last she said, 'It is your life or his. I will spare him on condition that you sacrifice your own life.' Sister Maddelena accepted the terms joyfully, wrote a last farewell to Michele, fastened the note to the rope, and with her own hands cut the rope and saw it fall coiling down to the valley bed far below.

"Then she silently prepared for death; and at midnight, while her lover was wandering, mad with the horror of impotent fear, around the white walls of the convent, Sister Maddelena, for love of Michele, gave up her life. How, was never known. That she was indeed dead was only a suspicion, for when Biscari finally compelled the civil authorities to enter the convent, claiming that murder had been done there, they found no sign. Sister Maddelena had been sent to the parent house of the barefoot Carmelites at Avila in Spain, so the Superior stated, because of her incorrigible contumacy. The old Duke of Castiglione refused to stir hand or foot in the matter, and Michele, after fruitless attempts to prove that the Superior of Sta. Catarina had caused the death, was forced to leave Sicily. He sought in Spain for very long; but no sign of the girl was to be found, and at last he died, exhausted with suffering and sorrow.

"Even the name of Sister Maddelena was forgotten, and it was not until the convents were suppressed, and this house came into the hands of the Muxaros, that her story was remembered. It was then that the ghost began to appear; and, an explanation being necessary, the story, or legend, was obtained from one of the nuns who still lived after the suppression. I think the fact—for it is a fact—of the ghost rather goes to prove that Michele was right, and that poor Rosalia gave her life a sacrifice for love,—whether in accordance with the terms of the legend or not, I cannot say. One or the other of you will probably see her to-night. You might ask her for the facts. Well, that is all the story of Sister Maddelena, known in the world as Rosalia di Castiglione. Do you like it?"

"It is admirable," said Rendel, enthusiastically. "But I fancy I should rather look on it simply as a story, and not as a warning of what is going to happen. I don't much fancy real ghosts myself."

"But the poor Sister is quite harmless;" and Valguanera rose, stretching himself. "My servants say she wants a mass said over her, or something of that kind; but I haven't much love for such priestly hocus-pocus,—I beg your pardon" (turning to me), "I had forgotten that you were a Catholic: forgive my rudeness."

"My dear Cavaliere, I beg you not to apologize. I am sorry you cannot see things as I do; but don't for a moment think I am hypersensitive."

"I have an excuse,—perhaps you will say only an explanation; but I live where I see all the absurdities and corruptions of the Church."

"Perhaps you let the accidents blind you to the essentials; but do not let us quarrel to-night,—see, the storm is close on us. Shall we go in?"

The stars were blotted out through nearly all the sky; low, thunderous clouds, massed at the head of the valley, were sweeping over so close that they seemed to brush the black pines on the mountain above us. To the south and east the storm-clouds had shut down almost to the sea, leaving a space of black sky where the moon in its last quarter was rising just to the left of Monte Pellegrino,—a black silhouette against the pallid moonlight. The rosy lightning flashed almost incessantly, and through the fitful darkness came the sound of bells across the valley, the rushing torrent below, and the dull roar of the approaching rain, with a deep organ point of solemn thunder through it all.

We fled indoors from the coming tempest, and taking our candles, said "good-night," and sought each his respective room.

My own was in the southern part of the old convent, giving on the terrace we had just quitted, and about over the main doorway. The rushing storm, as it swept down the valley with the swelling torrent beneath, was very fascinating, and after wrapping myself in a dressing-gown I stood for some time by the deeply embrasured window, watching the blazing lightning and the beating rain whirled by fitful gusts of wind around the spurs of the mountains. Gradually the violence of the shower seemed to decrease, and I threw myself down on my bed in the hot air, wondering if I really was to experience the ghostly visit the Cavaliere so confidently predicted.

I had thought out the whole matter to my own satisfaction, and fancied I knew exactly what I should do, in case Sister Maddelena came to visit me. The story touched me: the thought of the poor faithful girl who sacrificed herself for her lover,—himself, very likely, quite unworthy,—and who now could never sleep for reason of her unquiet soul, sent out into the storm of eternity without spiritual aid or counsel. I could not sleep; for the still vivid lightning, the crowding thoughts of the dead nun, and the shivering anticipation of my possible visitation, made slumber quite out of the question. No suspicion of sleepiness had visited me, when, perhaps an hour after midnight, came a sudden vivid flash of lightning, and, as my dazzled eyes began to regain the power of sight, I saw her as plainly as in life,—a tall figure, shrouded in the white habit of the Carmelites, her head bent, her hands clasped before her. In another flash of lightning she slowly raised her head and looked at me long and earnestly. She was very beautiful, like the Virgin of Beltraffio in the National Gallery,—more beautiful than I had supposed possible, her deep, passionate eyes very tender and pitiful in their pleading, beseeching glance. I hardly think I was frightened, or even startled, but lay looking steadily at her as she stood in the beating lightning.

Then she breathed, rather than articulated, with a voice that almost brought tears, so infinitely sad and sorrowful was it, "I cannot sleep!" and the liquid eyes grew more pitiful and questioning as bright tears fell from them down the pale dark face.

The figure began to move slowly towards the door, its eyes fixed on mine with a look that was weary and almost agonized. I leaped from the bed and stood waiting. A look of utter gratitude swept over the face, and, turning, the figure passed through the doorway.

Out into the shadow of the corridor it moved, like a drift of pallid storm-cloud, and I followed, all natural and instinctive fear or nervousness quite blotted out by the part I felt I was to play in giving rest to a tortured soul. The corridors were velvet black; but the pale figure floated before me always, an unerring guide, now but a thin mist on the utter night, now white and clear in the bluish lightning through some window or doorway.

Down the stairway into the lower hall, across the refectory, where the great frescoed Crucifixion flared into sudden clearness under the fitful lightning, out into the silent cloister.

It was very dark. I stumbled along the heaving bricks, now guiding myself by a hand on the whitewashed wall, now by a touch on a column wet with the storm. From all the eaves the rain was dripping on to the pebbles at the foot of the arcade: a pigeon, startled from the capital where it was sleeping, beat its way into the cloister close. Still the white thing drifted before me to the farther side of the court, then along the cloister at right angles, and paused before one of the many doorways that led to the cells.

A sudden blaze of fierce lightning, the last now of the fleeting trail of storm, leaped around us, and in the vivid light I saw the white face turned again with the look of overwhelming desire, of beseeching pathos, that had choked my throat with an involuntary sob when first I saw Sister Maddelena. In the brief interval that ensued after the flash, and before the roaring thunder burst like the crash of battle over the trembling convent, I heard again the sorrowful words, "I cannot sleep," come from the impenetrable darkness. And when the lightning came again, the white figure was gone.

I wandered around the courtyard, searching in vain for Sister Maddelena, even until the moonlight broke through the torn and sweeping fringes of the storm. I tried the door where the white figure vanished: it was locked; but I had found what I sought, and, carefully noting its location, went back to my room, but not to sleep.

In the morning the Cavaliere asked Rendel and me which of us had seen the ghost, and I told him my story; then I asked him to grant me permission to sift the thing to the bottom; and he courteously gave the whole matter into my charge, promising that he would consent to anything.

I could hardly wait to finish breakfast; but no sooner was this done than, forgetting my morning pipe, I started with Rendel and the Cavaliere to investigate.

"I am sure there is nothing in that cell," said Valguanera, when we came in front of the door I had marked. "It is curious that you should have chosen the door of the very cell that tradition assigns to Sister Maddelena; but I have often examined that room myself, and I am sure that there is no chance for anything to be concealed. In fact, I had the floor taken up once, soon after I came here, knowing the room was that of the mysterious Sister, and thinking that there, if anywhere, the monastic crime would have taken place; still, we will go in, if you like."

He unlocked the door, and we entered, one of us, at all events, with a beating heart. The cell was very small, hardly eight feet square. There certainly seemed no opportunity for concealing a body in the tiny place; and although I sounded the floor and walls, all gave a solid, heavy answer,—the unmistakable sound of masonry.

For the innocence of the floor the Cavaliere answered. He had, he said, had it all removed, even to the curving surfaces of the vault below; yet somewhere in this room the body of the murdered girl was concealed,—of this I was certain. But where? There seemed no answer; and I was compelled to give up the search for the moment, somewhat to the amusement of Valguanera, who had watched curiously to see if I could solve the mystery.

But I could not forget the subject, and towards noon started on another tour of investigation. I procured the keys from the Cavaliere, and examined the cells adjoining; they were apparently the same, each with its window opposite the door, and nothing— Stay, were they the same? I hastened into the suspected cell; it was as I thought: this cell, being on the corner, could have had two windows, yet only one was visible, and that to the left, at right angles with the doorway. Was it imagination? As I sounded the wall opposite the door, where the other window should be, I fancied that the sound was a trifle less solid and dull. I was becoming excited. I dashed back to the cell on the right, and, forcing open the little window, thrust my head out.

It was found at last! In the smooth surface of the yellow wall was a rough space, following approximately the shape of the other cell windows, not plastered like the rest of the wall, but showing the shapes of bricks through its thick coatings of whitewash. I turned with a gasp of excitement and satisfaction: yes, the embrasure of the wall was deep enough; what a wall it was!—four feet at least, and the opening of the window reached to the floor, though the window itself was hardly three feet square. I felt absolutely certain that the secret was solved, and called the Cavaliere and Rendel, too excited to give them an explanation of my theories.

They must have thought me mad when I suddenly began scraping away at the solid wall in front of the door; but in a few minutes they understood what I was about, for under the coatings of paint and plaster appeared the original bricks; and as my architectural knowledge had led me rightly, the space I had cleared was directly over a vertical joint between firm, workmanlike masonry on one hand, and rough amateurish work on the other, bricks laid anyway, and without order or science.

Rendel seized a pick, and was about to assail the rude wall, when I stopped him.

"Let us be careful," I said; "who knows what we may find?" So we set to work digging out the mortar around a brick at about the level of our eyes.

How hard the mortar had become! But a brick yielded at last, and with trembling fingers I detached it. Darkness within, yet beyond question there was a cavity there, not a solid wall; and with infinite care we removed another brick. Still the hole was too small to admit enough light from the dimly illuminated cell. With a chisel we pried at the sides of a large block of masonry, perhaps eight bricks in size. It moved, and we softly slid it from its bed.

Valguanera, who was standing watching us as we lowered the bricks to the floor, gave a sudden cry, a cry like that of a frightened woman,—terrible, coming from him. Yet there was cause.

Framed by the ragged opening of the bricks, hardly seen in the dim light, was a face, an ivory image, more beautiful than any antique bust, but drawn and distorted by unspeakable agony: the lovely mouth half open, as though gasping for breath; the eyes cast upward; and below, slim chiselled hands crossed on the breast, but clutching the folds of the white Carmelite habit, torture and agony visible in every tense muscle, fighting against the determination of the rigid pose.

We stood there breathless, staring at the pitiful sight, fascinated, bewitched. So this was the secret. With fiendish ingenuity, the rigid ecclesiastics had blocked up the window, then forced the beautiful creature to stand in the alcove, while with remorseless hands and iron hearts they had shut her into a living tomb. I had read of such things in romance; but to find the verity here, before my eyes—

Steps came down the cloister, and with a simultaneous thought we sprang to the door and closed it behind us. The room was sacred; that awful sight was not for curious eyes. The gardener was coming to ask some trivial question of Valguanera. The Cavaliere cut him short. "Pietro, go down to Parco and ask Padre Stefano to come here at once." (I thanked him with a glance.) "Stay!" He turned to me: "Signore, it is already two o'clock and too late for mass, is it not?"

I nodded.

Valguanera thought a moment, then he said, "Bring two horses; the Signor Americano will go with you,—do you understand?" Then, turning to me, "You will go, will you not? I think you can explain matters to Padre Stefano better than I."

"Of course I will go, more than gladly." So it happened that after a hasty luncheon I wound down the mountain to Parco, found Padre Stefano, explained my errand to him, found him intensely eager and sympathetic, and by five o'clock had him back at the convent with all that was necessary for the resting of the soul of the dead girl.

In the warm twilight, with the last light of the sunset pouring into the little cell through the window where almost a century ago Rosalia had for the last time said farewell to her lover, we gathered together to speed her tortured soul on its journey, so long delayed. Nothing was omitted; all the needful offices of the Church were said by Padre Stefano, while the light in the window died away, and the flickering flames of the candles carried by two of the acolytes from San Francesco threw fitful flashes of pallid light into the dark recess where the white face had prayed to Heaven for a hundred years.

Finally, the Padre took the asperge from the hands of one of the acolytes, and with a sign of the cross in benediction while he chanted the *Asperges*, gently sprinkled the holy water on the upturned face. Instantly the whole vision crumbled to dust, the face was gone, and where once the candlelight had flickered on the perfect semblance of the girl dead so very long, it now fell only on the rough bricks which closed the window, bricks laid with frozen hearts by pitiless hands.

But our task was not done yet. It had been arranged that Padre Stefano should remain at the convent all night, and that as soon as midnight made it possible he should say the first mass for the repose of the girl's soul. We sat on the terrace talking over the strange events of the last crowded hours, and I noted with satisfaction that the Cavaliere no longer spoke of the Church with that hardness, which had hurt me so often. It is true that the Padre was with us nearly all the time; but not only was Valguanera courteous, he was almost sympathetic; and I wondered if it might not prove that more than one soul benefited by the untoward events of the day.

With the aid of the astonished and delighted servants, and no little help as well from Signora Valguanera, I fitted up the long cold Altar in the chapel, and by midnight we had the gloomy sanctuary beautiful with flowers and candles. It was a curiously solemn service, in the first hour of the new day, in the midst of blazing candles and the thick incense, the odor of the opening orange-blooms drifting up in the fresh morning air, and mingling with the incense smoke and the perfume of flowers within. Many prayers were said that night for the soul of the dead girl, and I think many afterwards; for after the benediction I remained for a little time in my place, and when I rose from my knees and went towards the chapel door, I saw a figure kneeling still, and, with a start, recognized the form of the Cavaliere. I smiled with quiet satisfaction and gratitude, and went away softly, content with the chain of events that now seemed finished.

The next day the alcove was again walled up, for the precious dust could not be gathered together for transportation to consecrated ground; so I went down to the little cemetery at Parco for a basket of earth, which we cast in over the ashes of Sister Maddelena.

By and by, when Rendel and I went away, with great regret, Valguanera came down to Palermo with us; and the last act that we performed in Sicily was assisting him to order a tablet of marble, whereon was carved this simple inscription:—

HERE LIES THE BODY OF
ROSALIA DI CASTIGLIONI,
CALLED
SISTER MADDELENA.
HER SOUL
IS WITH HIM WHO GAVE IT.

To this I added in thought:—

"Let him that is without sin among you cast the first stone."

THE SOUTHWEST CHAMBER

MARY ELEANOR WILKINS FREEMAN

"That school-teacher from Acton is coming to-day," said the elder Miss Gill, Sophia.

"So she is," assented the younger Miss Gill, Amanda.

"I have decided to put her in the southwest chamber," said Sophia.

Amanda looked at her sister with an expression of mingled doubt and terror. "You don't suppose she would—" she began hesitatingly.

"Would what?" demanded Sophia, sharply. She was more incisive than her sister. Both were below the medium height, and stout, but Sophia was firm where Amanda was flabby. Amanda wore a baggy old muslin (it was a hot day), and Sophia was uncompromisingly hooked up in a starched and boned cambric over her high shelving figure.

"I didn't know but she would object to sleeping in that room, as long as Aunt Harriet died there such a little time ago," faltered Amanda.

"Well!" said Sophia, "of all the silly notions! If you are going to pick out rooms in this house where nobody has died, for the boarders, you'll have your hands full. Grandfather Ackley had seven children; four of them died here to my certain knowledge, besides grandfather and grandmother. I think Great-grandmother Ackley, grandfather's mother, died here, too; she must have; and Great-grandfather Ackley, and grandfather's unmarried sister, Great-aunt Fanny Ackley. I don't believe there's a room nor a bed in this house that somebody hasn't passed away in."

"Well, I suppose I am silly to think of it, and she had better go in there," said Amanda.

"I know she had. The northeast room is small and hot, and she's stout and likely to feel the heat, and she's saved money and is able to board out summers, and maybe she'll come here another year if she's well accommodated," said Sophia. "Now I guess you'd better go in there and see if any dust has settled on anything since it was cleaned, and open the west windows and let the sun in, while I see to that cake."

Amanda went to her task in the southwest chamber while her sister stepped heavily down the back stairs on her way to the kitchen.

"It seems to me you had better open the bed while you air and dust, then make it up again," she called back.

"Yes, sister," Amanda answered, shudderingly.

Nobody knew how this elderly woman with the untrammeled imagination of a child dreaded to enter the southwest chamber, and yet she could not have told why she had the dread. She had entered and occupied rooms which had been once tenanted by persons now dead. The room which had been hers in the little house in which she and her sister had lived before coming here had been her dead mother's. She had never reflected upon the fact with anything but loving awe and reverence. There had never been any fear. But this was different. She entered and her heart beat thickly in her ears. Her hands were cold. The room was a very large one. The four windows, two facing south, two west, were closed, the blinds also. The room was in a film of green gloom. The furniture loomed out vaguely. The gilt frame of a blurred old engraving on the wall caught a little light. The white counterpane on the bed showed like a blank page.

Amanda crossed the room, opened with a straining motion of her thin back and shoulders one of the west windows, and threw back the blind. Then the room revealed itself an apartment full of an aged and worn but no less valid state. Pieces of old mahogany swelled forth; a peacock-patterned chintz draped the bedstead. This chintz also covered a great easy chair which had been the favourite seat of the former occupant of the room. The closet door stood ajar. Amanda noticed that with wonder. There was a glimpse of purple drapery floating from a peg inside the closet. Amanda went across and took down the garment hanging there. She wondered how her sister had happened to leave it when she cleaned the room. It was an old loose gown which had belonged to her aunt. She took it down, shuddering, and closed the closet door after a fearful glance into its dark depths. It was a long closet with a strong odour of lovage. The Aunt Harriet had had a habit of eating lovage and had carried it constantly in her pocket. There was very likely some of the pleasant root in the pocket of the musty purple gown which Amanda threw over the easy chair.

Amanda perceived the odour with a start as if before an actual presence. Odour seems in a sense a vital part of a personality. It can survive the flesh to which it has clung like a persistent shadow, seeming to have in itself something of the substance of that to which it pertained. Amanda was always conscious of this fragrance of lovage as she tidied the room. She dusted the heavy mahogany pieces punctiliously after she had opened the bed as her sister had directed. She spread fresh towels over the wash-stand and the bureau; she made the bed. Then she thought to take the purple gown from the easy chair and carry it to the garret and put it in the trunk with the other articles of the dead woman's wardrobe which had been packed away there; BUT THE PURPLE GOWN WAS NOT ON THE CHAIR!

Amanda Gill was not a woman of strong convictions even as to her own actions. She directly thought that possibly she had been mistaken and had not removed it from the closet. She glanced at the closet door and saw with surprise that it was open, and she had thought she had closed it, but she instantly was not sure of that. So she entered the closet and looked for the purple gown. IT WAS NOT THERE!

Amanda Gill went feebly out of the closet and looked at the easy chair again. The purple gown was not there! She looked wildly around the room. She went down on her trembling knees and peered under the bed, she opened the bureau drawers, she looked again in the closet. Then she stood in the middle of the floor and fairly wrung her hands.

"What does it mean?" she said in a shocked whisper.

She had certainly seen that loose purple gown of her dead Aunt Harriet's.

There is a limit at which self-refutation must stop in any sane person. Amanda Gill had reached it. She knew that she had seen that purple gown in that closet; she knew that she had removed it and put it on the easy chair. She also knew that she had not taken it out of the room. She felt a curious sense of being inverted mentally. It was as if all her traditions and laws of life were on their heads. Never in her simple record had any garment not remained where she had placed it unless removed by some palpable human agency.

Then the thought occurred to her that possibly her sister Sophia might have entered the room unobserved while her back was turned and removed the dress. A sensation of relief came over her. Her blood seemed to flow back into its usual channels; the tension of her nerves relaxed.

"How silly I am," she said aloud.

She hurried out and downstairs into the kitchen where Sophia was making cake, stirring with splendid circular sweeps of a wooden spoon a creamy yellow mass. She looked up as her sister entered.

"Have you got it done?" said she.

"Yes," replied Amanda. Then she hesitated. A sudden terror overcame her. It did not seem as if it were at all probable that Sophia had left that foamy cake mixture a second to go to Aunt Harriet's chamber and remove that purple gown.

"Well," said Sophia, "if you have got that done I wish you would take hold and string those beans. The first thing we know there won't be time to boil them for dinner."

Amanda moved toward the pan of beans on the table, then she looked at her sister.

"Did you come up in Aunt Harriet's room while I was there?" she asked weakly.

She knew while she asked what the answer would be.

"Up in Aunt Harriet's room? Of course I didn't. I couldn't leave this cake without having it fall. You know that well enough. Why?"

"Nothing," replied Amanda.

Suddenly she realized that she could not tell her sister what had happened, for before the utter absurdity of the whole thing her belief in her own reason quailed. She knew what Sophia would say if she told her. She could hear her.

"Amanda Gill, have you gone stark staring mad?"

She resolved that she would never tell Sophia. She dropped into a chair and begun shelling the beans with nerveless fingers. Sophia looked at her curiously.

"Amanda Gill, what on earth ails you?" she asked.

"Nothing," replied Amanda. She bent her head very low over the green pods.

"Yes, there is, too! You are as white as a sheet, and your hands are shaking so you can hardly string those beans. I did think you had more sense, Amanda Gill."

"I don't know what you mean, Sophia."

"Yes, you do know what I mean, too; you needn't pretend you don't. Why did you ask me if I had been in that room, and why do you act so queer?"

Amanda hesitated. She had been trained to truth. Then she lied.

"I wondered if you'd noticed how it had leaked in on the paper over by the bureau, that last rain," said she.

"What makes you look so pale then?"

"I don't know. I guess the heat sort of overcame me."

"I shouldn't think it could have been very hot in that room when it had been shut up so long," said Sophia.

She was evidently not satisfied, but then the grocer came to the door and the matter dropped.

For the next hour the two women were very busy. They kept no servant. When they had come into possession of this fine old place by the death of their aunt it had seemed a doubtful blessing. There was not a cent with which to pay for repairs and taxes and insurance, except the twelve hundred dollars which they had obtained from the sale of the little house in which they had been born and lived all their lives. There had been a division in the old Ackley family years before. One of the daughters had married against her mother's wish and had been disinherited. She had married a poor man by the name of Gill, and shared his humble lot in sight of her former home and her sister and mother living in prosperity, until she had borne three daughters; then she died, worn out with overwork and worry.

The mother and the elder sister had been pitiless to the last. Neither had ever spoken to her since she left her home the night of her marriage. They were hard women.

The three daughters of the disinherited sister had lived quiet and poor, but not actually needy lives. Jane, the middle daughter, had married, and died in less than a year. Amanda and Sophia had taken the girl baby she left when the father married again. Sophia had taught a primary school for many years; she had saved enough to buy the little house in which they lived. Amanda had crocheted lace, and embroidered flannel, and made tidies and pincushions, and had earned enough for her clothes and the child's, little Flora Scott.

Their father, William Gill, had died before they were thirty, and now in their late middle life had come the death of the aunt to whom they had never spoken, although they had often seen her, who had lived in solitary state in the old Ackley mansion until she was more than eighty. There had been no will, and they were the only heirs with the exception of young Flora Scott, the daughter of the dead sister.

Sophia and Amanda thought directly of Flora when they knew of the inheritance.

"It will be a splendid thing for her; she will have enough to live on when we are gone," Sophia said.

She had promptly decided what was to be done. The small house was to be sold, and they were to move into the old Ackley house and take boarders to pay for its keeping. She scouted the idea of selling it. She had an enormous family pride. She had always held her head high when she had walked past that fine old mansion, the cradle of her race, which she was forbidden to enter. She was unmoved when the lawyer who was advising her disclosed to her the fact that Harriet Ackley had used every cent of the Ackley money.

"I realize that we have to work," said she, "but my sister and I have determined to keep the place."

That was the end of the discussion. Sophia and Amanda Gill had been living in the old Ackley house a fortnight, and they had three boarders: an elderly widow with a comfortable income, a young congregationalist clergyman, and the middle-aged single woman who had charge of the village library. Now the school-teacher from Acton, Miss Louisa Stark, was expected for the summer, and would make four.

Sophia considered that they were comfortably provided for. Her wants and her sister's were very few, and even the niece, although a young girl, had small expenses, since her wardrobe was supplied for years to come from that of the deceased aunt. There were stored away in the garret of the Ackley house enough voluminous black silks and satins and bombazines to keep her clad in somber richness for years to come.

Flora was a very gentle girl, with large, serious blue eyes, a seldom-smiling, pretty mouth, and smooth flaxen hair. She was delicate and very young—sixteen on her next birthday.

She came home soon now with her parcels of sugar and tea from the grocer's. She entered the kitchen gravely and deposited them on the table by which her Aunt Amanda was seated stringing beans. Flora wore an obsolete turban-shaped hat of black straw which had belonged to the dead aunt; it set high like a crown, revealing her forehead. Her dress was an ancient purple-and-white print, too long and too large except over the chest, where it held her like a straight waistcoat.

"You had better take off your hat, Flora," said Sophia. She turned suddenly to Amanda. "Did you fill the water-pitcher in that chamber for the schoolteacher?" she asked severely. She was quite sure that Amanda had not filled the water-pitcher.

Amanda blushed and started guiltily. "I declare, I don't believe I did," said she.

"I didn't think you had," said her sister with sarcastic emphasis.

"Flora, you go up to the room that was your Great-aunt Harriet's, and take the water-pitcher off the wash-stand and fill it with water. Be real careful, and don't break the pitcher, and don't spill the water."

"In THAT chamber?" asked Flora. She spoke very quietly, but her face changed a little.

"Yes, in that chamber," returned her Aunt Sophia sharply. "Go right along."

Flora went, and her light footstep was heard on the stairs. Very soon she returned with the blue-and-white water-pitcher and filled it carefully at the kitchen sink.

"Now be careful and not spill it," said Sophia as she went out of the room carrying it gingerly.

Amanda gave a timidly curious glance at her; she wondered if she had seen the purple gown.

Then she started, for the village stagecoach was seen driving around to the front of the house. The house stood on a corner.

"Here, Amanda, you look better than I do; you go and meet her," said Sophia. "I'll just put the cake in the pan and get it in the oven and I'll come. Show her right up to her room."

Amanda removed her apron hastily and obeyed. Sophia hurried with her cake, pouring it into the baking-tins. She had just put it in the oven, when the door opened and Flora entered carrying the blue water-pitcher.

"What are you bringing down that pitcher again for?" asked Sophia.

"She wants some water, and Aunt Amanda sent me," replied Flora.

Her pretty pale face had a bewildered expression.

"For the land sake, she hasn't used all that great pitcherful of water so quick?"

"There wasn't any water in it," replied Flora.

Her high, childish forehead was contracted slightly with a puzzled frown as she looked at her aunt.

"Wasn't any water in it?"

"No, ma'am."

"Didn't I see you filling the pitcher with water not ten minutes ago, I want to know?"

"Yes, ma'am."

"What did you do with that water?"

"Nothing."

"Did you carry that pitcherful of water up to that room and set it on the washstand?"

"Yes, ma'am."

"Didn't you spill it?"

"No, ma'am."

"Now, Flora Scott, I want the truth! Did you fill that pitcher with water and carry it up there, and wasn't there any there when she came to use it?"

"Yes, ma'am."

"Let me see that pitcher." Sophia examined the pitcher. It was not only perfectly dry from top to bottom, but even a little dusty. She turned severely on the young girl. "That shows," said she, "you did not fill the pitcher at all. You let the water run at the side because you didn't want to carry it upstairs. I am ashamed of you. It's bad enough to be so lazy, but when it comes to not telling the truth—"

The young girl's face broke up suddenly into piteous confusion, and her blue eyes became filmy with tears.

"I did fill the pitcher, honest," she faltered, "I did, Aunt Sophia. You ask Aunt Amanda."

"I'll ask nobody. This pitcher is proof enough. Water don't go off and leave the pitcher dusty on the inside if it was put in ten minutes ago. Now you fill that pitcher full quick, and you carry it upstairs, and if you spill a drop there'll be something besides talk."

Flora filled the pitcher, with the tears falling over her cheeks. She sniveled softly as she went out, balancing it carefully against her slender hip. Sophia followed her.

"Stop crying," said she sharply; "you ought to be ashamed of yourself. What do you suppose Miss Louisa Stark will think. No water in her pitcher in the first place, and then you come back crying as if you didn't want to get it."

In spite of herself, Sophia's voice was soothing. She was very fond of the girl. She followed her up the stairs to the chamber where Miss Louisa Stark was waiting for the water to remove the soil of travel. She had removed her bonnet, and its tuft of red geraniums lightened the obscurity of the mahogany dresser. She had placed her little beaded cape carefully on the bed. She was replying to a tremulous remark of Amanda's, who was nearly fainting from the new mystery of the water-pitcher, that it was warm and she suffered a good deal in warm weather.

Louisa Stark was stout and solidly built. She was much larger than either of the Gill sisters. She was a masterly woman inured to command from years of school-teaching. She carried her swelling bulk with majesty; even her face, moist and red with the heat, lost nothing of its dignity of expression.

She was standing in the middle of the floor with an air which gave the effect of her standing upon an elevation. She turned when Sophia and Flora, carrying the water-pitcher, entered.

"This is my sister Sophia," said Amanda tremulously.

Sophia advanced, shook hands with Miss Louisa Stark and bade her welcome and hoped she would like her room. Then she moved toward the closet. "There is a nice large closet in this room—the best closet in the house. You might have your trunk—" she said, then she stopped short.

The closet door was ajar, and a purple garment seemed suddenly to swing into view as if impelled by some wind.

"Why, here is something left in this closet," Sophia said in a mortified tone. "I thought all those things had been taken away."

She pulled down the garment with a jerk, and as she did so Amanda passed her in a weak rush for the door.

"I am afraid your sister is not well," said the school-teacher from Acton. "She looked very pale when you took that dress down. I noticed it at once. Hadn't you better go and see what the matter is? She may be going to faint."

"She is not subject to fainting spells," replied Sophia, but she followed Amanda.

She found her in the room which they occupied together, lying on the bed, very pale and gasping. She leaned over her.

"Amanda, what is the matter; don't you feel well?" she asked.

"I feel a little faint."

Sophia got a camphor bottle and began rubbing her sister's forehead.

"Do you feel better?" she said.

Amanda nodded.

"I guess it was that green apple pie you ate this noon," said Sophia. "I declare, what did I do with that dress of Aunt Harriet's? I guess if you feel better I'll just run and get it and take it up garret. I'll stop in here again when I come down. You'd better lay still. Flora can bring you up a cup of tea. I wouldn't try to eat any supper."

Sophia's tone as she left the room was full of loving concern. Presently she returned; she looked disturbed, but angrily so. There was not the slightest hint of any fear in her expression.

"I want to know," said she, looking sharply and quickly around, "if I brought that purple dress in here, after all?"

"I didn't see you," replied Amanda.

"I must have. It isn't in that chamber, nor the closet. You aren't lying on it, are you?"

"I lay down before you came in," replied Amanda.

"So you did. Well, I'll go and look again."

Presently Amanda heard her sister's heavy step on the garret stairs. Then she returned with a queer defiant expression on her face.

"I carried it up garret, after all, and put it in the trunk," said she. "I declare, I forgot it. I suppose your being faint sort of put it out of my head. There it was, folded up just as nice, right where I put it."

Sophia's mouth was set; her eyes upon her sister's scared, agitated face were full of hard challenge.

"Yes," murmured Amanda.

"I must go right down and see to that cake," said Sophia, going out of the room. "If you don't feel well, you pound on the floor with the umbrella."

Amanda looked after her. She knew that Sophia had not put that purple dress of her dead Aunt Harriet in the trunk in the garret.

Meantime Miss Louisa Stark was settling herself in the southwest chamber. She unpacked her trunk and hung her dresses carefully in the closet. She filled the bureau drawers with nicely folded linen and small articles of dress. She was a very punctilious woman. She put on a black India silk dress with purple flowers. She combed her grayish-blond hair in smooth ridges back from her broad forehead. She pinned her lace at her throat with a brooch, very handsome, although somewhat obsolete—a bunch of pearl grapes on black onyx, set in gold filagree. She had purchased it several years ago with a considerable portion of the stipend from her spring term of school-teaching.

As she surveyed herself in the little swing mirror surmounting the old-fashioned mahogany bureau she suddenly bent forward and looked closely at the brooch. It seemed to her that something was wrong with it. As she looked she became sure. Instead of the familiar bunch of pearl grapes on the black onyx, she saw a knot of blonde and black hair under glass surrounded by a border of twisted gold. She felt a thrill of horror, though she could not tell why. She unpinned the brooch, and it was her own familiar one, the pearl grapes and the onyx. "How very foolish I am," she thought. She thrust the pin in the laces at her throat and again looked at herself in the glass, and there it was again—the knot of blond and black hair and the twisted gold.

Louisa Stark looked at her own large, firm face above the brooch and it was full of terror and dismay which were new to it. She straightway began to wonder if there could be anything wrong with her mind. She remembered that an aunt of her mother's had been insane. A sort of fury with herself possessed her. She stared at the brooch in the glass with eyes at once angry and terrified. Then she removed it again and there was her own old brooch. Finally she thrust the gold pin through the lace again, fastened it and turning a defiant back on the glass, went down to supper.

At the supper table she met the other boarders—the elderly widow, the young clergyman and the middle-aged librarian. She viewed the elderly widow with reserve, the clergyman with respect, the middle-aged librarian with suspicion. The latter wore a very youthful shirt-waist, and her hair in a girlish fashion which the school-teacher, who twisted hers severely from the straining roots at the nape of her neck to the small, smooth coil at the top, condemned as straining after effects no longer hers by right.

The librarian, who had a quick acridness of manner, addressed her, asking what room she had, and asked the second time in spite of the school-teacher's evident reluctance to hear her. She even, since she sat next to her, nudged her familiarly in her rigid black silk side.

"What room are you in, Miss Stark?" said she.

"I am at a loss how to designate the room," replied Miss Stark stiffly.

"Is it the big southwest room?"

"It evidently faces in that direction," said Miss Stark.

The librarian, whose name was Eliza Lippincott, turned abruptly to Miss Amanda Gill, over whose delicate face a curious colour compounded of flush and pallour was stealing.

"What room did your aunt die in, Miss Amanda?" asked she abruptly.

Amanda cast a terrified glance at her sister, who was serving a second plate of pudding for the minister.

"That room," she replied feebly.

"That's what I thought," said the librarian with a certain triumph. "I calculated that must be the room she died in, for it's the best room in the house, and you haven't put anybody in it before. Somehow the room that anybody has died in lately is generally the last room that anybody is put in. I suppose YOU are so strong-minded you don't object to sleeping in a room where anybody died a few weeks ago?" she inquired of Louisa Stark with sharp eyes on her face.

"No, I do not," replied Miss Stark with emphasis.

"Nor in the same bed?" persisted Eliza Lippincott with a kittenish reflection.

The young minister looked up from his pudding. He was very spiritual, but he had had poor pickings in his previous boarding place, and he could not help a certain abstract enjoyment over Miss Gill's cooking.

"You would certainly not be afraid, Miss Lippincott?" he remarked, with his gentle, almost caressing inflection of tone. "You do not for a minute believe that a higher power would allow any manifestation on the part of a disembodied spirit—who we trust is in her heavenly home—to harm one of His servants?"

"Oh, Mr. Dunn, of course not," replied Eliza Lippincott with a blush. "Of course not. I never meant to imply—"

"I could not believe you did," said the minister gently. He was very young, but he already had a wrinkle of permanent anxiety between his eyes and a smile of permanent ingratiation on his lips. The lines of the smile were as deeply marked as the wrinkle.

"Of course dear Miss Harriet Gill was a professing Christian," remarked the widow, "and I don't suppose a professing Christian would come back and scare folks if she could. I wouldn't be a mite afraid to sleep in that room; I'd rather have it than the one I've got. If I was afraid to sleep in a room where a good woman died, I wouldn't tell of it. If I saw things or heard things I'd think the fault must be with my own guilty conscience." Then she turned to Miss Stark. "Any time you feel timid in that room I'm ready and willing to change with you," said she.

"Thank you; I have no desire to change. I am perfectly satisfied with my room," replied Miss Stark with freezing dignity, which was thrown away upon the widow.

"Well," said she, "any time, if you should feel timid, you know what to do. I've got a real nice room; it faces east and gets the morning sun, but it isn't so nice as yours, according to my way of thinking. I'd rather take my chances any day in a room anybody had died in than in one that was hot in summer. I'm more afraid of a sunstroke than of spooks, for my part."

Miss Sophia Gill, who had not spoken one word, but whose mouth had become more and more rigidly compressed, suddenly rose from the table, forcing the minister to leave a little pudding, at which he glanced regretfully.

Miss Louisa Stark did not sit down in the parlour with the other boarders. She went straight to her room. She felt tired after her journey, and meditated a loose wrapper and writing a few letters quietly before she went to bed. Then, too, she was conscious of a feeling that if she delayed, the going there at all might assume more terrifying proportions. She was full of defiance against herself and her own lurking weakness.

So she went resolutely and entered the southwest chamber. There was through the room a soft twilight. She could dimly discern everything, the white satin scroll-work on the wall paper and the white counterpane on the bed being most evident. Consequently both arrested her attention first. She saw against the wall-paper directly facing the door the waist of her best black satin dress hung over a picture.

"That is very strange," she said to herself, and again a thrill of vague horror came over her.

She knew, or thought she knew, that she had put that black satin dress waist away nicely folded between towels in her trunk. She was very choice of her black satin dress.

She took down the black waist and laid it on the bed preparatory to folding it, but when she attempted to do so she discovered that the two sleeves were firmly sewed together. Louisa Stark stared at the sewed sleeves. "What does this mean?" she asked herself. She examined the sewing carefully; the stitches were small, and even, and firm, of black silk.

She looked around the room. On the stand beside the bed was something which she had not noticed before: a little old-fashioned work-box with a picture of a little boy in a pinafore on the top. Beside this work-box lay, as if just laid down by the user, a spool of black silk, a pair of scissors, and a large steel thimble with a hole in the top, after an old style. Louisa stared at these, then at the sleeves of her dress. She moved toward the door. For a moment she thought that this was something legitimate about which she might demand information; then she became doubtful. Suppose that work-box had been there all the time; suppose she had forgotten; suppose she herself had done this absurd thing, or suppose that she had not, what was to hinder the others from thinking so; what was to hinder a doubt being cast upon her own memory and reasoning powers?

Louisa Stark had been on the verge of a nervous breakdown in spite of her iron constitution and her great will power. No woman can teach school for forty years with absolute impunity. She was more credulous as to her own possible failings than she had ever been in her whole life. She was cold with horror and terror, and yet not so much horror and terror of the supernatural as of her own self. The weakness of belief in the supernatural was nearly impossible for this strong nature. She could more easily believe in her own failing powers.

"I don't know but I'm going to be like Aunt Marcia," she said to herself, and her fat face took on a long rigidity of fear.

She started toward the mirror to unfasten her dress, then she remembered the strange circumstance of the brooch and stopped short. Then she straightened herself defiantly and marched up to the bureau and looked in the glass. She saw reflected therein, fastening the lace at her throat, the old-fashioned thing of a large oval, a knot of fair and black hair under glass, set in a rim of twisted gold. She unfastened it with trembling fingers and looked at it. It was her own brooch, the cluster of pearl grapes on black onyx. Louisa Stark placed the trinket in its little box on the nest of pink cotton and put it away in the bureau drawer. Only death could disturb her habit of order.

Her fingers were so cold they felt fairly numb as she unfastened her dress; she staggered when she slipped it over her head. She went to the closet to hang it up and recoiled. A strong smell of lovage came in her nostrils; a purple gown near the door swung softly against her face as if impelled by some wind from within. All the pegs were filled with garments not her own, mostly of somber black, but there were some strange-patterned silk things and satins.

Suddenly Louisa Stark recovered her nerve. This, she told herself, was something distinctly tangible. Somebody had been taking liberties with her wardrobe. Somebody had been hanging some one else's clothes in her closet. She hastily slipped on her dress again and marched straight down to the parlour. The people were seated there; the widow and the minister were playing backgammon. The librarian was watching them. Miss Amanda Gill was mending beside the large lamp on the centre table. They all looked up with amazement as Louisa Stark entered. There was something strange in her expression. She noticed none of them except Amanda.

"Where is your sister?" she asked peremptorily of her.

"She's in the kitchen mixing up bread," Amanda quavered; "is there anything—" But the school-teacher was gone.

She found Sophia Gill standing by the kitchen table kneading dough with dignity. The young girl Flora was bringing some flour from the pantry. She stopped and stared at Miss Stark, and her pretty, delicate young face took on an expression of alarm.

Miss Stark opened at once upon the subject in her mind.

"Miss Gill," said she, with her utmost school-teacher manner, "I wish to inquire why you have had my own clothes removed from the closet in my room and others substituted?"

Sophia Gill stood with her hands fast in the dough, regarding her. Her own face paled slowly and reluctantly, her mouth stiffened.

"What? I don't quite understand what you mean, Miss Stark," said she.

"My clothes are not in the closet in my room and it is full of things which do not belong to me," said Louisa Stark.

"Bring me that flour," said Sophia sharply to the young girl, who obeyed, casting timid, startled glances at Miss Stark as she passed her. Sophia Gill began rubbing her hands clear of the dough. "I am sure I know nothing about it," she said with a certain tempered asperity. "Do you know anything about it, Flora?"

"Oh, no, I don't know anything about it, Aunt Sophia," answered the young girl, fluttering.

Then Sophia turned to Miss Stark. "I'll go upstairs with you, Miss Stark," said she, "and see what the trouble is. There must be some mistake." She spoke stiffly with constrained civility.

"Very well," said Miss Stark with dignity. Then she and Miss Sophia went upstairs. Flora stood staring after them.

Sophia and Louisa Stark went up to the southwest chamber. The closet door was shut. Sophia threw it open, then she looked at Miss Stark. On the pegs hung the schoolteacher's own garments in ordinary array.

"I can't see that there is anything wrong," remarked Sophia grimly.

Miss Stark strove to speak but she could not. She sank down on the nearest chair. She did not even attempt to defend herself. She saw her own clothes in the closet. She knew there had been no time for any human being to remove those which she thought she had seen and put hers in their places. She knew it was impossible. Again the awful horror of herself overwhelmed her.

"You must have been mistaken," she heard Sophia say.

She muttered something, she scarcely knew what. Sophia then went out of the room. Presently she undressed and went to bed. In the morning she did not go down to breakfast, and when Sophia came to inquire, requested that the stage be ordered for the noon train. She said that she was sorry, but was ill, and feared lest she might be worse, and she felt that she must return home at once. She looked ill, and could not take even the toast and tea which Sophia had prepared for her. Sophia felt a certain pity for her, but it was largely mixed with indignation. She felt that she knew the true reason for the school-teacher's illness and sudden departure, and it incensed her.

"If folks are going to act like fools we shall never be able to keep this house," she said to Amanda after Miss Stark had gone; and Amanda knew what she meant.

Directly the widow, Mrs. Elvira Simmons, knew that the school-teacher had gone and the southwest room was vacant, she begged to have it in exchange for her own. Sophia hesitated a moment; she eyed the widow sharply. There was something about the large, roseate face worn in firm lines of humour and decision which reassured her.

"I have no objection, Mrs. Simmons," said she, "if—"

"If what?" asked the widow.

"If you have common sense enough not to keep fussing because the room happens to be the one my aunt died in," said Sophia bluntly.

"Fiddlesticks!" said the widow, Mrs. Elvira Simmons.

That very afternoon she moved into the southwest chamber. The young girl Flora assisted her, though much against her will.

"Now I want you to carry Mrs. Simmons' dresses into the closet in that room and hang them up nicely, and see that she has everything she wants," said Sophia Gill. "And you can change the bed and put on fresh sheets. What are you looking at me that way for?"

"Oh, Aunt Sophia, can't I do something else?"

"What do you want to do something else for?"

"I am afraid."

"Afraid of what? I should think you'd hang your head. No; you go right in there and do what I tell you."

Pretty soon Flora came running into the sitting-room where Sophia was, as pale as death, and in her hand she held a queer, old-fashioned frilled nightcap.

"What's that?" demanded Sophia.

"I found it under the pillow."

"What pillow?"

"In the southwest room."

Sophia took it and looked at it sternly.

"It's Great-aunt Harriet's," said Flora faintly.

"You run down street and do that errand at the grocer's for me and I'll see that room," said Sophia with dignity. She carried the nightcap away and put it in the trunk in the garret where she had supposed it stored with the rest of the dead woman's belongings. Then she went into the southwest chamber and made the bed and assisted Mrs. Simmons to move, and there was no further incident.

The widow was openly triumphant over her new room. She talked a deal about it at the dinner-table.

"It is the best room in the house, and I expect you all to be envious of me," said she.

"And you are sure you don't feel afraid of ghosts?" said the librarian.

"Ghosts!" repeated the widow with scorn. "If a ghost comes I'll send her over to you. You are just across the hall from the southwest room."

"You needn't," returned Eliza Lippincott with a shudder. "I wouldn't sleep in that room, after—" she checked herself with an eye on the minister.

"After what?" asked the widow.

"Nothing," replied Eliza Lippincott in an embarrassed fashion.

"I trust Miss Lippincott has too good sense and too great faith to believe in anything of that sort," said the minister.

"I trust so, too," replied Eliza hurriedly.

"You did see or hear something—now what was it, I want to know?" said the widow that evening when they were alone in the parlour. The minister had gone to make a call.

Eliza hesitated.

"What was it?" insisted the widow.

"Well," said Eliza hesitatingly, "if you'll promise not to tell."

"Yes, I promise; what was it?"

"Well, one day last week, just before the school-teacher came, I went in that room to see if there were any clouds. I wanted to wear my gray dress, and I was afraid it was going to rain, so I wanted to look at the sky at all points, so I went in there, and—"

"And what?"

"Well, you know that chintz over the bed, and the valance, and the easy chair; what pattern should you say it was?"

"Why, peacocks on a blue ground. Good land, I shouldn't think any one who had ever seen that would forget it."

"Peacocks on a blue ground, you are sure?"

"Of course I am. Why?"

"Only when I went in there that afternoon it was not peacocks on a blue ground; it was great red roses on a yellow ground."

"Why, what do you mean?"

"What I say."

"Did Miss Sophia have it changed?"

"No. I went in there again an hour later and the peacocks were there."

"You didn't see straight the first time."

"I expected you would say that."

"The peacocks are there now; I saw them just now."

"Yes, I suppose so; I suppose they flew back."

"But they couldn't."

"Looks as if they did."

"Why, how could such a thing be? It couldn't be."

"Well, all I know is those peacocks were gone for an hour that afternoon and the red roses on the yellow ground were there instead."

The widow stared at her a moment, then she began to laugh rather hysterically.

"Well," said she, "I guess I sha'n't give up my nice room for any such tomfoolery as that. I guess I would just as soon have red roses on a yellow ground as peacocks on a blue; but there's no use talking, you couldn't have seen straight. How could such a thing have happened?"

"I don't know," said Eliza Lippincott; "but I know I wouldn't sleep in that room if you'd give me a thousand dollars."

"Well, I would," said the widow, "and I'm going to."

When Mrs. Simmons went to the southwest chamber that night she cast a glance at the bed-hanging and the easy chair. There were the peacocks on the blue ground. She gave a contemptuous thought to Eliza Lippincott.

"I don't believe but she's getting nervous," she thought. "I wonder if any of her family have been out at all."

But just before Mrs. Simmons was ready to get into bed she looked again at the hangings and the easy chair, and there were the red roses on the yellow ground instead of the peacocks on the blue. She looked long and sharply. Then she shut her eyes, and then opened them and looked. She still saw the red roses. Then she crossed the room, turned her back to the bed, and looked out at the night from the south window. It was clear and the full moon was shining. She watched it a moment sailing over the dark blue in its nimbus of gold. Then she looked around at the bed hangings. She still saw the red roses on the yellow ground.

Mrs. Simmons was struck in her most vulnerable point. This apparent contradiction of the reasonable as manifested in such a commonplace thing as chintz of a bed-hanging affected this ordinarily unimaginative woman as no ghostly appearance could have done. Those red roses on the yellow ground were to her much more ghostly than any strange figure clad in the white robes of the grave entering the room.

She took a step toward the door, then she turned with a resolute air. "As for going downstairs and owning up I'm scared and having that Lippincott girl crowing over me, I won't for any red roses instead of peacocks. I guess they can't hurt me, and as long as we've both of us seen 'em I guess we can't both be getting loony," she said.

Mrs. Elvira Simmons blew out her light and got into bed and lay staring out between the chintz hangings at the moonlit room. She said her prayers in bed always as being more comfortable, and presumably just as acceptable in the case of a faithful servant with a stout habit of body. Then after a little she fell asleep; she was of too practical a nature to be kept long awake by anything which had no power of actual bodily effect upon her. No stress of the spirit had ever disturbed her slumbers. So she slumbered between the red roses, or the peacocks, she did not know which.

But she was awakened about midnight by a strange sensation in her throat. She had dreamed that some one with long white fingers was strangling her, and she saw bending over her the face of an old woman in a white cap. When she waked there was no old woman, the room was almost as light as day in the full moonlight, and looked very peaceful; but the strangling sensation at her throat continued, and besides that, her face and ears felt muffled. She put up her hand and felt that her head was covered with a ruffled nightcap tied under her chin so tightly that it was exceedingly uncomfortable. A great qualm of horror shot over her. She tore the thing off frantically and flung it from her with a convulsive effort as if it had been a spider. She gave, as she did so, a quick, short scream of terror. She sprang out of bed and was going toward the door, when she stopped.

It had suddenly occurred to her that Eliza Lippincott might have entered the room and tied on the cap while she was asleep. She had not locked her door. She looked in the closet, under the bed; there was no one there. Then she tried to open the door, but to her astonishment found that it was locked—bolted on the inside. "I must have locked it, after all," she reflected with wonder, for she never locked her door. Then she could scarcely conceal from herself that there was something out of the usual about it all. Certainly no one could have entered the room and departed locking the door on the inside. She could not control the long shiver of horror that crept over her, but she was still resolute. She resolved that she would throw the cap out of the window. "I'll see if I have tricks like that played on me, I don't care who does it," said she quite aloud. She was still unable to believe wholly in the supernatural. The idea of some human agency was still in her mind, filling her with anger.

She went toward the spot where she had thrown the cap—she had stepped over it on her way to the door—but it was not there. She searched the whole room, lighting her lamp, but she could not find the cap. Finally she gave it up. She extinguished her lamp and went back to bed. She fell asleep again, to be again awakened in the same fashion. That time she tore off the cap as before, but she did not fling it on the floor as before. Instead she held to it with a fierce grip. Her blood was up.

Holding fast to the white flimsy thing, she sprang out of bed, ran to the window which was open, slipped the screen, and flung it out; but a sudden gust of wind, though the night was calm, arose and it floated back in her face. She brushed it aside like a cobweb and she clutched at it. She was actually furious. It eluded her clutching fingers. Then she did not see it at all. She examined the floor, she lighted her lamp again and searched, but there was no sign of it.

Mrs. Simmons was then in such a rage that all terror had disappeared for the time. She did not know with what she was angry, but she had a sense of some mocking presence which was silently proving too strong against her weakness, and she was aroused to the utmost power of resistance. To be baffled like this and resisted by something which was as nothing to her straining senses filled her with intensest resentment.

Finally she got back into bed again; she did not go to sleep. She felt strangely drowsy, but she fought against it. She was wide awake, staring at the moonlight, when she suddenly felt the soft white strings of the thing tighten around her throat and realized that her enemy was again upon her. She seized the strings, untied them, twitched off the cap, ran with it to the table where her scissors lay and furiously cut it into small bits. She cut and tore, feeling an insane fury of gratification.

"There!" said she quite aloud. "I guess I sha'n't have any more trouble with this old cap."

She tossed the bits of muslin into a basket and went back to bed. Almost immediately she felt the soft strings tighten around her throat. Then at last she yielded, vanquished. This new refutal of all laws of reason by which she had learned, as it were, to spell her theory of life, was too much for her equilibrium. She pulled off the clinging strings feebly, drew the thing from her head, slid weakly out of bed, caught up her wrapper and hastened out of the room. She went noiselessly along the hall to her own old room: she entered, got into her familiar bed, and lay there the rest of the night shuddering and listening, and if she dozed, waking with a start at the feeling of the pressure upon her throat to find that it was not there, yet still to be unable to shake off entirely the horror.

When daylight came she crept back to the southwest chamber and hurriedly got some clothes in which to dress herself. It took all her resolution to enter the room, but nothing unusual happened while she was there. She hastened back to her old chamber, dressed herself and went down to breakfast with an imperturbable face. Her colour had not faded. When asked by Eliza Lippincott how she had slept, she replied with an appearance of calmness which was bewildering that she had not slept very well. She never did sleep very well in a new bed, and she thought she would go back to her old room.

Eliza Lippincott was not deceived, however, neither were the Gill sisters, nor the young girl, Flora. Eliza Lippincott spoke out bluntly.

"You needn't talk to me about sleeping well," said she. "I know something queer happened in that room last night by the way you act."

They all looked at Mrs. Simmons, inquiringly—the librarian with malicious curiosity and triumph, the minister with sad incredulity, Sophia Gill with fear and indignation, Amanda and the young girl with unmixed terror. The widow bore herself with dignity.

"I saw nothing nor heard nothing which I trust could not have been accounted for in some rational manner," said she.

"What was it?" persisted Eliza Lippincott.

"I do not wish to discuss the matter any further," replied Mrs. Simmons shortly. Then she passed her plate for more creamed potato. She felt that she would die before she confessed to the ghastly absurdity of that nightcap, or to having been disturbed by the flight of peacocks off a blue field of chintz after she had scoffed at the possibility of such a thing. She left the whole matter so vague that in a fashion she came off the mistress of the situation. She at all events impressed everybody by her coolness in the face of no one knew what nightly terror.

After breakfast, with the assistance of Amanda and Flora, she moved back into her old room. Scarcely a word was spoken during the process of moving, but they all worked with trembling haste and looked guilty when they met one another's eyes, as if conscious of betraying a common fear.

That afternoon the young minister, John Dunn, went to Sophia Gill and requested permission to occupy the southwest chamber that night.

"I don't ask to have my effects moved there," said he, "for I could scarcely afford a room so much superior to the one I now occupy, but

I would like, if you please, to sleep there to-night for the purpose of refuting in my own person any unfortunate superstition which may have obtained root here."

Sophia Gill thanked the minister gratefully and eagerly accepted his offer.

"How anybody with common sense can believe for a minute in any such nonsense passes my comprehension," said she.

"It certainly passes mine how anybody with Christian faith can believe in ghosts," said the minister gently, and Sophia Gill felt a certain feminine contentment in hearing him. The minister was a child to her; she regarded him with no tincture of sentiment, and yet she loved to hear two other women covertly condemned by him and she herself thereby exalted.

That night about twelve o'clock the Reverend John Dunn essayed to go to his nightly slumber in the southwest chamber. He had been sitting up until that hour preparing his sermon.

He traversed the hall with a little night-lamp in his hand, opened the door of the southwest chamber, and essayed to enter. He might as well have essayed to enter the solid side of a house. He could not believe his senses. The door was certainly open; he could look into the room full of soft lights and shadows under the moonlight which streamed into the windows. He could see the bed in which he had expected to pass the night, but he could not enter. Whenever he strove to do so he had a curious sensation as if he were trying to press against an invisible person who met him with a force of opposition impossible to overcome. The minister was not an athletic man, yet he had considerable strength. He squared his elbows, set his mouth hard, and strove to push his way through into the room. The opposition which he met was as sternly and mutely terrible as the rocky fastness of a mountain in his way.

For a half hour John Dunn, doubting, raging, overwhelmed with spiritual agony as to the state of his own soul rather than fear, strove to enter that southwest chamber. He was simply powerless against this uncanny obstacle. Finally a great horror as of evil itself came over him. He was a nervous man and very young. He fairly fled to his own chamber and locked himself in like a terror-stricken girl.

The next morning he went to Miss Gill and told her frankly what had happened, and begged her to say nothing about it lest he should have injured the cause by the betrayal of such weakness, for he actually had come to believe that there was something wrong with the room.

"What it is I know not, Miss Sophia," said he, "but I firmly believe, against my will, that there is in that room some accursed evil power at work, of which modern faith and modern science know nothing."

Miss Sophia Gill listened with grimly lowering face. She had an inborn respect for the clergy, but she was bound to hold that southwest chamber in the dearly beloved old house of her fathers free of blame.

"I think I will sleep in that room myself to-night," she said, when the minister had finished.

He looked at her in doubt and dismay.

"I have great admiration for your faith and courage, Miss Sophia," he said, "but are you wise?"

"I am fully resolved to sleep in that room to-night," said she conclusively. There were occasions when Miss Sophia Gill could put on a manner of majesty, and she did now.

It was ten o'clock that night when Sophia Gill entered the southwest chamber. She had told her sister what she intended doing and had been proof against her tearful entreaties. Amanda was charged not to tell the young girl, Flora.

"There is no use in frightening that child over nothing," said Sophia.

Sophia, when she entered the southwest chamber, set the lamp which she carried on the bureau, and began moving about the rooms pulling down the curtains, taking off the nice white counterpane of the bed, and preparing generally for the night.

As she did so, moving with great coolness and deliberation, she became conscious that she was thinking some thoughts that were foreign to her. She began remembering what she could not have remembered, since she was not then born: the trouble over her mother's marriage, the bitter opposition, the shutting the door upon her, the ostracizing her from heart and home. She became aware of a most singular sensation as of bitter resentment herself, and not against the mother and sister who had so treated her own mother, but against her own mother, and then she became aware of a like bitterness extended to her own self. She felt malignant toward her mother as a young girl whom she remembered, though she could not have remembered, and she felt malignant toward her own self, and her sister Amanda, and Flora. Evil suggestions surged in her brain—suggestions which turned her heart to stone and which still fascinated her. And all the time by a sort of double consciousness she knew that what she thought was strange and not due to her own volition. She knew that she was thinking the thoughts of some other person, and she knew who. She felt herself possessed.

But there was tremendous strength in the woman's nature. She had inherited strength for good and righteous self-assertion, from the evil strength of her ancestors. They had turned their own weapons against themselves. She made an effort which seemed almost mortal, but was conscious that the hideous thing was gone from her. She thought her own thoughts. Then she scouted to herself the idea of anything supernatural about the terrific experience. "I am imagining everything," she told herself. She went on with her preparations; she went to the bureau to take down her hair. She looked in the glass and saw, instead of her softly parted waves of hair, harsh lines of iron-gray under the black borders of an old-fashioned head-dress. She saw instead of her smooth, broad forehead, a high one wrinkled with the intensest concentration of selfish reflections of a long life; she saw instead of her steady blue eyes, black ones with depths of malignant reserve, behind a broad meaning of ill will; she saw instead of her firm, benevolent mouth one with a hard, thin line, a network of melancholic wrinkles. She saw instead of her own face, middle-aged and good to see, the expression of a life of honesty and good will to others and patience under trials, the face of a very old woman scowling forever with unceasing hatred and misery at herself and all others, at life, and death, at that which had been and that which was to come. She saw instead of her own face in the glass, the face of her dead Aunt Harriet, topping her own shoulders in her own well-known dress!

Sophia Gill left the room. She went into the one which she shared with her sister Amanda. Amanda looked up and saw her standing there. She had set the lamp on a table, and she stood holding a handkerchief over her face. Amanda looked at her with terror.

"What is it? What is it, Sophia?" she gasped.

Sophia still stood with the handkerchief pressed to her face.

"Oh, Sophia, let me call somebody. Is your face hurt? Sophia, what is the matter with your face?" fairly shrieked Amanda.

Suddenly Sophia took the handkerchief from her face.

"Look at me, Amanda Gill," she said in an awful voice.

Amanda looked, shrinking.

"What is it? Oh, what is it? You don't look hurt. What is it, Sophia?"

"What do you see?"

"Why, I see you."

"Me?"

"Yes, you. What did you think I would see?"

Sophia Gill looked at her sister. "Never as long as I live will I tell you what I thought you would see, and you must never ask me," said she.

"Well, I never will, Sophia," replied Amanda, half weeping with terror.

"You won't try to sleep in that room again, Sophia?"

"No," said Sophia; "and I am going to sell this house."

IN THE TUBE

EDWARD FREDERIC BENSON

'It's a convention,' said Anthony Carling cheerfully, 'and not a very convincing one. Time, indeed! There's no such thing as Time really; it has no actual existence. Time is nothing more than an infinitesimal point in eternity, just as space is an infinitesimal point in infinity. At the most, Time is a sort of tunnel through which we are accustomed to believe that we are travelling.

'There's a roar in our ears and a darkness in our eyes which makes it seem real to us. But before we came into the tunnel we existed for ever in an infinite sunlight, and after we have got through it we shall exist in an infinite sunlight again. So why should we bother ourselves about the confusion and noise and darkness which only encompass us for a moment?'

For a firm-rooted believer in such immeasurable ideas as these, which he punctuated with brisk application of the poker to the brave sparkle and glow of the fire, Anthony has a very pleasant appreciation of the measurable and the finite, and nobody with whom I have acquaintance has so keen a zest for life and its enjoyments as he. He had given us this evening an admirable dinner, had passed round a port beyond praise, and had illuminated the jolly hours with the light of his infectious optimism. Now the small company had melted away, and I was left with him over the fire in his study. Outside the tattoo of wind-driven sleet was audible on the window-panes, over-scoring now and again the flap of the flames on the open hearth, and the thought of the chilly blasts and the snow-covered pavement in Brompton Square, across which, to skidding taxicabs, the last of his other guests had scurried, made my position, resident here till tomorrow morning, the more delicately delightful. Above all there was this stimulating and suggestive companion, who, whether he talked of the great abstractions which were so intensely real and practical to him, or of the very remarkable experiences which he had encountered among these conventions of time and space, was equally fascinating to the listener.

'I adore life,' he said. 'I find it the most entrancing plaything. It's a delightful game, and, as you know very well, the only conceivable way to play a game is to treat it extremely seriously. If you say to yourself, "It's only a game," you cease to take the slightest interest in it. You have to know that it's only a game, and behave as if it was the one object of existence. I should like it to go on for many years yet. But all the time one has to be living on the true plane as well, which is eternity and infinity. If you come to think of it, the one thing which the human mind cannot grasp is the finite, not the infinite, the temporary, not the eternal.'

'That sounds rather paradoxical,' said I.

'Only because you've made a habit of thinking about things that seem bounded and limited.

'Look it in the face for a minute. Try to imagine finite Time and Space, and you find you can't.

'Go back a million years, and multiply that million of years by another million, and you find that you can't conceive of a beginning. What happened before that beginning? Another beginning and another beginning? And before that? Look at it like that, and you find that the only solution comprehensible to you is the existence of an eternity, something that never began and will never end. It's the same about space. Project yourself to the farthest star, and what comes beyond that?

'Emptiness? Go on through the emptiness, and you can't imagine it being finite and having an end. It must needs go on for ever: that's the only thing you can understand. There's no such thing as before or after, or beginning or end, and what a comfort that is! I should fidget myself to death if there wasn't the huge soft cushion of eternity to lean one's head against. Some people say – I believe I've heard you say it yourself – that the idea of eternity is so tiring; you feel that you want to stop. But that's because you are thinking of eternity in terms of Time, and mumbling in your brain, "And after that, and after that?" Don't you grasp the idea that in eternity there isn't any "after," any more than there is any "before"? It's all one. Eternity isn't a quantity: it's a quality.'

Sometimes, when Anthony talks in this manner, I seem to get a glimpse of that which to his mind is so transparently clear and solidly real, at other times (not having a brain that readily envisages abstractions) I feel as though he was pushing me over a precipice, and my intellectual faculties grasp wildly at anything tangible or comprehensible. This was the case now, and I hastily interrupted.

'But there is a "before" and "after,"' I said. 'A few hours ago you gave us an admirable dinner, and after that – yes, after – we played bridge. And now you are going to explain things a little more clearly to me, and after that I shall go to bed—'

He laughed.

'You shall do exactly as you like,' he said, 'and you shan't be a slave to Time either to-night or tomorrow morning. We won't even mention an hour for breakfast, but you shall have it in eternity whenever you awake. And as I see it is not midnight yet, we'll slip the bonds of Time, and talk quite infinitely. I will stop the clock, if that will assist you in getting rid of your illusion, and then I'll tell you a story, which to my mind, shows how unreal so-called realities are; or, at any rate, how fallacious are our senses as judges of what is real and what is not.'

'Something occult, something spookish?' I asked, pricking up my ears, for Anthony has the strangest clairvoyances and visions of things unseen by the normal eye.

'I suppose you might call some of it occult,' he said, 'though there's a certain amount of rather grim reality mixed up in it.'

'Go on; excellent mixture,' said I.

He threw a fresh log on the fire.

'It's a longish story,' he said. 'You may stop me as soon as you have had enough. But there will come a point for which I claim your consideration. You, who cling to your "before" and "after," has it ever occurred to you how difficult it is to say when an incident takes place? Say that a man commits some crime of violence, can we not, with a good deal of truth, say that he really commits that crime when he definitely plans and determines upon it, dwelling on it with gusto? The actual commission of it, I think we can reasonably argue, is the mere material sequel of his resolve: he is guilty of it when he makes that determination. When, therefore, in the term of "before" and "after," does the crime truly take place? There is also in my story a further point for your consideration. For it seems certain that the spirit of a man, after the death of his body, is obliged to reenact such a crime, with a view, I suppose we may guess, to his remorse and his eventual redemption. Those who have second sight have seen such reenactments. Perhaps he may have done his deed blindly in this life; but then his spirit recommits it with its spiritual eyes open, and able to comprehend its enormity. So, shall we view the man's original determination and the material commission of his crime only as preludes to the real commission of it, when with eyes unsealed he does it and repents of it? ... That all sounds very obscure when I speak in the abstract, but I think you will see what I mean, if you follow my tale. Comfortable? Got everything you want? Here goes, then.'

He leaned back in his chair, concentrating his mind, and then spoke:

'The story that I am about to tell you,' he said, 'had its beginning a month ago, when you were away in Switzerland. It reached its conclusion, so I imagine, last night. I do not, at any rate expect to experience any more of it. Well, a month ago I was returning late on a very wet night from dining out. There was not a taxi to be had, and I hurried through the pouring rain to the tube-station at Piccadilly Circus, and thought myself very lucky to catch the last train in this direction. The carriage into which I stepped was quite empty except for one other passenger, who sat next the door immediately opposite to me. I had never, to my knowledge, seen him before, but I found my attention vividly fixed on him, as if he somehow concerned me. He was a man of middle age, in dress-clothes, and his face wore an expression of intense thought, as if in his mind he was pondering some very significant matter, and his hand which was resting on his knee clenched and unclenched itself. Suddenly he looked up and stared me in the face, and I saw there suspicion and fear, as if I had surprised him in some secret deed.

'At that moment we stopped at Dover Street, and the conductor threw open the doors, announced the station and added, "Change here for Hyde Park Corner and Gloucester Road." That was all right for me since it meant that the train would stop at Brompton Road, which was my destination. It was all right apparently, too, for my companion, for he certainly did not get out, and after a moment's stop, during which no one else got in, we went on. I saw him, I must insist, after the doors were closed and the train had started. But when I looked again, as we rattled on, I saw that there was no one there. I was quite alone in the carriage.

'Now you may think that I had had one of those swift momentary dreams which flash in and out of the mind in the space of a second, but I did not believe it was so myself, for I felt that I had experienced some sort of premonition or clairvoyant vision. A man, the semblance of whom, astral body or whatever you may choose to call it, I had just seen, would sometime sit in that seat opposite to me, pondering and planning.'

'But why?' I asked. 'Why should it have been the astral body of a living man which you thought you had seen? Why not the ghost of a dead one?'

'Because of my own sensations. The sight of the spirit of someone dead, which has occurred to me two or three times in my life, has always been accompanied by a physical shrinking and fear, and by the sensation of cold and of loneliness. I believed, at any rate, that I had seen a phantom of the living, and that impression was confirmed, I might say proved, the next day. For I met the man himself. And the next night, as you shall hear, I met the phantom again. We will take them in order.

'I was lunching, then, the next day with my neighbour Mrs. Stanley: there was a small party, and when I arrived we waited but for the final guest. He entered while I was talking to some friend, and presently at my elbow I heard Mrs. Stanley's voice – "Let me introduce you to Sir Henry Payle," she said.

'I turned and saw my vis-à-vis of the night before. It was quite unmistakably he, and as we shook hands he looked at me I thought with vague and puzzled recognition.

'"Haven't we met before, Mr. Carling?" he said. 'I seem to recollect—'

'For the moment I forgot the strange manner of his disappearance from the carriage, and thought that it had been the man himself whom I had seen last night.

'"Surely, and not so long ago," I said. "For we sat opposite each other in the last tube-train from Piccadilly Circus yesterday night."

'He still looked at me, frowning, puzzled, and shook his head.

'"That can hardly be," he said. "I only came up from the country this morning."

'Now this interested me profoundly, for the astral body, we are told, abides in some half-conscious region of the mind or spirit, and has recollections of what has happened to it, which it can convey only very vaguely and dimly to the conscious mind. All lunch-time I could see his eyes again and again directed to me with the same puzzled and perplexed air, and as I was taking my departure he came up to me.

'"I shall recollect some day," he said, "where we met before, and I hope we may meet again. Was it not—?" – and he stopped. "No: it has gone from me," he added.'

The log that Anthony had thrown on the fire was burning bravely now, and its high-flickering flame lit up his face.

'Now, I don't know whether you believe in coincidences as chance things,' he said, 'but if you do, get rid of the notion. Or if you can't at once, call it a coincidence that that very night I again caught the last train on the tube going westwards. This time, so far from my being a solitary passenger, there was a considerable crowd waiting at Dover Street, where I entered, and just as the noise of the approaching train began to reverberate in the tunnel I caught sight of Sir Henry Payle standing near the opening from which the train would presently emerge, apart from the rest of the crowd. And I thought to myself how odd it was that I should have seen the phantom of him at this very hour last night and the man himself now, and I began walking towards him with the idea of saying, "Anyhow, it is in the tube that we meet to-night." … And then a terrible and awful thing happened. Just as the train emerged from the tunnel he jumped down on to the line in front of it, and the train swept along over him up the platform.

'For a moment I was stricken with horror at the sight, and I remember covering my eyes against the dreadful tragedy. But then I perceived that, though it had taken place in full sight of those who were waiting, no one seemed to have seen it except myself. The driver, looking out from his window, had not applied his brakes, there was no jolt from the advancing train, no scream, no cry, and the rest of the passengers began boarding the train with perfect nonchalance.

'I must have staggered, for I felt sick and faint with what I had seen, and some kindly soul put his arm round me and supported me into the train. He was a doctor, he told me, and asked if I was in pain, or what ailed me. I told him what I thought I had seen, and he assured me that no such accident had taken place.

'It was clear then to my own mind that I had seen the second act, so to speak, in this psychical drama, and I pondered next morning over the problem as to what I should do. Already I had glanced at the morning paper, which, as I knew would be the case, contained no mention whatever of what I had seen. The thing had certainly not happened, but I knew in myself that it would happen. The flimsy veil of Time had been withdrawn from my eyes, and I had seen into what you would call the future. In terms of Time of course it was the future, but from my point of view the thing was just as much in the past as it was in the future. It existed, and waited only for its material fulfilment. The more I thought about it, the more I saw that I could do nothing.'

I interrupted his narrative.

'You did nothing?' I exclaimed. 'Surely you might have taken some step in order to try to avert the tragedy.'

He shook his head.

'What step precisely?' he said. 'Was I to go to Sir Henry and tell him that once more I had seen him in the tube in the act of committing suicide? Look at it like this. Either what I had seen was pure illusion, pure imagination, in which case it had no existence or significance at all, or it was actual and real, and essentially it had happened. Or take it, though not very logically, somewhere between the two. Say that the idea of suicide, for some cause of which I knew nothing, had occurred to him or would occur. Should I not, if that was the case, be doing a very dangerous thing, by making such a suggestion to him? Might not the fact of my telling him what I had seen put the idea into his mind, or, if it was already there, confirm it and strengthen it? "It's a ticklish matter to play with souls," as Browning says.'

'But it seems so inhuman not to interfere in any way,' said I, 'not to make any attempt.'

'What interference?' asked he. 'What attempt?'

The human instinct in me still seemed to cry aloud at the thought of doing nothing to avert such a tragedy, but it seemed to be beating itself against something austere and inexorable. And cudgel my brain as I would, I could not combat the sense of what he had said. I had no answer for him, and he went on.

'You must recollect, too,' he said, 'that I believed then and believe now that the thing had happened. The cause of it, whatever that was, had begun to work, and the effect, in this material sphere, was inevitable. That is what I alluded to when, at the beginning of my story, I asked you to consider how difficult it was to say when an action took place. You still hold that this particular action, this suicide of Sir Henry, had not yet taken place, because he had not yet thrown himself under the advancing train. To me that seems a materialistic view. I hold that in all but the endorsement of it, so to speak, it had taken place. I fancy that Sir Henry, for instance, now free from the material dusks, knows that himself.'

Exactly as he spoke there swept through the warm lit room a current of ice-cold air, ruffling my hair as it passed me, and making the wood flames on the hearth to dwindle and flare. I looked round to see if the door at my back had opened, but nothing stirred there, and over the closed window the curtains were fully drawn. As it reached Anthony, he sat up quickly in his chair and directed his glance this way and that about the room.

'Did you feel that?' he asked.

'Yes: a sudden draught,' I said. 'Ice-cold.'

'Anything else?' he asked. 'Any other sensation?'

I paused before I answered, for at the moment there occurred to me Anthony's differentiation of the effects produced on the beholder by a phantasm of the living and the apparition of the dead. It was the latter which accurately described my sensations now, a certain physical shrinking, a fear, a feeling of desolation. But yet I had seen nothing. 'I felt rather creepy,' I said.

As I spoke I drew my chair rather closer to the fire, and sent a swift and, I confess, a somewhat apprehensive scrutiny round the walls of the brightly lit room. I noticed at the same time that Anthony was peering across to the chimney-piece, on which, just below a sconce holding two electric lights, stood the clock which at the beginning of our talk he had offered to stop. The hands I noticed pointed to twenty-five minutes to one.

'But you saw nothing?' he asked.

'Nothing whatever,' I said. 'Why should I? What was there to see? Or did you—'

'I don't think so,' he said.

Somehow this answer got on my nerves, for the queer feeling which had accompanied that cold current of air had not left me. If anything it had become more acute.

'But surely you know whether you saw anything or not?' I said.

'One can't always be certain,' said he. 'I say that I don't think I saw anything. But I'm not sure, either, whether the story I am telling you was quite concluded last night. I think there may be a further incident. If you prefer it, I will leave the rest of it, as far as I know it, unfinished till tomorrow morning, and you can go off to bed now.'

His complete calmness and tranquillity reassured me.

'But why should I do that?' I asked.

Again he looked round on the bright walls.

'Well, I think something entered the room just now,' he said, 'and it may develop. If you don't like the notion, you had better go. Of course there's nothing to be alarmed at; whatever it is, it can't hurt us. But it is close on the hour when on two successive nights I saw what I have already told you, and an apparition usually occurs at the same time. Why that is so, I cannot say, but certainly it looks as if a spirit that is earth-bound is still subject to certain conventions, the conventions of time for instance. I think that personally I shall see something before long, but most likely you won't. You're not such a sufferer as I from these – these delusions—'

I was frightened and knew it, but I was also intensely interested, and some perverse pride wriggled within me at his last words. Why, so I asked myself, shouldn't I see whatever was to be seen? …

'I don't want to go in the least,' I said. 'I want to hear the rest of your story.'

'Where was I, then? Ah, yes: you were wondering why I didn't do something after I saw the train move up to the platform, and I said that there was nothing to be done. If you think it over, I fancy you will agree with me … A couple of days passed, and on the third morning I saw in the paper that there had come fulfilment to my vision. Sir Henry Payle, who had been waiting on the platform of Dover Street Station for the last train to South Kensington, had thrown himself in front of it as it came into the station. The train had been pulled up in a couple of yards, but a wheel had passed over his chest, crushing it in and instantly killing him.

'An inquest was held, and there emerged at it one of those dark stories which, on occasions like these, sometimes fall like a midnight shadow across a life that the world perhaps had thought prosperous. He had long been on bad terms with his wife, from whom he had lived apart, and it appeared that not long before this he had fallen desperately in love with another woman. The night before his suicide he had appeared very late at his wife's house, and had a long and angry scene with her in which he entreated her to divorce him, threatening otherwise to make her life a hell to her. She refused, and in an ungovernable fit of passion he attempted to strangle her. There was a struggle and the noise of it caused her manservant to come up, who succeeded in overmastering him. Lady Payle threatened to proceed against him for assault with the intention to murder her. With this hanging over his head, the next night, as I have already told you, he committed suicide.'

He glanced at the clock again, and I saw that the hands now pointed to ten minutes to one.

The fire was beginning to burn low and the room surely was growing strangely cold.

'That's not quite all,' said Anthony, again looking round. 'Are you sure you wouldn't prefer to hear it tomorrow?'

The mixture of shame and pride and curiosity again prevailed.

'No: tell me the rest of it at once,' I said.

Before speaking, he peered suddenly at some point behind my chair, shading his eyes. I followed his glance, and knew what he meant by saying that sometimes one could not be sure whether one saw something or not. But was that an outlined shadow that intervened between me and the wall? It was difficult to focus; I did not know whether it was near the wall or near my chair. It seemed to clear away, anyhow, as I looked more closely at it.

'You see nothing?' asked Anthony.

'No: I don't think so,' said I. 'And you?'

'I think I do,' he said, and his eyes followed something which was invisible to mine. They came to rest between him and the chimney-piece. Looking steadily there, he spoke again.

'All this happened some weeks ago,' he said, 'when you were out in Switzerland, and since then, up till last night, I saw nothing further. But all the time I was expecting something further. I felt that, as far as I was concerned, it was not all over yet, and last night, with the intention of assisting any communication to come through to me from – from beyond, I went into the Dover Street tube-station at a few minutes before one o'clock, the hour at which both the assault and the suicide had taken place. The platform when I arrived on it was absolutely empty, or appeared to be so, but presently, just as I began to hear the roar of the approaching train, I saw there was the figure of a man standing some twenty yards from me, looking into the tunnel. He had not come down with me in the lift, and the moment before he had not been there. He began moving towards me, and then I saw who it was, and I felt a stir of wind icy-cold coming towards me as he approached. It was not the draught that heralds the approach of a train, for it came from the opposite direction. He came close up to me, and I saw there was recognition in his eyes. He raised his face towards me and I saw his lips move, but, perhaps in the increasing noise from the tunnel, I heard nothing come from them. He put out his hand, as if entreating me to do something, and with a cowardice for which I cannot forgive myself, I shrank from him, for I knew, by the sign that I have told you, that this was one from the dead, and my flesh quaked before him, drowning for the moment all pity and all desire to help him, if that was possible.

'Certainly he had something which he wanted of me, but I recoiled from him. And by now the train was emerging from the tunnel, and next moment, with a dreadful gesture of despair, he threw himself in front of it.'

As he finished speaking he got up quickly from his chair, still looking fixedly in front of him.

I saw his pupils dilate, and his mouth worked.

'It is coming,' he said. 'I am to be given a chance of atoning for my cowardice. There is nothing to be afraid of: I must remember that myself...'

As he spoke there came from the panelling above the chimney-piece one loud shattering crack, and the cold wind again circled about my head. I found myself shrinking back in my chair with my hands held in front of me as instinctively I screened myself against something which I knew was there but which I could not see. Every sense told me that there was a presence in the room other than mine and Anthony's, and the horror of it was that I could not see it. Any vision, however terrible, would, I felt, be more tolerable than this clear certain knowledge that close to me was this invisible thing. And yet what horror might not be disclosed of the face of the dead and the crushed chest ... But all I could see, as I shuddered in this cold wind, was the familiar walls of the room, and Anthony standing in front of me stiff and firm, making, as I knew, a call on his courage. His eyes were focused on something quite close to him, and some semblance of a smile quivered on his mouth. And then he spoke again.

'Yes, I know you,' he said. 'And you want something of me. Tell me, then, what it is.'

There was absolute silence, but what was silence to my ears could not have been so to his, for once or twice he nodded, and once he said, 'Yes: I see. I will do it.' And with the knowledge that, even as there was someone here whom I could not see, so there was speech going on which I could not hear, this terror of the dead and of the unknown rose in me with the sense of powerlessness to move that accompanies nightmare. I could not stir, I could not speak. I could only strain my ears for the inaudible and my eyes for the unseen, while the cold wind from the very valley of the shadow of death streamed over me. It was not that the presence of death itself was terrible; it was that from its tranquillity and serene keeping there had been driven some unquiet soul unable to rest in peace for whatever ultimate awakening rouses the countless generations of those who have passed away, driven, no less, from whatever activities are theirs, back into the material world from which it should have been delivered. Never, until the gulf between the living and the dead was thus bridged, had it seemed so immense and so unnatural. It is possible that the dead may have communication with the living, and it was not that exactly that so terrified me, for such communication, as we know it, comes voluntarily from them. But here was something icy-cold and crime-laden, that was chased back from the peace that would not pacify it.

And then, most horrible of all, there came a change in these unseen conditions. Anthony was silent now, and from looking straight and fixedly in front of him, he began to glance sideways to where I sat and back again, and with that I felt that the unseen presence had turned its attention from him to me. And now, too, gradually and by awful degrees I began to see …

There came an outline of shadow across the chimney-piece and the panels above it. It took shape: it fashioned itself into the outline of a man. Within the shape of the shadow details began to form themselves, and I saw wavering in the air, like something concealed by haze, the semblance of a face, stricken and tragic, and burdened with such a weight of woe as no human face had ever worn. Next, the shoulders outlined themselves, and a stain livid and red spread out below them, and suddenly the vision leaped into clearness. There he stood, the chest crushed in and drowned in the red stain, from which broken ribs, like the bones of a wrecked ship, protruded. The mournful, terrible eyes were fixed on me, and it was from them, so I knew, that the bitter wind proceeded …

Then, quick as the switching off of a lamp, the spectre vanished, and the bitter wind was still, and opposite to me stood Anthony, in a quiet, bright-lit room. There was no sense of an unseen presence any more; he and I were then alone, with an interrupted conversation still dangling between us in the warm air. I came round to that, as one comes round after an anesthetic. It all swam into sight again, unreal at first, and gradually assuming the texture of actuality.

'You were talking to somebody, not to me,' I said. 'Who was it? What was it?'

He passed the back of his hand over his forehead, which glistened in the light.

'A soul in hell,' he said.

Now it is hard ever to recall mere physical sensations, when they have passed. If you have been cold and are warmed, it is difficult to remember what cold was like: if you have been hot and have got cool, it is difficult to realise what the oppression of heat really meant. Just so, with the passing of that presence, I found myself unable to recapture the sense of the terror with which, a few moments ago only, it had invaded and inspired me.

'A soul in hell?' I said. 'What are you talking about?'

He moved about the room for a minute or so, and then came and sat on the arm of my chair.

'I don't know what you saw,' he said, 'or what you felt, but there has never in all my life happened to me anything more real than what these last few minutes have brought. I have talked to a soul in the hell of remorse, which is the only possible hell. He knew, from what happened last night, that he could perhaps establish communication through me with the world he had quitted, and he sought me and found me. I am charged with a mission to a woman I have never seen, a message from the contrite … You can guess who it is …'

He got up with a sudden briskness.

'Let's verify it anyhow,' he said. 'He gave me the street and the number. Ah, there's the telephone book! Would it be a coincidence merely if I found that at No. 20 in Chasemore Street, South Kensington, there lived a Lady Payle?'

He turned over the leaves of the bulky volume.

'Yes, that's right,' he said.

ARE THE DEAD DEAD?

EMMA FRANCES DAWSON

Who shall determine the power of sympathy,
or assign to that power its limit?

My story is so strange that I cannot expect many to believe it. Only a short time ago I myself would have scoffed at such a tale. I would not tell it, but for the faint hope that it may lead others if such there be to own to any like experience; for I cannot think that I alone, of all the world, have had such glimpse of the mysterious outlying region usually veiled from mortals. Whoever you are, now about to read what comes, I implore you comfort me, if you can, by writing: "I, too, have heard and seen!" Come forward and share my burden before I lose my mind.

Marvel not that I grant the request of the club which asked for this statement. Since that awful experience I feel lifted above the paltry secret-keeping of this world. I own our spiritual kinship. On the Day of Judgment all will be known; why should I hesitate to give now a brief account of what, after all, might have happened to any one? For we are all tangled in strange meshes of circumstance.

But it must be seldom that one is allowed to see how one's thoughts or acts here may, long after one is gone, affect people one may not have known; to see how, before unguessed, life might have been different; to find that one's passions last as strong as in life, or stronger. But are they not one's self! Without them we might as well be lost in the Universal Spirit of the Brahmins.

That no one has seen and heard such proof of this until now weighs nothing against it. Sir John Herschel has said, that of all the fusions that might be of the fifty or sixty elements which chemistry shows there are on the earth, it is likely—nay, almost sure—that some have not been made. Those who cannot understand my story should remember that to the blind the touch of ice or fire is the same. Those who doubt this tale are like the Indian prince told of by Hume, who would not think there could be ice.

I have another reason for writing this; I owe it to the club upon which I rather forced myself to tell the cause of my abject terror when they saw nothing. I know some of them thought I was crazed; they will feel sure of it, perhaps, when I say that, so far as human judgment could go, it seemed to me at first that my joining them sprang from the wealth of bloom this year on the great heliotrope under my parlor-window, and from a chance call; but now these seem but links in a chain, running into past and future beyond our ken.

I filled a vase on my piano with the flowers, whose strong, sweet, wine-like odor led me to rhymes. Then I played and sang till, through the dreamful scent and the charm of music, I was rapt in clouds far above the world, and so little pleased to have a caller that I paid slight heed to him; and, on the plea of playing for him, did some hard practice, till, with aching arms, I turned round to find he had caught up the leaf of note-paper I had written on, and was placing his eyeglass to see what it was.

With some notion that it was a joke to do so, he read aloud my

RONDEL

Strange depth of passion freights the heavy scent
Of heliotrope; there breathes a discontent
From pallid purple upon snow upthrown,
Like haze of hills afar with white cloud blent;
All vague regret and mad desire seem loan
From odor blown.

Sweet things that never were pervade my thought,
As when sad music sounds, with yearning fraught,
That makes the present pass behind two tears,
All that the future may unfold seem naught.
Some past unknown was blest.
Too quickly veers
The lapse of years.

I cannot read nor sing—
I only sigh.
A haunting presence in my room is nigh;
I suffocate with a delicious dole.
What spirit stronger than my own is by?
Is this fierce will, that can my mind control,
The flower's soul?

"Humph!" said he. "You ought to join the Ghost Club."

"What do you mean?" I asked. "I had not heard of one."

"Well, it is kept quiet," he said; "but it is a small club, whose members go to houses said to be haunted, to see what truth there may be in the tales. You know that one out on Valencia street, near Fifteenth? They have spent some time there; and in the large house here in town, on Sutter street, which was vacant so long, and at last taken, with its fine grounds, for a beer-garden."

"What happened?" I asked. "Was any one frightened into a fit?"

"No," said he; "they have seen nothing yet. But if you watch to-morrow night, you will see them marching up here to the house over the way."

I began to be interested. "That house!" I said. "I did not know anything was the matter with it. But I know it has long been to let." I did not tell him what a part of my reveries it had been—not only for its picturesque look, but because of the music I had once heard from its windows.

"It is not easy to let," he went on, "because the first owner poisoned himself there. Why don't you join the club ? You are fanciful enough. I can give you letters to the chief members."

"I might—for fun," I said; "I have no faith."

"Neither have they; they call it a quest for truth."

I let him write the letters—two to women, one to a man—three out of the seven who formed the club. The last thing that night I paused by my window to look over at the house—square, high, dark, outlined against the stars, far above the street, which was cut through the hill at some date since the building of the house, which stands near the head of about a hundred zigzag steps, with landings here and there at the turns, the first flight boarded from the street, and looking like a switch-tender's hut on a railroad.

Behind an uncared-for garden of dusty evergreens, and half-hidden in yellow and white jasmine, the lonely house, with its closed windows, made me think of a giant with shut eyes lying in a garden under a spell. Did it ever dream? Sometimes I half-believed in flitting lights and changeful shadows behind one shutterless window upstairs, but thought it must be the reflection of the headlight of a passing street-car dummy.

That house had long been like a conscious comrade in my day-dreams. It was linked in my mind with an offer of marriage I once had from one for whom I cared very little, but whom circumstances nearly brought me to accept. But through the open windows came such a strain of warning music that, creatures of chance impulses that we are, swayed by a look or a tone, my mind changed in spite of me. I was lifted out of my usual self, and had strength to do right. I never knew anything of the unseen singer but his love for his art as shown by daily study which I heard. That "sound which was a soul" surely saved me from making my life a mere hard, rude outline, from losing all the picturesque effects of light and shade which romance, hope, and feeling give. But it was strangely done, by making the man at my feet so suddenly hateful to me.

I could not help wishing to join the Ghost Club, though I thought our pains would be vain. I felt a strange interest in the plan. It made me restless that night. While dressing in the morning, I looked up again at the lonesome-looking house, and, nodding gayly toward it, cried: "*You* have haunted *me!*"

No one could have felt lighter-hearted and more free from dread than I, as during the day I presented my letters, and gained consent to my joining the club "for that one house." Heaven knows I have now no wish to thus visit another!

When the club gathered that night at the doorway to the steps over the way, I joined them. A queer group. A believer, a doubter, an inquirer, a strict church member, and others who came, as I did, for pastime. Some were late, and had not yet come when we wound up the long stairs, and waited at the door for some one who was to bring the key.

"Nothing is too strange to happen," said the inquirer, who, with his wife, seemed gravely exploring a strange region. "There is nothing which may not be in the wide margin of the unknown around all we know."

"The Bible tells us," said the pious man, "'There is a universe to us invisible, but not, therefore, unreal.'"

"But I cannot think," said the doubter, "that those who have gone there think of us; for 'Death remembers to forget.'"

"Yet Isaac Taylor thought," said the believer, "the human and extra-human crowd might be within any given bounds; but as they are commonly unseen and unheard by us, so we may be the same to them."

"Like the voices the Talmud tells of," said a Jewess, laden with flesh and lace and diamonds, "the sounds which pass through the world, and are not heard by any creatures in it."

He nodded, and went on: "Jung Stilling and Oberlin also held, we can be only ghosts to them, as they to us."

"No one ever saw a ghost not made by his fancy," said the doubter—a Jew. "It is always like that German tale of a student who fought a duel with a spectre, who, when he dropped the cloak from his face, was seen to be himself!"

"That is why the club was formed," said the believer; "doctors own that more than one may have an illusion, but say there is no such thing as delusion for a group of people."

The pious man patted my Spitz dog. "He may see more than we can," said he, "as Balaam's ass saw the angel."

"Yes," said the joker, "to 'speak by the card,' when we are within an ace of meeting hobgoblins, and the deuce is to pay, Tray will knock spots out of them."

As we went into the house, I found in the man who had the key an old neighbor.

"Why, Mr. H—!" I cried.

He started nervously, and looked around in great surprise. "Miss W—!" said he, "are *you* here? with those asking eyes of yours?"

"Oh, I don't believe in it," I laughed; "I am only curious, like the rest."

Not so much then as since, I have thought of his strange look at me, and the shrug of his shoulders, which seemed to lift me off his mind, for he paid no more heed to me that night.

The others glanced here and there through the open doors, with an eager air, in marked contrast with Mr. H—'s studied unconcern. They noticed his manner, and spoke of it.

"I never look about me in *this* house," he said, gravely, "or in any of these old places," he added, and hurried off.

The inquirer plunged down the steps, caught him on the first landing, and cried: "Why? Why not?"

Mr. H— hesitated. "Well—you might look for the ghosts of the restless, roving folks who wandered to California," he answered, and ran down.

As we stood in the hall, the believer made us a speech about being in a fit state, and urged that we should be placed in rooms by ourselves, or no more than two together. Though, after some wrangling, we were allowed a light in each room, we were to sit idle and not speak. I was left in a small room, with a window on the street. The others went where he told them. The silence which soon reigned made it seem as if there was no one in the house. Fearless as I had always boasted of being, a strange dread at last settled on me. I could not lose that feeling as of some one just at the door, which we know in vacant furnished houses. I tried to forget why we came. I counted, each way, the figures in carpet and curtains. I noticed all in the room, the common and uncommon, from chairs, table, and sofa to a veiled picture and an old-fashioned secretary, whose torn green silk behind the glass doors showed some stray leaves of manuscript.

I wondered in which room the old owner took poison. Supposing it to be true, as some have thought, that suicide chains the spirit to earth, why should we know it? What right had we to pry into the unknown? I shrank from the test, and was seized with nervous trembling. Even my dog grew restless, and ran home just as, much to my relief, a late-comer entered the house.

He came in the room where I was—a shy, quiet young man, who went toward the window, but, suddenly seeing me, started, stared, and dropped into a seat. It struck me some way that he was in awe of me. I was half-amused to think he might be taking a stranger for a ghost.

Long we sat amid the shadows, silent and strange, as if both by some spell called up from the shades by the club. The oil-lamp burned dimly. I faintly saw my companion's glowing eyes, and fine profile, like that on antique vase or coin, and the small spray of the breath-of-heaven's snow-flake flowers that, with a blood-red pink, he wore as a buttonhole bouquet.

The floor cracked like a goblin telegraph. The banisters creaked as if people were going up and down the stairs. The wind in sudden gusts rattled the tin roof till it seemed like the tramp of an army. But I heard with my mind's ear once more the passionate love-songs and snatches from operas which had of old so charmed me from this very window.

I could not keep my eyes off this man. Dazed, I looked at him. Where had I known him? I seemed flooded by a tidal wave of memories of what? bits of dreams? sleeping or waking ones? Was it a tide of inherited memories surging through my veins with the hot blood of some ancestress who had, like me now, loved at first sight one like him, this man of graceful movement and head like an antique bust? Who could tell? I gazed at him, mad with vague, keen longing and remembrance, excited as with wine by the new and piquant charm of feeling the overwhelming power of his presence, yet seeing him wholly unaware of it, and even shy. I was under a spell subtle as the scent of the blossoms which nestled where I longed to lay my head, upon his breast.

When the hours of our fruitless waiting had passed, and we all stumbled down the winding, grass-grown steps, from starlight through shadow into the gas-lit street, I was dizzy with the intoxication of his glances, and lay awake the rest of the night. Who was he? One of this crazy club. I wanted nothing to do with them. I resolved not to join them again. But just as I had waked all night, I dreamed all day. This, then, was love, to look into eyes of such dazzling enchantment that all else became dull. I could do nothing but think of him. I envied the girls in the "Arabian Nights," who could always send an old woman to tell a young man he was loved, and bring him. I longed for the freedom of the birds of the air, who are not held in check by the straight-jacket of custom which keeps us from blows or kisses at first sight. As the day wore on, I could not keep from going up there to look about in the light. The key had been left with me. I took it, but hardly meant to use it. I thought I would walk in the garden. The still, old place had an odd charm for me. San Francisco was gone; its hum sounded faint, like a distant sea; it seemed far off, as if one of the vanished Five Cities of the Plain, to me on this hilltop, alone, with the fierce wind and dazzling sky, better comrades and more akin than the breathless, thronged streets and crowding buildings. The clouds floated near. The garden shrubs whispered their secrets. It was so solitary that, though the sunshine was over all, and an army of wall-flowers formed their torch-lit ranks round the door, there seemed to be no relief from a weight of loneliness. It seemed almost remote enough for Death to overlook. Was it haunted? The house looked at me with its pleasant windows, and lured me to go in. The sense of intrusion was too strong for me to go all over it. I went into the room where I sat the night before. I had not paused to mark the dusty gloom, or to feel nervous, when I happened to glance through the glass of the secretary. I bent to admire the writing thrust behind the worn green silk. I saw my own Christian name. I opened the doors. Fragments which had lain there by chance so long, plainly worthless, at the mercy of the next tenant, whoever it might be. I took them by right of my name of Rose. They were leaves torn from a note-book, mostly the record of a singer's daily practice; so many minutes to these exercises or to those, or to songs, and so much time to French and Italian.

But here and there came these entries:

> Rose! sweet blossom in the wilderness of names, freighted with fragrance of lovers' vows folded in it, with hints of passionate meetings and farewells embalmed in amber moonlights, of dusky old gardens at nightfall, whose satin-cheeked flowers—wakeful, pale, and tearful, or crumpled, flushed, and warm, tossing in their dreams—all sigh their hearts out for the day who loved and rode away—for a Rose should have an ardent soul. She would not look at me now; but when skilled in my art, famous, rich—who knows?
>
> This evening I saw her sitting in her window, looking lonely and sad, for her drooping head reminded me of a heavy-hearted flower. Could I but be her sheltering and supporting leaf! But I am like the ground at the feet of my Rose—no more able to come near her sweet lips, or touch her dainty hand! Soon her curtains were drawn. Into the moon-lit space between our houses, from the depths of my heart, I sang Fesca's impassioned "Maiden at the Window."

I love her; but how can that serve *her* the love of one with no wealth beyond his silver tenor and his golden hope. She might as well be the wild rose who blushes in lonely woodlands, her sweet soul unblessing and unblest, and dies with no knowledge of bliss that might have been hers. She may never know of the kisses I long to give her. It is strange to think of our cool unconsciousness of precious treasures of heart and soul in those around us whom we never know.

How hard is my fate! My mind is like a phantom battle-field, with this conflict carried on in silence—an awful, noiseless war, as of shadows; but, to me, what dread realities! Sometimes I think I must break my bond with my cousin. What a cursed fool I was to bargain away my freedom for the sake of her money, for study here and in Europe! But love was to me only a name. When I made that contract I had not seen Rose.

To see Rose sitting here before me, to hear her say, "I love you!" would be enough to come back for from another world. But what we miss here must be gone forever.

"We shall go down to earth,
And be raised again from her;
But there is no resurrection birth
For the things that never were."

Sometimes I seem to live but to see her shadow on her curtain, her flitting form in the garden, or going in or out. Bliss and woe! Then I force myself to scales and exercises of the like sameness, that may dull my senses like a narcotic.

Last night, at my open window, I poured out my whole soul in the love-songs of Beethoven and Schubert. Edith supposed I was making out my hours of practice. The only neighbors near enough to hear may have thought me mad, but I did not care. I had seen her lighted room grow dark; I knew my voice rang through her dreams. The nightingale singing to the rose, I thought; and was I not also leaning my breast against a thorn?

My God! What an awful feeling is jealousy! Three days ago, through our open windows, I watched Rose with a suitor. It was plain that he was wooing, and that she, though, it seemed, not much caring, still she listened. I thought of the "Malediction" from Halévy's "Charles the Sixth." My teacher, an old opera-singer, had told me how the spell of this fatal air followed the pointing finger of a tenor of the Grand Opera at Paris: now it was one of the audience who dropped in a fit; then he signed downward, and the shock was upon a carpenter under a trap-door; again, reaching up, a scene-shifter fell senseless. I burst into the solemn air. If ever such subtle influence worked, I meant it should now. I wished there could be poison in sound. I hated that unknown man. I willed him to lose his cause. I thought how Stradella's heavenly tones in his own hymn, the prayer of a bruised and rueful soul, changed the minds of those who had come to slay him. Could I make mine evil enough to crush that man's hopes? My song should be an alembic through which passion, hate, and despair could distill a strong and malign force. I shook. I grew afraid of my own voice, of my own soul. The man rose as if unwilling to leave. I willed him to go. I quaked from head to foot. Cold drops beaded my brow. In the glass I caught sight of my uplifted, menacing hand, and of my eyes, which were strange to me, blazing with a fierce, inward fire, like those of a wild beast that sees its prey. He went. I drew free breath. I felt as if I had been out of my body. And I did not find my voice for two days after. Can there be truth in the old saying that curses come home?

How can I bear to drift away with no anchor in her life? Oh, it is too, too hard. I have studied so long; I owe too much to Cousin Edith. I must keep on. But I must earn enough to pay her, and then, *when I return, I shall be free!* O Rose! shall I find you here the same? Heaven grant it! I go—to study, to sing, so Edith thinks; but *I*—I am sure of but one thing; I go—to return. *I shall come back!*

This was all of the journal. There was nothing else in the secretary, except a book of poems by the Countess Hahn-Hahn. Side by side with her "Playful Love" was pinned a page of note-paper, which bore the last of her verses, in a version made by the writer of the diary:

Must I die?—straight will soar
My soul above to thee;
And thou new life will lend,
New light to me. And I—
Could I with thee quite blend,
I should not fear to die.

Shall I with spirits keep?
No; though I soar, depart
As spirits heavenward sweep,
Yet th' heaven is thy heart.
Thou wilt thy truant shield,
And ever sympathize,
And ope to him the field
Of that calm paradise.

And then the portal golden
Soft, softly close again,
Where I, in peace enfolden,
Shall ever rest from pain.
As, of a morn, the bee
In tulip lies apart,
I sleep all hid in thee,
Swayed of and in thy heart.

I was amazed at these bits of a shattered romance; for the writer had long been known abroad, and I had read of his being made court-singer for life in a far-off country. It was like too late looking down some charming road one might have taken. I sighed. Was my sigh echoed, or was it the sound of the swaying boughs of the old gum-trees? I could not stay. I ran home to think it over. I remembered the weird music which had so strangely mingled with my thoughts when I refused the man whom he saw. I was still lost in wonder over it when, in spite of my resolves, I joined the club at night. Neither my companion of the night before nor my old neighbor were there this time.

"This is a risky scheme," said the believer; "it is playing with edged tools."

"We fail to see anything," said the inquirer, "because visions must come without being evoked, as by the witches in the play."

"Shut off in different rooms," said the joker, "who knows which is witch."

"What I can not make agree with there being ghosts," said the learned-looking inquirer, "is this: Heraclitus says, 'Nothing is, but all flows; being is not a station, but a motion, a constant becoming.' So those out of the flesh are not the same as when in it. Always moving on, no one crosses the same stream or sees the same picture twice."

"Then," cried the joker, "debtor and creditor of yesterday lose that relation to-day. Owe, let us be joyful!"

"Buddha," said the doubter, "called the soul a current of states; when the mechanism goes to pieces, the soul is gone. It was only the mass of associations, experience, and memory."

"That," said the believer, "puts man on a level with a table or chair."

"Yes," said the joker, "let us be chary of that unstable belief."

"Life *is* a current of states," said I; "it is not in our frames, or in years, but in moments of bliss or woe, hope or despair, pain, disgust, strength, or weakness. Those who have not known 'raptures and desolations' have no spirit to come back."

We were placed as before, but not without much dispute.

I thought of the odd folks now in these rooms, queer as the thoughts that lurk in the cells of a madman's brain. I waited, like them, but not for the same reason. I was anxious for *his* coming, though I felt faint and ready to run home to shun meeting his eyes. What if he did not come? At the thought, a weight on my spirits changed the look of the room, as a cloud dulls the sunny landscape. With a thrill, a shiver of delight, I heard him enter.

As he stood for a moment, looking at me over the lamp on the table, the faint radiance making his statuesque beauty glow out of the dimness as if conjured by a spell, the scent of the breath-of-heaven and clove-pink in his button-hole might have been that of spices burned for an incantation. What was it I saw in those fine eyes? Neither scorn nor pity; they were kind, but full of an overwhelming surprise.

"Again!" he murmured; then kept the club rule of silence.

I was confused. I could scarcely breathe. My head whirled. I reeled to a chair. The flickering rays of the lamp danced about him, like my restless thoughts, while we waited. Waited? I forgot the club, the house, that I was in the city, in the world. I knew only that the man I loved sat before me. I could not love those who sought me. How was it that my heart leaped at a glance from this stranger's eyes? Stranger? Had we not known each other from the first of creation? The king had come to his own again!

After even the little I had known of the club disputes, I was not surprised to see the pale young man shun the others when we all left. As we went out into the windy night, the well-known street and view seemed new. I felt as if I had left the real world behind; that, truly, one "lived" only in "raptures and desolations." San Francisco, the club, were vague phantoms, dreams within dreams. I roused to myself at my own gate, with Mr. H—'s voice in my ear:

"Are these all?" he asked, looking after the members going down the street. And watching, with a pang of regret, their vanishing forms, I forgot to answer.

Then I cried: "Mr. H—, it has just come back to me how you urged my folks not to take that very house a year or two ago. Why did you do so?"

"I don't want to see any one live in it," he answered. "My friend K—, the rare tenor, used to be there. Poor fellow! He was to have married a cousin, whose money helped him to study music; but I have always thought his heart was elsewhere. She held him in a thrall, which wore upon him; and the voice, most frail of all instruments, is hurt by worry. His was, and at last left him. This shock, and disappointment, killed him."

"Oh, I am so sorry!" I cried. "I never saw him, but I shall not forget his voice. In 'Robin Adair' it was like 'the flute of the twilight wind.'"

"Yes," said Mr. H—. "As I stood by his grave, I thought of what Antipater said over the tomb of Orpheus: 'Here lies a poet; here lies a soul that sang; here lies the sound of the wind.' He did not want to die, though he would say to me, '*Then* I shall be free!' His cousin, a spiteful woman, seemed to hate to have him escape her control, though he did that whenever he sang. His voice raised a magic wall around him—we could only listen afar. After his death, she said to me, 'He has got away from me now—but *wait till I die!*' with a motion that was a threat. She would not return here, and has been trying to have the house sold."

"But why did you not want us to move there?" I asked.

"He once said to me," Mr. H— went on: "'If, when I dream, I can see the old house, go over it, see her in the window across the way, may it not be that such pleasure, felt by me now through none of the nerves of sense, will be known to my spirit after I die? Perhaps, unheard, unseen, the two worlds blend, and we shall move along our old paths, with rare visions of the living, who will seem unreal and awful to us. I wonder if my soul could then affect one I loved, or must I be a flitting spectre with no power. We shall see.'"

"Then you believe?" I began.

"I have no belief," he said, quickly. "It seems to me nothing is too strange to happen," unconsciously repeating the words of a club-member.

"No," I thought, after he left me, "I should wonder at nothing after feeling this sudden deep interest in two strangers, such regret for the singer, and such absorbing passion for my companion of the last two evenings." Why had I not asked Mr. H— who he was?

The next night I meant should be my last with the club, shrunk this time to the inquirer and wife, and the joker.

"I half believe," said the inquirer, "shadows are bound to go through tragedies whose scenes shift with no lookers-on, night after night, year after year, as if the hour could not forget, and would not let the place do so. It is the horror of Doom. But it is not for all to have it proved to them. Our inner sense has its bounds, like our other senses."

The joker wound the great hall-clock, which began to work with convulsive gasps, as if it had been scared into silence. "Too frightened," he said, "to cover its face with its hands."

The small room where I sat had at once a charm and a sadness for me. I was filled with the vain desire to have known its old tenant.

I wondered about the end of such strong passions as his. Can they cease here? Are they merely to brighten our path, like vivid colors in flowers and sky? In fancy I heard again the lovely tenor airs from "Lucia," "Faust," and "Martha" which had of old rung through this window. I thought of his journal, and his translation of the German love-song. And I was haunted—haunted by two lines of Jean Ingelow's—

"I have no place on sea or shore,
But only in thy heart."

But through it all ran the stronger undercurrent of longing for the coming of the pale young member of the club—a longing that made me blame my fickle heart, so touched by one stranger's love and grief, and just as much thrilled by another's sweet eyes; a longing that made me tremble, and made my heart, at the sound of his step, feel as if clutched by Fate, and nearly powerless to beat.

He started at seeing me, and, pausing an instant, murmured, "Once more!" and sank into a chair which stood back to the door; and again I was spellbound by his shy but ardent gaze, by the scent of the same sweet flowers he wore.

With none of my suitors, thronging like bees about the honey of my wealth, had I ever felt this tumult of emotion. I was glad of the club rule of silence. I could have thrown myself into his arms, but I could not speak.

What was the fatal enigma his eyes held? They had a mystic spell, as if they had seen deeper than most eyes. Looking into them, my soul was lured down an unknown tide, on and on, voyaging through their unspeakable glory, with glimpse of a new world behind them, dropping through endless gulfs, till only by a fierce strain I turned my head away, blinded, breathless, dazed, and awed; for far down in those fathomless depths I touched eternity—I found the immortal—Love!

Sitting there so long, so still, it seemed to my strained nerves that we were like ghosts, and only the pictures on the wall had life and motion. The hall-clock groaned twelve times, but my watch lacked ten minutes of twelve. A cold draught rushed in as at the opening and closing of some of the doors. A nameless fear seized me. But a woman I had not yet seen with the club looked in at the open door, surprise, doubt, and scorn in her intent face.

A woman more to be feared than a ghost, I thought, as I marked her evil look. She paused in amaze at sight of us. Suddenly the dim light wholly failed. To be in the dark was to recall the errand here of the club. It could not be borne, even with others near me. After crossing what seemed an endless space, I reached the mantel, felt for a match, found one, and groped back to the centre-table.

As I lighted the lamp, I saw him watching me with questioning eyes, as if unmoved by the loss of thc light or its return. I saw her looking in with a wicked smile. A jealous woman, I judged all the more as she drew back before he could turn to find the cause of my changed looks. But he was curious enough to leave the room. Was she his wife? Was I bewitched by a man bound to another woman? Has each case its like? Was another man in this very house held in bonds? These questions perplexed me all night.

The next afternoon I went over to look for a favorite lace handkerchief, dropped in coming out with the club. I found it caught on a thistle, near the top stair. It was Sunday, and the chimes of Saint Patrick's Church came to me clear and sweet. Some of the words which are sung to the air they played ran through my mind:

"A realm of shadowy forms out yonder lies.

Faint sounds of friendly voices come and go,
That seem to lure us forth into the air;
But whence they come perchance no ear may know,
And where they go perchance no foot may dare."

I looked at the old house, longed and yet did not like to go in. But I knew none of the club were likely to come until night, when they were to make their last visit—and as for ghosts, had we not tested it? What worse than to be haunted by vain yearnings after a different past, or to know a present not to be shaped by my will because a woman may not speak first. Perhaps I was to fade—the ungathered rose that cannot seek its lover's hand! Surely, if he felt as I did, he could not long rest without seeking me outside of the club.

I pushed in through the dreary hall. I passed on into the small front room. It gave me the same feeling of sorrow and regret. It was like the return from a funeral. How sorry I now felt that I had never known the people who used to live here! I had often thought, perhaps the friends we never meet might have been the dearest. I could not tear myself away. For the first time by daylight I looked from the window, which, to my surprise, had a full view of my own room across the way. They must have known more of me than I ever knew about them.

The house shook in the wind, as if stirred by unseen hands, but in the room all was still as if in a picture. There were the rusty nails and black moss in the grass-grown garden, and stairs, as at the "moated grange"; but no fly buzzed in the window, no mouse squeaked in the wainscot, no bird chirped on the roof. Nothing moved but the clock in the hall, and the shadow of a gum-tree across the floor. My little dog and I sat still as statues.

As in the gloom of Gérome's pictures, ragged beggar and peddler, in the softened light of oriental canvas-covered streets, become grand and suggestive ideals, so in this dim, lonely room common things had a weird, unreal look; the lounge took coffin-shape; the tall, narrow secretary loomed like a monument near it. I could fancy the veil over the picture stirred. The chairs gave sudden creaks, as if bearing unseen burdens.

I looked out of the window, and saw the buildings of the city far below stand out in the light of the sinking sun, with sudden sharp lines, as long-forgotten things start up in the mind of one dying. Why were my thoughts all of death? Then a line of phantoms of silent tunes, long since sung here, passed by my ears.

I thought of the surprise and dislike in that woman's face the night before, and of what slight ground for jealousy she had, when he and I sat in such silence,—but recalling his speaking eyes, my heart's quickened beating, and the flushes I felt mount my cheeks, I knew she had good cause.

I was vexed at myself, both for being here almost against my will, and for a nervous fear which had come over me when once inside the house. I would not yield to it. There was a scrap of paper on the table. I drew a pencil from my pocket, and tried to forget by writing about

THE GHOST OF YESTERDAY.

Faint in the cloudless sky yet shows
The last night's moon, whose phantom white
Has haunted dawn's pale-blue and rose
With thrilling gleam of lost delight,

And lingers through the blaze of noon,
Like Banquo's ghost at Macbeth's feast.
Avaunt, O Spectre whose weird rune
Appears to me when thought of least!

Though clouds from out life's sky seem furled
By dazzling bliss, to me is clear—
Far off and dreamlike—my own world
Burnt out, my yesterday thus here!

A long-drawn sigh, which sounded close by me, made me look up. Bravely as I had tried to think only of the words I wrote, I was startled. My dog crouched at my feet and barked. Had I left the front door on the latch? I rushed to see. Turning in the hall with the feeling of being watched, I saw a woman's head peering round a distant door. There was a familiar look about her. Thinking it must be one of the club, I started toward her, but she drew back and closed the door, which she held against me.

Was she afraid of me? I laughed, a little nervously, wrenched it open—but no one was in sight! I called, no answer, but, glancing up, saw the same head hanging over the banisters upstairs, and part of her dress. I was struck with something so wicked in her look that my little Spitz ran cowering and whining to the street-door. But, thinking I ought to explain my presence there, I went upstairs. To my surprise, the woman, without waiting for me, passed down the long hall and turned a corner.

I hurried after, thinking I might have frightened her, if she were a nervous member, and, in my haste, nearly fell through to the lower story, for at the turning yawned an opening where stairs had been taken down. My dress caught on a nail in the floor, and held me back just in time. As I freed my skirt, I saw that from the hall-window, just beyond the pitfall, my house could be seen better than from downstairs. A smothered chuckle, followed by a cry of rage, made me look down. The woman was watching me from below. There must be some other flight, I thought, yet found none, and went to the lower room, but she had hidden.

My verses, dropped as I ran out, were torn into shreds, and strewed on the floor. Thinking it was one of my dog's tricks, I felt I ought not to have brought him, that I must wait and excuse myself to her. I turned to look for him. What was this fluffy mass by the halldoor? Not my gay little comrade? This poor creature in spasms! Some evil power was at work here. Even that cruel-faced woman would be welcome company. I called. No reply. I tried to open the outer door, but it seemed barred by the rusty, large lock, to which there was no key.

I strove to be brave. I went through the lower part. The back door was fast. I thought she must have fled that way. It was awful to be alone there! I saw nothing strange, but felt as if dogged, doors opening behind me as soon as I closed them. I tried to think it was caused by the jar of my steps and the uneven flooring, but I felt the Bible was right to forbid the calling of spirits. Had not the Ghost Club brought all this horror upon me? It made no odds that they had been searching to prove there was no such thing. There was the ugly story of the hanged man, whose body was dissected and his skull ground to dust; yet in the night the bits were seen to join, one by one, till the man was whole, and went out of the door.

I went back to the front room. Trying to forget my fears, I raised the gauze screen from the portrait over the mantel. It was not unlike the face of the strange woman! In my vexation toward her, I flung the veil against it again. The next instant, my elbows were fiercely gripped from behind. I was rushed swiftly toward the window I had opened when I first came in. My heart nearly stopped beating. Years of torture seemed crowded into that one moment. I was to be thrown out, to fall from that great height to the street. I shrieked in hopeless terror. I was suddenly cast on the floor, and, when I could look round, I saw that woman near the door, with her hard face turned as if to listen.

Some one was on the steps. She glided out, and was upstairs, as the front door, forced by stronger hand than mine, opened, and, to my deep relief and joy, the pale young man came in. Braced by the relief of his coming, then I could talk to him. He only nodded once in a while, but his eyes again held mine. To my questions about the woman, he shook his head, and seemed surprised when I said, "She was here last night."

So she had gone when he went out. I did not wonder she was jealous, as I stood there, hardly conscious of anything but the charm of his presence, and the scent of the bit of breath-of-heaven and blood-red pink he wore. And he—he kept the club rule of silence. But I thought I knew what he was thinking. I had not slept since I had last seen him. I passed the night watching, as I lay in bed, the old house—looming dim and large against the starry sky,—or, half-dozing, dreamed of flitting lights in the windows and echoing strains of music.

I had not slept for thinking of him. Fancying what bliss his kisses might be, waked me as fully as a real draught of wine. Heaven help me! And he knew it—he knew it; his eyes told me that.

Those wonderful eyes! They seemed so near and dear a part of myself, that I forgot we were, as the world goes, strangers. Surely we had known each other for eternities. I forgot that it was not a woman's part to woo. I thought only of my love—my love, fierce as the wind, resistless as the sea, wide-spreading as the sky! I lost my senses.

"Where have you been all these years?" I cried. "We must have known each other before, for I love you, I *love* you, and it is no new feeling. My life has been a dream, a nightmare—at last I am awake! Do not leave me again, for I could not bear it. Stay! Stay!"

"Oh, if it might only be!" he murmured.

He came nearer, bent over as if to kiss me, when a white hand was laid on his shoulder. He turned in amazement. *She* stood beside him.

"*You*," he groaned, with a gesture of despair, and reeled back. He grew, if possible, more bloodless than ever. I could see him tremble. Dismay and dread in his face, and a hunted look came into his eyes.

With a look of triumph at me, she beckoned him. Making a motion toward me, as of mingled farewell and warning, he slowly went after her, though often turning to look back. I followed. They passed along the hall, where my dog lay dead, out of the front door, and slowly down the long steps. At each landing he stopped and gazed back, then followed her into the dusk through which the members of the club were toiling up—among them Mr. H—, with a lighted lantern. They paid no heed to the figures going down, and were surprised at my wild agitation.

"Look! Look!"I cried to Mr. H—.

"Why! Your eyes have been answered!" he muttered, staring at me.

"What is it?" "Where?" "When?" "What happened?" "What's the matter, H—?" urged the club.

"Let us get away from this house!" he cried, looking uneasily behind him, and signing to the doubter to lock the door. His hand trembled so that the lantern shook, as he said:

"I came over, in case any of you were here, to warn you. I have just heard Miss Edith L—, who lived here, died in Paris last night."

"Last night!—at ten minutes of twelve o'clock?" I gasped, suddenly faint.

"Well—," he thought a moment, "yes—ten minutes past nine there would just make it—how did you know of it?"

"Tall,—light eyes, a set, stern face—not without malice?" I stammered.

"I thought you never saw her?" he said.

"Tall,—dark,—with a face like an antique bust,—divine eyes?" I went on.

"Then you *had* seen him," said he. Struck by a sudden thought, he added: "Do you mean—can it be that you—how—where?"

I caught his arm. "See there!" I cried, pointing where the two forms one looking up over his shoulder—had paused on the lowest landing, but now moved on. Could it be that my touch made him see as I did?

"My God!" he cried, his nerveless hand dropping the lantern. "Then I was too late!"

I sank, limp and helpless, on the top stair. The glare of the lantern on the club's eager faces round me, with their various looks of wonder, doubt, content, fear, and pity; the jeering sound of the fog-horn; the shock of such an end to my romance; a keen sense of life's "raptures and desolations,"—all made me hysterical, as I burst forth: "You you think—?"

"I *know*,"—he answered, with awe-struck face, white to the very lips that could scarcely say the words, "*you* have seen the ghosts!"

The Boarded Window

AMBROSE BIERCE

IN 1830, only a few miles away from what is now the great city of Cincinnati, lay an immense and almost unbroken forest. The whole region was sparsely settled by people of the frontier—restless souls who no sooner had hewn fairly habitable homes out of the wilderness and attained to that degree of prosperity which to-day we should call indigence than impelled by some mysterious impulse of their nature they abandoned all and pushed farther westward, to encounter new perils and privations in the effort to regain the meagre comforts which they had voluntarily renounced. Many of them had already forsaken that region for the remoter settlements, but among those remaining was one who had been of those first arriving. He lived alone in a house of logs surrounded on all sides by the great forest, of whose gloom and silence he seemed a part, for no one had ever known him to smile nor speak a needless word. His simple wants were supplied by the sale or barter of skins of wild animals in the river town, for not a thing did he grow upon the land which, if needful, he might have claimed by right of undisturbed possession. There were evidences of "improvement"—a few acres of ground immediately about the house had once been cleared of its trees, the decayed stumps of which were half concealed by the new growth that had been suffered to repair the ravage wrought by the ax. Apparently the man's zeal for agriculture had burned with a failing flame, expiring in penitential ashes.

The little log house, with its chimney of sticks, its roof of warping clapboards weighted with traversing poles and its "chinking" of clay, had a single door and, directly opposite, a window. The latter, however, was boarded up—nobody could remember a time when it was not. And none knew why it was so closed; certainly not because of the occupant's dislike of light and air, for on those rare occasions when a hunter had passed that lonely spot the recluse had commonly been seen sunning himself on his doorstep if heaven had provided sunshine for his need. I fancy there are few persons living to-day who ever knew the secret of that window, but I am one, as you shall see.

The man's name was said to be Murlock. He was apparently seventy years old, actually about fifty. Something besides years had had a hand in his aging. His hair and long, full beard were white, his gray, lustreless eyes sunken, his face singularly seamed with wrinkles which appeared to belong to two intersecting systems. In figure he was tall and spare, with a stoop of the shoulders—a burden bearer. I never saw him; these particulars I learned from my grandfather, from whom also I got the man's story when I was a lad. He had known him when living near by in that early day.

One day Murlock was found in his cabin, dead. It was not a time and place for coroners and newspapers, and I suppose it was agreed that he had died from natural causes or I should have been told, and should remember. I know only that with what was probably a sense of the fitness of things the body was buried near the cabin, alongside the grave of his wife, who had preceded him by so many years that local tradition had retained hardly a hint of her existence. That closes the final chapter of this true story excepting, indeed, the circumstance that many years afterward, in company with an equally intrepid spirit, I penetrated to the place and ventured near enough to the ruined cabin to throw a stone against it, and ran away to avoid the ghost which every well-informed boy thereabout knew haunted the spot. But there is an earlier chapter—that supplied by my grandfather.

When Murlock built his cabin and began laying sturdily about with his ax to hew out a farm—the rifle, meanwhile, his means of support—he was young, strong and full of hope. In that eastern country whence he came he had married, as was the fashion, a young woman in all ways worthy of his honest devotion, who shared the dangers and privations of his lot with a willing spirit and light heart. There is no known record of her name; of her charms of mind and person tradition is silent and the doubter is at liberty to entertain his doubt; but God forbid that I should share it! Of their affection and happiness there is abundant assurance in every added day of the man's widowed life; for what but the magnetism of a blessed memory could have chained that venturesome spirit to a lot like that?

One day Murlock returned from gunning in a distant part of the forest to find his wife prostrate with fever, and delirious. There was no physician within miles, no neighbor; nor was she in a condition to be left, to summon help. So he set about the task of nursing her back to health, but at the end of the third day she fell into unconsciousness and so passed away, apparently, with never a gleam of returning reason.

From what we know of a nature like his we may venture to sketch in some of the details of the outline picture drawn by my grandfather. When convinced that she was dead, Murlock had sense enough to remember that the dead must be prepared for burial. In performance of this sacred duty he blundered now and again, did certain things incorrectly, and others which he did correctly were done over and over. His occasional failures to accomplish some simple and ordinary act filled him with astonishment, like that of a drunken man who wonders at the suspension of familiar natural laws. He was surprised, too, that he did not weep—surprised and a little ashamed; surely it is unkind not to weep for the dead. "To-morrow," he said aloud, "I shall have to make the coffin and dig the grave; and then I shall miss her, when she is no longer in sight; but now—she is dead, of course, but it is all right—it *must* be all right, somehow. Things cannot be so bad as they seem."

He stood over the body in the fading light, adjusting the hair and putting the finishing touches to the simple toilet, doing all mechanically, with soulless care. And still through his consciousness ran an undersense of conviction that all was right—that he should have her again as before, and everything explained. He had had no experience in grief; his capacity had not been enlarged by use. His heart could not contain it all, nor his imagination rightly conceive it. He did not know he was so hard struck; *that* knowledge would come later, and never go. Grief is an artist of powers as various as the instruments upon which he plays his dirges for the dead, evoking from some the sharpest, shrillest notes, from others the low, grave chords that throb recurrent like the slow beating of a distant drum. Some natures it startles; some it stupefies. To one it comes like the stroke of an arrow, stinging all the sensibilities to a keener life; to another as the blow of a bludgeon, which in crushing benumbs. We may conceive Murlock to have been that way affected, for (and here we are upon surer ground than that of conjecture) no sooner had he finished his pious work than, sinking into a chair by the side of the table upon which the body lay, and noting how white the profile showed in the deepening gloom, he laid his arms upon the table's edge, and dropped his face into them, tearless yet and unutterably weary. At that moment came in through the open window a long, wailing sound like the cry of a lost child in the far deeps of the darkening wood! But the man did not move. Again, and nearer than before, sounded that unearthly cry upon his failing sense. Perhaps it was a wild beast; perhaps it was a dream. For Murlock was asleep.

Some hours later, as it afterward appeared, this unfaithful watcher awoke and lifting his head from his arms intently listened—he knew not why. There in the black darkness by the side of the dead, recalling all without a shock, he strained his eyes to see—he knew not what. His senses were all alert, his breath was suspended, his blood had stilled its tides as if to assist the silence. Who—what had waked him, and where was it?

Suddenly the table shook beneath his arms, and at the same moment he heard, or fancied that he heard, a light, soft step—another—sounds as of bare feet upon the floor!

He was terrified beyond the power to cry out or move. Perforce he waited—waited there in the darkness through seeming centuries of such dread as one may know, yet live to tell. He tried vainly to speak the dead woman's name, vainly to stretch forth his hand across the table to learn if she were there. His throat was powerless, his arms and hands were like lead. Then occurred something most frightful. Some heavy body seemed hurled against the table with an impetus that pushed it against his breast so sharply as nearly to overthrow him, and at the same instant he heard and felt the fall of something upon the floor with so violent a thump that the whole house was shaken by the impact. A scuffling ensued, and a confusion of sounds impossible to describe. Murlock had risen to his feet. Fear had by excess forfeited control of his faculties. He flung his hands upon the table. Nothing was there!

There is a point at which terror may turn to madness; and madness incites to action. With no definite intent, from no motive but the wayward impulse of a madman, Murlock sprang to the wall, with a little groping seized his loaded rifle, and without aim discharged it. By the flash which lit up the room with a vivid illumination, he saw an enormous panther dragging the dead woman toward the window, its teeth fixed in her throat! Then there were darkness blacker than before, and silence; and when he returned to consciousness the sun was high and the wood vocal with songs of birds.

The body lay near the window, where the beast had left it when frightened away by the flash and report of the rifle. The clothing was deranged, the long hair in disorder, the limbs lay anyhow. From the throat, dreadfully lacerated, had issued a pool of blood not yet entirely coagulated. The ribbon with which he had bound the wrists was broken; the hands were tightly clenched. Between the teeth was a fragment of the animal's ear.

The Shell of Sense

Olivia Howard Dunbar

It was intolerably unchanged, the dim, dark-toned room. In an agony of recognition my glance ran from one to another of the comfortable, familiar things that my earthly life had been passed among. Incredibly distant from it all as I essentially was. I noted sharply that the very gaps that I myself had left in my bookshelves still stood unfilled; that the delicate fingers of the ferns that I had tended were still stretched futilely toward the light; that the soft agreeable chuckle of my own little clock, like some elderly woman with whom conversation has become automatic, was undiminished.

Unchanged—or so it seemed at first. But there were certain trivial differences that shortly smote me. The windows were closed too tightly; for I had always kept the house very cool, although I had known that Theresa preferred warm rooms. And my work-basket was in disorder; it was preposterous that so small a thing should hurt me so. Then, for this was my first experience of the shadow-folded transition, the odd alteration of my emotions bewildered me. For at one moment the place seemed so humanly familiar, so distinctly my own proper envelope, that for love of it I could have laid my cheek against the wall; while in the next I was miserably conscious of strange new shrillnesses. How could they be endured—and had I ever endured them?—those harsh influences that I now perceived at the window; light and color so blinding that they obscured the form of the wind, tumult so discordant that one could scarcely hear the roses open in the garden below?

But Theresa did not seem to mind any of these things. Disorder, it is true, the dear child had never minded. She was sitting all this time at my desk—at *my* desk—occupied, I could only too easily surmise how.

In the light of my own habits of precision it was plain that that sombre correspondence should have been attended to before; but I believe that I did not really reproach Theresa, for I knew that her notes, when she did write them, were perhaps less perfunctory than mine. She finished the last one as I watched her, and added it to the heap of black-bordered envelopes that lay on the desk. Poor girl! I saw now that they had cost her tears. Yet, living beside her day after day, year after year, I had never discovered what deep tenderness my sister possessed. Toward each other it had been our habit to display only a temperate affection, and I remember having always thought it distinctly fortunate for Theresa, since she was denied my happiness, that she could live so easily and pleasantly without emotions of the devastating sort... And now, for the first time, I was really to behold her... Could it be Theresa, after all, this tangle of subdued turbulences? Let no one suppose that it is an easy thing to bear, the relentlessly lucid understanding that I then first exercised; or that, in its first enfranchisement, the timid vision does not yearn for its old screens and mists.

Suddenly, as Theresa sat there, her head, filled with its tender thoughts of me, held in her gentle hands, I felt Allan's step on the carpeted stair outside. Theresa felt it, too,—but how? for it was not audible. She gave a start, swept the black envelopes out of sight, and pretended to be writing in a little book. Then I forgot to watch her any longer in my absorption in Allan's coming. It was he, of course, that I was awaiting. It was for him that I had made this first lonely, frightened effort to return, to recover... It was not that I had supposed he would allow himself to recognize my presence, for I had long been sufficiently familiar with his hard and fast denials of the invisible. He was so reasonable always, so sane—so blindfolded. But I had hoped that because of his very rejection of the ether that now contained me I could perhaps all the more safely, the more secretly, watch him, linger near him. He was near now, very near,—but why did Theresa, sitting there in the room that had never belonged to her, appropriate for herself his coming? It was so manifestly I who had drawn him, I whom he had come to seek.

The door was ajar. He knocked softly at it "Are you there, Theresa?" he called. He expected to find her, then, there in my room? I shrank back, fearing, almost, to stay.

"I shall have finished in a moment," Theresa told him, and he sat down to wait for her.

No spirit still unreleased can understand the pang that I felt with Allan sitting almost within my touch. Almost irresistibly the wish beset me to let him for an instant feel my nearness. Then I checked myself, remembering—oh, absurd, piteous human fears!—that my too unguarded closeness might alarm him. It was not so remote a time that I myself had known them, those blind, uncouth timidities. I came, therefore, somewhat nearer—but I did not touch him. I merely leaned toward him and with incredible softness whispered his name. That much I could not have forborne; the spell of life was still too strong in me.

But it gave him no comfort, no delight. "Theresa!" he called, in a voice dreadful with alarm—and in that instant the last veil fell, and desperately, scarce believingly, I beheld how it stood between them, those two.

She turned to him that gentle look of hers.

"Forgive me," came from him hoarsely. "But I had suddenly the most—unaccountable sensation. Can there be too many windows open? There is such a—chill—about."

"There are no windows open," Theresa assured him. "I took care to shut out the chill. You are not well, Allan!"

"Perhaps not." He embraced the suggestion. "And yet I feel no illness apart from this abominable sensation that persists—persists... Theresa, you must tell me: do I fancy it, or do you, too, feel—something—strange here?"

"Oh, there is something very strange here," she half sobbed. "There always will be."

"Good heavens, child, I didn't mean that!" He rose and stood looking about him. "I know, of course, that you have your beliefs, and I respect them, but you know equally well that I have nothing of the sort! So—don't let us conjure up anything inexplicable."

I stayed impalpably, imponderably near him. Wretched and bereft though I was, I could not have left him while he stood denying me.

"What I mean," he went on, in his low, distinct voice, "is a special, an almost ominous sense of cold. Upon my soul, Theresa,"—he paused—"if I *were* superstitious, if I *were* a woman, I should probably imagine it to seem—a presence!"

He spoke the last word very faintly, but Theresa shrank from it nevertheless.

"*Don't* say that, Allan!" she cried out. "Don't think it, I beg of you! I've tried so hard myself not to think it—and you must help me. You know it is only perturbed, uneasy spirits that wander. With her it is quite different. She has always been so happy—she must still be."

I listened, stunned, to Theresa's sweet dogmatism. From what blind distances came her confident misapprehensions, how dense, both for her and for Allan, was the separating vapor!

Allan frowned. "Don't take me literally, Theresa," he explained; and I, who a moment before had almost touched him, now held myself aloof and heard him with a strange untried pity, new born in me. "I'm not speaking of what you call—spirits. It's something much more terrible." He allowed his head to sink heavily on his chest. "If I did not positively know that I had never done her any harm, I should suppose myself to be suffering from guilt, from remorse... Theresa, you know better than I, perhaps. Was she content, always? Did she believe in me?"

"Believe in you?—when she knew you to be so good!—when you adored her!"

"She thought that? She said it? Then what in Heaven's name ails me?—unless it is all as you believe, Theresa, and she knows now what she didn't know then, poor dear, and minds——"

"Minds what? What do you mean, Allan?"

I, who with my perhaps illegitimate advantage saw so clear, knew that he had not meant to tell her: I did him that justice, even in my first jealousy. If I had not tortured him so by clinging near him, he would not have told her. But the moment came, and overflowed, and he did tell her—passionate, tumultuous story that it was. During all our life together, Allan's and mine, he had spared me, had kept me wrapped in the white cloak of an unblemished loyalty. But it would have been kinder, I now bitterly thought, if, like many husbands, he had years ago found for the story he now poured forth some clandestine listener; I should not have known. But he was faithful and good, and so he waited till I, mute and chained, was there to hear him. So well did I know him, as I thought, so thoroughly had he once been mine, that I saw it in his eyes, heard it in his voice, before the words came. And yet, when it came, it lashed me with the whips of an unbearable humiliation. For I, his wife, had not known how greatly he could love.

And that Theresa, soft little traitor, should, in her still way, have cared too! Where was the iron in her, I moaned within my stricken spirit, where the steadfastness? From the moment he bade her, she turned her soft little petals up to him—and my last delusion was spent. It was intolerable; and none the less so that in another moment she had, prompted by some belated thought of me, renounced him. Allan was hers, yet she put him from her; and it was my part to watch them both.

Then in the anguish of it all I remembered, awkward, untutored spirit that I was, that I now had the Great Recourse. Whatever human things were unbearable, I had no need to bear. I ceased, therefore, to make the effort that kept me with them. The pitiless poignancy was dulled, the sounds and the light ceased, the lovers faded from me, and again I was mercifully drawn into the dim, infinite spaces.

There followed a period whose length I cannot measure and during which I was able to make no progress in the difficult, dizzying experience of release. "Earth-bound" my jealousy relentlessly kept me. Though my two dear ones had forsworn each other, I could not trust them, for theirs seemed to me an affectation of a more than mortal magnanimity. Without a ghostly sentinel to prick them with sharp fears and recollections, who could believe that they would keep to it? Of the efficacy of my own vigilance, so long as I might choose to exercise it, I could have no doubt, for I had by this time come to have a dreadful exultation in the new power that lived in me. Repeated delicate experiment had taught me how a touch or a breath, a wish or a whisper, could control Allan's acts, could keep him from Theresa. I could manifest myself as palely, as transiently, as a thought. I could produce the merest necessary flicker, like the shadow of a just-opened leaf, on his trembling, tortured consciousness. And these unrealized perceptions of me he interpreted, as I had known that he would, as his soul's inevitable penance. He had come to believe that he had done evil in silently loving Theresa all these years, and it was my vengeance to allow him to believe this, to prod him ever to believe it afresh.

I am conscious that this frame of mind was not continuous in me. For I remember, too, that when Allan and Theresa were safely apart and sufficiently miserable I loved them as dearly as I ever had, more dearly perhaps. For it was impossible that I should not perceive, in my new emancipation, that they were, each of them, something more and greater than the two beings I had once ignorantly pictured them. For years they had practiced a selflessness of which I could once scarcely have conceived, and which even now I could only admire without entering into its mystery. While I had lived solely for myself, these two divine creatures had lived exquisitely for me. They had granted me everything, themselves nothing. For my undeserving sake their lives had been a constant torment of renunciation—a torment they had not sought to alleviate by the exchange of a single glance of understanding. There were even marvelous moments when, from the depths of my newly informed heart, I pitied them—poor creatures, who, withheld from the infinite solaces that I had come to know, were still utterly within that

> Shell of sense
> So frail, so piteously contrived for pain.

Within it, yes; yet exercising qualities that so sublimely transcended it. Yet the shy, hesitating compassion that thus had birth in me was far from being able to defeat the earlier, earthlier emotion. The two, I recognized, were in a sort of conflict; and I, regarding it, assumed that the conflict would never end; that for years, as Allan and Theresa reckoned time, I should be obliged to withhold myself from the great spaces and linger suffering, grudging, shamed, where they lingered.

It can never have been explained, I suppose, what, to devitalized perception such as mine, the contact of mortal beings with each other appears to be. Once to have exercised this sense-freed perception is to realize that the gift of prophecy, although the subject of such frequent marvel, is no longer mysterious. The merest glance of our sensitive and uncloyed vision can detect the strength of the relation between two beings, and therefore instantly calculate its duration. If you see a heavy weight suspended from a slender string, you can know, without any wizardry, that in a few moments the string will snap; well, such, if you admit the analogy, is prophecy, is foreknowledge. And it was thus that I saw it with Theresa and Allan. For it was perfectly visible to me that they would very little longer have the strength to preserve, near each other, the denuded impersonal relation that they, and that I, behind them, insisted on; and that they would have to separate. It was my sister, perhaps the more sensitive, who first realized this. It had now become possible for me to observe them almost constantly, the effort necessary to visit them had so greatly diminished; so that I watched her, poor, anguished girl, prepare to leave him. I saw each reluctant movement that she made. I saw her eyes, worn from self-searching; I heard her step grown timid from inexplicable fears; I entered her very heart and heard its pitiful, wild beating. And still I did not interfere.

For at this time I had a wonderful, almost demoniacal sense of disposing of matters to suit my own selfish will. At any moment I could have checked their miseries, could have restored happiness and peace. Yet it gave me, and I could weep to admit it, a monstrous joy to know that Theresa thought she was leaving Allan of her own free intention, when it was I who was contriving, arranging, insisting... And yet she wretchedly felt my presence near her; I am certain of that.

A few days before the time of her intended departure my sister told Allan that she must speak with him after dinner. Our beautiful old house branched out from a circular hall with great arched doors at either end; and it was through the rear doorway that always in summer, after dinner, we passed out into the garden adjoining. As usual, therefore, when the hour came, Theresa led the way. That dreadful daytime brilliance that in my present state I found so hard to endure was now becoming softer. A delicate, capricious twilight breeze danced inconsequently through languidly whispering leaves. Lovely pale flowers blossomed like little moons in the dusk, and over them the breath of mignonette hung heavily. It was a perfect place—and it had so long been ours, Allan's and mine. It made me restless and a little wicked that those two should be there together now.

For a little they walked about together, speaking of common, daily things. Then suddenly Theresa burst out:

"I am going away, Allan. I have stayed to do everything that needed to be done. Now your mother will be here to care for you, and it is time for me to go."

He stared at her and stood still. Theresa had been there so long, she so definitely, to his mind, belonged there. And she was, as I also had jealously known, so lovely there, the small, dark, dainty creature, in the old hall, on the wide staircases, in the garden... Life there without Theresa, even the intentionally remote, the perpetually renounced

Theresa—he had not dreamed of it, he could not, so suddenly, conceive of it.

"Sit here," he said, and drew her down beside him on a bench, "and tell me what it means, why you are going. Is it because of something that I have been—have done?"

She hesitated. I wondered if she would dare tell him. She looked out and away from him, and he waited long for her to speak.

The pale stars were sliding into their places. The whispering of the leaves was almost hushed. All about them it was still and shadowy and sweet. It was that wonderful moment when, for lack of a visible horizon, the not yet darkened world seems infinitely greater—a moment when anything can happen, anything be believed in. To me, watching, listening, hovering, there came a dreadful purpose and a dreadful courage. Suppose for one moment, Theresa should not only feel, but *see* me—would she dare to tell him then?

There came a brief space of terrible effort, all my fluttering, uncertain forces strained to the utmost. The instant of my struggle was endlessly long and the transition seemed to take place outside me—as one sitting in a train, motionless, sees the leagues of earth float by. And then, in a bright, terrible flash I knew I had achieved it—I had *attained visibility*. Shuddering, insubstantial, but luminously apparent, I stood there before them. And for the instant that I maintained the visible state I looked straight into Theresa's soul.

She gave a cry. And then, thing of silly, cruel impulses that I was, I saw what I had done. The very thing that I wished to avert I had precipitated. For Allan, in his sudden terror and pity, had bent and caught her in his arms. For the first time they were together; and it was I who had brought them.

Then, to his whispered urging to tell the reason of her cry, Theresa said:

"Frances was here. You did not see her, standing there, under the lilacs, with no smile on her face?"

"My dear, my dear!" was all that Allan said. I had so long now lived invisibly with them, he knew that she was right.

"I suppose you know what it means?" she asked him, calmly.

"Dear Theresa," Allan said, slowly, "if you and I should go away somewhere, could we not evade all this ghostliness? And will you come with me?"

"Distance would not banish her," my sister confidently asserted. And then she said, softly: "Have you thought what a lonely, awesome thing it must be to be so newly dead? Pity her, Allan. We who are warm and alive should pity her. She loves you still,—that is the meaning of it all, you know—and she wants us to understand that for that reason we must keep apart. Oh, it was so plain in her white face as she stood there. And you did not see her?"

"It was your face that I saw," Allan solemnly told her—oh, how different he had grown from the Allan that I had known!—"and yours is the only face that I shall ever see." And again he drew her to him.

She sprang from him. "You are defying her, Allan!" she cried. "And you must not. It is her right to keep us apart, if she wishes. It must be as she insists. I shall go, as I told you. And, Allan, I beg of you, leave me the courage to do as she demands!"

They stood facing each other in the deep dusk, and the wounds that I had dealt them gaped red and accusing. "We must pity her," Theresa had said. And as I remembered that extraordinary speech, and saw the agony in her face, and the greater agony in Allan's, there came the great irreparable cleavage between mortality and me. In a swift, merciful flame the last of my mortal emotions—gross and tenacious they must have been—was consumed. My cold grasp of Allan loosened and a new unearthly love of him bloomed in my heart.

I was now, however, in a difficulty with which my experience in the newer state was scarcely sufficient to deal. How could I make it plain to Allan and Theresa that I wished to bring them together, to heal the wounds that I had made?

Pityingly, remorsefully, I lingered near them all that night and the next day. And by that time had brought myself to the point of a great determination. In the little time that was left, before Theresa should be gone and Allan bereft and desolate, I saw the one way that lay open to me to convince them of my acquiescence in their destiny.

In the deepest darkness and silence of the next night I made a greater effort than it will ever be necessary for me to make again. When they think of me, Allan and Theresa, I pray now that they will recall what I did that night, and that my thousand frustrations and selfishnesses may shrivel and be blown from their indulgent memories.

Yet the following morning, as she had planned, Theresa appeared at breakfast dressed for her journey. Above in her room there were the sounds of departure. They spoke little during the brief meal, but when it was ended Allan said:

"Theresa, there is half an hour before you go. Will you come upstairs with me? I had a dream that I must tell you of."

"Allan!" She looked at him, frightened, but went with him. "It was of Frances you dreamed," she said, quietly, as they entered the library together.

"Did I say it was a dream? But I was awake—thoroughly awake. I had not been sleeping well, and I heard, twice, the striking of the clock. And as I lay there, looking out at the stars, and thinking—thinking of you, Theresa,—she came to me, stood there before me, in my room. It was no sheeted specter, you understand; it was Frances, literally she. In some inexplicable fashion I seemed to be aware that she wanted to make me know something, and I waited, watching her face. After a few moments it came. She did not speak, precisely. That is, I am sure I heard no sound. Yet the words that came from her were definite enough. She said: 'Don't let Theresa leave you. Take her and keep her.' Then she went away. Was that a dream?"

"I had not meant to tell you," Theresa eagerly answered, "but now I must. It is too wonderful. What time did your clock strike, Allan?"

"One, the last time."

"Yes; it was then that I awoke. And she had been with me. I had not seen her, but her arm had been about me and her kiss was on my cheek. Oh. I knew; it was unmistakable. And the sound of her voice was with me."

"Then she bade you, too—"

"Yes, to stay with you. I am glad we told each other." She smiled tearfully and began to fasten her wrap.

"But you are not going—*now!*" Allan cried. "You know that you cannot, now that she has asked you to stay."

"Then you believe, as I do, that it was she?" Theresa demanded.

"I can never understand, but I know," he answered her. "And now you will not go?"

I am freed. There will be no further semblance of me in my old home, no sound of my voice, no dimmest echo of my earthly self. They have no further need of me, the two that I have brought together. Theirs is the fullest joy that the dwellers in the shell of sense can know. Mine is the transcendent joy of the unseen spaces.

THURNLEY ABBEY

PERCEVAL LANDON

Three years ago I was on my way out to the East, and as an extra day in London was of some importance, I took the Friday evening mail-train to Brindisi instead of the usual Thursday morning Marseilles express. Many people shrink from the long forty-eight-hour train journey through Europe, and the subsequent rush across the Mediterranean on the nineteen-knot *Isis* or *Osiris*; but there is really very little discomfort on either the train or the mail-boat, and unless there is actually nothing for me to do, I always like to save the extra day and a half in London before I say goodbye to her for one of my longer tramps. This time – it was early, I remember, in the shipping season, probably about the beginning of September – there were few passengers, and I had a compartment in the P. & O. Indian express to myself all the way from Calais. All Sunday I watched the blue waves dimpling the Adriatic, and the pale rosemary along the cuttings; the plain white towns, with their flat roofs and their bold 'duomos', and the grey-green gnarled olive orchards of Apulia. The journey was just like any other. We ate in the dining-car as often and as long as we decently could. We slept after luncheon; we dawdled the afternoon away with yellow-backed novels; sometimes we exchanged platitudes in the smoking-room, and it was there that I met Alastair Colvin.

Colvin was a man of middle height, with a resolute, well-cut jaw; his hair was turning grey; his moustache was sun-whitened, otherwise he was clean-shaven – obviously a gentleman, and obviously also a preoccupied man. He had no great wit. When spoken to, he made the usual remarks in the right way, and I dare say he refrained from banalities only because he spoke less than the rest of us; most of the time he buried himself in the Wagon-lit Company's time-table, but seemed unable to concentrate his attention on any one page of it. He found that I had been over the Siberian railway, and for a quarter of an hour he discussed it with me. Then he lost interest in it, and rose to go to his compartment. But he came back again very soon, and seemed glad to pick up the conversation again.

Of course this did not seem to me to be of any importance. Most travellers by train become a trifle infirm of purpose after thirty-six hours' rattling. But Colvin's restless way I noticed in somewhat marked contrast with the man's personal importance and dignity; especially ill suited was it to his finely made large hand with strong, broad, regular nails and its few lines. As I looked at his hand I noticed a long, deep, and recent scar of ragged shape. However, it is absurd to pretend that I thought anything was unusual. I went off at five o'clock on Sunday afternoon to sleep away the hour or two that had still to be got through before we arrived at Brindisi.

Once there, we few passengers transhipped our hand baggage, verified our berths – there were only a score of us in all – and then, after an aimless ramble of half an hour in Brindisi, we returned to dinner at the Hotel International, not wholly surprised that the town had been the death of Virgil. If I remember rightly, there is a gaily painted hall at the International – I do not wish to advertise anything, but there is no other place in Brindisi at which to await the coming of the mails – and after dinner I was looking with awe at a trellis overgrown with blue vines, when Colvin moved across the room to my table. He picked up *Il Secolo*, but almost immediately gave up the pretence of reading it. He turned squarely to me and said:

'Would you do me a favour?'

One doesn't do favours to stray acquaintances on Continental expresses without knowing something more of them than I knew of Colvin. But I smiled in a noncommittal way, and asked him what he wanted. I wasn't wrong in part of my estimate of him; he said bluntly:

'Will you let me sleep in your cabin on the *Osiris*?' And he coloured a little as he said it.

Now, there is nothing more tiresome than having to put up with a stable-companion at sea, and I asked him rather pointedly:

'Surely there is room for all of us?' I thought that perhaps he had been partnered off with some mangy Levantine, and wanted to escape from him at all hazards.

Colvin, still somewhat confused, said: 'Yes; I am in a cabin by myself. But you would do me the greatest favour if you would allow me to share yours.'

This was all very well, but, besides the fact that I always sleep better when alone, there had been some recent thefts on board English liners, and I hesitated, frank and honest and self-conscious as Colvin was. Just then the mail-train came in with a clatter and a rush of escaping steam, and I asked him to see me again about it on the boat when we started. He answered me curtly – I suppose he saw the mistrust in my manner – 'I am a member of White's and the Beefsteak.' I smiled to myself as he said it, but I remembered in a moment that the man – if he were really what he claimed to be, and I make no doubt that he was – must have been sorely put to it before he urged the fact as a guarantee of his respectability to a total stranger at a Brindisi hotel.

That evening, as we cleared the red and green harbour-lights of Brindisi, Colvin explained. This is his story in his own words.

'When I was travelling in India some years ago, I made the acquaintance of a youngish man in the Woods and Forests. We camped out together for a week, and I found him a pleasant companion. John Broughton was a light-hearted soul when off duty, but a steady and capable man in any of the small emergencies that continually arise in that department. He was liked and trusted by the natives, and though a trifle over-pleased with himself when he escaped to civilization at Simla or Calcutta, Broughton's future was well assured in Government service, when a fair-sized estate was unexpectedly left to him, and he joyfully shook the dust of the Indian plains from his feet and returned to England. For five years he drifted about London. I saw him now and then. We dined together about every eighteen months, and I could trace pretty exactly the gradual sickening of Broughton with a merely idle life. He then set out on a couple of long voyages, returned as restless as before, and at last told me that he had decided to marry and settle down at his place, Thurnley Abbey, which had long been empty. He spoke about looking after the property and standing for his constituency in the usual way. Vivien Wilde, his fiancée, had, I suppose, begun to take him in hand. She was a pretty girl with a deal of fair hair and rather an exclusive manner; deeply religious in a narrow school, she was still kindly and high-spirited, and I thought that Broughton was in luck. He was quite happy and full of information about his future.

'Among other things, I asked him about Thurnley Abbey. He confessed that he hardly knew the place. The last tenant, a man called Clarke, had lived in one wing for fifteen years and seen no one. He had been a miser and a hermit. It was the rarest thing for a light to be seen at the Abbey after dark. Only the barest necessities of life were ordered, and the tenant himself received them at the side-door. His one half-caste manservant, after a month's stay in the house, had abruptly left without warning, and had returned to the Southern States. One thing Broughton complained bitterly about: Clarke had wilfully spread the rumour among the villagers that the Abbey was haunted, and had even condescended to play childish tricks with spirit-lamps and salt in order to scare trespassers away at night. He had been detected in the act of this tomfoolery, but the story spread, and no one, said Broughton, would venture near the house except in broad daylight. The hauntedness of Thurnley Abbey was now, he said with a grin, part of the gospel of the countryside, but he and his young wife were going to change all that. Would I propose myself any time I liked? I, of course, said I would, and equally, of course, intended to do nothing of the sort without a definite invitation.

'The house was put in thorough repair, though not a stick of the old furniture and tapestry were removed. Floors and ceilings were relaid: the roof was made watertight again, and the dust of half a century was scoured out. He showed me some photographs of the place. It was called an Abbey, though as a matter of fact it had been only the infirmary of the long-vanished Abbey of Closter some five miles away. The larger part of this building remained as it had been in pre-Reformation days, but a wing had been added in Jacobean times, and that part of the house had been kept in something like repair by Mr. Clarke. He had in both the ground and first floors set a heavy timber door, strongly barred with iron, in the passage between the earlier and the Jacobean parts of the house, and had entirely neglected the former. So there had been a good deal of work to be done.

'Broughton, whom I saw in London two or three times about this period, made a deal of fun over the positive refusal of the workmen to remain after sundown. Even after the electric light had been put into every room, nothing would induce them to remain, though, as Broughton observed, electric light was death on ghosts. The legend of the Abbey's ghosts had gone far and wide, and the men would take no risks. They went home in batches of five and six, and even during the daylight hours there was an inordinate amount of talking between one and another, if either happened to be out of sight of his companion. On the whole, though nothing of any sort or kind had been conjured up even by their heated imaginations during their five months' work upon the Abbey, the belief in the ghosts was rather strengthened than otherwise in Thurnley because of the men's confessed nervousness, and local tradition declared itself in favour of the ghost of an immured nun.

'"Good old nun!" said Broughton.

'I asked him whether in general he believed in the possibility of ghosts, and, rather to my surprise, he said that he couldn't say he entirely disbelieved in them. A man in India had told him one morning in camp that he believed that his mother was dead in England, as her vision had come to his tent the night before. He had not been alarmed, but had said nothing, and the figure vanished again. As a matter of fact, the next possible dak-walla brought on a telegram announcing the mother's death. "There the thing was," said Broughton. But at Thurnley he was practical enough. He roundly cursed the idiotic selfishness of Clarke, whose silly antics had caused all the inconvenience. At the same time, he couldn't refuse to sympathize to some extent with the ignorant workmen. "My own idea," said he, "is that if a ghost ever does come in one's way, one ought to speak to it."

'I agreed. Little as I knew of the ghost world and its conventions, I had always remembered that a spook was in honour bound to wait to be spoken to. It didn't seem much to do, and I felt that the sound of one's own voice would at any rate reassure oneself as to one's wakefulness. But there are few ghosts outside Europe – few, that is, that a white man can see – and I had never been troubled with any. However, as I have said, I told Broughton that I agreed.

'So the wedding took place, and I went to it in a tall hat which I bought for the occasion, and the new Mrs. Broughton smiled very nicely at me afterwards. As it had to happen, I took the Orient Express that evening and was not in England again for nearly six months. Just before I came back I got a letter from Broughton. He asked if I could see him in London or come to Thurnley, as he thought I should be better able to help him than anyone else he knew. His wife sent a nice message to me at the end, so I was reassured about at least one thing. I wrote from Budapest that I would come and see him at Thurnley two days after my arrival in London, and as I sauntered out of the Pannonia into the Kerepesi Utcza to post my letters, I wondered of what earthly service I could be to Broughton. I had been out with him after tiger on foot, and I could imagine few men better able at a pinch to manage their own business. However, I had nothing to do, so after dealing with some small accumulations of business during my absence, I packed a kit-bag and departed to Euston.

'I was met by Broughton's great limousine at Thurnley Road station, and after a drive of nearly seven miles we echoed through the sleepy streets of Thurnley village, into which the main gates of the park thrust themselves, splendid with pillars and spreadeagles and tom-cats rampant atop of them. I never was a herald, but I know that the Broughtons have the right to supporters – Heaven knows why! From the gates a quadruple avenue of beech-trees led inwards for a quarter of a mile. Beneath them a neat strip of fine turf edged the road and ran back until the poison of the dead beech-leaves killed it under the trees. There were many wheel-tracks on the road, and a comfortable little pony trap jogged past me laden with a country parson and his wife and daughter. Evidently there was some garden party going on at the Abbey. The road dropped away to the right at the end of the avenue, and I could see the Abbey across a wide pasturage and a broad lawn thickly dotted with guests.

'The end of the building was plain. It must have been almost mercilessly austere when it was first built, but time had crumbled the edges and toned the stone down to an orange-lichened grey wherever it showed behind its curtain of magnolia, jasmine, and ivy. Further on was the three-storeyed Jacobean house, tall and handsome. There had not been the slightest attempt to adapt the one to the other, but the kindly ivy had glossed over the touching-point. There was a tall flèche in the middle of the building, surmounting a small bell tower. Behind the house there rose the mountainous verdure of Spanish chestnuts all the way up the hill.

'Broughton had seen me coming from afar, and walked across from his other guests to welcome me before turning me over to the butler's care. This man was sandy-haired and rather inclined to be talkative. He could, however, answer hardly any questions about the house; he had, he said, only been there three weeks. Mindful of what Broughton had told me, I made no enquiries about ghosts, though the room into which I was shown might have justified anything. It was a very large low room with oak beams projecting from the white ceiling. Every inch of the walls, including the doors, was covered with tapestry, and a remarkably fine Italian fourpost bedstead, heavily draped, added to the darkness and dignity of the place. All the furniture was old, well made and dark. Underfoot there was a plain green pile carpet, the only new thing about the room except the electric light fittings and the jugs and basins. Even the looking-glass on the dressing-table was an old pyramidal Venetian glass set in a heavy repoussé frame of tarnished silver.

'After a few minutes' cleaning up, I went downstairs and out upon the lawn, where I greeted my hostess. The people gathered there were of the usual country type, all anxious to be pleased and roundly curious as to the new master of the Abbey. Rather to my surprise, and quite to my pleasure, I rediscovered Glenham, whom I had known well in old days in Barotseland: he lived quite close, as, he remarked with a grin. I ought to have known. "But," he added, "I don't live in a place like this." He swept his hand to the long, low lines of the Abbey in obvious admiration, and then, to my intense interest, muttered beneath his breath, "Thank God!" He saw that I had overheard him, and turning to me said decidedly, "Yes, 'thank God' I said, and I meant it. I wouldn't live at the Abbey for all Broughton's money."

'"But surely," I demurred, "you know that old Clarke was discovered in the very act of setting light to his bug-a-boos?"

'Glenham shrugged his shoulders. "Yes, I know about that. But there is something wrong with the place still. All I can say is that Broughton is a different man since he has lived here. I don't believe that he will remain much longer. But – you're staying here? – well, you'll hear all about it tonight. There's a big dinner, I understand." The conversation turned off to old reminiscences, and Glenham soon after had to go.

'Before I went to dress that evening I had twenty minutes' talk with Broughton in his library. There was no doubt that the man was altered, gravely altered. He was nervous and fidgety, and I found him looking at me only when my eye was off him. I naturally asked him what he wanted of me. I told him I would do anything I could, but that I couldn't conceive what he lacked that I could provide. He said with a lustreless smile that there was, however, something, and that he would tell me the following morning. It struck me that he was somehow ashamed of himself and perhaps ashamed of the part he was asking me to play. However, I dismissed the subject from my mind and went up to dress in my palatial room. As I shut the door a draught blew out the Queen of Sheba from the wall, and I noticed that the tapestries were not fastened to the wall at the bottom. I have always held very practical views about spooks, and it has often seemed to me that the slow waving in firelight of loose tapestry upon a wall would account for ninety-nine per cent of the stories one hears. Certainly the dignified undulation of this lady with her attendants and huntsmen – one of whom was untidily cutting the throat of a fallow deer upon the very steps on which King Solomon, a grey-faced Flemish nobleman with the order of the Golden Fleece, awaited his fair visitor – gave colour to my hypothesis.

'Nothing much happened at dinner. The people were very much like those of the garden party. A young woman next to me seemed anxious to know what was being read in London. As she was far more familiar than I with the most recent magazines and literary supplements, I found salvation in being myself instructed in the tendencies of modern fiction. All true art, she said, was shot through and through with melancholy. How vulgar were the attempts at wit that marked so many modern books! From the beginning of literature it had always been tragedy that embodied the highest attainment of every age. To call such works morbid merely begged the question. No thoughtful man – she looked sternly at me through the steel rim of her glasses – could fail to agree with me. Of course, as one would, I immediately and properly said that I slept with Pett Ridge and Jacobs under my pillow at night, and that if *Jorrocks* weren't quite so large and cornery, I would add him to the company. She hadn't read any of them, so I was saved – for a time. But I remember grimly that she said that the dearest wish of her life was to be in some awful and soul-freezing situation of horror, and I remember that she dealt hardly with the hero of Nat Paynter's vampire story, between nibbles at her brown-bread ice. She was a cheerless soul, and I couldn't help thinking that if there were many such in the neighbourhood, it was not surprising that old Glenham had been stuffed with some nonsense or other about the Abbey. Yet nothing could well have been less creepy than the glitter of silver and glass, and the subdued lights and cackle of conversation all round the dinner-table.

'After the ladies had gone I found myself talking to the rural dean. He was a thin, earnest man, who at once turned the conversation to old Clarke's buffooneries. But, he said, Mr Broughton had introduced such a new and cheerful spirit, not only into the Abbey, but, he might say, into the whole neighbourhood, that he had great hopes that the ignorant superstitions of the past were from henceforth destined to oblivion. Thereupon his other neighbour, a portly gentleman of independent means and position, audibly remarked "Amen", which damped the rural dean, and we talked of partridges past, partridges present, and pheasants to come. At the other end of the table Broughton sat with a couple of his friends, red-faced hunting men. Once I noticed that they were discussing me, but I paid no attention to it at the time. I remembered it a few hours later.

'By eleven all the guests were gone, and Broughton, his wife, and I were alone together under the fine plaster ceiling of the Jacobean drawing-room. Mrs Broughton talked about one or two of the neighbours, and then, with a smile, said that she knew I would excuse her, shook hands with me, and went off to bed. I am not very good at analysing things, but I felt that she talked a little uncomfortably and with a suspicion of effort, smiled rather conventionally, and was obviously glad to go. These things seem trifling enough to repeat, but I had throughout the faint feeling that everything was not square. Under the circumstances, this was enough to set me wondering what on earth the service could be that I was to render – wondering also whether the whole business were not some ill-advised jest in order to make me come down from

London for a mere shooting-party.

'Broughton said little after she had gone. But he was evidently labouring to bring the conversation round to the so-called haunting of the Abbey. As soon as I saw this, of course I asked him directly about it. He then seemed at once to lose interest in the matter. There was no doubt about it: Broughton was somehow a changed man, and to my mind he had changed in no way for the better. Mrs Broughton seemed no sufficient cause. He was clearly very fond of her, and she of him. I reminded him that he was going to tell me what I could do for him in the morning, pleaded my journey, lighted a candle, and went upstairs with him. At the end of the passage leading into the old house he grinned weakly and said, "Mind, if you see a ghost, do talk to it; you said you would." He stood irresolutely a moment and then turned away. At the door of his dressing-room he paused once more: "I'm here," he called out, "if you should want anything. Good night," and he shut his door.

'I went along the passage to my room, undressed, switched on a lamp beside my bed, read a few pages of *The Jungle Book*, and then, more than ready for sleep, turned the light off and went fast asleep.

'Three hours later I woke up. There was not a breath of wind outside. There was not even a flicker of light from the fireplace. As I lay there, an ash tinkled slightly as it cooled, but there was hardly a gleam of the dullest red in the grate. An owl cried among the silent Spanish chestnuts on the slope outside. I idly reviewed the events of the day, hoping that I should fall off to sleep again before I reached dinner. But at the end I seemed as wakeful as ever. There was no help for it. I must read my *Jungle Book* again till I felt ready to go off, so I fumbled for the pear at the end of the cord that hung down inside the bed, and I switched on the bedside lamp. The sudden glory dazzled me for a moment. I felt under my pillow for my book with half-shut eyes. Then, growing used to the light, I happened to look down to the foot of my bed.

'I can never tell you really what happened then. Nothing I could ever confess in the most abject words could even faintly picture to you what I felt. I know that my heart stopped dead, and my throat shut automatically. In one instinctive movement I crouched back up against the head-boards of the bed, staring at the horror. The movement set my heart going again, and the sweat dripped from every pore. I am not a particularly religious man, but I had always believed that God would never allow any supernatural appearance to present itself to man in such a guise and in such circumstances that harm, either bodily or mental, could result to him. I can only tell you that at that moment both my life and my reason rocked unsteadily on their seats.'

The other *Osiris* passengers had gone to bed. Only he and I remained leaning over the starboard railing, which rattled uneasily now and then under the fierce vibration of the over-engined mail-boat. Far over, there were the lights of a few fishing-smacks riding out the night, and a great rush of white combing and seething water fell out and away from us overside.

At last Colvin went on:

'Leaning over the foot of my bed, looking at me, was a figure swathed in a rotten and tattered veiling. This shroud passed over the head, but left both eyes and the right side of the face bare. It then followed the line of the arm down to where the hand grasped the bed-end. The face was not entirely that of a skull, though the eyes and the flesh of the face were totally gone. There was a thin, dry skin drawn tightly over the features, and there was some skin left on the hand. One wisp of hair crossed the forehead. It was perfectly still. I looked at it, and it looked at me, and my brains turned dry and hot in my head. I had still got the pear of the electric lamp in my hand, and I played idly with it; only I dared not turn the light out again. I shut my eyes, only to open them in a hideous terror the same second. The thing had not moved.

My heart was thumping, and the sweat cooled me as it evaporated. Another cinder tinkled in the grate, and a panel creaked in the wall.

'My reason failed me. For twenty minutes, or twenty seconds. I was able to think of nothing else but this awful figure, till there came, hurtling through the empty channels of my senses, the remembrance that Broughton and his friends had discussed me furtively at dinner. The dim possibility of its being a hoax stole gratefully into my unhappy mind, and once there, one's pluck came creeping back along a thousand tiny veins. My first sensation was one of blind unreasoning thankfulness that my brain was going to stand the trial. I am not a timid man, but the best of us needs some human handle to steady him in time of extremity, and in this faint but growing hope that after all it might be only a brutal hoax, I found the fulcrum that I needed. At last I moved.

'How I managed to do it I cannot tell you, but with one spring towards the foot of the bed I got within arm's-length and struck out one fearful blow with my fist at the thing. It crumbled under it, and my hand was cut to the bone. With a sickening revulsion after my terror, I dropped half-fainting across the end of the bed. So it was merely a foul trick after all. No doubt the trick had been played many a time before: no doubt Broughton and his friends had had some large bet among themselves as to what I should do when I discovered the gruesome thing. From my state of abject terror I found myself transported into an insensate anger. I shouted curses upon Broughton. I dived rather than climbed over the bed-end on to the sofa. I tore at the robed skeleton – how well the whole thing had been carried out, I thought – I broke the skull against the floor, and stamped upon its dry bones. I flung the head away under the bed, and rent the brittle bones of the trunk in pieces. I snapped the thin thigh-bones across my knee, and flung them in different directions. The shin-bones I set up against a stool and broke with my heel. I raged like a Berserker against the loathly thing, and stripped the ribs from the backbone and slung the breastbone against the cupboard. My fury increased as the work of destruction went on.

I tore the frail rotten veil into twenty pieces, and the dust went up over everything, over the clean blotting-paper and the silver inkstand. At last my work was done. There was but a raffle of broken bones and strips of parchment and crumbling wool. Then, picking up a piece of the skull – it was the check and temple bone of the right side, I remember – I opened the door and went down the passage to Broughton's dressing-room. I remember still how my sweat-dripping pyjamas clung to me as I walked. At the door I kicked and entered.

'Broughton was in bed. He had already turned the light on and seemed shrunken and horrified. For a moment he could hardly pull himself together. Then I spoke. I don't know what I said. Only I know that from a heart full and over-full with hatred and contempt, spurred on by shame of my own recent cowardice, I let my tongue run on. He answered nothing. I was amazed at my own fluency. My hair still clung lankily to my wet temples, my hand was bleeding profusely, and I must have looked a strange sight. Broughton huddled himself up at the head of the bed just as I had. Still he made no answer, no defence. He seemed preoccupied with something besides my reproaches, and once or twice moistened his lips with his tongue. But he could say nothing, though he moved his hands now and then, just as a baby who cannot speak moves its hands.

'At last the door into Mrs Broughton's room opened and she came in, white and terrified. "What is it? What is it? Oh, in God's name! what is it?" she cried again and again, and then she went up to her husband and sat on the bed in her night-dress, and the two faced me. I told her what the matter was. I spared her husband not a word for her presence there. Yet he seemed hardly to understand. I told the pair that I had spoiled their cowardly joke for them. Broughton looked up.

'"I have smashed the foul thing into a hundred pieces," I said. Broughton licked his lips again and his mouth worked. "By God!" I shouted, "it would serve you right if I thrashed you within an inch of your life. I will take care that not a decent man or woman of my acquaintance ever speaks to you again. And there," I added, throwing the broken piece of the skull upon the floor beside his bed, "there is a souvenir for you, of your damned work tonight!"

'Broughton saw the bone, and in a moment it was his turn to frighten me. He squealed like a hare caught in a trap. He screamed and screamed till Mrs Broughton, almost as bewildered as myself, held on to him and coaxed him like a child to be quiet. But Broughton – and as he moved I thought that ten minutes ago I perhaps looked as terribly ill as he did – thrust her from him, and scrambled out of the bed on to the floor, and still screaming put out his hand to the bone. It had blood on it from my hand. He paid no attention to me whatever. In truth I said nothing. This was a new turn indeed to the horrors of the evening. He rose from the floor with the bone in his hand and stood silent. He seemed to be listening. "Time, time, perhaps," he muttered, and almost at the same moment fell at full length on the carpet, cutting his head against the fender. The bone flew from his hand and came to rest near the door. I picked Broughton up, haggard and broken, with blood over his face. He whispered hoarsely and quickly, "Listen, listen!" We listened.

'After ten seconds' utter quiet, I seemed to hear something. I could not be sure, but at last there was no doubt. There was a quiet sound as of one moving along the passage. Little regular steps came towards us over the hard oak flooring. Broughton moved to where his wife sat, white and speechless, on the bed, and pressed her face into his shoulder.

'Then, the last thing that I could see as he turned the light out, he fell forward with his own head pressed into the pillow of the bed. Something in their company, something in their cowardice, helped me, and I faced the open doorway of the room, which was outlined fairly clearly against the dimly lighted passage. I put out one hand and touched Mrs Broughton's shoulder in the darkness. But at the last moment I too failed. I sank on my knees and put my face in the bed. Only we all heard. The footsteps came to the door, and there they stopped. The piece of bone was lying a yard inside the door. There was a rustle of moving stuff, and the thing was in the room. Mrs Broughton was silent: I could hear Broughton's voice praying, muffled in the pillow: I was cursing my own cowardice. Then the steps moved out again on the oak boards of the passage, and I heard the sounds dying away. In a flash of remorse I went to the door and looked out. At the end of the corridor I thought I saw something that moved away. A moment later the passage was empty. I stood with my forehead against the jamb of the door almost physically sick.

'"You can turn the light on," I said, and there was an answering flare. There was no bone at my feet. Mrs Broughton had fainted. Broughton was almost useless, and it took me ten minutes to bring her to. Broughton only said one thing worth remembering. For the most part he went on muttering prayers. But I was glad afterwards to recollect that he had said that thing. He said in a colourless voice, half as a question, half as a reproach, "You didn't speak to her."

'We spent the remainder of the night together. Mrs Broughton actually fell off into in a kind of sleep before dawn, but she suffered so horribly in her dreams that I shook her into consciousness again. Never was dawn so long in coming. Three or four times Broughton spoke to himself. Mrs Broughton would then just tighten her hold on his arm, but she could say nothing. As for me, I can honestly say that I grew worse as the hours passed and the light strengthened. The two violent reactions had battered down my steadiness of view, and I felt that the foundations of my life had been built upon the sand. I said nothing, and after binding up my hand with a towel, I did not move. It was better so. They helped me and I helped them, and we all three knew that our reason had gone very near to ruin that night. At last, when the light came in pretty strongly, and the birds outside were chattering and singing, we felt that we must do something. Yet we never moved. You might have thought that we should particularly dislike being found as we were by the servants: yet nothing of that kind mattered a straw, and an overpowering listlessness bound us as we sat, until Chapman,

Broughton's man, actually knocked and opened the door. None of us moved. Broughton, speaking hardly and stiffly, said, "Chapman, you can come back in five minutes." Chapman was a discreet man, but it would have made no difference to us if he had carried his news to the "room" at once.

'We looked at each other and I said I must go back. I meant to wait outside till Chapman returned. I simply dared not re-enter my bedroom alone. Broughton roused himself and said that he would come with me. Mrs Broughton agreed to remain in her own room for five minutes if the blinds were drawn up and all the doors left open.

'So Broughton and I, leaning stiffly one against the other, went down to my room. By the morning light that filtered past the blinds we could see our way, and I released the blinds. There was nothing wrong in the room from end to end, except smears of my own blood on the end of the bed, on the sofa, and on the carpet where I had torn the thing to pieces.'

Colvin had finished his story. There was nothing to say. Seven bells stuttered out from the fo'c'sle, and the answering cry wailed through the darkness. I took him downstairs.

'Of course I am much better now, but it is a kindness of you to let me sleep in your cabin.'

THE PHANTOM COACH

AMELIA B. EDWARDS

The circumstances I am about to relate to you have truth to recommend them. They happened to myself, and my recollection of them is as vivid as if they had taken place only yesterday. Twenty years, however, have gone by since that night. During those twenty years I have told the story to but one other person. I tell it now with a reluctance which I find it difficult to overcome. All I entreat, meanwhile, is that you will abstain from forcing your own conclusions upon me. I want nothing explained away. I desire no arguments. My mind on this subject is quite made up, and, having the testimony of my own senses to rely upon, I prefer to abide by it.

Well! It was just twenty years ago, and within a day or two of the end of the grouse season. I had been out all day with my gun, and had had no sport to speak of. The wind was due east; the month, December; the place, a bleak wide moor in the far north of England. And I had lost my way. It was not a pleasant place in which to lose one's way, with the first feathery flakes of a coming snowstorm just fluttering down upon the heather, and the leaden evening closing in all around. I shaded my eyes with my hand, and stared anxiously into the gathering darkness, where the purple moorland melted into a range of low hills, some ten or twelve miles distant. Not the faintest smoke-wreath, not the tiniest cultivated patch, or fence, or sheep-track, met my eyes in any direction. There was nothing for it but to walk on, and take my chance of finding what shelter I could, by the way. So I shouldered my gun again, and pushed wearily forward; for I had been on foot since an hour after daybreak, and had eaten nothing since breakfast.

Meanwhile, the snow began to come down with ominous steadiness, and the wind fell. After this, the cold became more intense, and the night came rapidly up. As for me, my prospects darkened with the darkening sky, and my heart grew heavy as I thought how my young wife was already watching for me through the window of our little inn parlour, and thought of all the suffering in store for her throughout this weary night. We had been married four months, and, having spent our autumn in the Highlands, were now lodging in a remote little village situated just on the verge of the great English moorlands. We were very much in love, and, of course, very happy. This morning, when we parted, she had implored me to return before dusk, and I had promised her that I would. What would I not have given to have kept my word!

Even now, weary as I was, I felt that with a supper, an hour's rest, and a guide, I might still get back to her before midnight, if only guide and shelter could be found.

And all this time, the snow fell and the night thickened. I stopped and shouted every now and then, but my shouts seemed only to make the silence deeper. Then a vague sense of uneasiness came upon me, and I began to remember stories of travellers who had walked on and on in the falling snow until, wearied out, they were fain to lie down and sleep their lives away. Would it be possible, I asked myself, to keep on thus through all the long dark night? Would there not come a time when my limbs must fail, and my resolution give way? When I, too, must sleep the sleep of death. Death! I shuddered. How hard to die just now, when life lay all so bright before me! How hard for my darling, whose whole loving heart but that thought was not to be borne! To banish it, I shouted again, louder and longer, and then listened eagerly. Was my shout answered, or did I only fancy that I heard a far-off cry? I halloed again, and again the echo followed. Then a wavering speck of light came suddenly out of the dark, shifting, disappearing, growing momentarily nearer and brighter. Running towards it at full speed, I found myself, to my great joy, face to face with an old man and a lantern.

'Thank God!' was the exclamation that burst involuntarily from my lips.

Blinking and frowning, he lifted his lantern and peered into my face.

'What for?' growled he, sulkily.

'Well – for you. I began to fear I should be lost in the snow.'

'Eh, then, folks do get cast away hereabouts fra' time to time, an' what's to hinder you from bein' cast away likewise, if the Lord's so minded?'

'If the Lord is so minded that you and I shall be lost together, friend, we must submit,' I replied; 'but I don't mean to be lost without you. How far am I now from Dwolding?'

'A gude twenty mile, more or less.'

'And the nearest village?'

'The nearest village is Wyke, an' that's twelve mile t'other side.'

'Where do you live, then?'

'Out yonder,' said he, with a vague jerk of the lantern.

'You're going home, I presume?'

'Maybe I am.'

'Then I'm going with you.'

The old man shook his head, and rubbed his nose reflectively with the handle of the lantern.

'It ain't o' no use,' growled he. 'He 'ont let you in – not he.'

'We'll see about that,' I replied, briskly. 'Who is He?'

'The master.'

'Who is the master?'

'That's nowt to you,' was the unceremonious reply.

'Well, well; you lead the way, and I'll engage that the master shall give me shelter and a supper to-night.'

'Eh, you can try him!' muttered my reluctant guide; and, still shaking his head, he hobbled, gnome-like, away through the falling snow. A large mass loomed up presently out of the darkness, and a huge dog rushed out, barking furiously.

'Is this the house?' I asked.

'Ay, it's the house. Down, Bey!' And he fumbled in his pocket for the key.

I drew up close behind him, prepared to lose no chance of entrance, and saw in the little circle of light shed by the lantern that the door was heavily studded with iron nails, like the door of a prison. In another minute he had turned the key and I had pushed past him into the house.

Once inside, I looked round with curiosity, and found myself in a great raftered hall, which served, apparently, a variety of uses. One end was piled to the roof with corn, like a barn. The other was stored with flour-sacks, agricultural implements, casks, and all kinds of miscellaneous lumber; while from the beams overhead hung rows of hams, flitches, and bunches of dried herbs for winter use. In the centre of the floor stood some huge object gauntly dressed in a dingy wrapping-cloth, and reaching half way to the rafters. Lifting a corner of this cloth, I saw, to my surprise, a telescope of very considerable size, mounted on a rude movable platform, with four small wheels. The tube was made of painted wood, bound round with bands of metal rudely fashioned; the speculum, so far as I could estimate its size in the dim light, measured at least fifteen inches in diameter. While I was yet examining the instrument, and asking myself whether it was not the work of some self-taught optician, a bell rang sharply.

'That's for you,' said my guide, with a malicious grin. 'Yonder's his room.'

He pointed to a low black door at the opposite side of the hall. I crossed over, rapped somewhat loudly, and went in, without waiting for an invitation. A huge, white-haired old man rose from a table covered with books and papers, and confronted me sternly.

'Who are you?' said he. 'How came you here? What do you want?'

'James Murray, barrister-at-law. On foot across the moor. Meat, drink, and sleep.'

He bent his bushy brows into a portentous frown.

'Mine is not a house of entertainment,' he said, haughtily. 'Jacob, how dared you admit this stranger?'

'I didn't admit him,' grumbled the old man. 'He followed me over the muir, and shouldered his way in before me. I'm no match for six foot two.'

'And pray, sir, by what right have you forced an entrance into my house?'

'The same by which I should have clung to your boat, if I were drowning. The right of self-preservation.'

'Self-preservation?'

'There's an inch of snow on the ground already,' I replied, briefly; 'and it would be deep enough to cover my body before daybreak.'

He strode to the window, pulled aside a heavy black curtain, and looked out.

'It is true,' he said. 'You can stay, if you choose, till morning. Jacob, serve the supper.'

With this he waved me to a seat, resumed his own, and became at once absorbed in the studies from which I had disturbed him.

I placed my gun in a corner, drew a chair to the hearth, and examined my quarters at leisure. Smaller and less incongruous in its arrangements than the hall, this room contained, nevertheless, much to awaken my curiosity. The floor was carpetless. The whitewashed walls were in parts scrawled over with strange diagrams, and in others covered with shelves crowded with philosophical instruments, the uses of many of which were unknown to me. On one side of the fireplace, stood a bookcase filled with dingy folios; on the other, a small organ, fantastically decorated with painted carvings of mediæval saints and devils. Through the half-opened door of a cupboard at the further end of the room, I saw a long array of geological specimens, surgical preparations, crucibles, retorts, and jars of chemicals; while on the mantelshelf beside me, amid a number of small objects, stood a model of the solar system, a small galvanic battery, and a microscope. Every chair had its burden. Every corner was heaped high with books. The very floor was littered over with maps, casts, papers, tracings, and learned lumber of all conceivable kinds.

I stared about me with an amazement increased by every fresh object upon which my eyes chanced to rest. So strange a room I had never seen; yet seemed it stranger still, to find such a room in a lone farmhouse amid those wild and solitary moors! Over and over again, I looked from my host to his surroundings, and from his surroundings back to my host, asking myself who and what he could be? His head was singularly fine; but it was more the head of a poet than of a philosopher. Broad in the temples, prominent over the eyes, and clothed with a rough profusion of perfectly white hair, it had all the ideality and much of the ruggedness that characterises the head of Louis van Beethoven. There were the same deep lines about the mouth, and the same stern furrows in the brow. There was the same concentration of expression. While I was yet observing him, the door opened, and Jacob brought in the supper. His master then closed his book, rose, and with more courtesy of manner than he had yet shown, invited me to the table.

A dish of ham and eggs, a loaf of brown bread, and a bottle of admirable sherry, were placed before me.

'I have but the homeliest farmhouse fare to offer you, sir,' said my entertainer. 'Your appetite, I trust, will make up for the deficiencies of our larder.'

I had already fallen upon the viands, and now protested, with the enthusiasm of a starving sportsman, that I had never eaten anything so delicious.

He bowed stiffly, and sat down to his own supper, which consisted, primitively, of a jug of milk and a basin of porridge. We ate in silence, and, when we had done, Jacob removed the tray. I then drew my chair back to the fireside. My host, somewhat to my surprise, did the same, and turning abruptly towards me, said:

'Sir, I have lived here in strict retirement for three-and-twenty years. During that time, I have not seen as many strange faces, and I have not read a single newspaper. You are the first stranger who has crossed my threshold for more than four years. Will you favour me with a few words of information respecting that outer world from which I have parted company so long?'

'Pray interrogate me,' I replied. 'I am heartily at your service.'

He bent his head in acknowledgment; leaned forward, with his elbows resting on his knees and his chin supported in the palms of his hands; stared fixedly into the fire; and proceeded to question me.

His inquiries related chiefly to scientific matters, with the later progress of which, as applied to the practical purposes of life, he was almost wholly unacquainted. No student of science myself, I replied as well as my slight information permitted; but the task was far from easy, and I was much relieved when, passing from interrogation to discussion, he began pouring forth his own conclusions upon the facts which I had been attempting to place before him. He talked, and I listened spell-bound. He talked till I believe he almost forgot my presence, and only thought aloud. I had never heard anything like it then; I have never heard anything like it since. Familiar with all systems of all philosophies, subtle in analysis, bold in generalisation, he poured forth his thoughts in an uninterrupted stream, and, still leaning forward in the same moody attitude with his eyes fixed upon the fire, wandered from topic to topic, from speculation to speculation, like an inspired dreamer. From practical science to mental philosophy; from electricity in the wire to electricity in the nerve; from Watts to Mesmer, from Mesmer to Reichenbach, from Reichenbach to Swedenborg, Spinoza, Condillac, Descartes, Berkeley, Aristotle, Plato, and the Magi and mystics of the East, were transitions which, however bewildering in their variety and scope, seemed easy and harmonious upon his lips as sequences in music. By-and-by – I forget now by what link of conjecture or illustration – he passed on to that field which lies beyond the boundary line of even conjectural philosophy, and reaches no man knows whither. He spoke of the soul and its aspirations; of the spirit and its powers; of second sight; of prophecy; of those phenomena which, under the names of ghosts, spectres, and supernatural appearances, have been denied by the sceptics and attested by the credulous, of all ages.

'The world,' he said, 'grows hourly more and more sceptical of all that lies beyond its own narrow radius; and our men of science foster the fatal tendency. They condemn as fable all that resists experiment. They reject as false all that cannot be brought to the test of the laboratory or the dissecting-room. Against what superstition have they waged so long and obstinate a war, as against the belief in apparitions? And yet what superstition has maintained its hold upon the minds of men so long and so firmly? Show me any fact in physics, in history, in archæology, which is supported by testimony so wide and so various. Attested by all races of men, in all ages, and in all climates, by the soberest sages of antiquity, by the rudest savage of to-day, by the Christian, the Pagan, the Pantheist, the Materialist, this phenomenon is treated as a nursery tale by the philosophers of our century. Circumstantial evidence weighs with them as a feather in the balance. The comparison of causes with effects, however valuable in physical science, is put aside as worthless and unreliable. The evidence of competent witnesses, however conclusive in a court of justice, counts for nothing. He who pauses before he pronounces, is condemned as a trifler. He who believes, is a dreamer or a fool.'

He spoke with bitterness, and, having said thus, relapsed for some minutes into silence. Presently he raised his head from his hands, and added, with an altered voice and manner, 'I, sir, paused, investigated, believed, and was not ashamed to state my convictions to the world. I, too, was branded as a visionary, held up to ridicule by my contemporaries, and hooted from that field of science in which I had laboured with honour during all the best years of my life. These things happened just three-and-twenty years ago. Since then, I have lived as you see me living now, and the world has forgotten me, as I have forgotten the world. You have my history.'

'It is a very sad one,' I murmured, scarcely knowing what to answer.

'It is a very common one,' he replied. 'I have only suffered for the truth, as many a better and wiser man has suffered before me.'

He rose, as if desirous of ending the conversation, and went over to the window.

'It has ceased snowing,' he observed, as he dropped the curtain, and came back to the fireside.

'Ceased!' I exclaimed, starting eagerly to my feet. 'Oh, if it were only possible – but no! it is hopeless. Even if I could find my way across the moor, I could not walk twenty miles to-night.'

'Walk twenty miles to-night!' repeated my host. 'What are you thinking of?'

'Of my wife,' I replied, impatiently. 'Of my young wife, who does not know that I have lost my way, and who is at this moment breaking her heart with suspense and terror.'

'Where is she?'

'At Dwolding, twenty miles away.'

'At Dwolding,' he echoed, thoughtfully. 'Yes, the distance, it is true, is twenty miles; but – are you so very anxious to save the next six or eight hours?'

'So very, very anxious, that I would give ten guineas at this moment for a guide and a horse.'

'Your wish can be gratified at a less costly rate,' said he, smiling. 'The night mail from the north, which changes horses at Dwolding, passes within five miles of this spot, and will be due at a certain cross-road in about an hour and a quarter. If Jacob were to go with you across the moor, and put you into the old coach-road, you could find your way, I suppose, to where it joins the new one?'

'Easily – gladly.'

He smiled again, rang the bell, gave the old servant his directions, and, taking a bottle of whisky and a wineglass from the cupboard in which he kept his chemicals, said:

'The snow lies deep, and it will be difficult walking to-night on the moor. A glass of usquebaugh before you start?'

I would have declined the spirit, but he pressed it on me, and I drank it. It went down my throat like liquid flame, and almost took my breath away.

'It is strong,' he said; 'but it will help to keep out the cold. And now you have no moments to spare. Good night!'

I thanked him for his hospitality, and would have shaken hands, but that he had turned away before I could finish my sentence. In another minute I had traversed the hall, Jacob had locked the outer door behind me, and we were out on the wide white moor.

Although the wind had fallen, it was still bitterly cold. Not a star glimmered in the black vault overhead. Not a sound, save the rapid crunching of the snow beneath our feet, disturbed the heavy stillness of the night. Jacob, not too well pleased with his mission, shambled on before in sullen silence, his lantern in his hand, and his shadow at his feet. I followed, with my gun over my shoulder, as little inclined for conversation as himself. My thoughts were full of my late host. His voice yet rang in my ears. His eloquence yet held my imagination captive. I remember to this day, with surprise, how my over-excited brain retained whole sentences and parts of sentences, troops of brilliant images, and fragments of splendid reasoning, in the very words in which he had uttered them. Musing thus over what I had heard, and striving to recall a lost link here and there, I strode on at the heels of my guide, absorbed and unobservant. Presently – at the end, as it seemed to me, of only a few minutes – he came to a sudden halt, and said:

'Yon's your road. Keep the stone fence to your right hand, and you can't fail of the way.'

'This, then, is the old coach-road?'

'Ay, 'tis the old coach-road.'

'And how far do I go, before I reach the cross-roads?'

'Nigh upon three mile.'

I pulled out my purse, and he became more communicative.

'The road's a fair road enough,' said he, 'for foot passengers; but 'twas over steep and narrow for the northern traffic. You'll mind where the parapet's broken away, close again the sign-post. It's never been mended since the accident.'

'What accident?'

'Eh, the night mail pitched right over into the valley below – a gude fifty feet an' more – just at the worst bit o' road in the whole county.'

'Horrible! Were many lives lost?'

'All. Four were found dead, and t'other two died next morning.'

'How long is it since this happened?'

'Just nine year.'

'Near the sign-post, you say? I will bear it in mind. Good night.'

'Gude night, sir, and thankee.' Jacob pocketed his half-crown, made a faint pretence of touching his hat, and trudged back by the way he had come.

I watched the light of his lantern till it quite disappeared, and then turned to pursue my way alone. This was no longer matter of the slightest difficulty, for, despite the dead darkness overhead, the line of stone fence showed distinctly enough against the pale gleam of the snow. How silent it seemed now, with only my footsteps to listen to; how silent and how solitary! A strange disagreeable sense of loneliness stole over me. I walked faster. I hummed a fragment of a tune. I cast up enormous sums in my head, and accumulated them at compound interest. I did my best, in short, to forget the startling speculations to which I had but just been listening, and, to some extent, I succeeded.

Meanwhile the night air seemed to become colder and colder, and though I walked fast I found it impossible to keep myself warm. My feet were like ice. I lost sensation in my hands, and grasped my gun mechanically. I even breathed with difficulty, as though, instead of traversing a quiet north country highway, I were scaling the uppermost heights of some gigantic Alp. This last symptom became presently so distressing, that I was forced to stop for a few minutes, and lean against the stone fence. As I did so, I chanced to look back up the road, and there, to my infinite relief, I saw a distant point of light, like the gleam of an approaching lantern. I at first concluded that Jacob had retraced his steps and followed me; but even as the conjecture presented itself, a second light flashed into sight – a light evidently parallel with the first, and approaching at the same rate of motion. It needed no second thought to show me that these must be the carriage-lamps of some private vehicle, though it seemed strange that any private vehicle should take a road professedly disused and dangerous.

There could be no doubt, however, of the fact, for the lamps grew larger and brighter every moment, and I even fancied I could already see the dark outline of the carriage between them. It was coming up very fast, and quite noiselessly, the snow being nearly a foot deep under the wheels.

And now the body of the vehicle became distinctly visible behind the lamps. It looked strangely lofty. A sudden suspicion flashed upon me. Was it possible that I had passed the cross-roads in the dark without observing the sign-post, and could this be the very coach which I had come to meet?

No need to ask myself that question a second time, for here it came round the bend of the road, guard and driver, one outside passenger, and four steaming greys, all wrapped in a soft haze of light, through which the lamps blazed out, like a pair of fiery meteors.

I jumped forward, waved my hat, and shouted. The mail came down at full speed, and passed me. For a moment I feared that I had not been seen or heard, but it was only for a moment. The coachman pulled up; the guard, muffled to the eyes in capes and comforters, and apparently sound asleep in the rumble, neither answered my hail nor made the slightest effort to dismount; the outside passenger did not even turn his head. I opened the door for myself, and looked in. There were but three travellers inside, so I stepped in, shut the door, slipped into the vacant corner, and congratulated myself on my good fortune.

The atmosphere of the coach seemed, if possible, colder than that of the outer air, and was pervaded by a singularly damp and disagreeable smell. I looked round at my fellow-passengers. They were all three, men, and all silent. They did not seem to be asleep, but each leaned back in his corner of the vehicle, as if absorbed in his own reflections. I attempted to open a conversation.

'How intensely cold it is to-night,' I said, addressing my opposite neighbour.

He lifted his head, looked at me, but made no reply.

'The winter,' I added, 'seems to have begun in earnest.'

Although the corner in which he sat was so dim that I could distinguish none of his features very clearly, I saw that his eyes were still turned full upon me. And yet he answered never a word.

At any other time I should have felt, and perhaps expressed, some annoyance, but at the moment I felt too ill to do either. The icy coldness of the night air had struck a chill to my very marrow, and the strange smell inside the coach was affecting me with an intolerable nausea. I shivered from head to foot, and, turning to my left-hand neighbour, asked if he had any objection to an open window?

He neither spoke nor stirred.

I repeated the question somewhat more loudly, but with the same result. Then I lost patience, and let the sash down. As I did so, the leather strap broke in my hand, and I observed that the glass was covered with a thick coat of mildew, the accumulation, apparently, of years. My attention being thus drawn to the condition of the coach, I examined it more narrowly, and saw by the uncertain light of the outer lamps that it was in the last stage of dilapidation. Every part of it was not only out of repair, but in a condition of decay. The sashes splintered at a touch. The leather fittings were crusted over with mould, and literally rotting from the woodwork. The floor was almost breaking away beneath my feet. The whole machine, in short, was foul with damp, and had evidently been dragged from some outhouse in which it had been mouldering away for years, to do another day or two of duty on the road.

I turned to the third passenger, whom I had not yet addressed, and hazarded one more remark.

'This coach,' I said, 'is in a deplorable condition. The regular mail, I suppose, is under repair?'

He moved his head slowly, and looked me in the face, without speaking a word. I shall never forget that look while I live. I turned cold at heart under it. I turn cold at heart even now when I recall it. His eyes glowed with a fiery unnatural lustre. His face was livid as the face of a corpse. His bloodless lips were drawn back as if in the agony of death, and showed the gleaming teeth between.

The words that I was about to utter died upon my lips, and a strange horror – a dreadful horror – came upon me. My sight had by this time become used to the gloom of the coach, and I could see with tolerable distinctness. I turned to my opposite neighbour. He, too, was looking at me, with the same startling pallor in his face, and the same stony glitter in his eyes. I passed my hand across my brow. I turned to the passenger on the seat beside my own, and saw – oh Heaven! how shall I describe what I saw? I saw that he was no living man – that none of them were living men, like myself! A pale phosphorescent light – the light of putrefaction – played upon their awful faces; upon their hair, dank with the dews of the grave; upon their clothes, earth-stained and dropping to pieces; upon their hands, which were as the hands of corpses long buried. Only their eyes, their terrible eyes, were living; and those eyes were all turned menacingly upon me!

A shriek of terror, a wild unintelligible cry for help and mercy, burst from my lips as I flung myself against the door, and strove in vain to open it.

In that single instant, brief and vivid as a landscape beheld in the flash of summer lightning, I saw the moon shining down through a rift of stormy cloud – the ghastly sign-post rearing its warning finger by the wayside – the broken parapet – the plunging horses – the black gulf below. Then, the coach reeled like a ship at sea. Then, came a mighty crash – a sense of crushing pain – and then, darkness.

It seemed as if years had gone by when I awoke one morning from a deep sleep, and found my wife watching by my bedside. I will pass over the scene that ensued, and give you, in half a dozen words, the tale she told me with tears of thanksgiving. I had fallen over a precipice, close against the junction of the old coach-road and the new, and had only been saved from certain death by lighting upon a deep snowdrift that had accumulated at the foot of the rock beneath. In this snowdrift I was discovered at daybreak, by a couple of shepherds, who carried me to the nearest shelter, and brought a surgeon to my aid. The surgeon found me in a state of raving delirium, with a broken arm and a compound fracture of the skull. The letters in my pocket-book showed my name and address; my wife was summoned to nurse me; and, thanks to youth and a fine constitution, I came out of danger at last. The place of my fall, I need scarcely say, was precisely that at which a frightful accident had happened to the north mail nine years before.

I never told my wife the fearful events which I have just related to you. I told the surgeon who attended me; but he treated the whole adventure as a mere dream born of the fever in my brain. We discussed the question over and over again, until we found that we could discuss it with temper no longer, and then we dropped it. Others may form what conclusions they please – I know that twenty years ago I was the fourth inside passenger in that Phantom Coach.

THE COLD EMBRACE

MARY ELIZABETH BRADDON

He was an artist – such things as happened to him happen sometimes to artists.

He was a German – such things as happened to him happen sometimes to Germans.

He was young, handsome, studious, enthusiastic, metaphysical, reckless, unbelieving, heartless.

And being young, handsome and eloquent, he was beloved.

He was an orphan, under the guardianship of his dead father's brother, his uncle Wilhelm, in whose house he had been brought up from a little child; and she who loved him was his cousin – his cousin Gertrude, whom he swore he loved in return.

Did he love her? Yes, when he first swore it. It soon wore out, this passionate love; how threadbare and wretched a sentiment it became at last in the selfish heart of the student! But in its first golden dawn, when he was only nineteen, and had just returned from his apprenticeship to a great painter at Antwerp, and they wandered together in the most romantic outskirts of the city at rosy sunset, by holy moonlight, or bright and joyous morning, how beautiful a dream!

They keep it a secret from Wilhelm, as he has the father's ambition of a wealthy suitor for his only child – a cold and dreary vision beside the lover's dream.

So they are betrothed; and standing side by side when the dying sun and the pale rising moon divide the heavens, he puts the betrothal ring upon her finger, the white and tapered finger whose slender shape he knows so well. This ring is a peculiar one, a massive golden serpent, its tail in its mouth, the symbol of eternity; it had been his mother's, and he would know it amongst a thousand. If he were to become blind tomorrow, he could select it from amongst a thousand by the touch alone.

He places it on her finger, and they swear to be true to each other for ever and ever – through trouble and danger – sorrow and change – in wealth or poverty. Her father must needs be won to consent to their union by-and-by, for they were now betrothed, and death alone could part them.

But the young student, the scoffer at revelation, yet the enthusiastic adorer of the mystical asks:

'Can death part us? I would return to you from the grave, Gertrude. My soul would come back to be near my love. And you – you, if you died before me – the cold earth would not hold you from me; if you loved me, you would return, and again these fair arms would be clasped round my neck as they are now.'

But she told him, with a holier light in her deep-blue eyes than had ever shone in his – she told him that the dead who die at peace with God are happy in heaven, and cannot return to the troubled earth; and that it is only the suicide – the lost wretch on whom sorrowful angels shut the door of Paradise – whose unholy spirit haunts the footsteps of the living.

The first year of their betrothal is passed, and she is alone, for he has gone to Italy, on a commission for some rich man, to copy Raphaels, Titians, Guidos, in a gallery at Florence. He has gone to win fame, perhaps; but it is not the less bitter – he is gone!

Of course her father misses his young nephew, who has been as a son to him; and he thinks his daughter's sadness no more than a cousin should feel for a cousin's absence.

In the meantime, the weeks and months pass. The lover writes – often at first, then seldom – at last, not at all.

How many excuses she invents for him! How many times she goes to the distant little post-office, to which he is to address his letters! How many times she hopes, only to be disappointed!

How many times she despairs, only to hope again!

But real despair comes at last, and will not be put off any more. The rich suitor appears on the scene, and her father is determined. She is to marry at once. The wedding-day is fixed – the fifteenth of June.

The date seems burnt into her brain.

The date, written in fire, dances for ever before her eyes.

The date, shrieked by the Furies, sounds continually in her ears.

But there is time yet – it is the middle of May – there is time for a letter to reach him at Florence; there is time for him to come to Brunswick, to take her away and marry her, in spite of her father – in spite of the whole world.

But the days and weeks fly by, and he does not write – he does not come. This is indeed despair which usurps her heart, and will not be put away.

It is the fourteenth of June. For the last time she goes to the little post-office; for the last time she asks the old question, and they give her for the last time the dreary answer, 'No; no letter.'

For the last time – for tomorrow is the day appointed for her bridal. Her father will hear no entreaties; her rich suitor will not listen to her prayers. They will not be put off a day – an hour; tonight alone is hers – this night, which she may employ as she will.

She takes another path than that which leads home; she hurries through some by-streets of the city, out on to a lonely bridge, where he and she had stood so often in the sunset, watching the rose-coloured light glow, fade, and die upon the river.

He returns from Florence. He had received her letter. That letter, blotted with tears, entreating, despairing – he had received it, but he loved her no longer. A young Florentine, who has sat to him for a model, had bewitched his fancy – that fancy which with him stood in place of a heart – and Gertrude had been half-forgotten. If she had a rich suitor, good; let her marry him; better for her, better far for himself.

He had no wish to fetter himself with a wife. Had he not his art always? – his eternal bride, his unchanging mistress.

Thus he thought it wiser to delay his journey to Brunswick, so that he should arrive when the wedding was over – arrive in time to salute the bride.

And the vows – the mystical fancies – the belief in his return, even after death, to the embrace of his beloved? O, gone out of his life; melted away for ever, those foolish dreams of his boyhood.

So on the fifteenth of June he enters Brunswick, by that very bridge on which she stood, the stars looking down on her, the night before. He strolls across the bridge and down by the water's edge, a great rough dog at his heels, and the smoke from his short meerschaum-pipe curling in blue wreaths fantastically in the pure morning air. He has his sketch-book under his arm, and attracted now and then by some object that catches his artist's eye, stops to draw: a few weeds and pebbles on the river's brink – a crag on the opposite shore – a group of pollard willows in the distance. When he has done, he admires his drawing, shuts his sketch-book, empties the ashes from his pipe, refills from his tobacco-pouch, sings the refrain of a gay drinking-song, calls to his dog, smokes again, and walks on. Suddenly he opens his sketch-book again; this time that which attracts him is a group of figures: but what is it? It is not a funeral, for there are no mourners.

It is not a funeral, but a corpse lying on a rough bier, covered with an old sail, carried between two bearers.

It is not a funeral, for the bearers are fishermen – fishermen in their everyday garb.

About a hundred yards from him they rest their burden on a bank – one stands at the head of the bier, the other throws himself down at the foot of it.

And thus they form a perfect group; he walks back two or three paces, selects his point of sight, and begins to sketch a hurried outline. He has finished it before they move; he hears their voices, though he cannot hear their words, and wonders what they can be talking of. Presently he walks on and joins them.

'You have a corpse there, my friends?' he says.

'Yes; a corpse washed ashore an hour ago.'

'Drowned?'

'Yes, drowned. A young girl, very handsome.'

'Suicides are always handsome,' says the painter; and then he stands for a little while idly smoking and meditating, looking at the sharp outline of the corpse and the stiff folds of the rough canvas covering.

Life is such a golden holiday for him – young, ambitious, clever – that it seems as though sorrow and death could have no part in his destiny.

At last he says that, as this poor suicide is so handsome, he should like to make a sketch of her.

He gives the fishermen some money, and they offer to remove the sailcloth that covers her features.

No; he will do it himself. He lifts the rough, coarse, wet canvas from her face. What face?

The face that shone on the dreams of his foolish boyhood; the face which once was the light of his uncle's home. His cousin Gertrude – his betrothed!

He sees, as in one glance, while he draws one breath, the rigid features – the marble arms – the hands crossed on the cold bosom; and, on the third finger of the left hand, the ring which had been his mother's – the golden serpent; the ring which, if he were to become blind, he could select from a thousand others by the touch alone.

But he is a genius and a metaphysician – grief, true grief, is not for such as he. His first thought is flight – flight anywhere out of that accursed city – anywhere far from the brink of that hideous river – anywhere away from remorse – anywhere to forget.

He is miles on the road that leads away from Brunswick before he knows that he has walked a step.

It is only when his dog lies down panting at his feet than he feels how exhausted he is himself, and sits down upon a bank to rest. How the landscape spins round and round before his dazzled eyes, while his morning's sketch of the two fishermen and the canvas-covered bier glares redly at him out of the twilight!

At last, after sitting a long time by the roadside, idly playing with his dog, idly smoking, idly lounging, looking as any idle, light-hearted travelling student might look, yet all the while acting over that morning's scene in his burning brain a hundred times a minute; at last he grows a little more composed, and tries presently to think of himself as he is, apart from his cousin's suicide.

Apart from that, he was no worse off than he was yesterday. His genius was not gone; the money he had earned at Florence still lined his pocket-book; he was his own master, free to go whither he would.

And while he sits on the roadside, trying to separate himself from the scene of that morning – trying to put away the image of the corpse covered with the damp canvas sail – trying to think of what he should do next, where he should go, to be farthest away from Brunswick and remorse, the old diligence comes rumbling and jingling along. He remembers it; it goes from Brunswick to Aix-la-Chapelle.

He whistles to his dog, shouts to the postillion to stop, and springs into the coupé.

During the whole evening, through the long night, though he does not once close his eyes, he never speaks a word; but when morning dawns, and the other passengers awake and begin to talk to each other, he joins in the conversation. He tells them that he is an artist, that he is going to Cologne and to Antwerp to copy Rubenses, and the great picture by Quentin Matsys, in the museum. He remembered afterwards that he talked and laughed boisterously, and that when he was talking and laughing loudest, a passenger, older and graver than the rest, opened the window near him, and told him to put his head out. He remembered the fresh air blowing in his face, the singing of the birds in his ears, and the flat fields and roadside reeling before his eyes. He remembered this, and then falling in a lifeless heap on the floor of the diligence.

It is a fever that keeps him for six long weeks on a bed at a hotel in Aix-la-Chapelle.

He gets well, and, accompanied by his dog, starts on foot for Cologne. By this time he is his former self once more. Again the blue smoke from his short meerschaum curls upwards in the morning air – again he sings some old university drinking-song – again stops here and there, meditating and sketching.

He is happy, and has forgotten his cousin – and so on to Cologne.

It is by the great cathedral he is standing, with his dog at his side. It is night, the bells have just chimed the hour, and the clocks are striking eleven; the moonlight shines full upon the magnificent pile, over which the artist's eye wanders, absorbed in the beauty of form.

He is not thinking of his drowned cousin, for he has forgotten her and is happy.

Suddenly some one, something from behind him, puts two cold arms round his neck, and clasps its hands on his breast.

And yet there is no one behind him, for on the flags bathed in the broad moonlight there are only two shadows, his own and his dog's. He turns quickly round – there is no one – nothing to be seen in the broad square but himself and his dog; and though he feels, he cannot see the cold arms clasped round his neck.

It is not ghostly, this embrace, for it is palpable to the touch – it cannot be real, for it is invisible.

He tries to throw off the cold caress. He clasps the hands in his own to tear them asunder, and to cast them off his neck. He can feel the long delicate fingers cold and wet beneath his touch, and on the third finger of the left hand he can feel the ring which was his mother's – the golden serpent – the ring which he has always said he would know among a thousand by the touch alone. He knows it now!

His dead cousin's cold arms are round his neck – his dead cousin's wet hands are clasped upon his breast. He asks himself if he is mad. 'Up, Leo!' he shouts. 'Up, up, boy!' and the Newfoundland leaps to his shoulders – the dog's paws are on the dead hands, and the animal utters a terrific howl, and springs away from his master.

The student stands in the moonlight, the dead arms around his neck, and the dog at a little distance moaning piteously.

Presently a watchman, alarmed by the howling of the dog, comes into the square to see what is wrong.

In a breath the cold arms are gone.

He takes the watchman home to the hotel with him and gives him money; in his gratitude he could have given that man half his little fortune.

Will it ever come to him again, this embrace of the dead?

He tries never to be alone; he makes a hundred acquaintances, and shares the chamber of another student. He starts up if he is left by himself in the public room at the inn where he is staying, and runs into the street. People notice his strange actions, and begin to think that he is mad.

But, in spite of all, he is alone once more; for one night the public room being empty for a moment, when on some idle pretence he strolls into the street, the street is empty too, and for the second time he feels the cold arms round his neck, and for the second time, when he calls his dog, the animal slinks away from him with a piteous howl.

After this he leaves Cologne, still travelling on foot – of necessity now, for his money is getting low. He joins travelling hawkers, he walks side by side with labourers, he talks to every foot-passenger he falls in with, and tries from morning till night to get company on the road.

At night he sleeps by the fire in the kitchen of the inn at which he stops; but do what he will, he is often alone, and it is now a common thing for him to feel the cold arms around his neck.

Many months have passed since his cousin's death – autumn, winter, early spring. His money is nearly gone, his health is utterly broken, he is the shadow of his former self, and he is getting near to Paris. He will reach that city at the time of the Carnival. To this he looks forward. In Paris, in Carnival time, he need never, surely, be alone, never feel that deadly caress; he may even recover his lost gaiety, his lost health, once more resume his profession, once more earn fame and money by his art.

How hard he tries to get over the distance that divides him from Paris, while day by day he grows weaker, and his step slower and more heavy!

But there is an end at last; the long dreary roads are passed. This is Paris, which he enters for the first time – Paris, of which he has dreamed so much – Paris, whose million voices are to exorcise his phantom.

To him tonight Paris seems one vast chaos of lights, music, and confusion – lights which dance before his eyes and will not be still – music that rings in his ears and deafens him – confusion which makes his head whirl round and round.

But, in spite of all, he finds the opera-house, where there is a masked ball. He has enough money left to buy a ticket of admission, and to hire a domino to throw over his shabby dress. It seems only a moment after his entering the gates of Paris that he is in the very midst of all the wild gaiety of the opera-house ball.

No more darkness, no more loneliness, but a mad crowd, shouting and dancing, and a lovely Débardeuse hanging on his arm.

The boisterous gaiety he feels surely is his old light-heartedness come back. He hears the people round him talking of the outrageous conduct of some drunken student, and it is to him they point when they say this to him, who has not moistened his lips since yesterday at noon, for even now he will not drink; though his lips are parched, and his throat burning, he cannot drink.

His voice is thick and hoarse, and his utterance indistinct; but still this must be his old light-heartedness come back that makes him so wildly gay.

The little Débardeuse is wearied out – her arm rests on his shoulder heavier than lead – the other dancers one by one drop off.

The lights in the chandeliers one by one die out.

The decorations look pale and shadowy in that dim light which is neither night nor day.

A faint glimmer from the dying lamps, a pale streak of cold grey light from the new-born day, creeping in through half-opened shutters.

And by this light the bright-eyed Débardeuse fades sadly. He looks her in the face. How the brightness of her eyes dies out! Again he looks her in the face. How white that face has grown!

Again – and now it is the shadow of a face alone that looks in his.

Again – and they are gone – the bright eyes, the face, the shadow of the face. He is alone; alone in that vast saloon.

Alone, and, in the terrible silence, he hears the echoes of his own footsteps in that dismal dance which has no music.

No music but the beating of his breast. For the cold arms are round his neck – they whirl him round, they will not be flung off, or cast away; he can no more escape from their icy grasp than he can escape from death. He looks behind him – there is nothing but himself in the great empty salle; but he can feel – cold, deathlike, but O, how palpable! – the long slender fingers, and the ring which was his mother's.

He tries to shout, but he has no power in his burning throat. The silence of the place is only broken by the echoes of his own footsteps in the dance from which he cannot extricate himself.

Who says he has no partner? The cold hands are clasped on his breast, and now he does not shun their caress. No! One more polka, if he drops down dead.

The lights are all out, and, half an hour after, the gendarmes come in with a lantern to see that the house is empty; they are followed by a great dog that they have found seated howling on the steps of the theatre. Near the principal entrance they stumble over— The body of a student, who has died from want of food, exhaustion, and the breaking of a blood-vessel.

The Shadows on the Wall

Mary Eleanor Wilkins Freeman

"Henry had words with Edward in the study the night before Edward died," said Caroline Glynn.

She spoke not with acrimony, but with grave severity. Rebecca Ann Glynn gasped by way of assent. She sat in a wide flounce of black silk in the corner of the sofa, and rolled terrified eyes from her sister Caroline to her sister Mrs. Stephen Brigham, who had been Emma Glynn, the one beauty of the family. The latter was beautiful still, with a large, splendid, full-blown beauty; she filled a great rocking-chair with her superb bulk of femininity, and swayed gently back and forth, her black silks whispering and her black frills fluttering. Even the shock of death—for her brother Edward lay dead in the house—could not disturb her outward serenity of demeanor.

But even her expression of masterly placidity changed before her sister Caroline's announcement and her sister Rebecca Ann's gasp of terror and distress in response.

"I think Henry might have controlled his temper, when poor Edward was so near his end," she said with an asperity which disturbed slightly the roseate curves of her beautiful mouth.

"Of course he did not *know*," murmured Rebecca Ann in a faint tone strangely out of keeping with her appearance.

"Of course he did not know it," said Caroline quickly. She turned on her sister with a strange, sharp look of suspicion. Then she shrank as if from the other's possible answer. "Of course you and I both know he could not," said she conclusively, but her pale face was paler than it had been before.

Rebecca gasped again. The married sister, Mrs. Emma Brigham, was now sitting up straight in her chair; she had ceased rocking, and was eyeing them both intently with a sudden accentuation of family likeness in her face. Given one common intensity of emotion and similar lines showed forth, and the three sisters of one race were evident.

"What do you mean?" said she impartially to them both. Then she, too, seemed to shrink before a possible answer. She even laughed an evasive sort of laugh. "I guess you don't mean anything," said she, but her face wore still the expression of shrinking horror.

"Nobody means anything," said Caroline firmly. She rose and crossed the room toward the door with grim decisiveness.

"Where are you going?" asked Mrs. Brigham.

"I have something to see to," replied Caroline, and the others at once knew by her tone that she had some solemn and sad duty to perform in the chamber of death.

"Oh," said Mrs. Brigham.

After the door had closed behind Caroline, she turned to Rebecca.

"Did Henry have many words with him?" she asked.

"They were talking very loud," replied Rebecca evasively, yet with an answering gleam of ready response to the other's curiosity in the quick lift of her soft blue eyes.

Mrs. Brigham looked at her. She had not resumed rocking. She still sat up straight, with a slight knitting of intensity on her fair forehead, between the pretty rippling curves of her auburn hair.

"Did you—ever hear anything?" she asked in a low voice with a glance toward the door.

"I was just across the hall in the south parlor, and that door was open and this door ajar," replied Rebecca with a slight flush.

"Then you must have——"

"I couldn't help it."

"Everything?"

"Most of it."

"What was it?"

"The old story."

"I suppose Henry was mad, as he always was, because Edward was living on here for nothing, when he had wasted all the money father left him."

Rebecca nodded, with a fearful glance at the door.

When Emma spoke again her voice was still more hushed. "I know how he felt," said she. "He had always been so prudent himself, and worked hard at his profession, and there Edward had never done anything but spend, and it must have looked to him as if Edward was living at his expense, but he wasn't."

"No, he wasn't."

"And Edward had a right here according to the terms of father's will, and Henry ought to have remembered it."

"Yes, he ought."

"Did he say hard things?"

"Pretty hard, from what I heard."

"What?"

"I heard him tell Edward that he had no business here at all, and he thought he had better go away."

"What did Edward say?"

"That he would stay here as long as he lived and afterward, too, if he was a mind to, and he would like to see Henry get him out; and then—"

"What?"

"Then he laughed."

"What did Henry say?"

"I didn't hear him say anything, but—"

"But what?"

"I saw him when he came out of this room."

"He looked mad?"

"You've seen him when he looked so."

Emma nodded. The expression of horror on her face had deepened.

"Do you remember that time he killed the cat because she had scratched him?"

"Yes. Don't!"

Then Caroline reentered the room; she went up to the stove, in which a wood fire was burning—it was a cold, gloomy day of fall—and she warmed her hands, which were reddened from recent washing in cold water.

Mrs. Brigham looked at her and hesitated. She glanced at the door, which was still ajar; it did not easily shut, being still swollen with the damp weather of the summer. She rose and pushed it together with a sharp thud, which jarred the house. Rebecca started painfully with a half-exclamation. Caroline looked at her disapprovingly.

"It is time you controlled your nerves, Rebecca," she said.

"I can't help it," replied Rebecca with almost a wail. "I am nervous. There's enough to make me so, the Lord knows."

"What do you mean by that?" asked Caroline with her old air of sharp suspicion, and something between challenge and dread of its being met.

Rebecca shrank.

"Nothing," said she.

"Then I wouldn't keep speaking in such a fashion."

Emma, returning from the closed door, said imperiously that it ought to be fixed, it shut so hard.

"It will shrink enough after we have had the fire a few days," replied Caroline.

"I think Henry ought to be ashamed of himself for talking as he did to Edward," said Mrs. Brigham abruptly, but in an almost inaudible voice.

"Hush," said Caroline, with a glance of actual fear at the closed door.

"Nobody can hear with the door shut."

"He must have heard it shut, and—"

"Well, I can say what I want to before he comes down, and I am not afraid of him."

"I don't know who is afraid of him! What reason is there for anybody to be afraid of Henry?" demanded Caroline.

Mrs. Brigham trembled before her sister's look. Rebecca gasped again. "There isn't any reason of course. Why should there be?"

"I wouldn't speak so, then. Somebody might overhear you and think it was queer. Miranda Joy is in the south parlour sewing, you know."

"I thought she went upstairs to stitch on the machine."

"She did, but she has come down again."

"Well, she can't hear."

"I say again I think Henry ought to be ashamed of himself. I shouldn't think he'd ever get over it, having words with poor Edward the very night before he died. Edward was enough sight better disposition than Henry, with all his faults."

"I never heard him speak a cross word, unless he spoke cross to Henry that last night. I don't know but he did from what Rebecca overheard."

"Not so much cross, as sort of soft, and sweet, and aggravating," sniffed Rebecca.

"What do you really think ailed Edward?" asked Emma in hardly more than a whisper. She did not look at her sister.

Caroline sat down in a nearby armchair, and clutched the arms convulsively until her thin knuckles whitened.

"I told you," said she.

Rebecca held her handkerchief over her mouth, and looked at them above it with terrified, streaming eyes.

"I know you said that he had terrible pains in his stomach, and had spasms, but what do you think made him have them?"

"Henry called it gastric trouble. You know Edward has always had dyspepsia."

Mrs. Brigham hesitated a moment. "Was there any talk of an—examination?" said she.

Then Caroline turned on her fiercely.

"No," said she in a terrible voice. "No."

The three sisters' souls seemed to meet on one common ground of terrified understanding through their eyes.

The old-fashioned latch of the door was heard to rattle, and a push from without made the door shake ineffectually. "It's Henry," Rebecca sighed rather than whispered. Mrs. Brigham settled herself, after a noiseless rush across the floor, into her rocking-chair again, and was swaying back and forth with her head comfortably leaning back, when the door at last yielded and Henry Glynn entered. He cast a covertly sharp, comprehensive glance at Mrs. Brigham with her elaborate calm; at Rebecca quietly huddled in the corner of the sofa with her handkerchief to her face and only one small uncovered reddened ear as attentive as a dog's uncovered and revealing her alertness for his presence; at Caroline sitting with a strained composure in her armchair by the stove. She met his eyes quite firmly with a look of inscrutable fear, and defiance of the fear and of him.

Henry Glynn looked more like this sister than the others. Both had the same hard delicacy of form and feature, both were tall and almost emaciated, both had a sparse growth of gray blond hair far back from high intellectual foreheads, both had an almost noble aquilinity of feature. They confronted each other with the pitiless immovability of two statues in whose marble lineaments emotions were fixed for all eternity.

Then Henry Glynn smiled and the smile transformed his face. He looked suddenly years younger, and an almost boyish recklessness appeared in his face. He flung himself into a chair with a gesture which was bewildering from its incongruity with his general appearance. He leaned his head back, flung one leg over the other, and looked laughingly at Mrs. Brigham.

"I declare, Emma, you grow younger every year," he said.

She flushed a little, and her placid mouth widened at the corners. She was susceptible to praise.

"Our thoughts to-day ought to belong to the one of us who will *never* grow older," said Caroline in a hard voice.

Henry looked at her, still smiling. "Of course, we none of us forget that," said he, in a deep, gentle voice; "but we have to speak to the living, Caroline, and I have not seen Emma for a long time, and the living are as dear as the dead."

"Not to me," said Caroline.

She rose and went abruptly out of the room again. Rebecca also rose and hurried after her, sobbing loudly.

Henry looked slowly after them.

"Caroline is completely unstrung," said he.

Mrs. Brigham rocked. A confidence in him inspired by his manner was stealing over her. Out of that confidence she spoke quite easily and naturally.

"His death was very sudden," said she.

Henry's eyelids quivered slightly but his gaze was unswerving.

"Yes," said he, "it was very sudden. He was sick only a few hours."

"What did you call it?"

"Gastric."

"You did not think of an examination?"

"There was no need. I am perfectly certain as to the cause of his death."

Suddenly Mrs. Brigham felt a creep as of some live horror over her very soul. Her flesh prickled with cold, before an inflection of his voice. She rose, tottering on weak knees.

"Where are you going?" asked Henry in a strange, breathless voice.

Mrs. Brigham said something incoherent about some sewing which she had to do—some black for the funeral—and was out of the room. She went up to the front chamber which she occupied. Caroline was there. She went close to her and took her hands, and the two sisters looked at each other.

"Don't speak, don't, I won't have it!" said Caroline finally in an awful whisper.

"I won't," replied Emma.

That afternoon the three sisters were in the study, the large front room on the ground floor across the hall from the south parlour, when the dusk deepened.

Mrs. Brigham was hemming some black material. At last she laid her work on her lap.

"It's no use, I cannot see to sew another stitch until we have a light," said she.

Caroline, who was writing some letters at the table, turned to Rebecca, in her usual place on the sofa.

"Rebecca, you had better get a lamp," she said.

Rebecca started up; even in the dusk her face showed her agitation.

"It doesn't seem to me that we need a lamp quite yet," she said in a piteous, pleading voice like a child's.

"Yes, we do," returned Mrs. Brigham peremptorily. "I can't see to sew another stitch."

"Caroline can see to write letters, and she is farther from the window than you are," said Rebecca.

"Are you trying to save kerosene or are you lazy, Rebecca Glynn?" cried Mrs. Brigham. "I can go and get the light myself, but I have this work all in my lap."

Caroline's pen stopped scratching.

"Rebecca, we must have the light," said she.

"Had we better have it in here?" asked Rebecca weakly.

"Of course! Why not?" cried Caroline sternly.

"I am sure I don't want to take my sewing into the other room, when it is all cleaned up for to-morrow," said Mrs. Brigham.

"Why, I never heard such a to-do about lighting a lamp."

Rebecca rose and left the room. Presently she entered with a lamp. She set it on the table, an old-fashioned card-table which was placed against the opposite wall from the window. That opposite wall was taken up with three doors; the one small space was occupied by the table.

"What have you put that lamp over there for?" asked Mrs. Brigham, with more of impatience than her voice usually revealed. "Why didn't you set it in the hall, and have done with it? Neither Caroline nor I can see if it is on that table."

"I thought perhaps you would move," replied Rebecca hoarsely.

"If I do move, we can't both sit at that table. Caroline has her paper all spread around. Why don't you set the lamp on the study table in the middle of the room, then we can both see?"

Rebecca hesitated. Her face was very pale. She looked with an appeal that was fairly agonizing at her sister Caroline.

"Why don't you put the lamp on this table, as she says?" asked Caroline, almost fiercely. "Why do you act so, Rebecca?"

"I should think you *would* ask her that," said Mrs. Brigham. "She doesn't act like herself at all."

Rebecca took the lamp and set it on the table in the middle of the room without another word. Then she seated herself on the sofa and placed a hand over her eyes as if to shade them, and remained so.

"Does the light hurt your eyes, and is that the reason why you didn't want the lamp?" asked Mrs. Brigham kindly.

"I always like to sit in the dark," replied Rebecca chokingly. Then she snatched her handkerchief hastily from her pocket and began to weep. Caroline continued to write, Mrs. Brigham to sew.

Suddenly Mrs. Brigham as she sewed glanced at the opposite wall. The glance became a steady stare. She looked intently, her work suspended in her hands. Then she looked away again and took a few more stitches, then she looked again, and again turned to her task. At last she laid her work in her lap and stared concentratedly. She looked from the wall round the room, taking note of the various objects. Then she turned to her sisters.

"What *is* that?" said she.

"What?" asked Caroline harshly; her pen scratched loudly across the paper.

Rebecca gave one of her convulsive gasps.

"That strange shadow on the wall," replied Mrs. Brigham.

Rebecca sat with her face hidden; Caroline dipped her pen in the inkstand.

"Why don't you turn around and look?" asked Mrs. Brigham in a wondering and somewhat aggrieved way.

"I am in a hurry to finish this letter if Mrs. Wilson Ebbit is going to get word in time to come to the funeral," replied Caroline shortly.

Mrs. Brigham rose, her work slipping to the floor, and began walking round the room, moving various articles of furniture, with her eyes on the shadow.

Then suddenly she shrieked out:

"Look at this awful shadow! What is it? Caroline, look, look! Rebecca, look! *What is it*?"

All Mrs. Brigham's triumphant placidity was gone. Her handsome face was livid with horror. She stood stiffly pointing at the shadow.

"Look!" said she, pointing her finger at it. "Look! What is it?"

Then Rebecca burst out in a wild wail after a shuddering glance at the wall:

"Oh, Caroline, there it is again, there it is again!"

"Caroline Glynn, you look!" said Mrs. Brigham. "Look! What is that dreadful shadow?"

Caroline rose, turned, and stood confronting the wall.

"How should I know?" she said.

"It has been there every night since he died!" cried Rebecca.

"Every night?"

"Yes; he died Thursday and this is Saturday; that makes three nights," said Caroline rigidly. She stood as if holding her calm with a vise of concentrated will.

"It—it looks like—like—" stammered Mrs. Brigham in a tone of intense horror.

"I know what it looks like well enough," said Caroline. "I've got eyes in my head."

"It looks like Edward," burst out Rebecca in a sort of frenzy of fear. "Only—"

"Yes, it does," assented Mrs. Brigham, whose horror-stricken tone matched her sisters', "only—Oh, it is awful! What is it, Caroline?"

"I ask you again, how should I know?" replied Caroline. "I see it there like you. How should I know any more than you?"

"It *must* be something in the room," said Mrs. Brigham, staring wildly around.

"We moved everything in the room the first night it came," said Rebecca; "it is not anything in the room."

Caroline turned upon her with a sort of fury. "Of course it is something in the room," said she. "How you act! What do you mean talking so? Of course it is something in the room."

"Of course it is," agreed Mrs. Brigham, looking at Caroline suspiciously. "Of course it must be. It is only a coincidence. It just happens so. Perhaps it is that fold of the window curtain that makes it. It must be something in the room."

"It is not anything in the room," repeated Rebecca with obstinate horror.

The door opened suddenly and Henry Glynn entered. He began to speak, then his eyes followed the direction of the others. He stood stock still staring at the shadow on the wall. It was life size and stretched across the white parallelogram of a door, half across the wall space on which the picture hung.

"What is that?" he demanded in a strange voice.

"It must be due to something in the room," Mrs. Brigham said faintly.

"It is not due to anything in the room," said Rebecca again with the shrill insistency of terror.

"How you act, Rebecca Glynn," said Caroline.

Henry Glynn stood and stared a moment longer. His face showed a gamut of emotions—horror, conviction, then furious incredulity. Suddenly he began hastening hither and thither about the room. He moved the furniture with fierce jerks, turning ever to see the effect upon the shadow on the wall. Not a line of its terrible outlines wavered.

"It must be something in the room!" he declared in a voice which seemed to snap like a lash.

His face changed. The inmost secrecy of his nature seemed evident upon his face, until one almost lost sight of his lineaments. Rebecca stood close to her sofa, regarding him with woeful, fascinated eyes. Mrs. Brigham clutched Caroline's hand. They both stood in a corner out of his way. For a few moments he raged about the room like a caged wild animal. He moved every piece of furniture; when the moving of a piece did not affect the shadow, he flung it to the floor, the sisters watching.

Then suddenly he desisted. He laughed and began straightening the furniture which he had flung down.

"What an absurdity," he said easily. "Such a to-do about a shadow."

"That's so," assented Mrs. Brigham, in a scared voice which she tried to make natural. As she spoke she lifted a chair near her.

"I think you have broken the chair that Edward was fond of," said Caroline.

Terror and wrath were struggling for expression on her face. Her mouth was set, her eyes shrinking. Henry lifted the chair with a show of anxiety.

"Just as good as ever," he said pleasantly. He laughed again, looking at his sisters. "Did I scare you?" he said. "I should think you might be used to me by this time. You know my way of wanting to leap to the bottom of a mystery, and that shadow does look—queer, like—and I thought if there was any way of accounting for it I would like to without any delay."

"You don't seem to have succeeded," remarked Caroline dryly, with a slight glance at the wall.

Henry's eyes followed hers and he quivered perceptibly.

"Oh, there is no accounting for shadows," he said, and he laughed again. "A man is a fool to try to account for shadows."

Then the supper bell rang, and they all left the room, but Henry kept his back to the wall—as did, indeed, the others.

Mrs. Brigham pressed close to Caroline as she crossed the hall. "He looked like a demon!" she breathed in her ear.

Henry led the way with an alert motion like a boy; Rebecca brought up the rear. She could scarcely walk, her knees trembled so.

"I can't sit in that room again this evening," she whispered to Caroline after supper.

"Very well; we will sit in the south room," replied Caroline. "I think we will sit in the south parlor," she said aloud; "it isn't as damp as the study, and I have a cold."

So they all sat in the south room with their sewing. Henry read the newspaper, his chair drawn close to the lamp on the table. About nine o'clock he rose abruptly and crossed the hall to the study. The three sisters looked at one another. Mrs. Brigham rose, folded her rustling skirts compactly round her, and began tiptoeing toward the door.

"What are you going to do?" inquired Rebecca agitatedly.

"I am going to see what he is about," replied Mrs. Brigham cautiously.

As she spoke she pointed to the study door across the hall; it was ajar. Henry had striven to pull it together behind him, but it had somehow swollen beyond the limit with curious speed. It was still ajar and a streak of light showed from top to bottom.

"You had better stay where you are," said Caroline with guarded sharpness.

"I am going to see," repeated Mrs. Brigham firmly.

Then she folded her skirts so tightly that her bulk with its swelling curves was revealed in a black silk sheath, and she went with a slow toddle across the hall to the study door. She stood there, her eye at the crack.

In the south room Rebecca stopped sewing and sat watching with dilated eyes. Caroline sewed steadily. What Mrs. Brigham, standing at the crack in the study door, saw was this:

Henry Glynn, evidently reasoning that the source of the strange shadow must be between the table on which the lamp stood and the wall, was making systematic passes and thrusts with an old sword which had belonged to his father all over and through the intervening space. Not an inch was left unpierced. He seemed to have divided the space into mathematical sections. He brandished the sword with a sort of cold fury and calculation; the blade gave out flashes of light, the shadow remained unmoved. Mrs. Brigham, watching, felt herself cold with horror.

Finally Henry ceased and stood with the sword in hand and raised as if to strike, surveying the shadow on the wall threateningly. Mrs. Brigham toddled back across the hall and shut the south room door behind her before she related what she had seen.

"He looked like a demon," she said again. "Have you got any of that old wine in the house, Caroline? I don't feel as if I could stand much more."

Indeed, she looked overcome. Her handsome placid face was worn and strained and pale.

"Yes, there's plenty," said Caroline; "you can have some when you go to bed."

"I think we had all better take some," said Mrs. Brigham. "Oh, Caroline, what—"

"Don't ask; don't speak," said Caroline.

"No, I'm not going to," replied Mrs. Brigham; "but—"

Rebecca moaned aloud.

"What are you doing that for?" asked Caroline harshly.

"Poor Edward," returned Rebecca.

"That is all you have to groan for," said Caroline. "There is nothing else."

"I am going to bed," said Mrs. Brigham. "I sha'n't be able to be at the funeral if I don't."

Soon the three sisters went to their chambers and the south parlor was deserted. Caroline called to Henry in the study to put out the light before he came upstairs. They had been gone about an hour when he came into the room bringing the lamp which had stood in the study. He set it on the table, and waited a few minutes, pacing up and down. His face was terrible, his fair complexion showed livid, and his blue eyes seemed dark blanks of awful reflections.

Then he took up the lamp and returned to the library. He set the lamp on the center table and the shadow sprang out on the wall. Again he studied the furniture and moved it about, but deliberately, with none of his former frenzy. Nothing affected the shadow. Then he returned to the south room with the lamp and again waited. Again he returned to the study and placed the lamp on the table, and the shadow sprang out upon the wall. It was midnight before he went upstairs. Mrs. Brigham and the other sisters, who could not sleep, heard him.

The next day was the funeral. That evening the family sat in the south room. Some relatives were with them. Nobody entered the study until Henry carried a lamp in there after the others had retired for the night. He saw again the shadow on the wall leap to an awful life before the light.

The next morning at breakfast Henry Glynn announced that he had to go to the city for three days. The sisters looked at him with surprise. He very seldom left home, and just now his practice had been neglected on account of Edward's death. He was a physician.

"How can you leave your patients now?" asked Mrs. Brigham wonderingly.

"I don't know how to, but there is no other way," replied Henry easily. "I have had a telegram from Dr. Mitford."

"Consultation?" inquired Mrs. Brigham.

"I have business," replied Henry.

Doctor Mitford was an old classmate of his who lived in a neighboring city and who occasionally called upon him in the case of a consultation.

After he had gone, Mrs. Brigham said to Caroline that, after all, Henry had not said that he was going to consult with Doctor Mitford, and she thought it very strange.

"Everything is very strange," said Rebecca with a shudder.

"What do you mean?" inquired Caroline.

"Nothing," replied Rebecca.

Nobody entered the study that day, nor the next. The third day Henry was expected home, but he did not arrive and the last train from the city had come.

"I call it pretty queer work," said Mrs. Brigham. "The idea of a doctor leaving his patients at such a time as this, and the idea of a consultation lasting three days! There is no sense in it, and *now* he has not come. I don't understand it, for my part."

"I don't either," said Rebecca.

They were all in the south parlor. There was no light in the study; the door was ajar.

Presently Mrs. Brigham rose—she could not have told why; something seemed to impel her—some will outside her own. She went out of the room, again wrapping her rustling skirts round that she might pass noiselessly, and began pushing at the swollen door of the study.

"She has not got any lamp," said Rebecca in a shaking voice.

Caroline, who was writing letters, rose again, took a lamp (there were two in the room) and followed her sister. Rebecca had risen, but she stood trembling, not venturing to follow.

The doorbell rang, but the others did not hear it; it was on the south door on the other side of the house from the study. Rebecca, after hesitating until the bell rang the second time, went to the door; she remembered that the servant was out.

Caroline and her sister Emma entered the study. Caroline set the lamp on the table. They looked at the wall. "Oh, my God," gasped Mrs. Brigham, "there are—there are *two*—shadows." The sisters stood clutching each other, staring at the awful things on the wall. Then Rebecca came in, staggering, with a telegram in her hand. "Here is—a telegram," she gasped. "Henry is—dead."